THE DUKE'S CURSE

Darkened Kingdoms Collection

by Lola Knoes

I0670480

Table of Contents

To the ones who always stood beside me and never left.

Most importantly to my younger self. It took us much longer to achieve this, but despite the many faces of adversity we still managed to do it.

Paperback ISBN: 978-1-956668-49-0

Hardback ISBN: 978-1-956668-20-9

Ebook ISBN: 979-8-215412-95-4

Kindle ASIN: B0CDJG9GZZ

Permission Notice: All copyright holders of pictures included in this book have been contacted and permissions were granted to use this material.

Cover designed by Art Lynx Covers

Development Edits by Ashton Taylor

Catagrophy by RS Fantasy Maps

Author's Note

Welcome, dear reader, to the Darkened Kingdoms Collection universe. Each book is set in the same alternate universe, a smaller secondary world with a major landmass resembling a large Pangea, divided into twelve distinct kingdoms and several outlying islands. However, each story introduces a different cast of characters, with potential cameos in subsequent, all of whom will converge in the final book. These stories are written in a way that allows them to be picked up in any order, with the exception of the final book in the collection. Although narrated in the third person, *The Duke's Curse* primarily follows Princess Amirah on this quest to break a curse. During this she transitions from what she perceives as a prison-like life under the control of parental figures to a journey that nurtures her fiery streak of independence. The story also provides important perspectives on events happening in her absence through Prince Bradric and includes insights from our favorite dragon-shifting sorcerer, Nithe. If you enjoy a book playlist check out "The Duke's Curse" playlist on Spotify. Due to the contents, this book is recommended for those eighteen and older. Any names, places, details, and scenarios are strictly fiction fabricated from the author's imagination. This collection is written from a third person omniscient point of view. For all of the Darkened Kingdoms Collection's up-to-date book playlist, content, a list of possible triggers, and warnings please visit linktr.ee/LolaKnoes.

Kingdom & Character Index

The Twelve Kingdoms of the Continent

- Allerie/ˈæləri/ *al-uh-ree*

- Brizia/briːzjə/ *bree-zeh-uh*

- Ceraun/sɜʁaʊn/ *seh-ron*

- Isidris/ˈaɪsɪdˈres/ *eh-seh-dris*

- Navarre/naˈvar/ *nuh-vaar*

- Pruria/ˈpjʊɹzjə/ *proo-ree-uh*

- Rapplend/ɹæˈpɛlˈɛnd/ *ra-puh-el-end*

- Sevede/ˈsɛveɪd/ *seh-ved*

- Skadi/ˈskɛaːjɪ/ *skah-dee*

- Thorrel/ˈθɔrəl/ *thawr-reh-luh*

- Wolgast/ˈwoʊlgəst/ *wol-gazt*

- Yaeral/jeɪːɹəl/ *yay-ruhl*

- Khaos Wars: *(Pronounced same as 'chaos' with Latin/ Greek spelling) kay-aas*

Characters Names

- Princess Amirah Svanna Landry: Amirah /amiːra/ *a-meer-ah*, Svana /sca-na/ *s-vana*, Landry /'lændri/ *lan-dree*

- Lord Alonzo Macanay: Alonzo əˈlɑnzoʊ/ *uh-lon-zo*, Macanay /məkænejni/ *m-ahk-ahn-ay*

- Prince Bradrick Balthasar: Bradrick /bɹad ɹɪk/ *brad-rick*, Balthasar /bælˈθeɪzər/ *bal-thuh-zar*

- Elra /ˈel.ra/ *el-rah*

- Consort Foley Osman: Foley /ˈfoʊli/ *foh-lee*, Osman /ˈɑsmən/ *oz-maan*

- Cicely /ˈsɪsɪli/ *sis-eh-lee*

- Gabrielle "Gabbie" Paget: Gabrielle /ˌgabriˈɛl/ *gab-ree-el*, Gabbie /ˈgæbi/ *gab-ee*, Paget /ˈpædʒət/ *paj-it*

- Queen Indra Balthasar: Indra /ɪndɹə/ /ˈɪndrə/ *in-druh*, Balthasar /bælˈθeɪzər/ *bal-thuh-zar*

- Kamille /kəˈmil/ or /kaˈmɪlə/ *cuh-meal (like "Camille")*

- Lord Devon /ˈdɛv.ən/ *DEHV-ahN*

- Lady Mallory Devon: Mallory /ˈmæləɹi/ *mal-or-EE*, Devon /ˈdɛv.ən/ *DEHV-ahN*

- Duke-Heir Nithe Vivek : Nithe /naɪð/ *Nigh-th (like saying the kni in "Knife" with -ithe ending to "Lithe")*,Vivek /vɪ.veːk/ or /vajvɪk/ *viy-vihk*

- King Otis Landry: Otis /ˈoʊ tɪs/ *Oh-tis*, Landry /ˈlændri/ *lan-dree*

- Lord Paget/ˈpædʒət/ *paj-it*

- Queen Rana Landry: Rana /ˈrænə/ *ra-na*, Landry /ˈlændri/ *lan-dree*

- Roman /ˈroʊmən/ *row-man*

- Duke Sorgin Vivek: Sorgin /sɔr dʒɛn /sorgin/ s-awr-guh-ihn, Vivek /vɪ.veːk /vajvɪk/ *viy-vik*

- Lord Theorin /ˈθioʊrɪn/ *thee-o-rin*

- Sir Tristan/ˈtɹɪstən/ *tris-tan*

- The Astronomer, Venincio/vɛn ɪn sɪr oʊ /vɛnɪnsiow/ *vehn-ihn-see-o*

Prologue

Heavy boots sounded against wet cobblestone streets. A troop of Brizian soldiers clad in steel armor wove through the empty blocks of dilapidated buildings crowding the outskirts of the capital. The deepening gray evening skies matched the scowling face of the King that led the group. His thick red brows constantly knitted downward. His face remained fixated in such a way since his return from battlefields of the Khaos War.

The Captain of the compact unit rushed ahead as they rounded a corner to a dead-end street. The troop followed and split in two at the end. Six of the soldiers fanned out around a shabby wooden door of a dark thatch-roofed house with their swords drawn. The remaining four soldiers stationed themselves in front of King Landry. He tugged on the end of his red beard, which rested against his breastplate. The only pieces of armor he had elected to wear over his admiral blue aketon were a breastplate and a set of bracers. Standing beside the door, the Captain awaited his signal to proceed with trained patience. When King Landry dipped his head, the Captain rapped against the door with his gloved fist.

"Open the door in the name of the King!" he bellowed.

No answer came. The Captain rapped against the door once more before unrolling a scroll of tanned parchment. King Landry clenched his jaw as he waited.

"Open the door in the name of King Landry," the Captain repeated. "His Majesty has issued a warrant for the arrest of Duke Sorgin Vivek of Brizia on charges of dark sorcery! Present yourself!"

Silence answered them yet again. King Landry released an exasperated sigh and chopped his hand toward the door. At his signal, two of the six broke formation and headed for the door. A few kicks in unison sent it flying open, perhaps a bit too easy for someone accused of sorcery to be hiding behind. The six soldiers entered to find a large, dark room. Despite the lack of light, the emptiness of the space was apparent. Its dirt floor sat bare, with a single table and chair shoved into a corner. The earthen smell of rotted wood and damp walls hung in the air. Cobwebs were the sole life the place had seen in years.

They rejoined the troop outside and turned to their King for further direction. A susurration in the wind caught Landry's attention, and he noticed a slightly shorter figure standing where there had been an empty space moments before. The man chuckled, his narrow-set emerald green eyes glinting under the moonlight, a wide toothy grin spreading across his weathered tan face. Startled, some soldiers took an involuntary step back. King Landry unsheathed the sword at his waist as he turned to cautiously observe the Duke, whose disheveled black hair dusted the shoulders of his long burgundy noble coat, wrinkled from extended wear. The soldiers exchanged disconcerted looks amongst themselves.

"Otis," the Duke hissed the King's name through his teeth. "You call healing 'dark sorcery' nowadays? Old friend, you and I both know why you would cart me away to the slaughterhouse."

At the Captain's signal, the soldiers encircled them, swords drawn toward the Duke. King Landry rolled his eyes at their delayed response and raised his hand, signaling them to stand down. This fight was his alone. He and the Duke began to circle each other like two predators, each step mirroring the other's. The soldiers complied, lowering their swords and tightening the circle. Their bodies formed a makeshift arena as they stood shoulder-to-shoulder in the narrow, dead-end street. King Landry narrowed his eyes as the Duke produced a small dagger from his belt.

"The Continent has rid itself of the magic you cling to for power, no matter how much you have tried to hide it all of these years. How do I know you didn't kill her?" King Landry challenged.

"I would never kill someone I am loyal to, or that I love, unlike some of us."

A sneer spread over King Landry's face at the subtle accusation. Enraged, he charged at the Duke with his sword. The Duke dodged the first swing and effortlessly avoided the next three. A wild upward swing caught the Duke's side as he maneuvered to strike back. The dagger in the Duke's hand sliced against the exposed armpit of the King as he struggled to right himself. Without the aketon, the blade would have sunk deeper and become fatal. Both men stepped back, clasping their hands over their wounds.

The Duke swore under his breath when he looked at the blood coating his fingertips. Adrenaline made the cut feel as harmless as it appeared, but the amount of blood suggested more depth to the wound. Even with his abilities, he knew he had limited time. The King deflected the arching dagger with his sword. The two re-engaged in the dangerous dance, attempting to land a strike against the other—most of which they blocked or evaded. The few blows that they managed to land were worse than the next, but none were as intense as the Duke's initial wound. When they parted on the opposite side of the circle, the King smirked at the sight of his opponent. Compared to the Duke, who was covered in patches of blood, the King was relatively unscathed.

"Drop your weapon and we can end this peacefully," King Landry ordered.

He knew from his opponent's deep chuckle that the Duke would never surrender. The color leached from the Duke's eyes, morphing into the deep color of a haunted forest. The surrounding air stilled as the Duke executed a series of fluid gestures with his hands. King Landry's scowl deepened, and he signaled for his soldiers to capture their target. Two soldiers each grabbed an arm, halting the Duke's movement. Their comrades cheered as the King smirked.

The Duke muttered a chant in a fevered voice, his eyes ablaze with viridescent light as he fixed his gaze on King Landry. The King's smirk faded, replaced by wide-eyed shock, as an unseen energy flung the soldiers away from the Duke. The force was so powerful that a gust of wind knocked two soldiers to the ground as they attempted to approach him. With a simple motion of his hand, the Duke dispatched them effortlessly. Maintaining his focus on the King, he created a circular arm motion, forming an invisible barricade against the soldiers. The barrier hummed eerily as the wind whipped around it. Petrification and curiosity marred the soldiers' faces. Despite the Captain's orders to push through, their attempts to penetrate the barrier only resulted in being thrown into adjacent buildings.

King Landry raised his sword, poised to strike at the Duke. Yet, the Duke charged toward him, dagger raised in hand. A second before the sword pierced his flesh, the Duke lowered his weapon. A second before the two collided, the Duke shifted his stance, arms spread wide as if inviting an embrace, and dropped the dagger. With a sense of impending doom, King Landry watched as the Duke's eyes locked onto his, a chilling calm settling over him. King Landry's eyes widened in shock, but it was too late to halt his forward momentum. The sword plunged into the Duke, crimson liquid spilling forth like a blossoming flower over his abdomen. King Landry stammered in disbelief as he released the hilt of his sword, reaching out to catch the collapsing man.

"W-why in the Twelve Kingdoms...?"

King Landry eased the Duke to the ground, careful not to aggravate the protruding weapon. With a firm grip on the sword blade, he steadied it against the wound. The Duke's hands wrapped around Landry's and squeezed until it sliced deep into their skin. Their blood intermingled and oozed between his fingers. With a small burst of energy, the Duke jerked the sword free from his body, and the last of his strength seeped away as the sword fell beside them.

"Your blood is bound to mine," he cursed and spat blood on King Landry's face. The taste of copper flew into the King's gaped mouth.

The scowl returned to the King's face as he leaned close to the Duke to watch the light dim in his eyes.

"Yet it is your blood that spills, old friend."

"Yes," the Duke hissed.

He pooled his remaining strength to lift his head until his lips almost touched the King's ear. Landry froze as the Duke's warm breath tickled against his flesh. A dark chuckle rasped from the Duke's lips as blood slipped from the corner of his mouth. He shook his head as he spoke, causing a few crimson drops to add to the splatter on King Landry's face.

"Nevertheless, it is my blood alone that can undo the curse upon yours."

His head fell back to the ground. A smile splayed on his face, even as he choked on the liquid that bubbled from his mouth. Blood spread around them like the wings of a great beast. King Landry stood, collected his sword from the ground, and plunged it into the Duke's heart. With a sharp twist, he hastened an end of the decrepit moment.

"Farewell, old friend," he whispered sadly when he pulled it free.

The distant vacancy of death rested on the still-smiling face of the corpse he once called a friend. The invisible barricade fell, and the soldiers rushed to their King's side. He waved them off as he continued staring down at the Duke's remains. The Captain stooped down and closed the eyelids that stared vacantly at King Landry. The mission was done. King Landry wiped his sword on a kerchief from his pocket as the soldiers gathered the Duke's remains.

There should have been a sense of relief, some sense of elation over his sly victory. Instead, King Landry felt a deep-seated fear that clasped around his heart. Rather than celebrate, he was ready to forget the entire thing ever happened—forget the death of his wife and his once closest friend. He knew that the Duke's curse needed to be erased from the history of Brizia. Starting with every witness present.

CHAPTER 1

19 *years later.*
A metallic clang echoed throughout the castle courtyard. Amirah parried the soldier's swing and rolled into a counter as metal clattered against metal. She had persuaded a soldier to join her for a round of sword practice. Sweat made her wavy ginger hair and blue tunic cling to her body. If her father knew what she was doing, he would be unamused by her antics. Anything he deemed unsuitable for a princess had earned her more scoldings than she could count. Despite this, she allowed herself a final indulgence, knowing she would soon cease to be his burden. Much to the chagrin of her lady-in-waiting, who cast anxious eyes at the surrounding castle walls.

"Princess!" Gabrielle's voice pitched, unable to hide her distress. "We have to get ready. You're going to be late!"

"Alright, Gabbie," Amirah shouted and rolled her dark brown eyes in jest.

The soldier chuckled as she called an end to the sparring match. They bade farewell and clapped each other on the shoulder before turning to part ways. Amirah flashed a taunting grin at her fair companion as Gabbie snatched her arm and carted them away into the castle. Gabbie raved in a hushed panic about being ready on time and the King's potential wrath. It was reasonable for anyone to fear her father. King Otis Landry wasn't known for his leniency toward anyone, for any matter. Still, Amirah hid a devious smirk, knowing her procrastination would earn some trouble with her father. He always found something to scold her for, failing to understand the nature of her small rebellions. While they were something she enjoyed doing, it was more for the sake of survival than defiance.

She allowed Gabbie to vent her worries as they barreled toward her room. The gray stone walls of the home she might never see again offered distracting memories. Paintings, art, and decorative tapestries had once adorned them. Upon her mother's death, her father had the halls stripped bare and everything tucked away in a forgotten corner—a room she had long given up on her attempts to break into. The only portrait remaining in the castle was centered in the main hall. It depicted her father in a heroic stance at the end of the Khaos War.

Once Gabbie ushered them into the room, Amirah's attention returned to her surroundings. Gabbie groaned at the state of Amirah's mane. Her own pale golden hair would never be in such a state. Amirah shrugged and plucked the tie from her hair. Her sparring match had already enabled some of the frazzled ginger waves to escape.

"We don't have time for a proper bath," Gabbie grumbled aloud. With a sigh, she added rose-scented oil to the water in a porcelain washbowl. "Fortunately, we packed the trunks and the soldiers already took them down for transport. All we have to do is spruce you up a bit."

"I'll be spending the rest of my life being spruced up in Pruria. Here in Brizia, we only have my father to contend with. That's nothing compared to Queen Indra's scrutiny. Her son declares his despise for the profligacy he endures and that we'll both be living with."

"Empathy for your betrothed will not get you ready faster," Gabbie said in a near sing-song voice as she helped scrub Amirah's sweat-dried skin.

"Why would I ever want to get ready faster? These are the last moments of what little semblance of freedom I'll ever have," Amirah groaned.

They were going to be late for departure, no matter how quickly her lady-in-waiting could get her presentable. She still managed to do so within ample time. No one would have known by looking at her that moments before she was dripping with sweat in the courtyard. Amirah now donned a silken violet traveling dress, hidden away by an admiral blue cloak with an ermine fur collar. Gabbie checked her hair once more to ensure the ginger locks were secure enough for the arduous journey ahead.

As they raced through the castle halls toward the front doors, Gabbie mused between panting breaths, "It really is astounding that you and Prince Bradrick have so much in common, including the desire to be rid of each other."

They paused just before bursting through the oversized arched wooden front doors and wrapped each other in a warm hug. Gabbie pulled back and placed a simple golden crown on Amirah's head.

"Right as rain," she chirped.

The castle doors groaned open as they exited the castle to a sky set ablaze. The flaming orange sunset reflected off the procession line of carriages and two-by-two horse-mounted soldiers facing the gatehouse in the bailey. Amirah could see the half-admiral blue and half-emerald green banners waving in the wind as she approached. The design—a silver dragon wrapped around a shield with three red flowers—became clearer as she drew near. More to her annoyance, Lord Theorin stood outside of the gold-encrusted black King's carriage at the center of the waiting procession. The stout, old goat of a man with receding salt-white hair scowled at her with disapproval. His ruddy face reminded her of the twisted yellow-eyed dog featured on his house's emblem. Fortunately, he would not be accompanying them to Pruria. Much to Amirah's relief as she ignored him and climbed into the carriage, where her father waited with thinning patience.

There he sat, wrapped in a regal, fur-trimmed traveling cloak that matched hers, except for his gold trimming. She shifted on the plush cushioned seat and pretended not to notice the look of disapproval that seethed from beneath his bushy red-gray eyebrows. She envied the troops that surrounded them and Gabbie, who rode in a separate carriage behind them. At least they didn't have to be subject to his ire. The carriage gave a gentle jerk as the journey toward Pruria began and they left the city behind. Amirah craned her neck out her window to watch the summer sunlight fade in the distance.

Her father cleared his throat to draw her attention back to him. Amirah chewed the inside of her cheek as she braced for a lecture. But it never came. King Landry pursed his lips in an attempt to form the right words with his willful daughter. In the end, he settled on letting the matter rest for the moment. Everything he would have scolded her for had already been said repitiously on prior treks between the two kingdoms. These often ended in frustration and neither of them desired this last voyage to begin with another argument.

Although Amirah looked a great deal like her father, especially her long pale-ginger hair, she embodied the spirit of her mother. Queen Rana was a sour subject King Landry refused to entertain, despite his daughter's incessant questions over the years. All mentions of his late wife caused him to shudder as if haunted by her memory. She would have detested the marriage contract, as their daughter did. Amirah's childish protests were far more manageable in comparison to Queen Rana's willfulness. Still, it was evident King Landry detested the unwanted memories of a past life.

"I can't understand why it's imperative that we follow the same old traditions. Were you and Mother ever in love?" Amirah asked with faked nonchalance, looking out the window.

King Landry grunted, and she knew there wouldn't be an answer to her question. "These traditions have secured alliances between kingdoms for generations. It has kept this continent unified for centuries. You know this marriage will provide security for our people. Your duty is to them, above all else. We'll not discuss this further and make the journey any more unpleasant. Get some rest before we reach Pruria."

As was tradition, Amirah's twentieth birthday marked the start of her second season, and with it, her courting years. King Landry had already sought out advantageous options among their closest allies and narrowed them down to one—Pruria.

Queen Indra Balthasar had ruled Pruria for nineteen years, taking the throne after her husband's death until Prince Bradrick, their son, assumed it. Rather, if she ever allowed him to do so. The mutual contract benefited both kingdoms through the marriage of the royal children. Pruria was revered for its wealth, while Brizia was respected for its power. With their positions at the center of the Continent, their unity would reign above the twelve kingdoms for a millennium, the strongest alliance since the Khaos War. Amirah and Bradrick, however, ignored these facts as they railed against the contract.

For three years, the two families made regular journeys across the border to encourage the reluctant couple. The contract stipulated the couple would court for three years and a day. Despite their parents' urging, the courtship yielded nothing more than a close friendship. Amirah and Bradrick argued they bore no love for one another. Yet, according to Landry and Indra, things could be worse. They insisted this development promised a strong foundation for the marriage of their heirs. Amirah grew more rebellious in an effort to deter its fulfillment. Instead, she earned an increase in her father's scorn.

In truth, Amirah wanted nothing more than freedom from the invisible shackles that came with her position. This marriage traded one fortified stone cage for another. Her mood darkened over the voyage. Sleep offered the sole escape as the carriage rolled through Brizian countryside. Near the border, the tallest peak of a mountain range could be seen in the distance, peaking above the forest. The rest of the hidden mountain range stretched from Brisian's north and curved around the western border. Amirah always felt drawn to it whenever they passed through.

More than halfway through the voyage, they stopped at the border for a quick rest in a wide field surrounded by trees where an encampment of a company of soldiers awaited them. Many Brizian soldiers gathered around the procession to greet their dismounting peers. Gabbie quickly exited the carriage that followed the King's and stole Amirah away from her father's side. Together, they walked out of view, a trick she had several years of practice doing.

"Did you two argue the whole way, or are you simply both distraught about the marriage?" Gabbie asked, noting the look on both the royal's faces as they strolled farther into the rows of tents in the trodden grass.

"We hardly spoke a word to each other. I made the mistake of asking about my mother again, which, of course, he avoided. I suppose he is ready to be done with me, and we are now at the end of it," Amirah lamented.

Gabbie bit her lower lip with widened eyes at the mention of Amirah's mother. Everyone knew all discussion of the late Queen Rana was a sour subject with the King. Gabbie tucked a golden lock of hair behind an ear as they continued walking.

"He is still your father. I'm sure there is a part of him that mourns your leaving."

The words she offered were meant to be comforting but did little to relieve Amirah. "You know we aren't close like you are with your father. We're practically strangers residing under the same roof.

The nursemaids and nannies were in charge of my upbringing. Even Queen Indra has been closer to me than he has."

"That is true," Gabbie conceded.

The two had become the closest friends since the King handpicked Gabbie as her lady-in-waiting during their formative years. Gabbie came from the house of Paget, a house of lower nobility that ascended when her father joined the Brizian court. Lord Paget exceeded his peers in many areas, including being the living definition of noble. Despite her position, Gabrielle Paget flourished with the social grace and wit of the ladies who attended court their whole lives. Amirah admired her friend's loyal cunning, which helped shield them from the King's temper numerous times in the past.

As daylight fell on the camp, the two friends proceeded toward the crowds of rugged soldiers. They had gathered around campfires, rowdy with drink and song. Amirah had always enjoyed listening to their fireside tales interwoven with dragons and magic—Things that once laced the Continent before being claimed by the Khaos War. It sickened Amirah that her father had a hand in their decimation. Throughout the Twelve Kingdoms, people revered him as a hero among men for it—especially among the nobility. Compared to the snakes at court, she felt most comfortable among the soldiers. Despite the risk of the King's wrath, they had helped her in discrete acts of rebellion. In secret, she trained alongside them and took extra care to avoid injury. Such a thing would have brought an end to what she most enjoyed. Worse, the soldiers would have endured punishment for her selfish endeavors.

King Landry had meant Gabbie to act as a living leash for his daughter. His confidence in the Pagets, including Gabbie's rapport in court, allowed him to believe this to be the case. However, her presence further enabled Amirah's freedom to move without scrutiny. Lady Gabrielle Paget kept a watchful eye on Amirah, as the King hoped. However, he didn't realize he had also given his daughter a shield against him. By extension, Amirah's accomplices could aid her with lesser risk to their own necks.

The men passed them food and drinks when the two ladies sat on an empty log at a campfire. Their inclusion made it feel as if they had always belonged there. In the back of Amirah's mind, she remembered that the coming daylight meant it would soon be her birthday. A forgotten day, overshadowed like everything else by the looming wedding. She smirked, knowing this would be as close to celebrating as she would get. If Gabbie knew her birthday was today, she never gave it away. Her father had already retired without further ordering her to turn in for the night. *Perhaps he remembered and is allowing me to enjoy the moment,* she thought. She smiled to herself, taking comfort in the reprieve and enjoying the camaraderie before it ended.

Long into the night, Amirah sat among the soldiers with her friend until the air chilled and smelled of dew-covered earth. Before the dawn broke, she reluctantly climbed into the carriage. King Landry mumbled in his troubled sleep. She knew he fought with nightmares and assumed they came with memories from the Khaos War. He seldom spoke about the war, preferring to lock that era of their lives away. Whenever his past haunted him, Amirah carried on with her business, just as she intended to do after tucking his cloak around him.

As the procession rode off, the gentle thud of the horse's feet against the dirt road lulled her into a deep sleep. She awoke only when the carriage wheels rattled against stone streets. The sounds of jubilant life outside coaxed her to sit up, as her father also rubbed the cobwebs from his eyes. The hum of an anxious crowd chanted and cheered as they neared their destination.

Instead of trees and fields, there were pristine buildings and decorated roadways. Banners, streamers, and floral arrangements covered the main road of the city for the coming festivities. Throngs of citizens gathered to cheer the procession along as it rolled toward the palace. King Landry and Amirah cursed under their breath. The immaculate white stone palace with seven sharp towers and turrets came into view as the carriage passed through the open gates, and pulled to a stop before the doors of Amirah's future prison.

CHAPTER 2

Today began the traditional royal wedding celebrations that would exhaust Amirah's itinerary. Gabbie would have her hands full trying to keep her on schedule. If she could, Amirah intended to drag her feet at every moment.

Lavish decorations adorned the interior halls of the Prurian palace. An outrageous amount of floral arrangements and greenery were combined with golden ribbons, banners, candelabras, and other glittering objects on almost every surface. The color palette worked well with the Kingdom's banners of red and yellow diagonal stripes with a white stag head at the center. Queen Indra's reputation for throwing the most extravagant parties spread beyond any of the twelve kingdoms. The opulence and meticulous planning of her events drew nobles and dignitaries from beyond the Continent. The Queen had spared no expense to prepare for the long week of festivities, and it showed in every inch of the palace.

A steward ushered the Brizian royalty into a greeting room where none other than Queen Indra herself awaited them. She sat in a pale blue satin dress that consumed the cream sofa beneath her and complemented her sapphire blue eyes. A large chignon of golden hair was piled onto her head. As the steward announced the arrival of the Brizian royals, a generous red-lipped smile spread across her sharp porcelain face. Her Consort, Foley Osman, stood behind her, dressed to match in an elegant ensemble. It consisted of a vibrant azure habit, pants, white silk stockings, polished shoes, and a satin cravat tied into an oversized bow. Unlike King Landry, he had the build of a bean sprout. His clean-shaven chin and peach-colored cheeks sported a vibrant shade of rouge. No one could ascertain if his fine white hair belonged to him or if he wore a well-made periwig.

Amirah noticed her father's forced smile as the foppish man failed to give a proper greeting to him as King. Foley was far too concerned with the state of his manicured nails to be bothered with formalities. The struggle to remain civil increased each time they met. If he acted with intention, or if Indra noticed, remained uncertain. The wink Foley gave Amirah led her to assume it to be intentional.

"How was the journey?" Indra cooed.

"Uneventful, I am sorry to say." King Landry said, looking sideways at Amirah.

"No reason for apologies, Otis. It is better that everyone got enough sleep on their way in. Especially our dearest Amirah." Queen Indra smiled at her.

Amirah inclined her head to signify her agreement. Despite her intensity, Queen Indra proved to be easier to appease than her father. Before the marriage contract, the Brizian had spent several winters visiting Pruria. Indra had become the closest mother-like figure Amirah would know. However, her mother could never be replaced. Amirah knew what to expect from Indra as her mother-in-law from years of observation and maneuvering in the two royal courts. She did not envy Prince Bradrick's relationship with her and did not look forward to becoming Queen whenever Indra finally stepped aside. Amirah knew she would become a pawn among the courts as long as both Indra and her father were alive. She was doomed; in ways that might be worse than Bradrick.

"Where might Prince Bradrick be?" King Landry asked, scanning the room.

Foley rolled his eyes while Queen Indra pursed her lips at the question. King Landry masked his expression, already familiar with the Prince's insistent tardiness. Indra relaxed a second later and picked up a cup of tea from the serving tray on the small wooden table beside the sofa.

"My son should be preparing for the rehearsal, as should Amirah, once we finish our business here. Otis," Queen Indra started as she handed King Landry a flat, pristine set of parchment. "You should review the itinerary for the coming days to ensure that it is agreeable."

King Landry scanned the parchment as Amirah accepted an additional copy from Consort Foley. As tradition dictated, the rehearsal and wedding banquet took place prior to the wedding—the rehearsal during the day and the banquet at night. The next day held a dizzyingly detailed schedule for the wedding. King Landry agreed with the schedule, though Amirah's stomach churned as she reviewed the parchment. It solidified her unavoidable fate. She feigned agreement with a silent nod. A tight smile spread across the Queen's face. Appeased, Indra dismissed them to prepare for the scheduled rehearsal.

When Amirah stepped into the hallway, a heavy hand pulled on her shoulder. She spun around to face her father. If their relationship were more amicable, he might have hugged her or given her words of encouragement. Instead, he left her with stern warnings and commands. "Go straight to your chambers and prepare with haste. Your lady is already waiting there with Kamille. Do not cause trouble this night."

He gave her a final expectant look before heading off in the opposite direction. With that, a servant ushered Amirah to her chambers. The room offered a grateful amount of privacy away from the watchful eyes of their monarchical parents. However, the floral scent that permeated the entire palace served as an inescapable reminder of the reason for her presence. She tried focusing on other things, like the details of the cream-colored room. Its golden inlaid crown molding was equally as elaborate as the rest of the palace. A polished stone floor covered in plush rugs hosted fine furniture and luxurious textiles that were too pastel for her taste.

Gabbie waited inside the bedroom chamber with a maid that wrapped her in a warm embrace. Kamille had been born on the Prurian coast to a common family. She was a lovely brunette-haired maiden who was Gabbie's opposite in every way. Despite the young women's differences, they formed an inseparable trio during the long visits to Pruria. Amirah was unsure if she could have endured the past three years without them. The pair giggled with excitement as they began the work of unpacking the carriage trunks. Amirah observed their delight as they piled her dresses on the plush bed in the center of the room. They plucked out the ball gown for the banquet and a separate one for the rehearsal.

Her companions helped Amirah strip from the traveling clothes, wash her skin down, and climb into the dress for the rehearsal. Made of smooth eggshell-colored fabric with fabric buttons down the back, the dress hugged her upper waist and flowed around her ankles. She enjoyed the simplicity of this cap-sleeved dress compared to the extravagant ball gown she would wear later. Her friends prattled on through Amirah's silence as they fixed her hair with pearl drop pins and powdered her nose. Their easy musings became fervent banter and focused on the potential affairs of the night.

"Do you think you'll dance with one of the Lords tonight?" Kamille asked Gabbie as she began to put away the extra garments.

"No one in particular comes to mind, and I haven't been expeditiously looking for a match. While I am sure my father will allow me some say in whoever I end up paired with, I'm not in a rush to make a decision at the moment."

"Lucky," Amirah muttered.

Kamille gave her an empathetic pat. "I don't envy the children of nobility. Not that an arranged marriage never happens among the rest of us; it does. However, I've seen enough inner workings of this court to know it's not something I'd want to endure myself no matter how desirable a partner they might be."

Blush spread over Amirah's face as the subject drifted toward more deviant details. Being close friends, she was unprepared to think of Bradrick as a lover. She wondered if he felt the same conflict. Each step toward this inevitable future erased all hopes and dreams, leaving only the heavy weight of the duties expected of them. Despite three long years of protesting the arrangement, everything their parents wanted was coming to fruition.

When everything was finished, Gabbie escorted her into the overly decorated hallways. Years of practice had perfected Amirah's ability to mask her expression, just as she did now. Despite her appearance, a twinge of panic tightened within her chest as she faced the inevitability of her fate. She wondered if, by some chance, they could ever find happiness.

CHAPTER 3

It turned out Bradrick had become skilled at avoiding his mother. At least, that was the gist of what everyone overheard while Queen Indra grumbled to Consort Foley inside the throne room. Much of the Queen's irritation centered on her son being late for the rehearsal. Amirah had to strive to keep from smiling as she stood facing them. The Queen twisted her lips as her fingers tapped the arm of her golden throne that overlooked the rest of the rectangular room from a centered dais. Beside her in a matching chair, Consort Foley sat with a bored expression. The man would never become King, but Foley received the same treatment and luxuries as one. Few dared to question Queen Indra on that matter, least of all now.

The silence in the hall was uncomfortable. Even the priest avoided eye contact with the disgruntled Queen, convincingly staring at the smooth stone pillars on both sides of the near-empty room. Between them, a white runner stretched from the dais to the door. The small crowd exchanged awkward glances. King Landry stood on the lower step of the dais, observing the small crowd with a blank expression, his hands clasped behind his back. For the day's events he had changed into a fur-collared floor-length burgundy robe that hid most of his tunic. Everyone jumped when the throne room doors burst open, spilling light into the dreary room. Indra's face went from wide-eyed relief to a frosty glare at the person who was not her son.

Amirah met Alonzo's turquoise eyes as his brisk steps carried him forward until he stood beside her. His tight-cropped black curls, dark chiseled features, and firm build commanded attention. Consort Foley shifted in his chair with a grimace, most likely at the fact that Alonzo was always better dressed. Amirah cast a smile at Alonzo before returning her attention to the dais. She had known him from all her years at the Prurian court as a loyal second and best friend to Bradrick. Over the next few days, he would act as Bradrick's best man. The stout Master of Ceremonies scuttled in behind him.

He heaved to catch his breath as he attempted to carry out his duty. "Your highnesses, I present to you, Lord Alonzo Macanay—"

"Yes, yes, yes. I know who he is. You may return to your post." Queen Indra waved him off and squinted at Alonzo. "Where is Bradrick? He is late."

"On the way my Queen," Alonzo bowed. "He required a bath after his hunting trip and thought it best to be presentable for the occasion."

"I see. How long does he expect us to wait for, Lord Macanay?"

"No idea, Highness. He sent me ahead while he was dressing to inform you of his intent to come straight here."

"And here I am." Bradrick's voice sounded from the open doorway behind them.

Amirah turned to meet his soft brown eyes and the crooked, smug grin that showed off his left cheek dimples. He had combed back his short, loose, wavy blonde hair to appear more coiffed. The edges still curled behind his ear from dampness. Like Amirah's simpler dress, Bradrick wore a champagne-colored outfit trimmed in cream with sewn golden details. He nodded at Alonzo and Amirah before he looked at his mother. Her lips pursed as she examined him in silence.

"I suppose it is better late than never," she sighed. "Alonzo, make sure he is on time tomorrow. No excuses. Now, let us begin the rehearsal."

The Queen ordered Amirah to return to the hall and re-enter the throne room again. When she did, all eyes fell upon her, and once again, the tightness in her chest returned. It seemed to take ages to reach the dais. Alonzo gave her a wink from behind Bradrick, a reassurance that settled her nerves as the rehearsal began.

Bradrick took her hand as they shifted to kneel before the priest as directed. Neither looked at the other unless prompted by the priest. They rehearsed the nuptials without error. It could have been her imagination, but Bradrick's voice sounded as stiff as her own. Appeased with their performance, the priest praised the otherwise perfect rehearsal and took his leave. When he was gone, King Landry and Queen Indra let out a deep sigh of relief.

Alonzo bowed to Bradrick and Amirah as he excused himself to tend to errands. Before Bradrick could protest, Alonzo strode away, leaving them with a promise to see them at the banquet. The room had cleared, leaving the pair alone with their parents. The Queen instructed Foley to check the progress in the banquet hall, and as Bradrick turned around, he found himself nose-to-nose with his mother. A stare-down passed between them until the Queen relented with a sigh.

"It is bad enough you were late today. You could at least smile during the ceremonies," she nagged him as she smoothed the fabric at his shoulders.

Bradrick rolled his head back, staring at the ceiling in exasperation. "We have already been through this, Mother! Neither Amirah nor I want this!"

"Nonsense! This is not about 'wants' or other selfish desires. We will not go over this again! Both kingdoms are celebrating the unity this marriage represents. Your father would have never tolerated this disrespect toward us or our allies. Go apologize to King Landry for snubbing his gracious tolerance despite your continued disrespect!"

Bradrick chewed the interior of his cheek as she stalked away without another word. The palpable tension failed to ease in her wake. The last time he dared to speak up against his mother, she had threatened to lock Amirah and Bradrick together in his chambers for months. Amirah already felt trapped. She had endured similar treatments, or worse, from her father for her own acts of rebellion. At least, the ones he knew about.

Bradrick turned with a deep bow to King Landry, who strolled toward them. His dark, regal robe flowed around his feet and covered most of the long red tunic. A decorative golden belt kept it neatly in place around his waist. His sudden chuckle startled Amirah. *Is he smiling!?* she wondered, certain she detected a hint of one. Sure enough, one tugged at the corners of his mouth beneath the graying ginger beard. Almost no one had seen such jubilance on his face in years. Bradrick's brows reached toward the ceiling when the King patted his shoulder like they were old friends.

"No need to apologize," King Landry said as he straightened his crown—a simple heirloom of gold and silver.

Their surprise continued as he pulled both of them under each of his arms to hug their shoulders. Amirah went rigid. She strained to find a memory of him ever hugging her, but came up empty. Landry carried on, oblivious to her confusion. She rolled her eyes as he began 'the speech' at them, one of several variations that he had repeated often over the last three years. The joy in his voice was as unusual as his smile.

"I know this moment seems daunting to you both. Indra and I both faced the same beginnings before the Khaos War. We lived these same fears, albeit with quieter tongues, and survived hardships to see our kingdoms thrive. Peace and unity are fragile things, which is why our people are celebrating your marriage. It solidifies our alliance and unifies the center of the Continent. Your duty to them will always surpass your own desires. It comes with the life you were born into. In time, you will come to see that this is the best match." He clapped them on the shoulders. "Now, I need to prepare for this banquet. Some nobles freshly arrived from the southern kingdoms. They will be present at the banquet tonight and I hope to meet them."

Amirah and Bradrick stared at his retreating back back until he disappeared from the room. Both released a deep sigh. The weight of tension in the room eased as though a tight thread had snapped. Bradrick raked his hands through his hair, returning his tresses to their usual dishevelment. He examined the emptied space King Landry had stood until his eyes found hers. His troubled expression morphed into a defeated smile.

"Would you like to go to the library?"

Amirah's face brightened. She attempted to sequester her excitement with a simple nod of agreement. Bradrick gave her one of his dimpled grins before turning towards the doorway. Their feet hastily carried them from the throne room, eager to leave it behind them.

The Prurian palace library was larger than the one in the Brizian castle. It would take several years to read everything within the rectangular room filled with tall bookshelves and large study tables. It always smelled the same—aged wood mingled with leather and cloth. If nostalgia had a scent, it would match this room.

Amirah glided her hands along a waist-high shelf nonchalantly. Her soft steps paused only when she spotted a familiar viridian cover with faded gold lettering. She squatted down and plucked the book from the second lowest shelf. When she stood back up, she spun away from the bookcase in a dramatic twirl. Bradrick laughed at her antics.

"What?" Her eyebrows wiggled in a challenge.

"Nothing." He cleared his throat, attempting to feign seriousness.

Amirah leaped onto a table to sit, another fractious act their parents would chastise her for if they could see. They had spent many winter months here in the sanctuary of the smooth wooden shelfs. Alonzo and Gabbie had joined them sometimes. Their minds escaped into the pages of other worlds as they sat back to back in a circle, built forts from chairs, and told one another wild tales. Even now, they stole away to hide from their lives outside its sacred walls.

Amirah inhaled the woody scent of the aged pulp pages before she opened the book to the middle that was marked with an old, thin pink ribbon. Bradrick hopped up on the table beside her and pretended to read over her shoulder.

"Which story is it today?" He hummed with interest.

"You don't remember?" She tossed an incredulous expression in his direction. "No? This book is a famous collection written by a bard during the Khaos War. It's sad and beautiful, but a very satisfying story."

She began to read aloud from the book. The passages flowed like a gentle song, describing a ruthless warrior who met his end at the hands of a dragon who sought justice for the deaths of his brethren. It captured Bradrick's attention. He was absorbed into the story, pulled by the eb and flow of Amirah's voice. However, her tone softened with hints of empathy for the dragon.

When the story ended, she closed the book and turned to meet Bradrick's soft brown eyes. His brows creased as if a puzzle had baffled him. When he said nothing, she playfully nudged his shoulder and hopped off of the table.

As she replaced the book, Bradrick slid down as well, and thurned to place his palms down on the table's surface. Amirah noticed his strange stance from her crouched position by the bookshelf. She had no way to know what absurd question had formed in his mind. Although, it was easy to guess it was likely related to their parents' schemes. They had much to figure out before they continued to play along.

She re-shelved another book she had been considering and rounded the table, standing across from him with crossed arms. When his eyes raised to meet hers, she arched a questioning eyebrow.

"I think we should discuss what is happening," he blurted. "Maybe take time to consider what options we have some control over."

Amirah unfolded her arms. "There isn't much. Until you hold the crown, your mother gets an absolute final say and my father's a rock wall. His behavior today was...bizarre, but I suspect he is overjoyed with their victory."

"True, although I understand their position. Your father is an excellent strategist. He couldn't have led us out of the Khaos War without being able to see the bigger picture. Perhaps we need to approach this as he would."

Amirah crossed her arms again. Bradrick picked up on her frustration and circled to stand beside her. The feeling had eaten at them since being forced into the marriage contract.

"Although you are right. Until I have the crown, we have no actual power. All we can do is plan what will happen once I am on the throne."

"I am listening," she said, turning to face him directly.

"Once we are married, the crown will be ours. With it, we hold the power to do as we please. And, to be honest, I have yet to think of a way out of this whole thing, short of running away. There are too many in our kingdoms that depend upon us for that."

"We are beyond childhood, Bradrick," Amirah chastised, her words tinged with pessimism. Another dimpled grin spread across his face.

"Yes. We are needed by our people, by our friends, and even by our conniving parents. We could never abandon our friends. Alonzo? Gabbie? Kamille? Running is not the answer. That wouldn't be something they expected and it has too many unforeseeable consequences. When I have the crown, we can do anything, because the power transfers to me. It is a matter of outmaneuvering them before they can solidify new plans. We have a fighting chance since they have only envisioned this far."

Amirah considered this for a moment. "Okay. So we go through with their plan, with our own long-term plan of undoing it?"

"More or less. It depends on what we decide to do after we get the crown. That is something that will need our full focus first. Think of it in terms of the phases of a battle. If I learned nothing of strategy from my education, I made up for it with knowledge from our generals and your father. Now, there is something I wanted to try."

"What?" she dared to ask as he stepped closer.

Their bodies were so close that she could feel the warmth radiating from him. He wasn't as tall as her father, but he still stood a few inches above her. Time had given him a better scent—the gentle musk of pine and earth.

"Please let me know if you don't want to, or feel free to slap me afterward. The thing is, I would prefer our first kiss not be at the altar before the masses."

"Oh!" Amirah's eyebrows raised as her eyes fluttered rapidly with realization. "I hadn't considered that. Yeah. I don't think I want that either. I don't mind if we tried a kiss before—"

Bradrick pressed his lips against hers. The taste of sweet warmth teased her lips as he pulled her closer. Amirah followed his lead. Her arms reached up to his chest as he wrapped his arms around her waist. She hadn't kissed anyone in years. Since before their plight against the arranged marriage, to be exact.

When he finally broke away, their eyes searched one another, unable to read the other. He brushed away a ginger lock that had fallen over her eye. He let out an exasperated sigh with a curse, which amused Amirah. A subtle frown formed on his lips as they parted from each other.

"Anything for you?" The question revealed his opinion more than he intended.

"Not really, sorry. Maybe because I'm out of practice."

Now it was Bradrick's turn to raise an inquisitive eyebrow at her. He chuckled when she shrugged.

"She does have secrets! I can't say anything different. It's a strange thing. We really would be the perfect match. Brains, looks, strong heritages, childhood friends, and allied kingdoms."

"Perhaps we were born fools." Amirah joked.

"Perhaps we were."

CHAPTER 4

Alonzo pulled a wooden door shut, so nothing more than a gentle click sounded as he entered the guest hallway. A smug grin tugged the corners of his lips. He wandered away from the door, pulling a royal navy-colored dress coat with gold-spun designs over his lean torso. An unexpected whistle caused him to pause. When he turned, Bradrick stood him with a knowing smile plastered on his face. Alonzo's grin faded into a look of pressed curiosity.

"So, this was the errands you needed to run?" Bradrick teased, gesturing with his head toward the hall behind him and turning foot. Alonzo followed, matching his pace as they continued through the guest halls side-by-side. Bradrick glanced sideways at Alonzo. "Was that the guest room Lord—"

"Lord *and* Lady, yes. Am I so easy to find these days?"

"For me, always. Although it took a bit more work today."

Alonzo chuckled. "Then you're getting rusty. We have been having our private parties for a week now. Why are you searching for me at this hour anyways? You should be preparing for the banquet. Your mother will have both of our heads if you arrive late."

"I have plenty of time. Especially since your keen eyes have saved both of us more than once. However, I am worried I may have made a mess of things. I could use your sage advice."

"How could you have managed that in the time since I left your side?"

Alonzo stopped in front of a lesser-known staircase in the empty hall that eventually led to the gardens. Their voices dropped to a hush as Bradrick recounted the loose beginnings of a plan to change the fate he and Amirah would face tomorrow. Then he added the last detail.

"Also... I kissed Amirah."

"I am sorry, you did what now?" Alonzo shook his head in disbelief.

"I kissed her. It was nice, I suppose. Yet, it seemed to fall flat and stirred nothing for either of us."

Alonzo furled his lips and raised his eyebrows. His wordless expression spoke volumes. With an exasperated breath, he turned to lead them up the stairs and rubbed his forehead as if plagued by a sudden headache. The stairs rounded into another hall lined by a row of doors. Alonzo threw open a set of heavy doors in the center of the corridor. Inside Bradrick's private chambers, he flopped down onto a lounge chair near the oversized fireplace. Bradrick proceeded to his bedroom and began dressing for the banquet.

"I think we can work with your plan," Alonzo continued when Bradrick reemerged, "but we need to talk about this kiss. What were you thinking?"

"That tomorrow is terrible timing for our first kiss. I didn't tell her this, so I would appreciate it being kept between us, but I wanted to see if I could feel anything. I do care for her, but only in the same way I care for you. Thinking about all of it, I don't think I have ever felt anything romantic toward anyone. You and I both have experience—"

"—Me more than you."

Bradrick nodded in agreement and they both chuckled as he continued. "So, it's not that I am inexperienced. I just... I am not sure what to do from here."

"Well, what did you tell her?" Alonzo's eyebrows knitted in confusion. Bradrick tossed him a tunic to wear beneath his dress coat. "Thank you. Why do you think there's some befallen disaster?"

Bradrick sighed and smoothed down his pale gray evening jacket embroidered in gold and silver over his matching ensemble. His mother's choices always involved over-the-top golden exuberance that was not his preferred style. This was the least metallic attire he could get away with while still meeting her standards. He refused to reach the same heights of attire as Consort Foley.

"I asked her if she felt anything. An apologetic 'no' from her, of course. I couldn't deny it was the same for me. I feel a fool for it, but it's not something I can help. At some point, my mother will get the idea to demand we produce an heir next. It's an overall mess."

"There are viable solutions for that, just as there are solutions for what happens tomorrow—adoptions, lovers, and a plethora more options. If our planning goes as intended, it will never become a problem. Romance might not be your thing, Bradrick, but you still have a heart of gold. Your people will love you for not abandoning them and forsaking the kingdoms to unknown fates. The Continent would devolve into another war and be ruined by the lords vying for the thrones. I am not siding with your parents, but it's worthwhile to consider they could have chosen a far worse pairing to face this situation with."

"When you are right, you are right."

"I am always right. It's part of my charm." Alonzo laughed at his joke.

Though he laughed with him, Bradrick agreed with Alonzo's words of wisdom. At the core, their parents were monarchs. That forever meant they were politicians first, parents second, and sometimes even third. He knew his mother wanted to expand her influence and suspected King Landry would marry Amirah off to whoever offered him the highest advantage. Although the thought put a pit in his stomach. It fed his resolve to ensure their plans would succeed.

Time never seemed to be on their side. Pretending to go along with their parents' schemes carried risks. This aside, they were at the apex where drastic measures needed to be made. Bradrick had considered that, while he had no desire to marry, anyone less than Amirah would be an obstacle. Amirah was a friend, ally, and co-conspirator. While it didn't elude him how haphazardly they had thrown the plan together, taking the crown was their best chance. A plan was a plan, nonetheless.

"We'll talk more about this over dinner tonight. What better time to both convince our parents and everyone else while also gathering allies to support us in our future mischief?"

Alonzo laughed. "Now that's the spirit of a future King."

"Indeed. I'd already be King if my mother would step aside as she should have when I first reached my second season. There's always been some loophole she's used that likely had my father rolling over in his crypt. This marriage is the last one available, short of sending me off to war," Bradrick mused. He fussed with his hair and put on a lightweight golden crown that was smaller than the one he would eventually wear.

"Don't go giving her any ideas. Let's get past this first," Alonzo jokingly warned. He stood to put on the tunic. Once he had tucked it in and the dress coat pulled over it, they were ready. Together, he and Bradrick left the chambers. As they headed for the Banquet hall, Alonzo scoffed and nudged Bradrick's arm. "We might actually be on time for once."

CHAPTER 5

Amirah waited at the bottom of the wide, polished steps of the main stairway. Lush greenery intertwined with white flowers decorated the banisters. The fresh floral scent they exuded hung throughout the entire palace. Kamille had helped her slip into the white ivory ball gown she now wore. Its tight, square-necked bodice and flowing skirt had been fitted to her curves. The sleeves, however, billowed off her shoulders like layered feathers. She fiddled with the ribbon laced throughout the low, pulled-back, loose hairstyle. Kamille had painstakingly fixated the tresses with pearl-drop pins. A simple ringlet crown of gold rounded her head.

She scanned the vicinity for Gabbie, who had yet to arrive. Nothing else within sight moved except the flicker of candlelight against the evening's shadows. Soft voices around the corner caught her attention when she heard one mention Brizia. Curiosity piqued, she tiptoed closer to eavesdrop, careful to remain out of sight.

"What, have you never heard of it?" a gravelly voice demanded more than asked. "I don't believe you."

"It's an old rumor that no one believes anymore," a more gentle voice dismissed.

"Do you know why they don't speak of the curse?" the gravel voice prodded.

A third voice chimed in like an old bell, annoyance thick on their tongue. "Because the entire kingdom would've been affected! Everyone! It is an unfounded rumor lost in the winds of Brizia."

"No, it's because everyone who knew is dead!" the gravel voice chuckled as if they had won the argument.

"The rumor wouldn't have spread if that were true. It wasn't relevant then, and it isn't relevant now."

The voices continued their argument as they moved away into the distance. Amirah felt tempted to follow behind them. She wanted to know about the rumored curse and what it had to do with Brizia. Silence settled over the vacated hallway. She chanced a peek around the corner to glimpse their faded silhouettes.

Something sharp poked her side. Amirah jumped with a yelp, her hand clamped over the now tender spot. Gabrielle clapped her hands to her cheeks to hide a blush that was as pink as her flowing gown. A woven crown of flowers dangled from her wrist and she shuddered with her muted laughter. The pair hugged before Gabbie settled the floral crown on Amirah's head. Its large pastel blossoms with edges dipped in gold paint were big enough to conceal the crown that circled her head.

"Now you're ready," Gabbie grinned with approval.

"As ready as I can be," Amirah said with an indifferent shrug.

"Well, you look gorgeous," Gabbie cooed. "Let's get in there before they fuss."

Amirah sighed, reluctant to allow her lady-in-waiting to hook arms and lead her down the ethereal hallway that led to the banquet hall. They seemed to wander into an upside-down field of flowers. Ribbons, banners, and twinkling lanterns hung from the ceiling. Trees with white blossoms and jewels dangling from their branches sat between every few windows in giant golden planters. White and red petals littered the floors wherever guests might have ventured.

At the enormous double doors of the banquet hall, a pair of guards, whose armor served little purpose outside of the Queen's vanity, stood stationed on either side. Amirah hid her silent judgment with a tight smile. They waited there for only a moment until the Master of Ceremonies emerged. He looked up from an ornate scroll and bowed to Amirah before motioning them to follow. The heavy wooden doors opened to reveal the banquet hall, and a knot formed in Amirah's stomach as the guards closed the doors behind them, drawing every eye upon her.

Inside the banquet hall, the ethereal floral world continued on a grander scale. Petals scattered the floor around sturdy wooden tables laden with food. Amirah and Gabbie walked through the center of the open dance floor to the opposite end, where the Queen's high table sat on an elevated dais draped in a golden tablecloth. Below the dais, displayed before the entire room, was a small matching table where Bradrick stood from his chair upon her entrance. The Master of Ceremonies read through the announcement formalities from his scroll. When he finished, applause welcomed Amirah as Gabbie guided her to Bradrick's side. The trio bowed to King Landry and Queen Indra, who observed Amirah's every movement. Queen Indra's layered gold gown matched the crown nestled against her coiffured hair. Consort Foley sat on her left, dressed to match in fine clothes that almost swallowed him.

Her father gave a subtle nod of acknowledgment, despite the glint of wary suspicion that haunted his eyes. He nodded again, this time in approval, as Bradrick came to stand beside Amirah and joined the two women in a bow to the high table. Indra smiled approvingly and dismissed them with a flit of her right hand. Gabrielle departed from Amirah's side to seek a seat at one of the guest tables. Bradrick glided through the rehearsed steps and led her to their private table, where he pulled out her chair. Every eye was upon them until they were both seated.

The knot in Amirah's stomach untangled itself when the room filled with the murmur of pleasant conversation and laughter. Some eyes still flitted over them with open observation. Amirah felt the heat of their parents' gaze as they bore into their backs. A silver platter filled with food sat at the center of Bradrick and Amirah's table. Bradrick plucked items from it and piled them onto their plates.

He gestured to a servant, who circled the room with a large polished jorum, over to their table. Bradrick asked them to leave the entire thing when they began filling the pair of jeweled ornamental chalices. Amirah's face reflected that of the servant, who looked both shocked and horrified by Bradrick's déclassé behavior. The servant's eyebrows raised to the ceiling as he took the jorum, filled a chalice, and passed it to Amirah. She accepted it, watching the servant make a quick retreat from their table. Bradrick took a deep drink from his chalice and leaned in close enough that no one could decipher his words.

"If we are stuck in this together, then let us make the best of it. Drink our fill and party like it is the last we'll ever see. Let them think they have won. What do you think?"

"Well," she started, eyeing him sideways and catching the familiar mischievous glint in his eyes. "That sounds better than my ideas. Is Alonzo in league with us?"

"Always." He raised his glass for a toast.

Their parents perceived their exchange as a successful start to the evening. To them, this meant they had emerged victorious and could comfortably engage their attention elsewhere. Tomorrow's ceremony would be peaceful, followed by a string of events for the public, and end with another large feast. Indulging themselves as if they were, at last, compliant would prove to be a simple task.

"Do we have a detailed plan to execute?" Amirah questioned as she took a bite from her plate made from the pile of excess before them.

Bradrick refilled their drinks. "Not much more than what we discussed earlier, I'm afraid. We need a decent amount of political finesse to attain the crown from my mother. I doubt she will easily part with it."

"I almost can't blame her. Almost." Amirah drank from her chalice.

"Why is that? I never thought you'd have empathy for my mother."

"So few women will ever hold true positions of power that elevate them above their circumstances. To rule without a second—without a King above you and without question—is more freedom than most will ever achieve. What's more, she is loved as well as respected. A rare thing for any monarch in our recorded histories."

Bradrick chuckled and nodded his head in agreement. "That is true. However, peace and freedom come at a steep price. Most will pay through great sacrifices and far too many well-kept secrets. There is always more behind the curtain than the public perceives. That's true even for you and I. We plot the downfall of our parentage in hopes of freedom and peace from the system built long before their time. In so doing, we beget our own sacrifices and secrets."

"All too true."

Amirah hummed as she finished her drink, hoping to float without a care in the world for the rest of the night. She made the mistake of mentioning as much aloud to Bradrick, who took it as a literal invitation and filled her chalice again. Amirah balked when he stood up with a mischievous smile plastered to his face a few moments later. Silence surrounded them again when he turned upon his feet with his raised chalice to the high table, a signal they were ready to dance.

It drew Queen Indra's attention away from her conversation with nearby nobles. She squinted down at Bradrick with a smile plastered on her painted lips, eyes glinting with a mix of amusement and suspicion. With a final darting glance between Bradrick and Amirah, she finally dipped her head in approval. Bradrick took Amirah's hand and gently pulled her toward the center of the room.

"Let's really convince them of their win and that we're doing just what they asked," he whispered. "Ready?"

"Possibly more than you," she teased with a grin.

Once more, all eyes were upon them as they assumed their positions. From the outside, their convincing facade stole the hearts of the nobles present. They needed everyone to believe they were content, possibly even happy. Queen Indra clapped, signaling the band hidden away in the corner to begin playing.

A steady beat and a pleasant melody erupted. Amirah and Bradrick stepped in time, isolated in a world of their own. They parted, spun, and wove back together. Other couples joined, forming a circle of beautiful pairs that pranced around them. Their bodies glided with the song, while the high table sat in judgment of their graceful movements. When the song drew to a close, approving eyes fell upon Amirah and Bradrick. Their parents were confident that they had, at last, emerged triumphant. Now, they could all begin to enjoy the evening. Bradrick and Amirah entertained a few more dances, before he offered his arm to lead her back to their table.

Over full chalices, they discreetly observed the high table, which now ignored them. King Landry engaged in boisterous conversation with the nobility on his left, who had the dark complexion and bright-colored garb of the Southern Kingdoms. Queen Indra and Consort Foley resumed their deep conversations with the nobility on their right, dressed in equally exorbitant attire. Bradrick and Amirah smiled, pleased with the success of their ruse. Satisfied with their carousing on the dance floor, Bradrick excused himself to speak with Alonzo and the lords at a nearby table. Amirah wanted to keep dancing and found another dance partner to fill Bradrick's shoes.

The first song was energetic, with dancers spinning in circles around the floor. Amirah's head tipped back as laughter bubbled from her chest. Her focus shifted from the dance floor to a wraith-like figure standing at the entrance. His long, shaggy black hair spilled from beneath the hood that covered most of his olive-tan face. Her eyes locked with his dark forest green eyes that almost seemed to glow. She blinked, disoriented from the dances' rapid spinning. When she could look again, the black-clad stranger had vanished. Unable to find him, she wondered if he had been an apparition. The combination of drinks and dancing left her eyes heavy and her face flushed. She vowed to herself that the next song would be the last for a while.

When the new song started, the dancers wove through each other in counter circles. They moved faster and faster before breaking into pairs with whoever they landed hands with. Amirah found her fingers held by a leather glove. Still light-headed from the drink, her eyes widened in surprise as she met the forest-colored eyes of the stranger. She recovered a moment later and smiled up at him as he guided her their dance.

Not a word passed between them as she studied how his hair framed his chiseled cheekbones and spilled past his shoulders. Seemingly, he did the same, though his expression revealed nothing.

He appeared to be around the same age as herself. Seeing him this close, Amirah realized his garb was more refined than her first glance, including his handsomely tailored cloak. It draped over his fitted black Brizian noble traveling clothes and leather boots. Although not the usual attire for the event, he danced as well as the rest of the guests. The scent of spice and ginseng emanated from him. Something flashed in his eyes when their gaze locked before the song pulled their movements away from each other. She spotted a Prurian soldier in proper armor running toward the high table. Clenching her first, Amirah cursed herself for becoming distracted by the stranger.

CHAPTER 6

A high-pitched scream muted the banquet hall. Everyone searched for the source but found nothing alarming. A frigid gale lanced through the palace, making the candlelight flicker. Frantic bodies crowded away from the center of the banquet hall, pushing Amirah back with them. She scanned her surroundings for Bradrick, Alonzo, or Gabbie, to no avail. Everyone's attention focused on the high table where Queen Indra rose from her seat. A stone-cold, blank expression fell over her face, as unreadable as empty parchment. Her sapphire eyes fell upon a man who now stood center of the room.

Amirah sucked in a breath when she spotted him. Guilt chilled her blood from the recognition of the stranger she recognized as her last dance partner. The guests gawked in confusion at his sudden appearance. The man seemed unaffected by the audience. His leather boots echoed through the silent room with each measured step toward the high table. Queen Indra and the intruder stared at each other. They sized each other up as he approached, each revealing nothing. Amirah realized she had missed an opportunity to prevent whatever was about to happen. The sounds of metal scraping broke the heavy silence, and a rush of soldiers formed a line before the high table with drawn swords.

"I would put those away," the intruder warned. He remained locked in a stare-off with Indra. His cool, low voice sent a shiver down Amirah's spine. "Unless you want to end up like the guards outside the door."

Indra signaled her soldiers to hold their position. Confused looks and a few whispers spread through the crowd of guests. A thick sense of anticipation built in the air—for better or worse. The stare-down between the Queen and the mysterious intruder broke when King Landry struck his hand on the table. Queen Indra spared him a brief side glance while the room shifted their focus to him. He snarled through a mouth still full of food and his face reddened with annoyance. The southern guests he'd been conversing with shifted away from him in their seats. Unlike the wary nobles in the room, the intruder eyed him with boredom.

"Who in the Twelve Kingdoms are you!?" Landry demanded, his face reddening.

Everyone's eyes darted between Landry and the intruder. He responded with a dark chuckle and strolled closer to the high table. His eyes bore into King Landry with malicious amusement.

The bizarre exchange transfixed everyone, which helped provide additional concealment of Alonzo. His movements went unnoticed as he searched between the guests that crowded the walls and tables for Amirah. He spotted her pressed near the middle of the guests. She stood fixated on the mysterious man who came to a stop mere feet from the line of soldiers.

"After all these years, I'm surprised you don't see the resemblance," he mocked, clicking his tongue in disapproval.

King Landry's face contorted the longer he stared, processing the man who stood before them. Mock amusement twisted the corners of the man's face as he watched Landry become warped by disbelief. It carried his body into a slow stand.

"No!" Landry seethed.

Amirah spied Bradrick climbing onto a table on the opposite side of the banquet hall. Her heart pounded as she noticed him take

42

a silent position with a longbow in hand. All signs of amusement left the intruder's face.

"Yes, my father. Turns out, he had as many secrets as you do. Some things come back to haunt you, even when you bury them from memory."

Indra's soldiers glanced up from their positions, maintaining their offensive stance. The subtle movement of her hand paused when the man chuckled. He waggled a black, leather-gloved finger in warning at the Queen as the bow in Bradrick's hand creaked in protest. Its sound sent a wave of panic through Amirah.

She spotted the sheathed sword strapped to a noble standing beside her. Her movements were swift from training alongside her father's men. Even in a dress, capturing the hilt until drawing the sword was as easy as breathing. The noble realized too late what had happened, missing his chance to protest. Amirah had already set off and pushed her way through the crowd in front of her. Some guests startled back when Alonzo leaped after her. The tension in the air coiled around everyone in the room, threatening to erupt.

The sound of a bow can be silent to the untrained ear, but Amirah was no mere novice. She struggled through a tight throng of people, catching the faint hiss of Bradrick's arrow cutting the air. The intruder sidestepped it at the last moment. His hand flung up and closed into a fist. The arrow froze, suspended in midair above it, inches from his face. His sudden movement caused some of the soldiers to rush forward. His other hand sliced the air, and an unseen force threw the approaching soldiers back. A collective gasp sounded from the crowd. The man turned his focus back to King Landry, and the arrow turned with him.

"No! Father!" Amirah cried out.

She struggled against the last throng of people that were huddled together until she broke through. Her feet stumbled over her gown and she fell with the sword still in hand. Shocked, the man spun toward her as his fist unclenched, sending the arrow free. The arrow tip embedded in the table in front of King Landry. A line of blood formed against Amirah's cheek where the sword had nicked her flesh. She glared at her mysterious former dance partner. The shock that marred his otherwise sharp brooding features reflected in her own. A moment of bewilderment slipped over his face as his hand reached up to his cheek. Amirah noticed an odd, luminescent color flicker to life in his eyes. Long tendrils of hair spilled forward as his head tilted closer to examine his gloved fingers. His eyes darted between her and Landry.

The lighting in the room flickered and, at the same moment, the man was standing above Amirah. Their eyes locked as he pulled her up. Something unreadable crossed his face as he wiped the line of blood from her face. She froze at the bewildering warmth that tingled up the path of his thumb. What she had thought to be a small mark on his cheek disappeared. An alluring, wicked grin plastered his face as he turned back toward the high table.

"It's time to end this," he announced. "Almost two decades ago, your blood was bound to mine. I am here to stake my claim and end your curse."

"You have no power here! Guards! Guards!" Landry's voice bellowed.

The Brizian soldiers who had traveled to Pruria with them spilled into the center of the room. Queen Indra's soldiers joined them in a unified formation. The man smirked and cast a glance in Amirah's direction and her breath caught. A breeze billowed through the banquet hall until the lights flickered out and left everyone in darkness. The last thing that she saw of him was the glow of his viridescent eyes. When the candlelight sparked back to life a moment later, he was gone.

Brizian and Prurian soldiers encircled Amirah and the now emptied space. Everyone looked around them, bewildered. She stared at the vacant spot while suspicion clouded her mind. Alonzo interrupted her silent attempt to process the exchange between her father and the intruder. She hadn't realized that she held her breath until Bradrick joined them. The mark on her cheek was gone and without visible injury. Satisfied she was alright, Bradrick and Alonzo joined the soldiers to scour the palace.

Unlike Amirah, Queen Indra spared no breath before ordering an immediate search for the intruder. She was a steel wall of authority. Having assumed control in her husband's place during the Khaos War, her fortitude had been melded for situations far worse than this. She thanked everyone for attending the banquet and promised a grander feast tomorrow with fewer dramatics.

Reports were already coming in from the soldiers surveying the palace. Amirah gathered through her observations that something had happened outside the main doors. As a result, servants and soldiers worked in tandem to guide the guests through a separate exit behind a hidden wall by the high table.

"Just a rumor. Bah! I warned you, didn't I?" A vehement, deep, graveling voice goaded from the crowd.

Amirah recognized it and craned her neck, trying in vain to catch sight of the gossipers. Questions piled up in her mind that would go unanswered by anyone that surrounded her. Her father was keeping something from her that seemed to be related to her past. An observation that became more apparent as she watched him give whispered orders to his Captain, who departed in a hurry.

With the guests gone, the Prurian and Brizian royals followed behind the remaining soldiers through the banquet hall doors. Consort Foley gagged from beside her, and they all paused in disgust for a moment. The putrid copper smell that accompanied the tarnished hallway replaced the romantic floral scent. What had appeared as a beautiful inverted ethereal field had become a gruesome nightmare. Blood coated impossible places amongst the ruined, wet carnage of decorations. The guards' bodies lay on either side of the door in two mangled heaps, as the intruder warned. The state of the slashed armor boggled everyone. It looked as if claws had torn through them.

Queen Indra stepped into the bloodbath without hesitation. She gave no mind to the stains that formed against the fine golden fabrics of her gown and issued orders without pause. Bradrick was the only person who dared cross her at that moment. She forbade him from aiding in the search for the intruder, as he wanted. Instead, she ordered Alonzo to stay beside him at all times, both armed and with additional guards present.

Bradrick leaned against one of the blood-soaked walls near Amirah. She was keenly aware of the dark, brooding shadow that fell over his otherwise unreadable face. His soft brown eyes darted around the scene as if to search every dark corner. His gaze lingered for a moment on Foley, whose stomach was unaccustomed to grotesque scenes. A wave of nausea had the Consort braced against the wall for support. The Captain returned beside King Landry and gave an indicative nod. Amirah yelped as her father snatched her wrist and dragged her behind him. Amirah tried to pull away, unsure of what was going on. As he led her from the madness, Queen Indra's steely sapphire eyes fixed upon his back. She stopped Bradrick, who had bolted forward after them.

"King Landry!" Queen Indra's shout echoed off the halls.

Her air of superiority and controlled anger was apparent. Her tone alone stopped everyone, even Landry, who turned on his heel to face her. No one else would have dared to use such a tone with him. The sight of red flecks on her face and hands, paired with the blood-stained golden gown, gave him pause.

"There has been an attack upon my castle on the eve of our children's wedding." She all but stomped forward, splashing through the not yet dried puddles of blood as she approached. "Two of my men are dead. What I want to know is who that man was, why he was here, and why my men are dead for it. We have a contract, and you are attempting to flee! What do you know? Do you intend to put an end to our agreement?"

"No! You heard the madman's words," Landry retorted. "I have as many answers as you. The best promise of safety is to ride it out and retrieve my soldiers camped at our borders for additional security. We'll return by morning with them and proceed with the wedding as planned."

"Why take her with you when she's guarded here?"

"We don't know where he has gone, who he is, or what we are up against. You have seen what he has done here tonight. She is safest with my men until he's apprehended. Assigning additional soldiers to guard her would deplete the number of your men available for the search and your family's security. The soldiers that rode in with us will travel as our guard to the camp."

Queen Indra squinted at him in silent thought. Although her suspicion about the situation was apparent, she had no power over another monarch she could exert without ample risk, a factor King Landry was extorting. She nodded and turned away with a dismissive wave. Once more, King Landry jerked Amirah forward. *What isn't he telling me?* Amirah wondered, wrist burning from her father's grip.

The distance expanded between them and the blood-bathed halls. She tried to focus on the sound of Bradrick's angry voice as he argued with his mother behind her. Her ever-growing list of questions circled her mind. Of one thing she was certain: her father had lied to Queen Indra based on his earlier exchange with the intruder.

Outside, the Captain awaited them in front of the palace with the carriage and the now horse-mounted Brizian soldiers. Everyone else that came with them would remain at the palace while awaiting their return. *I hope Gabbie and Kamille are tucked away in the safety of their rooms,* she hoped silently. Her mind lingered on them as they shuffled into the carriage. She peeked out the window at the Prurian palace as they pulled away, only to be yanked back by her father. Bradrick and Alonzo emerged from the palace moments too late. Alonzo patted Bradrick's back as they watched the carriage fade from view.

CHAPTER 7

S everal hours later, King Landry still kept a vigilant eye on their surroundings. The deep lines on his face formed caverns, with a wrinkled nose, downward pointing eyebrows and gray eyes that darted around. He had been gazing out the window, searching the night, since they climbed into the carriage. Amirah sat with crossed arms, partly because of the chilly air and partly from her growing suspicion of her father. Whatever he was hiding had stirred him enough that they now fled into the frigid night. Her mind replayed what she had overheard about a curse, as if trying to assemble a puzzle without all the pieces.

The horses' gallop from the Prurian palace slowed into a steady canter. They would need a break soon if they were to make the trip King Landry proposed. The driver's patterned knock on the roof signaled that they were stopping. Landry grumbled as the carriage rolled to a standstill. The Captain opened the door to check with the King before attending to the troop. Amirah moved to climb out of the carriage, but her father blocked the door. He had no intention of letting either of them exit the carriage until they reached the camp. Amirah huffed as she crossed her arms again.

"Fine, but can you at least tell me what's going on? That man mentioned a curse. Before that, I overheard some guests mentioning one. What curse? Who was that man? What are you hiding from me?" Her questions rolled off her tongue in rapid succession.

"Do not take that tone with me! It's not for you to be concerned with! We're heading for safety, and that's all you need to know," Landry spat. He looked at his daughter as though she had sprouted multiple heads. Few dared to challenge the King's authority, and none raised their voice to him. His mouth opened and shut as he attempted to speak, his tongue failing him.

A high-pitched noise whistle overhead broke their stare-down. Landry's mouth clamped shut with an audible click. They heard soldiers scrambling, unsheathing swords, and the whining of horses that stamped their feet, rattling the carriage. Calls to protect the king echoed as soldiers screamed in pain. Amirah had never heard such an unsettling noise. She tried to peek out the window, but her father jerked her back. He shook his head with a stern warning glare. Beneath the robes, his hand wrapped around the hilt of his sword. Amirah's heart thudded in her ears, marking the slow seconds of sudden silence.

Thump, thump, thump.

Another whistle, followed by the sounds of metal clashing and an animalistic screech piercing the air. King Landry's eyes bulged. Somewhere, the Captain shouted orders to collect the horses. Landry and Amirah's ears strained to follow the fight they could not see outside of their cage. Moments later, the Captain threw open the carriage door. His pupils dilated, sweat beaded on his brow, while dirt and blood littered his armored uniform.

"Majesties! You mu—"

His body vanished, knocked away by something too quick for the royals to see. The door swung on its hinges in eerie silence. King Landry swore under his breath, but neither of them moved. A moment passed before he dared to push the door of the carriage open with the tip of his sword. When no immediate threat presented itself, he climbed out of the carriage and motioned for Amirah to follow.

Her dark brown eyes scanned the area as she emerged. The sun had yet to peek over the gray horizon, and they had stopped by the roadside where the dew-covered fields stretched to the tree-lined border. A small creek flowed within view alongside the road. Patches of morning fog drifted over the land. It would have been beautiful if not for the bodies of their soldiers and horses strewn around them. Blood pooled under and around each of the mangled remains. Flecks of red splattered the ground in various directions.

Amirah followed behind as her father wove careful steps around each corpse. He pointed in the direction they needed to head. The border in the distance had a sprawling tree line that stretched farther than the eye could see. She wondered if they had any chance of making it there as they maneuvered around the carnage. Most of the soldiers' bodies surrounded the carriage. Others had fallen beside the creek where they had tried to retrieve the horses they had left to water. The amount of blood staining the landscape lessened as they traipsed forward, and fewer corpses were scattered amongst the tall grass. Some had contorted limbs from being thrown, while others had fallen with their sword in hand, familiar slashes cut through them.

Her eyes met with the Captain's, who laid upon his back, struggling to breathe. It was impossible to tell where the bleeding came from, or what blood was his. The broken breastplate exposed his usually yellow-tan tunic beneath, stained as red as the rest of his armor. Blood choked his words as he tried to speak. She knelt beside him and cradled his head in her hands. The back of his head was slick with blood. Each breath rasped and gurgled as he tried to speak again. She leaned down to make sense of his weakened voice.

A sword slammed into his exposed chest, making Amirah jerk back. She gasped as blood droplets splattered her face and the Captain's eyes glazed over. King Landry jerked the sword free with a final twist. Amirah met her father's icy gaze with widened eyes.

She watched as he turned his back and stepped away, intent on continuing forward. Her eyes watered as she lowered the Captain's head onto the ground. Using her thumbs, she closed his eyelids and kissed his brow.

"Pax tecum." She whispered the words for a soldier's goodbye. One of many phrases she learned training alongside them, including the Captain.

Amirah's lips quivered in confused rage as she stood to follow her father. She intended to confront him, but the sound of bells halted their steps. They turned around in search of the source and found the mysterious man from the banquet. His venomous gaze latched onto King Landry eyes fading from a wicked glowing green to that of a deep forest. Not unlike her ruined dress, he wore the same black-clad outfit from the banquet, still wet with blood. His long black hair spilled out from beneath the hood of his cloak, revealing no obvious weapons. She supposed there could be a dagger tucked into his boots or the backside of his leather pants, hidden beneath the cloak. Ignoring the arms-reach distance between them, Amirah dislodged the Captain's sword from his lifeless hand.

"I never thought you would be the kind to flee, Otis," the man said, bemused. "You can't run forever."

Landry spat on the ground, shifting his sword to his dominant hand. "That is enough! I don't know who you think—"

"What in the Twelve Kingdoms is going on!?" Amirah demanded from both men that clearly knew something she did not. She had enough of being ignored. Soldiers, good men she had known most of her life, lay dead around them. Even now, as she kept the sword out of sight, she refused to tolerate more bloodshed without knowing the reason for it. Both men glanced at her.

The man smirked and turned his eyes back to King Landry. "I see nobody knows about the terrible things you have done and all the dark secrets you keep. Does your daughter even know about the curse? Worse yet, does she know how her mother died?"

Her father blanched. Amirah turned to him with bewilderment written on her face.

Everyone knew about the tragedy. Queen Rana died from an illness when Amirah was very young. It had caused the royal physician to keep an extra close eye on her for years. King Landry never spoke about his late wife. Amirah assumed it was caused by grief. A knot formed in her stomach as the overloaded list of questions swam around her head.

King Landry's face tinged close to the color of purple as rage overtook his body. He raised the sword and lunged at the stranger. The man dodged the swing with bored expertise. A flick of his hand forward sent out a wave of unseen energy. It seemed a strong wind had knocked King Landry back. After that, each attempted rage-driven swing by Amirah's father resulted in the same outcome until the man disarmed him, a factor that further enraged King Landry.

"There is only one way to end this, Otis. Remember the curse: Your blood is bound to mine!" The recital of those words boiled the blood inside Landry. His face contorted until realization drained the color from his face.

The man smiled. "Ah, so you figured it out. Then you know why I have to kill you."

A flicker of viridescent light consumed his eyes as he charged the King. Amirah jumped between them, swinging her sword, and missing the man;s chest by a mere fraction. She prepared to strike again, but a large hand yanked her back by the hair on her nape. Amirah yelped in pain as the weapon was wrenched from her hand.

King Landry released her hair and twisted her arm to anchor her in front of him. She froze, paralyzed by the cold, sharp edge of his sword that was pressed against her neck. She looked for something useful, but found nothing except the man standing before them. Disgust and a spark of anger licked the flames in his eyes.

"Why am I not surprised? You were always willing to murder those closest to you, and of course, you would murder your flesh and blood. The Continent may never know the depth of depravity you've wrought on this world, but I do. My name is Nithe Vivek, son of Duke Sorgin Vivek, and I am here to avenge him."

"Impossible," Landry bellowed. His sword pressed into Amirah's flesh and caused tears to threaten the corners of her eyes.

Nithe winced but didn't draw attention to the fresh cut as it formed on his neck. He didn't think it possible to loathe the King more until now. Without a doubt, the murderous brute wouldn't hesitate to kill his own daughter. This was a moment Nithe had looked forward to since he learned the details of his father's death. Now, her presence complicated everything. The curse left him short on time to consider other options. Before, when he realized that the beauty who had graced the floor like a swan was the daughter of his mortal enemy, he had the luxury of time. A luxury he no longer possessed. She looked now as if she would fly away, but the bloodstained hands of her father held her captive.

What King Landry still failed to notice was how much Nithe was like his father. Trained since he learned to walk, he didn't need man-made weaponry to wage war or take revenge. Now, the King's deranged threat against his own daughter, which presented a threat to his life, compelled him to respond. He had to improvise fast if they were going to survive.

Nithe glowered one last time at the King before he shut his eyes. He raised his arms so that his hands centered his body and began a fluid transition of his fingers that formed a series of hand gestures. They danced as they created the shape of his intent with each gesture.

Amirah felt the world shattering around her. Her vision blurred, taken over by darkness, and a scream caught in her throat as she curled into herself. King Landry lost his grip on her when white feathers battered his face. Her body seemed to shrink out of his grasp, replaced by the unorthodox flutters of an elegant bird.

Nithe opened his viridescent sparked eyes in time to observe her transformed body escape from the King. *Perfect,* he thought as he observed her clumsy movements. Although she had taken on the form of a swan, he could still hear her heartbroken cry.

He used the moment to his advantage. His hand transformed and shifted into a black-scaled claw with sharp talons. Seconds later, his inhuman speed landed him in front of Landry.

A look of horrific surprise consumed the King's face as the claw plunged into his chest. Landry's mouth gaped open and shut again as the claw tugged at an organ in his chest until it lurched free. Nithe ripped it out, allowing King Landry to look upon the still-beating heart before he dropped to the ground, dead.

It was over too quickly. Nithe's hand shifted back, and he bagged the heart in a sack he had scavenged off a fallen horse. The swan crashed into him the moment he looked up. She fell to the ground as Nithe regained his footing. He tilted his head, unsure of what to do with her while she cried and hissed at him.

He withdrew a cloth from beneath his cloak and began to clean himself. Somehow, he felt unsatisfied. Despite King Landry's blood caked onto one of his hands, something about the death of his enemy should have brought a sense of fulfillment to his hardened heart. He bent, hovering his hand over a small dip in the ground. Water droplets were summoned up from the earth, and swirled around his hand until it was cleaned. Now free of blood, he turned his attention back to the bird. Various bloodstains colored her plumage, worsening as she laid her long neck over her deceased father's body. She began busking when Nithe moved closer.

"Ungrateful," he muttered. "Be still for a moment."

She responded with a hiss. He stepped back from the disdainful bird and closed his eyes. With his hands centered and palms forward, he formed another set of gestures—fingers intertwining upward, then breaking away. When he opened his eyes, the bird remained staring back at him. He grunted and made another attempt, but to his perplexity, nothing happened.

"For the love of the Continent, why is this not working!?" He ran his hands through his hair and looked out at the horizon. The first rays of sunlight now danced behind the edge of the distant treeline—a reminder of the lack of time. Nithe approached her again with his hands raised. "I don't blame you for hating me or wanting to peck out my eyes, but as it stands, we're both in danger if we stay here. There isn't time right now to explain everything, but it's thanks to our fathers we are bound by this curse. To add to that problem, I can't seem to transform you back."

The swan launched herself at him. The clumsiness of her battering wings, as she adjusted to her new form, kept him a breath out of reach. That was, until she adapted to it and instinct took hold. As a typical side effect of new transformations, Nithe knew she would adapt within moments. Despite his ability to shift himself into a dragon, he didn't speak bird. Although he was certain a spell existed for that, he could guess what she said as she chased him through the field of corpses. As Amirah snapped at his backside, it struck Nithe that she was less intimidating in human form. He surrendered with his hands up.

"Wait, wait, wait! I have a solution! Well, a temporary one. I know this will be the last thing you want to do, but right now, it is our best option. My father's home—my home—has an enchanted lake. We can get you back into human form with it and work on a more permanent solution for the curse. Unless you think your prince would want a swan for a wife."

She snapped at him again, this time with more accuracy. Which was good; she was going to need it.

"I will take that as a reluctant *'yes'*."

He paced several steps backward. The wind picked up and spun around him until everything blurred. His change happened as suddenly as the strike of lighting. When his eyes opened, he towered over her in his now-massive form. The curious swan cocked its head from side to side. Her dark brown eyes took in the black, leathery-skinned being from its snout, all the way to the horns that sprouted between his short mane and went halfway down a long neck. She looked over his lean muscular body as he sat on his taloned hunches with a tail wrapped around him, much like an enormous cat would. The eyes that stared back at her possessed the same shade as Nithe's human form and swirled with the same viridescent light when he used his magic. Black feathered wings unfolded from his back and beat against the air.

Understanding his intent to leave, Amirah had no other option but to spread her white wings and copy the clapping movements of the dragon. With some great effort, she managed to lift into the sky. A few times she faltered toward the ground, but, as predicted, instinct took over. Content with her progress, the dragon took off toward the treeline that led into Brizia. Without better options, the swan followed him.

CHAPTER 8

T he next morning, King Landry failed to return to the Prurian palace as promised. Queen Indra was irate and raved about his betrayal, but Prince Bradrick felt something was terribly wrong in the pit of his stomach. He argued with his mother that the Brizian royals would never have abandoned members of their court, servants, and belongings without the intention of returning. The King was many things, but he wasn't someone without common intellect.

Even Amirah's loyal companion, Gabbie, remained behind. The court members, unaware of the Brizian royals' departure, still expected a wedding day. Gabbie, however, was sharp and astute at navigating her way through the two royal courts. She knew something was amiss when Amirah never returned to her chambers. Naturally, she alerted Kamille, and the two women sought information that the Prurian court did not have. No one did.

Although he avoided vocalizing it out loud to anyone other than his mother, Bradrick could not dismiss the concern for Amirah that nagged at his core. Under his mother's explicit orders, he remained under guard and kept away from the searches. Alonzo managed to slip away to help and gather intel for him. The searches revealed nothing about who the intruder was or where he came from. Alonzo reported finding no additional witnesses beyond those who were present at the banquet and the deceased. Inconsistent rumors began to spread among the civilians that someone had spotted a dragon circling at the edge of the capital. Bradrick dismissed the wild theory. The last time anyone had seen a dragon was during their eradication during the Khaos War.

It became clear the wedding would be, at the minimum, postponed. Bradrick approached his mother again, this time coming away with some modicum of success. Reluctantly, Queen Indra agreed to send a single scout. Her eagerness at the prospect of having King Landry's head on a stick as the hours passed drove the decision. Bradrick urged her to allow him to ride out with the scout, but she forbade it. Instead, she ordered his personal guard to ensure he returned to his chambers. Bradrick had predicted her reaction and was already prepared to escape the guards that trailed his every movement like shadows.

Inside his private-chambers-turned-prison-cell, Bradrick changed into plain clothes with a dark hooded cloak. His simple disguise had allowed him to sneak in and out of the palace on more than one occasion. He slipped over the side of his private balcony and onto the vine-covered trellis that descended into the gardens. Despite the increased presence of soldiers patrolling the palace, he evaded detection all the way to the stables. The ease with which a hooded man could slip in and out of the walls unnotice should have alarmed the entire kingdom. Bradrick had known this weakness from a young age and had exploited it too many times to count. *No wonder the intruder appeared and vanished without detection*, he thought.

Bradrick tailed the scout on horseback, careful that he hung far enough back to avoid being spotted. Predictably, the scout took the main road that connected the capitals of the two kingdoms. Being the most direct route meant King Landry wouldn't have sent his men another way.

The stone-paved road morphed into a dirt road outside of the Prurian capital. Bradrick maintained such a distance from the scout that the rider looked like a speck on the road ahead. They rode for hours into the early afternoon sun, even as the horses began sweating and their pace slowed. Just as he began worrying about his horse, the scout in the distance dismounted, and Bradrick drew closer.

The scout stood in the middle of the road, talking with another figure. The few remaining hours of daylight reflected off the figure from what could only be their armor. To the left, he could see the duo-colored Brizian banners posted in what he assumed was a small camp. Bradrick's heart hammered in his chest with a mixture of fear and hope as he urged his horse forward.

The scout eyed his approach with suspicion and the soldier that wore an admiral blue surcoat over his steely armor, drew his sword. When Bradrick threw back his hood and revealed himself as the Prurian Prince, they stooped into apologetic bows. Bradrick's gut sank upon seeing their somber expressions when they straightened, and he willed his eyes to survey the area off the road.

"It alerted us to trouble when unmounted horses arrived at our camp," the Brizian soldier explained. "We sent scouts out, and they discovered the carnage. More of my men are working to gather the bodies now."

As the soldier spoke, Bradrick dismounted and followed the tracks that led off into the flattened grass to where a gold-encrusted carriage sat. An ominous tapping of the door against the unblemished side drew his attention to the empty interior. The team of horses that had pulled royals was nowhere to be seen in the surrounding blood-soaked ground. Unquestionably, there had been an attack.

The world seemed to turn on its axis as Bradrick dismounted and handed the reins of his horse to the scout. He walked toward the carriage but stopped short. The aged smell of copper permeated the air closer to what appeared to be the corpses of the entire troop that had departed with King Landry. Their remains lay scattered in distorted positions, some crushed beneath the carcass of their horse. He peeled his eyes from one body to the next and noted wounds that no sword could have made. The dried blood splatter was reminiscent of the palace hallway. Bradrick looked toward the treeline in the distance where the borders of Pruria and Brizia collided to steady himself. The reality of the situation guided his attention back to the stained earth and the corpses that were being gathered by soldiers in front of him.

Bradrick kept his eyes peeled for any sign of Amirah as he ventured toward them. Although sickening, he was grateful none of the bodies the soldiers carried away seemed to be her. Ahead of him was a simple cart that had been pulled into the tall grass with a fur-lined bed. The care given to the body was one that only royalty received under the circumstances. The size of the pelt-covered corpse revealed that it could only be King Landry. Bradrick huffed against the internal war waging in his mind as he approached the cart.

For better or worse, he felt compelled to pull back the coverings. The sight of Landry's pallid corpse with an atrocious cavern in his chest churned Bradrick's stomach. He stepped away to empty its contents into the grass. Returning the coverings, he left the image that would forever burn in his mind.

Bradrick's mind spun, and his eyes darted around the area. He turned to a young soldier that was hooking the cart to a horse. "Where is the King's missing organ?"

"There's no trace of the King's heart, Your Highness. The only clues we have are the markings on the other soldiers and the hole in his chest." The soldier lowered his voice to a near whisper. "Everyone knows there's not a man-made weapon that can do damage like that. There is a rumor being whispered among the soldiers of a cursed beast in the night."

"What about the Princess? Is there any sign of Amirah or what happened to her?" Bradrick pressed the soldier.

"If it weren't for the footprints, we'd doubt she had been here at all." Somberly, the soldier guided Bradrick to where they had discovered King Landry. Before he left Bradrick, he added, "I'm not sure if it's important, Your Highness, but the Captain's sword laid near the King. He didn't make it this far and had wounds as bad as the rest. Maybe worse because he also had a wound from a sword."

Bradrick thanked the soldier and knelt closer to the ground, his eyes searching for any missed signs. Boot imprints indicated the ground's softness in the early hours before dawn. Under and between layers of smashed-down grass, he identified other footprints belonging to at least three people. He suspected the smallest set belonged to Amirah, though the positioning of them suggested she had followed close behind her father. Bradrick tried to trace her steps from the carriage to the field and became confused. He did this twice more but was left with more questions than results as he circled around where she appeared to have stood with King Landry where he had fallen. There, her footprints disappeared altogether, as if she had vanished with the morning fog.

More interesting were the pristine white feathers that scattered the ground. With one held up in the sunlight, he examined every detail. Perplexingly, he realized this wasn't a species of fowl he was familiar with. Such a peculiar thing to find scattered among the Brizian King's blood stains. Bradrick took the single feather with him as he returned to his scout's side. Both stood with slumped shoulders from the weight of the afternoon's discovery.

"What should I tell Queen Indra? She will ask about the Princess. Should I inform her they're all dead, Your Grace?" Worry tinged the scouts' voice.

"No," Bradrick shook his head. "Tell the Queen that there was an attack, and that Amirah is missing. Since there are no signs she shared the same fate, Pruria should help with the search. If I know nothing else, my mother will send aid if I remain here. When you return, please ask Lord Macanay to join me with my hunting bow, and to do so without telling my mother."

THE SCOUT DID AS THE Prince requested upon his return to the palace. As predicted, Queen Indra was reluctant to send aid to search for the Princess. She almost fell off of her throne when the scout informed her that Prince Bradrick had stayed behind to begin the search himself. Fury turned down her eyebrows, and she looked to Consort Foley, whose jaw gaped at the news. They mirrored each other as they agonized over the trivial inconveniences of the catastrophe. With a reluctant groan, she ordered a small dispatch of soldiers to aid in the search for Princess Amirah and to guard their Prince. Dismissed, the scout hurried from the throne room to search for Lord Macanay.

Alonzo was at the training grounds when the scout approached him with the news, and he wasted no time preparing to leave. He climbed onto a horse with a satchel of supplies and raced against the last rays of dying light, following the soldiers who departed the palace earlier.

Night had blanketed the sky for hours when he finally reached the scene. The stained ground was the only evidence that remained of the corpses, which were now on their way back to their homeland. Even the King's carriage had followed with the mutilated Sovereign. Alonzo found Bradrick standing beside his horse with a shadow darker than night cast over his face. His mouth was thin-lined, and his eyes were darkened with burdens. No words could bring comfort as they faced whatever blight had befallen allies.

Well-lit torches flamed to life around them as both the kingdom's soldiers surveyed the area. They traced Amirah's footprints alongside her father's. The two had gone from the carriage to the deceased Captain's side, then to a strange pattern of scuffling footprints where the King's corpse had fallen. Although the matted grass made it hard to follow, an altercation had occurred here. Then, her footprints ended, leaving no clue which direction she might have gone, which resulted in an expanded search.

Bradrick showed Alonzo the large white feathers he had collected earlier. Neither knew what species of fowl they had belonged to. Nearby, they discovered a set of unrecognizable tracks—four massive prints pressed into the earth. They gave the impression that a large, clawed creature had sat upon its tree-trunk-sized haunches. Bradrick's brow creased as he examined the prints with deepened suspicion.

Beside him, Alonzo rubbed his chin and mused, "In all my years of hunting, I have never seen animal prints as large as this. Do you think it might have been a wyvern?"

Alonzo's suggestion was a daring guess, but it challenged the history known throughout the Continent.

"No," Bradrick said, shaking his head. "I don't think any species of a dragon ever had white feathers. Plus, they went extinct during the Khaos War and Landry had a hand in their extinction. Although, there may be something to that line of thought. Some of the Brizian soldiers were killed in a similar way to the guards outside of the banquet hall. Perhaps the intruder has a 'pet'? A very large and dangerous pet."

"It could explain many things from these last two nights. It will be difficult to track, not knowing what it is. What should we do about Amirah?"

"Mother will give up the search within days and order the soldiers home. After that, it will be up to me to find her."

"Do you think she is still alive? I know we didn't find a body, but after a time, everyone will assume the worst has happened."

"I have to believe that she is. Unless there is some sign to suggest her death, I will keep searching. It's the only way I can atone for the mistakes I've made."

Alonzo patted Bradrick's back. "This is no fault of yours, but I will help you shoulder the burden. Whenever you search for her, I will be beside you."

Bradrick nodded. The weighted knot in his stomach eased a bit. Although he knew Alonzo was right, he still felt the burden of guilt. His mind had peeled back every scenario where he saw a chance he could've taken that would have changed the outcome. A voice in his head whispered, *The blood of these men, our allies, King Landry, and our people, are on our hands.* It was then that he felt the weight of the crown, long before it rested on his head.

CHAPTER 9

Daylight spilled over the Continent like a warm blanket as Amirah and Nithe soared above it. Instinct had taken over her body as she adjusted her wings to sail through gusts of air like the exquisite creature she had become. Nithe had adjusted to a slower speed that allowed Amirah to keep up in her new physical form. Though she had adjusted to her avian body, she still somehow maintained a keen sense of self. Her inner voice reminded her to memorize her surroundings and make an internalized map for when she was free. The elation from the soaring on the winds uninhibited came at a price she was certain would be her humanity. It didn't take long to pass from Pruria to Brizia. She recognized the final last village that looked as a speck nestled in the last expanse of trees on the borders.

The day passed as they carried forward. Brizia sat at the center of the Continent with luscious forests that spread over hills and valleys. Occasional clearings and wild fields dotted the land until they met the edge of the mountains that rose along its northern border. Had they flown south, there would've been farmlands and pockets of towns nestled against the edge of the forests. Instead, the mountain peaks before them rose from the expanse of thick sea of trees that had swallowed the remaining roads. The mountain at the end stood somewhat separate and was the tallest of the entire Continent. Its base tapered down into the woodlands, rolling into hills in the east that eventually met with the plains of Pruria.

THE DUKE'S CURSE

The Old Lore cited the regal ridges as the point of creation of the Continent—the gods having pulled them from the ocean floor. Snow dusted the highest points that stretched too close to the stars. In the aftermath of the Khaos War, the tree-covered valley at the mountain base had become a neutral territory inside the Brizian border. Though, few passed through its dense, dark forest.

Amirah remembered the peak from her travels between the kingdoms, though she had only ever seen it looming distantly over the forest. Those memories now felt tainted by grief and lies. Consumed by sadness, a single tear slid down her yellow-orange beak as her white-feathered head drooped, causing her to dip toward the ground. Startled by the change in altitude, she dipped her wings to correct. Nithe tilted his scaled black head to observe her recovery. He huffed as she attempted to catch up, unable to replicate the speed of his enormous body.

Night rose like a cool, dark blanket, chasing away the last fiery rays dancing on the horizon. As the light faded, Nithe became harder to see against the night sky. He stooped downward toward the valley with Amirah close at his tail when they neared the mountains. She blinked as a stone keep with a dark pointed roof emerged from the trees, where moments before there had been nothing. Four matching turrets attached to a pale stone castle followed it. The castle roof sloped from the carved fascia into a sharp apex. Every unlit window hinted that the place had long been abandoned.

A sizable arched gateway without doors was guarded by two stone alamy dragons, carved to peer down upon anyone who passed through. The gateway stood strong, as did most of the fortified wall surrounding the castle and its lands. However, some parts of the wall had collapsed into rubble, while nature consumed the others. Behind the castle, starlight danced over a rippling blanket of water—a lake.

Nithe's bestial body steered toward the ground, gliding into a landing that ended with a few steps in his human form. He waved her toward the pristine lake. Amirah doubted she could replicate his landing, much less on the water. The thought of the cool water both excited and inexplicably terrified her. She descended, her body gliding to a stop on the water's surface.

Her nerves eased as her wings folded to her back, her feathered body remaining buoyant on the rippling surface. Nithe watched from the lake's edge as she examined her surroundings. The ethereal face of the full moon shimmered on the lake's surface. As she swam through its glowing reflection, the water erupted. She sank below the water and rose again, gasping for air. Her human arms flailed in her effort to resurface, but her dress tangled around her limbs, and she sank deeper.

"I'm sure the water is wonderful, but will you come out?"

Nithe turned as the splashing stopped, the water's surface stilling as if Amirah had never been there. He cursed, tossed away his cloak, and jumped into the water. He cut through the darkness, familiar with the depths of the lake. Somehow, he found her still struggling below the surface, sinking away from the faint stream of moonlight. His hand latched onto the onto hers and yanked her upward.

Amirah gasped for air, choking as they broke through the surface. Nithe dragged their sodden bodies onto the bank of the lake where they lay, panting for air. Amirah's cheeks warmed, realizing their hands remained intertwined. Instinctively, she jerked her hand free and cradled it to her chest like a lost treasure. Her eyes locked onto his unreadable green depths.

"You could have let me drown," Amirah blurted.

"I should have. Probably would have if it wouldn't kill me too."

She frowned at his matter-of-fact tone. He gave no hint of noticing her reaction or concern as he shifted to his feet. When he offered her his hand, she stared at it in bewilderment. Her hesitation earned an eye roll and the loss of his proffered assistance. Shivers wracked her body as she struggled to her feet. A dark look flickered across his face, gone as instantaneously. Without warning, he tugged her up toward him. Heat pooled in her cheeks as she stumbled into his chest. As she straightened, his black cloak enveloped her like a warm blanket.

His movements paused, and she flinched when he tilted her chin upward. He studied her neck, his brows creased, as his other hand ventured to where the forgotten wound remained. She hissed at the initial sting of his touch, but the pain vanished. He released her chin and stepped back; her hand moved to her neck, feeling smooth skin. Only a faint silver scar remained. Her eyes widened and flicked to his. Without another word, he turned toward the castle. Bewildered and with no other options, Amirah followed.

They passed through the courtyard and entered the castle through the back door. Rich colors infused the interior wherever she looked. The walls had deep, vibrant greens, reds, yellows, and were contrasted by smooth-painted ceilings. All the woodwork was dark-stained and polished, withcolorful tiles inlaid in the floors. Each detail spilled out by the light of the candle Nithe lit. He led them through to the front entrance room and up an enormous staircase covered with a deep burgundy rug. At the top, they turned down a hallway that dead-ended with a wall centering a lattice window. Four identical wooden doors lined the hall, one of which they stopped in front of.

Nithe opened the door to a lightless room and found a candle to light on a nearby surface. It flickered to life, casting a gentle glow against the rich yellow walls of what appeared to be a bedroom. Amirah stepped in as he crossed the room to pull back the drapes from the windows. Moonlight spilled through the panes, conquering the remaining darkness. A cold fireplace took up the wall opposite a bed layered in various shades of pink-hued linens, with a fuchsia canopy trimmed in golden tassels. In one corner of the room, a faded plum chair faced the door. Other furniture, like the polished armoire and trunk, matched the dark woodwork throughout the castle. The brass candelabras that sat on the bedside table drew attention to the earthy artwork framed on the wall behind them. Another doorway led to a large round tub centered in a private washroom.

"You can rest here for now. I'll get some food from the kitchen while you change into something dry so we don't get sick," Nithe said, nodding toward the armoire. She raised a questioning eyebrow at the word 'we', and he continued as if reading her mind. "I don't know the extent of the curse, but it's better to err on the side of caution."

He left before she could respond, sending a wave of fresh agitation through her. If her gown didn't cling to her trembling body like a second wet skin, she would have refused to change into anything. It wasn't lost upon her that Nithe was her reluctant rescuer and also her father's murderer. Despite their strained relationship, he had still been her father. She brushed away the threat of tears and forced the unpleasant memories away as she approached the armoire.

It was entirely possible Nithe would do away with her after breaking the curse. The only comfort was that she was within Brizia's borders. All the burdens unintended for her were now thrust upon Amirah. With a bitter sigh, she threw open the doors of the armoire. Dust made her eyes flutter, but the sight of several gowns stole her breath.

Amirah pulled out a lace-trimmed linen nightdress but paused when a glint at the bottom of the armoire caught her attention. She made a mental note to come back to it, determined first to get out of the sodden trousseau and nearly damp cloak. Finding folded towels in the washroom, she dried herself and pulled on the fitted nightdress. With nowhere else to put her ruined ball gown, she tossed it into the empty washroom basket. The dresses in the armoire were plentiful enough until she could gather some of her own. *Oddly enough, it seems they fit me,* she thought.

The thought reminded her of what she had seen earlier. She returned to the bedroom and hung the cloak on the door of the armoire to dry before she resumed her exploration of its interior contents. The item at the bottom of the armoire glinted up at her from its strange location. Unable to contain her curiosity, she pulled out a small unframed portrait.

Amirah studied the painted details of the woman dressed in a regal blue gown. Her dark eyes burned back into Amirah as a dark-haired reflection of herself. The face was familiar. It elicited the faint memory of a large painting once been fixated on the walls of her father's castle with a subtle, mischievous smile hidden in the corners of the woman's mouth. She hadn't seen the likeness of her mother in more than a decade.

Amirah tucked the portrait back into the armoire with unease as more questions were added to the ever-growing list. The weight of exhaustion crept over her and she sought the warmth of the bed. Her mind searched for answers, for missed signs or moments that might have been a clue. She ventured to replay the events of the last two days until her eyes were heavy from tears, as was her heart. The tears slid down her cheeks, one after the other. There would be no questions asked tonight as she curled beneath the blankets.

Nithe returned to the room with a tray of food and drink in hand. His eyes landed on what appeared to be Amirah sleeping, nestled into a cocoon on the bed. With hushed steps, he placed the tray on a night-side table. Then, he gathered an extra blanket from the bottom of the armoire and placed it over her to ward against the chill of the room. He noted his cloak hung to dry against the armoire door and took it down. A frown tipped his mouth at the gentle care given to it. The day had concluded with unexpected difficulties that dared to taunt him. With one last look at her face, he blew out the candle and closed the door with a soft click.

CHAPTER 10

Sunbeams danced over Amirah through the windows. She stretched, sitting upright, and rubbed away the residual cobwebs clouding her vision. The sight of the room reminded her of everything that transpired until she cried herself to sleep. She grappled with the reality of being in the home of her father's murderer, though her father might also have murdered her mother. This reminded her of the portrait tucked away in the armoire.

Amirah held no tangible memories of her mother and no affectionate memories existed of her father, who was present as much as a King could be. He had long kept her at arm's length, unsatisfied whenever she would behave in ways that reminded him of her mother—which was often. All the while, he'd avoided any mention or questions about Queen Rana. All doubts about Otis Landry's feelings toward her vanished when he threatened Amirah's life.

On the verge of tears again, Amirah wrapped her arms around her knees, trying to bury the memories. She scanned the room, certain more clues were hidden somewhere, although none were within sight. Instead, a tray of fresh fruits, a pitcher of honey wine, and an empty glass sat on the bedside table, catching her attention. She felt disconcerted that she hadn't woken up when Nithe left it. A rebellious growl from her stomach protested her reluctance to eat. She reasoned with herself that he couldn't kill her. *Yet*.

After clearing the tray of food, Amirah turned to the pitcher of honey wine and poured herself a glass. The sweet notes of the drink helped settle the barrage of thoughts and questions. Moments later, a knock sounded at the door, just as she finished her glass. Returning it to the tray, she went to answer the door. When she opened it, Nithe stood there, dressed in an open black velvet long jacket and vest with silver embellishments fit for court life. His long, cascading black hair was groomed away from his face. Amirah's eyes scanned him from head to toe. When she looked back to his face, a tinge of pink tinted her cheeks. Whether it was from embarrassment or something else, she wasn't certain. Fortunately, he didn't seem to notice her assessment of him.

"Sorry, I must have slept in late." Other than it being later than when Gabbie normally burst into her chambers, she didn't know the time. Her heart ached, missing her friend already .

He nodded. "Well, it's afternoon Princess. I came to give you a tour and discuss a potential plan. We don't have any servants here, so you will need to dress yourself."

Amirah blushed, realizing she was still in her nightdress. She nodded and excused herself to change. The first thing she pulled out was a mint-colored gown that was soft to the touch and simple enough to put on without help. She tugged at the tightness of the sleeves around her wrist with a deep sigh and joined Nithe in the hallway. His gaze slid over her from head to toe, as she had done to him. When she cleared her throat, his eyes snapped to hers.

"How long will I be here?"

His eyes narrowed before he turned to lead the way. "Hopefully, not for long. Once, I employed a gardener, but he went back to his homelands. I don't like to keep guests. Follow me and I'll give you a tour of your temporary abode."

Amirah's eyes bulged and followed him. *Guests?* She mulled the idea over, remembering how abandoned the castle had looked the night before. In the daylight, the colorful details gave the castle walls new life. Her original impression was erased, as if she were seeing it anew.

They passed through the corridors of the two upper floors of the castle, which consisted of spare bedrooms and storage, including Nithe's bedroom and study. The two adjoined rooms were down the left hall, opposite the bedroom Amirah had slept in. Between the two halls, the enormous staircase descended to the entrance hall, a key feature of the castle. To either side of the staircase were hallways that connect in somewhat of a square. Both led to the gallery, parlor, and other rooms fit for entertaining guests—except for the keep's ground level and the kitchen quarters they had entered the evening before. Amirah could easily imagine the castle once bustling with life.

Nithe led the way outside to the courtyard where the fading sunset greeted them. Pale stone statues of opulent figures dotted the area within the overgrown garden beds. Cobblestone paths nestled between them, leading to a dais at the edge of the lake. Its stone steps disappeared into the calm water that waited for the lights of the night to dance upon its surface. Amirah wanted to dip her tired feet into the water's edge, despite the chilled breeze that tinged her cheeks and the tip of her nose with pink. She mentally kicked herself for not wearing a shawl as a shiver traveled down her spine.

Nithe cast a sidelong glance, catching sight of the shiver she tried to conceal. They barely spoke during the walk, and he grimced at the pang of guilt for not considering the weather. While being outside made discussing their predicament easier to breathe through, he had forgotten to consider it.

"It's colder than I expected. Let's go back inside. I have a fire lit in the study," he said, tone blank.

She nodded her agreement to his invitation. When Nithe turned his back, Amirah rolled her eyes, self-irritated by her easy compliance. She needed answers to the questions that refused to subside. As they ventured back into the castle, she studied his form from behind. He was not as tall as her father, though he towered above her more than Bradrick. They were all taller than her. Despite his intimidating and disconcertingly appealing height, he had shown no intention of harming her. Still, his coarse words after he pulled her from the lake lingered, reminding her of the possibility once they lifted the curse.

Earlier, they had avoided entering the study that now greeted them. Nithe strode in without hesitation, while Amirah's mouth dropped open. Ruby red walls complemented the dark woodwork of the room. Bookshelves lined the wall behind a large desk where Nithe stacked papers out of his way. Books and interesting trinkets Amirah was unfamiliar with were piled on the surface. A huge rug of intertwining red, blue, and gold layered most of the floor. In the middle of the room sat a rectangular wooden table with ornate emblems engraved around it and a small set of books scattered on its surface.

On the far wall, two navy blue cushioned chairs faced a large stone fireplace carved into the shape of a dragon. Its snout faced the fire, giving the illusion that it breathed the flames dancing upon the logs. A dark blue ceiling, painted with silver and gold stars forming the celestial bodies of the night sky glinted against the light. Windows with thick drapes flanked the fireplace. Nithe motioned for her to assume one of the chairs by the fireside and handed her a blanket when she sat down. He stoked the fire with a brass poker as she wrapped herself in the blanket. Her eyes trailed his movements until he took the other seat. Only a small table sat between them, and the angle of their chairs ensured her watchful gaze didn't go unnoticed.

"Should I reintroduce myself?" He arched an eyebrow, staring back at her.

"You can, if that's what you want." She shifted her gaze back to the fire. "I already caught your name."

"Humor me, Princess."

"Fine, but stop calling me Princess."

"I can't make any promises." ising steadily, Nithe took a few steps forward, standing in front of her. A glint of amusement flickered at the corners of his mouth before he stooped into a proper bow with his hand proffered. She suppressed the urge to roll her eyes and, instead, accepted his hand. "Pleasure to make Your Highness's acquaintance. I am Nithe Vivek, Duke-heir of the late Duke, Lord Sorgin Vivek of Brizia."

He placed a light kiss on her fingertips. She snatched her hand back from the unexpected contact and cleared her throat. Few people had placed their lips upon her skin; even following court etiquette. Nithe struggled to keep from grinning as he straightened back up.

""Right then. I am Princess Amirah Svana Landry of Brizia, heir—oh, for the love of the Continent!" She clapped her hands over her mouth. She looked at Nithe's bewildered expression with wide-eyed horror. "I am the sole blood heir to the blasted throne!"

"Sounds like you love your job." He chuckled, sitting back down.

"What about you? It's not like you've ever been to court," she snapped. "You don't understand what this could do to the kingdom!"

"Well, I don't have a proper title. My father kept my entire existence from everyone on the Continent and hid me here until just before his death. The King, your father, took everything that was his after he took his life. Who knows what would have become of me or our home if either had been discovered."

"I'm sorry. I wasn't aware of that. In truth, I asked so many questions over the years, but never received any answers. It's become apparent there's a lot that I don't know about."

They sat in silence for a moment, considering one another. Amirah chewed on her lower lip, eyes downcast. She had fewer happy memories of her past than she would like to admit, and no desire to delve into them now. Nithe rose from his seat and went to his desk, pouring two goblets of caramel-colored drink. When he returned, he handed one to her. She took a sip, nose wrinkling at the bite of it. After a few sips, she decided it was best to down the drink to get it over with.

With courage summoned, she looked up at him once again. "Why does my mother have a room here?"

"You're going to want another round for that," Nithe said, getting up again. "My father left a journal behind."

This time, he brought the decanter and a leather-bound journal back from the desk. He handed her the journal, refilled their cups, and settled back into his chair as she skimmed the name 'Sorgin Vivek' on the first of the age-stained pages.

"Reading it will give you some of the same information I have from someone who was there. After you've finished, we can talk about this curse that has somehow affected both of us."

After downing the remainder of her drink, Amirah set the cup on the side table and turned past the first page of the journal. It smelled aged, like the old books in the Prurian palace's library. Inside, the sharp lettering of the Duke's handwriting was scrawled over the pages. Amirah skimmed through the passages, each page recounting a time before and during the Khaos War. Some detailed the days when the Duke was friends with her father before he became King. In all matters, it appeared Sorgin Vivek was her father's right-hand man. Until they weren't. Amirah flipped back the entry that first mentioned her mother.

The old King has fallen ill and is in a hurry to see his heir married. Otis has many options, but there is one that sticks out from the rest. One that would make an exceptional future Queen for Brizia. My position allows me to advocate for my friend and future King...

So began the tale of how her father entered a year-long courtship with her mother, Rana. The strong-willed woman captured the Brizian hearts, including the Duke's, who wrote fondly of his new friend and his happiness for their match. Her grandfather was on his deathbed when her father received the crown. At the same time, the Duke received the terrible news that his wife had died. Thereafter, he removed himself from court life and kept everyone at arm's length. The Duke wrote fewer passages about King Landry, except for a single notation, written prior to the eruption of the Khaos War:

The weight of the crown has brought unforeseen changes within Landry. He has become unrecognizable from the man I once knew...

The passages carried on into the Khaos War that consumed the Continent. Queen Rana ruled in King Landry's stead while he was away on the battlefields. The Duke returned to his King's side, and they fought side-by-side on the battlefields. Soon, the war took its toll on them both. While the Duke grew tired of bloodshed, King Landry's blood-thirst ripened. The Duke advised against the unwarranted attacks on innocent villages, to no avail. Giving up, he left the King's side and returned home.

One night, the King returned to court alone after a particularly gruesome incident. He was full of icy rage and drenched in blood that was not only from enemy soldiers. Word had already spread across the Continent of his deeds to his infuriated Brizian allies. Queen Rana managed to maintain diplomacy, and he returned to the battlefields again. However, not long after, King Landry intercepted letters to Rana's family, revealing she planned to escape the Continent. Unable to leave the battlefield, he had limited options to prevent her departure. He burned the letters, unaware she kept the Duke abreast of the situation the entire time.

Days later, a sudden debilitating illness struck Queen Rana. The physician suspected poisoning, but none of them could remedy it. In those moments, she absconded from the Capitol to seek the Duke's assistance.

Rana arrived at my door this night as if delivering herself to death's door. I knew from her state there was little time. The blood on her lips was enough to determine this was not some unknown illness nor common poison. She would have had a quicker death if it were. The physicians at court are either fools or were paid off...

Saving the Queen revealed his secret. He was a sorcerer; one of the few magic wielders who had escaped the Continent-wide decimation. One with a panache for alchemic healing, and could concoct an antidote for Queen Rana. King Landry was seething when the Queen presented herself in perfect health upon his return. A couple of days later, servants discovered her dead in her private chambers.

Amirah gingerly closed the journal and set it in her lap, her brow furrowing as she gazed back at him. Tears threatened the edges of her eyes. Unable to bear more, she slammed the book shut. Nithe poured her another goblet. It quivered along with the slight tremor in her hands.

"It can't be true, can it?" she asked. "Why doesn't he mention you? It doesn't say why my mother had a room here."

"As a child, I used to think my father hid me because he hated me for my mother's death in childbirth. Later, I learned everything was to protect me. His knowledge of the ongoing politics gave him the foresight to err on the side of caution. Anyone with magic was being exterminated, and forcing those who survived into hiding. Fae-kind left the humans when the dragons began to be hunted nearer to extinction. Numerous innocents were slaughtered for their differences in the name of safety and power. My father knew that if the King murdedred Queen Rana, he would be next.

"So he sent me away to my mother's homelands, offshore from the Continent, and he went into hiding. It didn't take Landry long to hunt him down with the Khaos War drawing to a close. Knowing that King Landry would never be held accountable, my father went to his grave, cursing him. Now, here the two of us are." Nithe swung his goblet back and forth between them. "It's hard to say why, or even when her room happened. There is nothing written about it. They were all good friends for many years—more your mother than your father toward the end of the war. My father both loved and respected Queen Rana until his last breath."

Amirah swallowed the rest of her drink. Pieces of the puzzle began to click together. She couldn't deny the existence of the Duke's own written account, which was more than her father had ever given her. Her eyes glazed over as brittle numbness overtook the cracks that had formed in her heart by her father's betrayal. When her eyes met Nithe's again, a new understanding passed between them.

"So there's a curse? Tell me about it, because I don't quite understand what it means."

Nithe's finished his drink, setting his cup on the side table with a sigh. "Magic is not perfect. No one knows exactly how things unfolded on the day your father murdered mine. There's no one living who was present the day he finally hunted my father down in the very capital of Brizia. Sure, there are rumors—whispers that were almost forgotten to history. Intentionally, no doubt. What I do know is that my father cursed him as he lay dying in a pool of his own blood. Blood curses can only be carried out under certain conditions. They are easier to enact than they are to predict all of the possible outcomes."

"How do you know if it is a blood curse, or if there is a curse at all if no one was there?" Amirah asked.

"There's little magic able to be done while in a dying state. The rumors all mention the King being cursed, and some suggest the kingdom too. They cite the wording incorrectly, but close enough for me to guess the correct phrasing of part of it. I thought your father would be the end of everything, including the curse. But then, you appeared. It took a moment to piece together what happened when you fell and injured yourself. I was also injured, a replica of your own. Then again, before I cast the enchantment that turned you into a swan."

Her hand traced where the cut on her neck had been, the one Nithe had healed at the edge of the lake. She cleared her throat, tucking her hands back into her lap. "What exactly does that mean? How does it work?"

"I don't know everything about it yet. From what I can tell so far, there is a sort of pull between us. One I hadn't noticed until after we first met." Amirah nodded as he spoke. She recalled her eyes being drawn to him despite a room full of spinning bodies and the transfixion of their first meeting that followed. Nithe continued, "If you bleed, I bleed. Which means our fates, the very mortality of us, is tied together."

Amirah frowned. "We didn't notice before now. Is that even possible?"

"How often were you ever injured as a child?"

"Never. That is, I had several close calls, but fortunately for those around me, nothing my father could notice. Thanks to the mountain air, a long-sleeved dress could hide any bruises or scrapes without drawing suspicion. He wasn't known for his kindness, but he was very particular about how I was and wasn't to be. My father wanted the quintessential perfect royal daughter. Although, I failed to fulfill that hope. I was rarely ever ill—which happens when you're sheltered. Except for once, not long after the Khaos War ended and my father came home. I got sick with a terrible fever that would have made anyone think I had been at sea for months, but eventually, it went away. The physicians were under a lot of stress from my father over the entire ordeal. Afterward, he ensured it was clear not so much as a scratch was to befall me."

Nithe paled for a moment, then cleared his throat. "I was ill on the voyage to my mother's homeland, even after they got me off that forsaken ship. That may mean there is no factor in the distance between us. Once I recovered, my mother's family kept me safe and helped train me. I spent more time training than I ever did fighting. When I returned to the Continent, like anyone left with magic, I kept myself hidden from public attention. Physical harm, shared ailments, anything that could end either life seems to be part of the binding."

"How do we end this curse, Nithe?"

"That's something I'm still working on. I spent the time you slept going through the work my father left behind, but there is nothing specific to the particularities of this. I was unaware we were both affected until after our first encounter. Everything is... different from what I'd expected. First, I need to figure out why I wasn't able to turn you back from being a swan. It should've been as seamless as transforming you into one. Unfortunately, bathing in the moonlight of the lake every couple of days is only a temporary fix."

"Every couple days!?" Amirah shrieked, bolting up from her chair.

"Yes," he stated matter-of-factually. "A couple, a few, however many. I don't know the exact amount yet, but frequently enough. My father enchanted the lake when I was not yet a novice as a temporary solution for magical mishaps. I haven't had to use it since I returned to the Continent. We'll keep searching for answers here until Cicely returns to her home. She's an old friend of mine that might give us a solution or know where to find one. I promise to fix this if you give me time."

Amirah stared into his forest-colored eyes, unsure of what to believe. The world had crashed, burned her up with it, and sprinkled information that was kept in other people's graves. It was an overwhelming amount to digest. The chance at freedom was a siren's call that she couldn't resist. She nodded in agreement, exhaustion setting in, despite sleeping in late. With that, she excused herself and headed to bed. They were both ready to leave things where they were for the night. She needed time to herself to mourn the loss of her father, her shattered reality, and the girl she would never be again.

CHAPTER 11

Several uneventful nights passed. One night, Amirah floated her swan form onto the lake to return to her human body. As moonlight saturated her plumage, her body became engulfed in water. After Nithe had dragged her back onto the lake's bank a second time, he suggested they try swimming lessons. She couldn't deny it was a necessary survival skill and agreed. After a few days, and several mouthfuls of water, she had basic mastery of swimming. Or, at least, she could avoid immediate drowning. Besides that, they kept a cautious distance between each other.

Amirah passed time exploring the castle and wandering the courtyard garden. She favored sitting with her feet dipped in the lake's water as she reread the Duke's journal, carefully digesting each passage. However, Nithe's absence from its pages made her wonder about their undocumented childhood. She couldn't perceive Sorgin Vivek as the villain her father considered him in the end. She also noticed that there was no mention of herself. She had been a young child, a few years younger than Nithe, when her mother's life ended. *How different would everything have been if we had known one another as children?* She kept this questioning thought to herself as she studied the text.

In the mornings and late afternoons, Nithe left fresh meals with floral tea blends or water on the bedside table in what had become her room. She wasn't sure why he did it, other than perhaps to keep them both alive. The subtle gesture piqued her suspicion, even though Nithe kept himself distant. He busied himself with research as Amirah mourned and came to terms with the circumstances. In the study, Nithe poured over every resource the room contained. It seemed to be an endless search as stacks of books and journals began to pile on the table and desk.

In the end, his search proved futile.

The afternoon before Amirah's next expected transformation, her frustration mounted. She went in search of Nithe and, to her surprise, found him in the kitchen. The warm-colored room was fit for a full staff but was as empty as the rest of the castle. Nithe stood alone, focused on the work in front of him. A delectable aroma and curiosity drew her in.

His loosely pulled-back hair revealed the relaxed, sharp features of his face. He had rolled the sleeves of his tunic up to his elbows, allowing him to work diligently. Amirah watched his long fingers detail the surface of a pastry of sorts. She chewed on her lip to avoid licking them.

"I didn't take you for being a skilled cook," she stated, observing his handy work.

"I am full of surprises, Princess." He glanced at her with a smirk, noting her narrowed eyes. "The garden was overdue for a harvest, so I thought of something useful for a portion of it."

"Where did you learn to cook?" She hopped onto the countertop for a better view.

"Several people in many places taught me." He cleaned his hands off with a damp cloth and looked at her. "When I went to my mother's homelands, I learned a lot among her kin. When I was old enough to leave on my own, I ventured anywhere I could. You learn a thing or two while traveling the world. Then, there were a few kind hearts when I returned to the Continent. Even a handful here in Brizia."

She nodded, more from wonder than understanding. Her life had been one of strict regulation and isolation—the concept of leaving the Continent just beyond imagination. Her wide eyes followed Nithe with open curiosity, who appeared to take no notice as he focused on his work. He shifted the pastries into a basket, added other edibles, and covered them with a plain cloth.

When he offered an outstretched hand, she hesitated but eventually placed her hand in his. Her feet stumbled a little when she slid from the counter. He made no move to catch her and instead turned toward the door, gently pulling her behind him. She huffed but allowed him to lead her outside where the sunlight warmed her cheeks. They moved to the edge of the courtyard, where a clearing spread out. Nithe released her hand as she studied the sun sinking lower on the horizon in a pink-orange glow. When he cleared his throat, Amirah looked down to find a food-engulfed blanket set up.

Amirah mirrored his arched eyebrows as she sat opposite of him. She plucked at the fabric of her pale blue dress until she could sit comfortably. Nithe had arranged two plates with fresh fruits, sweet roasted nuts, honey, and one of his pastries. Amirah helped pour drinks from a dark glass decanter that smelled bittersweet. The arrangement looked akin to the paintings that hung in the noble houses she had visited across the central Continent.

"This is delicious!" Amirah mouthed over the first bite of pastry with a groan.

Nithe looked down and tried to hide a grin while he preoccupied himself with his plate. They ate in silence for a time, with only the gentle ripples of the lake in the almost natural melodious silence. Each had questions to ask the other, yet neither was prepared to breach that moment of peace. So they stayed in the quiet comfort of not-quite awkward silence, enjoying their meal. As she lay on her side, Amirah plopped a dark berry into her mouth, humming at the sweet taste. The pinkness of her cheeks could have been from the drink, the late afternoon breeze, or both. Nithe stared up at the darkening blue skies as if studying the stars above. Amirah tossed a berry at Nithe to catch his attention, and he shot a halfhearted glare in her direction that elicted a small laugh to escape her.

"What else do you know about them?" she asked. "My parents," she clarified at the confused look tossed in her direction.

"Only what's in the journal. Rumors, as with all kingdoms, are seldom worth their weight. Perhaps worth more in consideration of your father."

She frowned. "That seems to be the way of it. My father tried to erase as much of my mother as possible. He took down all of her portraits after she died. I found one in the room here. It's the first time I've seen her likeness in many years."

Nithe looked back at the sky, lost in unspoken thoughts. Fireflies twinkled at the edge of the forest, a sign that soon night would mingle their light with the starry night sky that descended over the lake. Amirah and Nithe both reached for the basket without looking at where their limbs were going. Each startled back when their hands grazed against one another. Amirah felt a jolt, a sensation not terribly different from the tingling that followed his magic. She snatched it back, clutching it to her heart with an apology.

Heart. Her mind hissed the reminder with the bitter memory of her father's death at Nithe's hands. A dark shadow crossed her face as she closed her eyes and turned away with her hand still clutched to her chest. Nithe cocked an eyebrow. She stood up and stepped away without looking back at him.

"I'm sorry." His words were slow, mixed with bewilderment and caution.

"Are you?" Amirah spat. "Are you really?"

Nithe hesitated to answer as he stood up. The air seemed to have thickened around them. His near-silent footsteps approached until his hand could reach out to her. She pushed it away and spun toward him.

"What did you do with his heart? My father's heart! Where is it?"

"Are you sure you want to know?"

"Where. Is. It. Nithe?" Her words came through gritted teeth.

"It's suspended in a jar. The magic of the jar keeps it from decaying further. I intended to use it as a spell to break the curse, but after further research, it won't work. Instead, it can be used as payment when we visit Cicely." He turned away with a sigh, face hidden by the long strands of his hair.

Amirah couldn't dismiss the nagging suspicion that secrets were still being kept and doubt beckoned to her like a spreading plague. She couldn't bring herself to look at him again. The ice in her veins chilled her voice as she excused herself for the evening.

Nithe stayed, staring at the space she had occupied. It was a strange thing, being bound to an enemy's daughter. He expected to hate everything tied to Landry's very existence. He wanted to loathe her, but that desire became conflicted when he'd first gazed upon her beaming face in Pruria. She was equally a victim of King Landry as her mother. The memory of the King threatening his daughter's life solidified that.

Nithe couldn't blame her for hating him for killing her father. Regardless of whether it saved their lives or not, it would have happened. While he deserved every bit of her ire, somehow, he had a glimmer of hope she might forgive him. But reality was always a bitter entity. He cursed his broken enchantment for keeping them closer together.

After he cleaned up, he made his way toward his study. In the corridor, a faint sound came from the direction of her room. A frown rumpled his face. All he could do now was oblige her need for space. Everything else could wait. He closed the study door and began pulling more books from the shelves in a fervor. Soon, the room had been immersed in layers of books, more off their shelves than on them. He poured himself into futile research until he fell into a deep slumber over a pile of dusty books.

CHAPTER 12

A lthough Amirah had cried herself to restless sleep, filled with tossing and turning through the night, her eyes cracked open without the expected crust of dried tears on her skin. She looked down at her body to find herself transformed. She pondered if the pristine plumage and clear sight were a perk of being a swan. Her heart, however, was unchanged. It had steeled with furious determination and the intent to get as far from the castle as she could. This form offered the chance at the freedom she sought.

The light gray shadows of her room hinted that dawn had not yet peeked over the horizon. Silence hung throughout the castle like a soft buzz. In this form, she didn't need to carry anything with her. She had arrived with nothing and she would leave with nothing. Leaving her room would be the easiest part since she left the door unlatched the night before. Alert for any sign that Nithe was awake, Amirah's web feet padded through the corridor. She navigated down the grand staircase to the main floor and made her way into the kitchen. The door in the kitchen had a frayed rope attached to the handle, making it easy to open.

It wasn't until she padded into the courtyard that she stopped and held her breath. Early rays of daylight crested over the dewy morning surface as she took off. Her wings beat against the chilled morning air and her heart burst with adrenaline as she climbed higher. A few times, she dared to look back at the fading castle. The sleeping windows looked as abandoned as they had when she arrived.

Each time she looked back, she felt surprised that Nithe was nowhere in sight. Worried that her luck would change, she beat her wings with more zeal.

Amirah used the glaring beauty of the rising sun to guide her over the land. She knew they had traveled somewhat northwest, based on the mountain. Although her memories from her flight to the Duke's castle were unreliable, she knew that using the sun as a guide would lead her somewhat southeast, closer to Pruria. At the very least, it would get her as far from the castle as possible, and then she could figure out the rest of her predicament.

Exhilaration at the sense of freedom she now had would have carried her feathered body if the wind did not. Despite this her stomach ached with hunger when the daylight was at its apex. The thought of food reminded her of the previous night. Regret bubbled in her stomach like acid, knowing Nithe would discover she had left without a goodbye. Not that any intelligible reason for the feeling existed. She shook her head and refocused on her location.

Her wings throbbed from flying such a far distance over the endless sea of trees. A factor she assumed contributed to the subtle tug in her chest. She stooped lower and found no signs of a village, farm, road, or even a body of water. Based on the surroundings, telling if she were in Brizia or Pruria was impossible. A hint of moisture tickled her beak. A second raindrop slid down her back, and another dripped off her webbed foot. With the sky overhead darkening both from the loss of sunlight and the approaching gray clouds, it became apparent she flew on the edge of a storm. By evening, she would need shelter or she would have to brave flying through a storm. Shelter was the preferable option.

A small clearing appeared as teh rain became steady, driving Amirah to land. Lightning clattered between the clouds and thunder rolled across the sky as she squeezed past a tree line. There, she found a thicket folded over to form a low canopy with dry earth nuzzled beneath it. She couldn't see much in the dark, other than its emptiness. This left nothing to do besides wait out the storm. Exhausted, Amirah nestled down with her head resting against her soft white wings. Soon, she fell asleep to the pitter-patter of the rain.

At some point, underbrush rustled near the thicket, and the sound startled Amirah out of her slumber. Dark shadows from the woods enveloped the thicket. Not yet dawn, the remaining overcast that hung in swaths in the sky dimmed the last of the stars. Alerted by the sound that had awakened her, she listened intently. An unsettling tug at her heart told her that something was coming. The world was silent except for her rapid heartbeat and the creature that shifted through the darkness somewhere. In this form, her sense of smell wasn't much improved. Still, it detected the subtle, earth-like musk that lingered around her.

Her eyes studied the surrounding shadows. Amirah caught an unfamiliar print outline with the impression of large, sharpened claws beside her. Despite the weather, it was dry and cracked from age. It occurred to her that this current shelter might be the home of another creature. *Perhaps a carnivorous one that likes a main course of fowl*, she thought sarcastically at the ominous conclusion. Slowly, she retreated from the sequestered confines of the thicket into the unfamiliar surroundings. Droplets of water had saturated the canopy from the storm and dripped down to the damp earth. Her plumage acted as a feathered cloak and let the water slide away to the ground.

Carefully Amirah stepped toward the edge of the trees. The saturated ground made it difficult to keep her padded footfalls silent. She emerged from the treeline, prepared to take to the sky, but the sound of a low growl made her freeze. When she dared to turn, a set of hungry eyes stared back at her. With each step, the green-scaled, serpent-like creature wove closer. It circled her with the clear intent of a hungry beast. She mirrored its movement so that her back never faced it.

By comparison, it at least doubled the size of her human form. Golden spikes trailed from the center of its two golden horns all the way down to its tail. Red spikes surrounded the tip of the tail, which flicked around like an irritated cat. Each movement of the scales sounded like the jingling of bells. Dark leathery wings folded back like a restless bird, waiting to spring into flight. The creature's lips pulled back, revealing sharp teeth.

Another growl slipped from the creature's throat and with it, a rancid smell that unsettled her stomach. *My human self would surely have vomited,* she thought queasily. Amirah dodged as it sprang toward her, its leathery snout smashing into the ground. When it shook its head, the tip of its golden horns grazed her feathered chest. A small tinge of red stained her white plumage from the scratch. She stumbled back further when a set of enormous claws swiped at her. Her wings splayed to correct the movement, and the creature missed its mark twice more. She hissed back as it snapped at her wings. More urgently, she felt the pull to take to the sky, the tug to flee, and the sense that something was coming.

Surely that something must have been certain death in the guise of this creature that followed, trained on her every movement. Another swipe caused Amirah to falter as she dodged and stumbled into the branches of a small briar bush. The thorns tore through her feathers and picked her skin. She ignored the pain from the impact as blood slowly blossomed over her plumage. It wasn't enough to kill her, and the adrenaline coursing through her veins fueled her determination to survive. With regained footing, she raised her battered wings skyward. The weight of the beast collided with her hollow-boned body. The air was knocked from her lungs as she struck the ground.

She snorted and bit fervently at the attacker. It made a terrible sound—something like a mix between a yelp and a strangled growl—when she batted her large wings. It feigned moving away to circle around for another attack. Amirah busked at each swipe until one claw tore her wings and chest and the creature sprang for a final blow. A high-pitched yelp of pain chirped from the beast as a larger creature collided with it.

Amirah's vision rippled like choppy water waves. Familiar viridescent lit eyes looked down at her battered form. Her pain-ridden mind filled with confusion and hope as she gagged on a noxious scent filling the air. The dragon above her whipped toward the beast with a snarl, and the smell receded as the two creatures stared each other down. In her confusion, Amirah used the last of her energy to fumble between them with a venomous hiss. A growl rumbled from Nithe as thin tendrils of smoke and embers curled from his snout. The creature whined in submission and retreated into the woods until it was no longer in sight. Nithe turned back towards Amirah as she collapsed onto the ground.

CHILLED AIR WAFTED through the dark room, making it difficult for Amirah to sleep. When her eyes opened, she found herself in a circular room she hadn't seen before, lying on an uncomfortable hard surface. Despite the pillow beneath her head, a dull pain throbbed in her skull. She moved to rub the ache in her temples but was yanked to a stop by the metal cuffs that encircled her wrist. A curse slipped from her lips as she bolted upright. The tight bandages wound around her chest and torso pinched painfully from the sudden adjustment. A chain anchored her shackles to the wall beneath the window behind her. They proved secure after a few tugs and careful examination. There was nothing within range that could pick a lock.

The circular room felt barren. A few crates and cloth-shrouded pictures were stacked against the opposite side of the room. Beside them was a dull and plain wooden door. A large circular rug covered the stone floor, and a small table was tucked against the right wall with a dusty cloth over its contents. The closest object to her was a simple wooden chair against the right wall. Amirah sat on a small stone ledge that gave a view out of a pointed arch window. The cuffs gave just enough range for her to strain, looking at the surroundings below. A familiar courtyard graced by the waters of a lake and a dense forest beyond the walls taunted her.

"I swear when you show your face Nithe I'm going to—"

The door opened, and Nithe strolled into the room. He paused when their eyes met. Concern tinged with relief flickered across his face, only to be wiped away and replaced by his usual blank expression. If he heard her, there were no telltale signs. He dragged the wooden chair closer to her and took a seat in it. Amirah glimpsed bandages like her own, hidden beneath his half-opened tunic. She wondered if the beast had injured him too or if his injuries were a byproduct of the curse. It did little to ease her irritation with him over the present situation. Amirah huffed and looked away from him with her arms crossed over her chest.

"If your nose were any higher in the air, a bird would fly into it." He chuckled to himself.

"It wouldn't be any of your concern if one did," she snapped.

"On the contrary, it would be my concern. You are the future queen of our kingdom. You should keep that in mind before running off into the woods to get yourself killed."

Her eyes threw daggers at him. "Really? Yet here I am, chained to a wall like a common prisoner. How did you find me out there anyway?"

"This was the only non-magical solution I could think of. I needed to make sure you wouldn't run off while you were healing. Did you forget?" She gave him a perplexed look, and he sighed. "Any harm that comes to you also comes to me. We are bound by this curse, as much as it pains both of us. Running off with reckless abandon to get yourself killed before we can even put an end to it endangers us both. Do you have any idea how worried I was to wake up and discover you were gone? No sign of where or why. The innumerable possibilities that plagued me when I couldn't find you in the castle or by the lake? When I took to the skies, I just flew wherever I felt pulled. Perhaps it was instinct, or maybe it was the curse. Whatever it was, I followed that pull. A good thing too, or we'd both be dead."

"Are you sure you aren't only keeping me as a prisoner for your own gain? You sound more concerned about yourself." She looked away, determined to ignore his arguments.

Nithe reached to the floor beside her and came up with a small iron key in hand. His voice softened as he unlocked her shackles.

"No. At least, not only myself, Princess. This kingdom teeters on the edge of war until you assume the throne. You are the sole heir, and not everyone from your father's court can be trusted to accept it. Title or not, I still have a duty to protect My Sovereign. Though, you put up a decent fight against the guivre... for a swan."

"The what?" Amirah asked, rubbing her freed wrists as the shackles tumbled away with a clatter.

Relieved at the lack of restraint, she stretched and rubbed her wrists. Nithe leaned close enough to her face that his breath tickled her skin. The sudden proximity caused her to shift backward, but the wall behind her prevented her from moving more than an inch. His dark forest-green eyes bore into her like dancing flames that dared her to look anywhere else.

"Guivre. A smaller species of dragon with gaseous breath that dwells deep in the forest. Their aggression makes up for their size, and they are quite territorial. Although, I think the incident revealed something more interesting about our bond."

"Oh?" the question came out little more than a breath as she kept his gaze.

"Yes," he said, his lips quirking upward in amusement.

"And what's that?" Amirah tried not to fidget and maintain focus on their discussion rather than on his lips.

"When the guivre injured you, my body replicated the injury as if I had been attacked. I tend to heal quicker than most, an ability inherited from my father, but it appears my ability doesn't transfer through our bond. Unless I heal you, the injury remains for both of us. I suspect that my ability to heal would be unhindered if it were me injured, thus you would also heal. Healing either of us might not prevent an infection, however, and that's not something we should test."

She considered the injuries she had sustained since meeting him and nodded. Despite her lack of knowledge about magic, everything she had witnessed added up. Yet something still troubled her.

"I thought dragons were wiped from the Continent."

Amirah knew little about dragons outside of the lore found in books in Pruria. The stories described them as vicious predators with a hunger for human flesh. Beyond that, the only other details about them came from tales told by old soldiers. Even her father's role in their erasure was told through fireside stories, rather than written records. Like magic and those that wielded it, they were driven into extinction and eradicated, slaughtered during the Khaos War. Most tales of war never made official records, but dragons were more than war. These were once thriving creatures, their existence was now reduced to nothing more than fairytales and the stories of old men.

"Apparently not. The forest keeps its secrets well, as you discovered. So, let's have an agreement." He straightened and paused, expecting her to protest. When none came, he continued, "Come with me to see Cicely. If we aren't any closer to breaking this curse afterward, I would understand if you didn't stay, and you are free to go if that's your wish. You are a guest here, not a prisoner. I know this place isn't your home, but the magic that conceals it keeps us both safe from those outside of it. You need to return to the Brizian court to assert your claim at some point. If nothing else, can we at least agree to be a bit more cautious?"

Amirah swallowed. Whether his concern for her was based on self-preservation or not, he had a point. Guest or not, the curse needed to be ended. She nodded curtly. "Fine. We have an agreement. For now."

CHAPTER 13

N ithe and Amirah traveled on foot to the other side of the lake the next day. Nature overran where they passed through the fallen portion of the far-end wall. Past the perimeter, the trees consumed the land all the way to the mountainsides, except a barren strip of trampled grass with patches of dirt dotting the way. Amirah realized it had once been a road as they followed it through the forest. Eventually, they came upon what appeared to be the ruins of buildings. Some had burned long ago, while others had collapsed in on themselves. All had been reclaimed by the forest as vines climbed over the fallen stone and rotting lumber. When the trail faded into the trees, Nithe guided them through the forest as if by second nature.

Before the sun set, a small cottage appeared, tucked away at the base of the mountainside. If not for the gentle glow that emanated from the windows, it would have remained camouflaged in the forest. Its thatch roof was as dark as the bark on the surrounding trees, and the half-stone walls blended with the mountainside that peeked from beneath the forest floor. A woman sat in a rocking chair beside the open doorway.

She observed their approach with bright cognac-colored eyes. Her dark, tight curls, adorned with golden trinkets, bounced with her movements. Her garb consisted of layered burgundy and gold robes over a red dress, a few shades darker than the robes, that split at each hip. Beneath it, she wore warm black pants tucked into short boots. A keen smile pulled her lips as her hands stopped plucking berries from a bunch of skinny twigs. She set aside her task and rose to greet them. Her eyes stayed on Amirah as she welcomed them with widespread arms. Nithe chuckled and wrapped her in a warm hug.

"Cicely." He greeted her with a toothy smile.

"I was wondering when you would get here." Her warm voice carried the thick accent of the southern kingdoms as her eyes snapped onto him. "You should have gotten to me sooner, child."

"I hope you don't mind that I brought company. This is Amirah."

Cicely clicked her tongue at him. "I know who she is! I also know what you have done, and I can already tell you that I don't have the answers you're hoping for. But let's go in for the night's meal. I've already pulled the food I prepared for you from the fire."

Amirah glanced between the two with piqued curiosity at their frank, kindred words, indicating a history of familial-like camaraderie. Cicely motioned for them to follow her with a long-nailed finger. They obliged and entered through the doorway with a curtain tied off to the side. Inside, a large open room smelling of warm spices greeted them. The hearth glowed against the darkening shadows as night approached.

Above the fireplace were shelves with various-sized glass containers of every color. Pots, pans, and an assortment of containers cluttered the kitchen counters. Herbs hung above a large table, already prepared with plates of food. Rich-colored furniture formed a sitting area that was nestled into one corner of the room. A bookshelf housing books, papers, and a collection of shiny objects sat nearby. Rugs layered the floor until they reached the base of a stairway that cut off a corner of the room. Amirah had never seen such a place.

Her eyes wandered over the home's details until she caught sight of Nithe. He tucked an object larger than his hands, wrapped in dark cloth, onto the back corner of a low shelf.. It was unmistakably jar-shaped. She frowned, remembering what he'd told her about payment. He gave her a questioning look when he took the seat opposite of her at the table. She repressed the ripples of irritation and the burn of questions as she adjusted her seat. Cicely passed out fresh herb rolls and placed an open jar of honey between them. The aroma was distraction enough as they bit into the honey-slathered bread. Amirah hummed with delight before sampling the bright dish before her. Cicely observed them with a smile as they consumed their meals.

"Thank you for such a delicious meal," Amirah finally said. "There were flavors that were new to me. Where did the ingredients come from?"

"I am glad it was to your liking, Your Majesty. I don't imagine the castle cooks used spices from the southern kingdoms often. However, I know they've never used herbs or spices harvested from these mountains."

"From the mountains?" Amirah asked, recalling the bland meals of her childhood before her forced courtship.

"A great many things can be found in the mountains," Cicely explained. "But ever since the Duke passed away, people don't come here anymore. Anyone who lived nearby left their homes under duress, and those who survived didn't dare return, not even to harvest from the natural wealth. One way I survive is by gathering those rare ingredients and trading them at the markets. Of course, I keep some to use for myself. The food here today had both spices from the mountainside and from traders who came to market from the southern kingdoms."

"I know you've recently returned from the markets. Did you hear any news while you were there?" Nithe asked.

"It's what you would expect," she stated with a bored sigh. "All of Brizia mourns the King, and there is a whisper among the citizens that a war is brewing over the throne within the Brizian court. Everything else was the usual rumor mill of any city. While I was there, a Prurian doctor was searching for specific herbs, including a rare one that few know of and that only grows on these mountains. Of course, I made a nice profit from him. That was the extent of anything interesting."

Nithe's eyes narrowed. "What kind of herbs?"

"The poisonous kind, if you don't know what you are doing." She gave him a pointed look over her cup.

An unspoken understanding passed between the pair. It didn't go unnoticed by Amirah, who considered what memories they might share. She recalled the Duke's journal entries regarding her mother's poisoning, and she continued her meal, lost in meandering thought.

When they had all finished, Amirah helped clear the table and clean up. Night blanketed the world and settled over the forest until the tree canopies were darker than the sky. Cicely invited them to stay for the night and sent Nithe to build the fire in the outside pit. Amirah helped Cicely finish the task she had been working on when they arrived. The two women talked over less important matters while they plucked berries from the sticks. The mysterious woman, who treated her with the warm kindness of an old friend, intrigued Amirah. Nithe's fondness for Cicely was understandable.

When they finished, they had two full baskets of berries. Cicely took one and Amirah followed behind her with the other through the dark. They didn't have to walk far to reach the door of a root cellar. Once opened, it looked to be a tight space, too small for both of them. Cicely settled her basket somewhere in the dark space below before taking the other from Amirah. She made a mental note to suggest building one back at the castle to Nithe.

"I appreciate your help," Cicely thanked Amirah as they began to walk back toward the fire. Amirah turned to face her when she felt the woman tug on her sleeve. Cicely's voice lowered to a near whisper. "Between you and I, there is nothing within my powers to solve either problem you two face. I have said as much already, but it is important you understand. Magic that forged the Duke's curse is outside of my capabilities, so I can only offer guidance. He was a powerful and gifted man, surpassed only by his son. With trouble brewing at court, you will need to return to claim the throne soon. As long as your life remains tied to Nithe's, I wouldn't trust anyone else."

"Is he like his father?" Amirah searched her eyes in the dark. Cicely's cognac-color seemed to give off a subtle golden glow against the night.It reminded her of how Nithe's eyes seemed to spark to life whenever his power was in use

"More than he'll ever know, except taller. He is just as powerful, with the potential to surpass the legacy left to him. I've had the fortune of knowing them both. The reason he can't prevent your transformation into a swan has more to do with you than his magic." She laughed at the confused look that twisted Amirah's face. "Magic is a fickle thing, Your Majesty. You're stuck, so the magic is stuck. You have to choose to release what binds you. That is the only way for the transformations to stop."

Amirah nodded. She understood, in part, but the rest of Cicely's words seemed to be a riddle. The two women resumed their walk to the fireside as Amirah asked, "How do I figure out what binds me?"

"That is an answer only you can find, Your Majesty."

"I see. Excuse my asking, but why did you require payment from Nithe?"

Cicely's eyes bulged with momentary surprise. She glanced at Amirah with an empathetic look. "You're wondering why he brought the old King's heart. It is customary to give something in exchange for another in our community. Those like Nithe and I rely on our own dwindling network to survive. We live on the outskirts of society for safety and our own comfort. The things we trade, be it goods or services, won't be found in any market. The heart of a living being, especially a human heart, can be used for numerous things. Its properties make it a most potent ingredient. You cannot hurt the dead, Your Majesty, but they can still do some good. I don't have any immediate use for the heart, but I will give it the utmost honor and respect when the time comes."

Amirah nodded in understanding. Her eyes shone, but no tears came as they continued to the campfire. She was aware of the terrible things her father had done during the war—or at least, some of them. Perhaps this could be one way in which restitution could be made. The rest she would do herself when she returned to the throne. Amirah found herself a place to sit closest to the fire. Nithe showed no sign of having heard their discussion. His eyes peered into the fire until Cicely turned to him.

"There are only a handful of ways to break a blood curse, most of which are unsavory, unsuitable, or equate to death," she said to both of them. "Any method would need to be done by you two alone. No one else can end this. It will take both of you."

"Any idea which one is best to start with?" Nithe asked.

"No. I do, however, know where you might find the answer. There is the Astronomer in the northern kingdom of Isidris. A man of Cunning that your father and I were both acquainted with. He goes by the name of Venincio. You'll be able to find him at his home, which happens to be an observatory. It's secretly used to house a number of books."

"The Forgotten Library," Nithe whispered.

Cicely nodded. "Better that it stays that way lest we lose any more knowledge in the wake of the Khaos War. Venincio may help you find the answers."

The two turned to Amirah, who couldn't hide her wide-eyed excitement at the mention of such a place. Her imagination and heart danced at the very idea of seeing this place. Even if they didn't break the curse, she would be happy to have found that a secret library existed somewhere within the twelve kingdoms.

She beamed at Nithe. "When do we leave?"

CHAPTER 14

B radrick wiped the sweat that beaded his brow. Curled strands of wavy blonde hair stuck to his forehead. The air that filled his lungs felt like a fire that scorched his esophagus with each inhale. Alonzo signaled his readiness to take a break from combat practice when their tunics finally clung to their heaving chests. Every afternoon they were at the palace; most often found in the rear bailey. Alonzo had always been the better swordsman, but Bradrick's drive was more relentless. The two could rival the best Prurian soldiers in combat, especially as a duo.

Today's session had gone until sunset haunted the horizon. Bradrick's distracted focus was obvious as they cleared the yard—a state that seemed to consume him whenever he wasn't busy. He had been this way since they returned from the bloodied fields without Amirah. The gruesome scene, bizarre circumstances, and his own mistakes haunted him. The attack had sent rippling effects through both kingdoms. Now, the summer was waning, and everyone other than Bradrick presumed Amirah to be dead as her father.

He refused to give up. Even when the search parties stopped, he continued. His search was ceaseless and without fresh leads. Whenever he wasn't searching, he dedicated his attention to training sessions. Alonzo's support was steadfast, his opinions unspoken to Bradrick. Queen Indra, already past the initial shock, did not offer any sympathy. She pressed her son to let the matter go and move on to other issues. With no one sitting on the throne of Brizia, the alliance was as dead as King Landry. Despite Bradrick's protest, she ordered the searches within Pruria stopped, and issued a period of mourning for the Princess.

Bradrick refused to comply. Instead, he trained, researched, or went out searching on his own. Now, he headed for his chambers, intending to bathe. However, before he could reach the chamber doors, a squire delivered him a summons to the throne room. With an exasperated sigh, he followed the squire, already aware of his mother's plans.

When he entered, the guards shut the doors behind him to leave him alone with his mother. Queen Indra sat in a regal red gown upon the throne with an elaborately dressed Consort Foley beside her. He was indifferent to Bradrick's arrival and examined his short-manicured nails while Indra quietly appraised her son's appearance. She pursed her lips in distaste and cleared her throat before speaking.

"Bradrick, I know things have been difficult for you since... the accident. It's natural for you to need time to overcome your feelings about it. That time has passed, and now we must put the priorities of Pruria at the forefront of our agenda. We are going to be hosting a ball, during which you will meet many eligible women, and of them, a future bride will be chosen. The kingdom depends upon a good marriage for their future king."

"Especially after the last one took years, then went straight into the gutters," mumbled Foley, still acutely focused on his digits.

Bradrick's fist clenched at his side, annoyed with the man who always wore too much rouge. The self-made noble had a habit of overstepping his boundaries with Bradrick. It was doubtless he hadn't helped scheme this arrangement. Foley Osman's ascension to his position was no doubt done through the same means, although nobody knew the details of his rise in rank. There were only rumors, like everything when it came to the Prurian court. However, in

Foley's case, some were believable. Whatever the truth, the man's character was that of schemes and manipulation hidden behind a flagrant face. He was a likable fop with the Queen's favor. Bradrick had mixed feelings about the man who had assumed his mother's affections after the Khaos War took his father. His word held weight with her, but he had developed a terrible habit of thinking he had power equal to the Queen.

"What if I don't like anyone at the ball?" Bradrick tested.

"Given your attachment to a dead girl, I wouldn't be surprised. Should your emotions prevent you from choosing a suitable bride, then we will make the selection for you," Indra said with a pointed look.

Bradrick had no opportunity to argue when the door to the throne room opened again. The royal physician was announced and a beady-eyed old man stuck his head in. The Queen waved him forward. He scampered his way to the throne with a dark-stained wooden box and pretty floral pattern engraved on the surface. With a deep bow, he presented the box to Queen Indra.

"Your Highness, I present the medicinal tea you ordered," the Physician croaked.

"Medicinal? What for?" Bradrick asked. Worry crept over him. The throne may have strained their relationship, but he still loved her as a son.

"For the headaches you're giving me," she retorted as she peeked at the contents. She closed it with a satisfied smirk at the Physician. "Thank you. The royal treasury has added a payment to your regular distributions."

"Was there any news from the market?" Foley inquired, eager for a bit of gossip. Queen Indra looked at Foley as if she might have kicked him for asking.

"Nothing that isn't to be expected. The Brizian people mourn their king while their court members are at each other's throats.

Some rumors are even saying there is a war brewing between them. Such a sad time in Brizia."

"Indeed." Indra looked at her son. She dismissed the Physician and waited for him to clear the room before she continued her conversation with Bradrick. "Had your marriage to Amirah been completed, then both kingdoms would be safe. Our job is to expand our influence and ensure the security of our kingdom. It is a delicate balance that requires favorable marriages to strengthen and build alliances. Without these necessities, kingdoms fall. I will not pass on this crown until you secure a favorable marriage. Your people need an alliance now, more than ever, with a war brewing on our borders."

"What if she comes back?" Bradrick challenged his mother.

"Too much time has passed, Bradrick. You have an opportunity to find someone you like more than you liked her; take it. If you do not choose, then I will choose for you. Again. You're dismissed." Briefly, her voice had held the softness of a mother who understood her son's pain. Then came the harsh words that nipped at the guilt that haunted Bradrick. The last words were stern and final as she turned her eyes away from him.

He left the room without another word. Behind him, he heard their conversation resume with renewed excitement. He paused for a moment, overhearing Foley speak.

"That will do nicely. However, with access lost, it may become unsavory. My dear, have you considered taking over if it goes in that direction?"

Bradrick didn't catch his mother's response when the servant closed the door behind him. What he heard from them before that was enough to confirm his suspicions they had their eyes set on Brizia. Anything was possible with their endless scheming to marry him off. His mother didn't need her Consort to conceive a plot, but he certainly enabled her. Bradrick knew the remaining days to find Amirah were numbered.

CHAPTER 15

Nithe and Amirah returned to the castle to prepare for the journey to Isidris. Amirah still beamed with excitement for the trip, which was an experience she had never had. Outside of Brizia and Pruria, the remaining twelve kingdoms were a mystery to her.

Nithe sourced two small bags to pack with the things they needed and pretended not to notice her radiant smile as she floated throughout the study. When they finished packing, he pulled a map of Isidris from a stack of scrolls on a corner bookshelf. Blowing the dust off of it, he untied a string and unfurled it onto the table. Amirah helped weigh each of the corners with a small book from the stacks on the floor. Amirah noticed the aged map looked different from the ones she had studied growing up. The most notable aspect was that the map depicted the Duke's castle and surrounding villages instead of the neutral territory. While she had never seen the other kingdoms, her father ensured she was at least educated. It further cemented her father's efforts to erase the past.

Oblivious to her silent assessment of this, Nithe plotted the best course from their location to the capital of Isidris. His fingers drew an invisible line from the depiction of the Duke's castle to a spot near the hill that dotted the coast of the Continent's central northern coast.

"The capital is here on the cliffs," Nithe said, pointing to a marked city. "The Astronomer resides in an observatory on the outskirts of the city atop a hill. We will fly over the mountains and land somewhere near the observatory with a body of water."

Amirah noted the first part of the journey required her to be in swan form, which piqued her concern. "How will I transform while we are away from the lake?"

"The lake is enchanted, so..." He pulled a vial that was shaped like a blue crystalline tube from his shirt and allowed it to dangle from the golden chain around his neck. It appeared already filled with clear water as it glistened in the light. "We carry it with us. If I add a few drops to another body of water, the magic will transfer, but only for a short time. Assuming my calculations are correct, which they should be, we'll have enough to transform you back into your human self twice. Moon phases don't seem to be anything to be worried about, but we should still err on the side of caution and leave Isidris before we need to use the second half. So if the Astronomer grants us access to the Forgotten Library, we'll only be able to stay for a night."

Amirah could hardly contain her delight. His plan was foolproof and afforded her an opportunity to see such a place. She threw her arms around Nithe like an eager child and he froze in shock at the sudden contact but did not push her away.

"Thank you!" she chirped. When she detached herself, she bit her lower lip, attempting to restrain the smile that wanted to remain plastered on her face.

Nithe recovered with a blink, and a mischievous smirk tugged his lips. "Don't thank me yet. We still don't know if this will work. The Astronomer might not let us in or even be there. Traveling will have some risks. Humans can be more of a threat than a guivre, toxic breath aside."

"Do you have a toxic breath when you're in dragon form?"

Nithe chuckled as he shook his head back and forth with his nose scrunched.

"What about fire?" Amirah pressed. "Can you breathe fire and brimstone like in the Old Lore books?"

"I can, but it is indescribably uncomfortable," he explained. "I learned from shifting into a dragon and from the few remaining dragons I've had the misfortune of meeting, that it's a defensive mechanism—a last resort. Some have fire, acid, toxic fumes, and a few have something akin to ice. It's not a limitless ability, like some of the older texts speculate."

Amirah wanted to ask more questions, but the day had faded into night, and she preferred not to be awake when her transformation happened. Although it wasn't painful, the change could be disorienting and uncomfortable while awake. The first time, it had happened abruptly, but now she sensed the oncoming change. More obviously, down feathers sprouted from unseemly little goose skin-like bumps on her skin. Then, within an hour or two, she would shift as suddenly as the first time—a bizarre moment she was keen to avoid.

They drank a final nightcap and Amirah excused herself to bed. Since Amirah and Nithe had not slept after their return from Cicely's home, sleep was quick to claim her.

HOURS LATER, THE SUN finally broke through the curtains in Amirah's room. She padded her way down to the courtyard yard where Nithe awaited her. The brisk air welcomed them and fresh rays of light glinted off the lake. It surprised Amirah that the cool, damp air didn't feel much different in her feathered form. She noticed the bags were nowhere in sight and cocked her head to the side. Nithe wrapped his thick black cloak around him to ward against the chill. When he spoke, a wisp of white air floated away from his lips.

"Don't worry, I have the bags," he replied to the unspoken question as he scanned the horizon before he turned to her. "Are you ready?"

A smirk twitched at the corner of Nithe's lips when her wings fluttered in an agreeable response.

"Alright then, let's go. Follow me."

Without looking back, he sprinted forward, his feet carrying him straight toward the lake. He shifted a moment before his boots hit the water. A burst of wind whipped around his body and blurred his image as he propelled forward. The water's surface rippled under the force above it. When the vortex faded, his sleek black dragon emerged and skimmed a front claw against the lake's surface before he arched into the sky.

Show off, Amirah thought as she flew after him.

The pair tilted their winged bodies away from the rising sun and headed toward the mountain peaks that spread along Brizia's northern border. When they passed them, the lush forest that spread over the hills and valleys of Brizia tapered to an end. Had they flown farther south into the borders, they would have eventually seen farmland nestled in the clearings. Instead, their path drew them closer to the regal ridges of the tallest peak that towered at the center of the Continent. It looked as tall and majestic up close as the Old Lore cited. The snow-dusted points were a sight to behold. Amirah had seen snow before during the winters that covered the central and northern kingdoms, but these were incomparable scenes.

Still, they continued forward. First, they sailed high over the borders of Rapplend with its rolling hills and valleys. Later, they would walk back through the edge of the hilly kingdom, which would give her time to see more of the land up close, another part of the trip that propelled her excited heart. She knew they neared Isidris when pockets of trees sprang up over the greater spaced sections of larger hills. By now, the sun had begun to sink below the surface, casting an orange glow over the land like a blaze.

When the starlight dotted the early night sky, they dove close to the land. Amirah could see the twinkling lights of a distant city against the darkening sky and knew they must be close to their destination. She recalled the map where Nithe had traced their route to a spot marked outside of the kingdom's capital city as Nithe circled a small woodland area beside a dirt road. In the center of it was a small pond with only enough room around it for him to land. He pulled out the vial he had shown her the night before, removed the stopper, and added a few drops to the pond water. Amirah floated down as he finished and saw that barely enough moonlight reached the surface for her to touch.

Swimming was still not a strength for her, but she could manage not to drown after transforming. Nithe waited for her at the water's edge with his hand extended. She clasped onto it and he helped pull her from the water. The shift dress she had fallen asleep in was soaking wet and did little to help against the cool night air. Nithe produced a small bundle from somewhere beneath his cloak and tossed it to her. The small burlap bag contained tight warm pantalets, a simple burgundy traveler's dress that slit up to the hips on both sides, and leather boots. Amirah changed into the outfit while Nithe set up a small tent. After wringing out the wet dress, she found a low branch to toss it over to dry before she turned toward the tent.

"How do you manage to fit all that into one little pack?" she asked Nithe as she eyed two small pallets of blankets that were squeezed side-by-side into the tight space of the tent.

The only response she received was a shrug from Nithe, followed by a subtle crooked grin. The bag at his feet still appeared to be full as he bent to rummage through its contents. He pulled out a small cotton bag and handed it to Amirah. She peeked inside to find it was filled with long strips of dried meat and fruits.

"I thought it best that we have food rations with us. Take what you'd like of it while I scout the perimeter."

"Thank—," she started, but he had already disappeared, a little trick she hadn't seen since he crashed the wedding banquet. Cicely had said he possessed as much, if not more, power than his father had. This gave Amirah the impression that she had yet to see the full extent of his abilities. Whenever he used it, it gave her the subtle reminder that he had mysteries of his own that perhaps she would uncover in time. Certain he would still hear her, she rolled her eyes and shouted it into the darkness. "Thank you!"

Amirah ate a strip of dried meat. The spicy-sweet seasoning of it and a complementing handful of dried berries pleased her taste buds. Satisfied, she returned it to Nithe's small bag that still sat beside the tent. The darkness of the woods crouched in around her with only the soft glow of moonlight to keep it at bay. Several nights, she had crept through the dark halls of her Brizian castle home, getting to and from her chambers. Yet, here in the little woods, she was keenly aware of her own lonesomeness. Amirah knew Nithe would return, but his absence brought uneasiness and perplexed her. *You don't miss him*, she told herself as she crawled into the tent. *You absolutely cannot and do not miss him.*

Amirah found it impossible to fall asleep and Nithe's near-silent footsteps outside of the tent startled her upright. He crawled into the tent and lay on the pile of blankets beside her. In the darkness, she could only make out the outline of his form—one arm slung over his eyes while the other served as a cushion beneath his head.

"Took you long enough," Amirah chastised him playfully as she laid back down.

"I had to increase the range after you shouted loud enough for the whole Continent to find you." He chuckled and rolled onto his side.

Amirah grinned, but it faltered when she noticed he wasn't beneath any blankets. Her voice was almost a whisper, yet still sounded loud in the darkness when she spoke. "You'll be warmer under the blankets."

"A blanket would be an obstacle if there was an attack or if we needed to move quickly. Plus, my cloak is plenty warm enough for the night." Nithe said without moving an inch. Amirah swore she felt his eyes boring into her from his shadowed figure. If he were to use magic, his eyes would be light all on their own.

She glanced toward the tent opening. Whether from the lack of light or her own tiredness, she was unable to see anything beyond the outline of her own feet. "Should we start a small fire?"

"No. It risks drawing attention, something we don't want to do while sleeping in unfamiliar territory. If we rest and continue uninterrupted in the morning, then we should arrive by tomorrow afternoon."

A soft hum was the only response from a near-asleep Amirah.

Through the darkness, Nithe could make out her frame huddled beneath the blankets that shuttered with her gentle breath. A peculiar feeling that gnawed away at him each time he looked at her. He couldn't explain it, but it increased the more time they were together. Perhaps it's the curse, Nithe reasoned. His father had gotten them into this mess, and it would be up to Nithe to put an end to it. Just as it should have been when he succeeded in his revenge. It was uncertain what would become of them when this was finished. He dared to consider, for a moment, the most unreasonable of hopes, but that was a fire he fought to stamp out. Something he failed to do as he studied her sleeping beside him, letting the peaceful moment burn into his memories until his own eyes closed.

The rest of the night passed without disturbance and Amirah awoke to the sound of bird chirps against the first light of morning and the sweet scent of the dewdrop inundating the earth. The air chilled her face, unlike the warmth that wrapped around her torso. She nuzzled her face beneath the blankets, but the fabric was difficult to move. The familiar, subtle scent of ginseng and spice lured her senses fully awake. Her heart rate increased when she realized the warm weight that curled around her was not from the blankets. She rolled over and, to her surprise, found herself face to face with a sleeping Nithe.

Amirah's movement caused his arm to tighten around her, pulling her closer to him. Her breath stuttered at first, but the steady pattern of his breath helped her to relax. She studied Nithe's serene face and features while trying to ignore the firm parts of his body that pressed against her. She smiled, even as the warning voice in her head cautioned against the warmth that ignited in her chest. Somehow, at this moment, in the middle of the woods in a foreign kingdom, she felt an unreasonable amount of comfort and security. *What in the Twelve Kingdoms is wrong with me?* Amirah wondered. Still, she remained there until her eyes grew heavy again as she hedged sleep in Nithe's arms.

A moment passed, and she felt his body stiffen. Her eyes snapped open to find his dark forest-green eyes narrowed on her. Unfamiliar darkness crossed out the serenity on his face. They laid there frozen together, staring at one another until the sound of twigs breaking near the tent interrupted the moment. Nithe jumped up and bolted from the tent faster than Amirah could. She followed behind him, cursing at not having a sword in hand.

Nithe glanced back at her, ready to tell her to run if needed, but noticed her readied stance and wondered if Amirah had training for hand-to-hand combat. It would be surprising that King Landry would have allowed that, but then again, Amirah had mentioned she failed to live up to his vision of a perfect daughter. He had seen Amirah twice with a sword, neither with enough time to gauge her ability to wield one. Yet, like himself, Amirah scanned the silent area around them for a threat in a stance that would be perfect, even without a blade. Without warning, a creature sprang from the brush and landed between them. They dodged, falling on their sides to avoid being trampled by hooves as the deer darted away into the woods. With all signs of danger gone, laughter erupted from Amirah.

Nithe gathered himself first and went to help her up. He rolled his eyes at the cheeky grin she flashed at him before she accepted his assistance. Recovered, they packed up their little campsite. When they were done, Nithe returned everything—the two bags and rolls of blankets—beneath his cloak. A crooked smile tugged at his lips when he caught Amirah watching him with wide-eyed interest. *Curious little bird,* he mused to himself as they turned their attention toward leaving their haven. He led the way to the road, not far from their hidden accommodation. As they set off on the road that wound through hills and valleys, the sun chased their heels. Before the day's end, they approached an unmissable grand building that sat on top of a hill.

CHAPTER 16

The observatory was a grandiose building that commanded attention. It sat on the outskirts of Isidris atop of the highest hill in the region. As Nithe and Amirah reached the top, the capital city came into view in the distance below. Nothing, not even the guard towers, spires, or polished buildings, not even the seaside castle that sat upon the distant cliff's edge stood out the way the dome-topped building before them did. Amirah marveled at the structure. It was a blend of sharp edges formed the squared white walls which were accented by carved pillars and tall arched windows. The dome at the top was made of dark glass panes. A dual-colored glass horologium was centered above the entryway, its hands moving with the tick of the gears toward each evenly placed symbol.

The tall front door itself was made of shining, dark-stained wood. Solid wood, judging by the sound of Nithe's knock against it. A long, deafening silence passed. Though they were on a limited amount of time, Amirah was about to propose they come back at a better hour the next day when the door finally groaned open. A moment later, a white-haired old man poked his head out. His eyes bulged with surprise at the sight of them standing there. When he emerged out of the doorway to gawk at them with curiosity, Amirah noticed he was only a few inches taller than herself. Deep blue and purple robes draped from his thin figure and tied at his waist. Without a visible shirt collar, it gave the impression that he, at least, wore no shirt.

"I was wondering when you would get here. Come in! Come in!" he cackled.

Nithe and Amirah exchanged a look as he disappeared inside. Uncertain, and with no other options, Amirah shrugged before following him. Nithe stayed close behind her, while his eyes scanned every inch of space around them. His habitual caution was tinged with a hint of curiosity. The pair looked behind them when the door shut on its own accord.

"Welcome to the observatory!" The old man spread his thin arms out in a wide gesture to the rich-colored enormous room. "Please, make yourselves at home."

The polished wood floor featured a gold inlaid depiction of the constellations. The starry pattern wound inward toward a brass-hued instrument that took up the center of the room. A geared telescope pointed toward the glass dome, which cast dwindling afternoon light into the room. There was a collection of cabinets that held metallic instruments and devices that gleamed against the fading sunbeams. A few chairs and tables sat along either wall. A wide grin splayed on the old man's face as he watched them look at everything in fascination.

Nithe remained fixated on the instruments in the cabinet as he spoke to the elderly man. "You're the Astronomer, Venincio, right? You knew we were coming?"

"Correct on both counts. In a way." Nithe and Amirah looked at him with brimming curiosity. He wore his frazzled white hair combed back, though it did little good to tame it, and his weathered face donned a short pointed goatee to match. Amirah noticed his kind, hazel eyes had a twinkle that reminded her of Cicely. He gave Nithe a perplexed look. "Although, I am surprised you didn't know that already yourself."

"The information given to us was limited," Nithe confessed.

"We are hoping you might help us," Amirah added. Her mind had already set to work, forming a million questions that would need to wait.

"Oh, that much I knew, Your Highness. Anyone who comes here needs something. There hasn't been a simple visitor since before the Khaos War. We, at least, still help one another where we can. You two came knowing I'm one of the Cunning, a wielder of sight and knowledge, but also you come seeking the knowledge within the Forgotten Library. I presume you know my abilities won't give you the solution. So, your answer is probably somewhere in the books, eh?" He gave Amirah a pointed look and a knowing smile when she nodded in response. "Follow me."

Venincio didn't wait for another response as he led them toward an identical set of tall wooden doors on the right side of the room. Through it, he led them into a short hall with a star-shaped light in the center of the ceiling. Amirah gazed in polarized fascination that almost made her run into the Astronomer. Venincio, who had stopped outside of another door, turned to cast a perplexed look upon her.

"I'm sorry," she apologized, then pointed upward at the object of her distraction. "I was looking at—well, what is that?"

"Another form of light." He chuckled warmly. "It's an old invention that is often forgotten, then remembered again throughout the ages."

"Not an oil lamp or candle? How does it work?"

"Not quite. In simplified words, harvested energy from the sun is converted into a circulating flame of sorts. The means of harvesting varies, but in the end, it produces the same results. Well, more or less anyways. Let's have a bite to eat while we discuss which books you might be needing."

They followed Venincio through the next door into what seemed to be actual living quarters. These rooms were rich in color and decorated. A large table acted as a desk that was piled with papers, metal trinkets that looked much like the ones in the main room of the observatory, and books. Of the items, the most interesting was an orrery with crystal orbs that spun around what looked like a representation of the sun. The next room over was a simple dining room with a polished table. Venincio pulled out one of the six chairs for Amirah before he found his own. Nithe took a seat beside her as Venincio removed the lids from the silver trays that were positioned at the center of the table.

Amirah's mouth watered at the warm aroma that filled the room. Venincio made his plate first, then gave the serving utensils to Amirah. Uncertain, she glanced at Nithe, who tilted his head toward the tray of food as a gesture of reassurance. Amirah put small portions of everything on her plate. First, she grabbed a soft but slightly flattened piece of herb topped bread. Beside it she placed long pasta noodles with an orange-brown sauce that was flecked with a red-colored spice. On the other half of her plate, a skewer of roasted vegetables chopped into squares sat beside a serving of fried vegetables drizzled over with a yellow sauce. After filling her plate, Amirah handed Nithe the utensils. Next, Venincio filled three translucent blue glasses with a cold tea and passed one to each of them. They began eating and talked between satisfying bites.

"Tell me about what books you need," Venincio asked as he swallowed a mouthful of food. "I'm sure you're aware that I have plenty."

Amirah glanced at Nithe. He passed his skewer of roasted vegetables to her plate and, after a moment of consideration, gave the least vague answer he could surmise. "Anything that might give us some direction on how to solve a magically inclined problem such as ours. Are you familiar with Cicely?"

"Yes, yes. Though, I haven't heard from her in some time. How does she fare these days?" Venincio asked before taking another bite of food.

"The same as ever, these last years. We sought her wisdom recently, and she advised us to seek you out about your library. She sends her regards."

"I knew it to be the case. Well, Cicely being the one who sent you here, anyway. Sometimes, that is the way with those of the Cunning." Venincio set down his eating utensils and then cupped his hands with his fingers laced together on top of the table. "The library here has been all but forgotten by the Continent—hence the name among those of us who remember. There are even fewer of us that remain that still make some use of it. It's one of the best-kept secrets of Isidris, and perhaps the Continent as a whole. What kind of problem are we dealing with, exactly?"

"The magical type," Amirah added while Nithe finished his drink. "We need to break a curse."

"A blood curse," Nithe elaborated. "One born from death that has passed down to the next generation."

Venincio nodded. "One of the most difficult. I am better suited to reading the futures and celestial bodies. All the Cunning in the world cannot break a curse, as you've been warned. However, I see why Cicely would send you in my direction. I shall take you to the library, but in exchange, I would like to request a favor in return."

Amirah beamed with excitement at the prospect of being closer to accomplishing their goal. Nithe raised an eyebrow at both of them, expecting more of a catch to this offer.

"What kind of favor?"

Venincio cleared his throat and sat back in his chair. "In exchange for the books, I ask that you deliver a letter to my son, Roman, after your departure tomorrow. I know you're both on borrowed time here, and it so happens you're going to be headed in his direction. After all, Ruya, his present location, is on the road back into Rapplend. Work keeps him away for long periods of time, and it is hard to find a trusted carrier who doesn't snoop. The Khaos War may be over, but as you know, there is still danger afoot."

"We'll do it!" Amirah cried with enthusiasm.

Her reaction earned surprised expressions from both men. Nithe frowned at the lost opportunity for further inquiry. However, Amirah had started the cultivation of a warm relationship with Venincio, which favored all of them. Amirah was the one person who could undo the things her father and other rulers had done during the Khaos War. Those like Venincio, Cicely, and Nithe would not survive another lifetime without change. Nithe recognized the innocent pride on Amirah's face at the prospect of having accomplished a task that meant as much to her as it did to him. It astonished him that, after everything she had been through, Amirah retained kindness. It was a favorable quality in a leader that could be equally dangerous if she didn't learn to be more careful with her trust. *And negotiation skills,* Nithe thought with a hint of amusement.

With the matter decided and their meal finished, Venincio led them back through the main room of the observatory to the opposing doorway. It opened to a room they hadn't seen before. On the far wall was a cozy seating arrangement gathered around a fireplace. Venincio advised them that guest bedrooms were through the two doors on the left wall. He walked up next to the fireplace and pressed his hands against the paneled wall. An audible pop followed, and the panel moved away like a door, revealing a stairwell. Amirah and Nithe followed behind Venincio as he ascended the staircase.

Amirah gasped at the sight of a large, open room at the top. Every wall was inlaid with rich wooden bookcases, except for the farthest. That wall had a set of ornate glass doors that were centered between arched windows that led to a balcony. Dark red and blue rugs scattered the room, with only a few cushioned seats and tables with globes rested upon them. The ceiling was arched and featured a deep indigo and gold painted ceiling that depicted the starlit night sky. At its center, a half-moon, half-sun glinted down on a chain that held a pendant light, resembling a star. It was a larger version of the one in the downstairs hallway.

"Feel free to browse the library," Venincio said and waved his hand toward the room. "If you need help, I will be glad to assist again in the morning. I'll bring the letter for my son with me. Now, if you will excuse me, these old bones require a nightcap and some rest. Goodnight."

"Goodnight," they bade him in unison as he left.

Amirah looked around in wonderment before turning to Nithe, who had a similar expression. "Have you ever seen such a place?"

"No, and I've seen many beautiful things." His eyes drifted from Amirah, arching toward the ceiling and then back toward the shelves. He looked toward the glass doors, speaking his thoughts aloud. "The balcony door should face the side we entered, but no windows or doors showed on the upper exterior. I suspect magic keeps them hidden. Perhaps it's glamoured, like back at the castle and lake."

Amirah hummed in agreement as she approached the bookcases in a trance-like state. To her, this library was a hidden gem filled with the forgotten treasures of the world. Nithe grabbed a few books from a shelf on the opposite wall and inspected them. There were more books than they had time to search through. Eager to narrow down the selection, he flicked his hand in the air. Several books floated from the shelves toward him. Amirah was so enamored that she hadn't noticed until one floated out of the pile that began accumulating in her arms. She cringed when a few hit the floor before she shot him a disapproving look. Nithe grabbed the offending book from the stack that was forming in front of him.

They were there for hours, thumbing through pages. Amirah had settled onto an evergreen couch while Nithe sat on the floor among the stacks of book. Some books were in foreign languages, of which only a few Amirah could read. Several had twisting runes that imbued the pages with patterns and symbols. A few books made it to a smaller stack beside Nithe, while others floated back to their designated shelf. Time passed in a comfortable silence as they searched for slivers of hope.

"I wish we had more time," Amirah groaned as she curled into the corner of the couch. She had read through several of the books and had yet to find anything helpful. "Do you think we'll find the answers here?"

The current tome sat open on the arm of the couch so that she could still read while her head rested. She had been fighting off sleep for the past hour. Nithe didn't look up. Instead, his glowing eyes remained transfixed upon the pages as he continued to skim, seeming unfazed. His stacks had dwindled at a considerably faster rate.

"We can only hope. Perhaps one day, we'll return, when you're no longer changing into a swan. There are a few promising leads here. When I finish this stack, I'll move on to reading them more thoroughly. If there is a way to break this curse, it's in here somewhere. If you are tired—"

When his eyes lifted, he found Amirah had already drifted to sleep. He clutched his cloak from the floor and covered her with it. A pang of guilt struck him as he watched her tranquil face. The same face he had seen when they camped beside the pond, but with a tinge of joy that tilted at the corner of her lips. That faint smile pushed at the darkness that consumed him for years. It was a cruel fate for them to be tied together.

If only our fates were different, he thought as he tucked a stray ginger lock away from her face. Lethargy pulled at him as he lay on the couch opposite of her and opened one of the unreturned books. Even as his determination pushed him to find the answer, his eyes grew heavier. Moments later, he lost the fight and fell asleep.

"There you two are!" Venincio's voice barked, causing Amirah and Nithe to rouse from their slumber. "I should have skipped the bedrooms and come up here first. When you're up and ready, please join me in the dining room for breakfast."

As Amirah sat up, she noticed Nithe's cloak slip off her shoulders into a pile in her lap. A smile tugged at the corner of her lips as she realized he had covered her with it at some point. The warning to her heart was slow, but she was still quick to rationalize the gesture. She stole a glance at him as he stretched like a cat while still sprawled out on the couch across from her. The image of which made her giggle and drew his attention. He shot her a quizical look.

"You look like a cat who's been sunbathing," she confessed.

"I imagine this is what they feel like too," he mused. "This old furniture is far too comfortable. I could laze here all day."

Amirah stood up and passed the cloak to Nithe. "Well, it's a pity we have to leave today."

Nithe looked at the shining morning sky outside the windows. "It is, but there's not much time left."

They left their books where they were and headed down to find a washroom before meeting Venincio at the dining table. Three plates sat with hearty portions of eggs and a fruit pastry. As they assumed the same seats as the prior night, Venincio studied them. When they settled into their chairs, he cleared his throat.

"I saw that you two were still sorting through some books this morning. I had suspected that might be the case. As a token of my personal gratitude," he motioned at both of them, "you may take the unread books with you."

Amirah looked at Nithe with surprise. Her wide eyes glinted with the same excitement he'd seen on her face numerous times since they learned of the Forgotten Library. Nithe, however, was already shaking his head before the words left his lips. "We couldn't possibly keep such things that belong to the library. They contain priceless knowledge that is best safeguarded here."

"Did I say keep? My word, of course not. However, you are an adept sorcerer, trustworthy of guarding such items. Your partner on the journey here is the most honorable royal I've had the pleasure to meet in some time. I would be remiss not to return the kindness extended to me." Venincio's eyes spun with a glowing silver that, once again, reminded Amirah of Cicely and Nithe. "Your futures, and that of the twelve kingdoms, rely upon the two of you finding an answer to your problems. So, you must borrow the books."

There was little other choice than to accept the offer. Amirah and Nithe were relieved that the time restriction had not prevented their success. The books were an offering of hope they needed for their journey home. Venincio explained that the road to Rapplend would lead to a small town called Ruya, where they would find his son, Roman. The directions themselves were simply to stick to the road until they got there. Amirah felt as if she could sit and talk with Venincio for hours. If allowed, she would ask question after question, but her transformations had settled them with a firm time constraint. The elderly Astronomer understood somewhat, thanks to the Cunning, and kindly pardoned their rushed visit.

After Nithe and Amirah finished breakfast, they returned to the library for the few items that needed to be gathered. Amirah returned the unneeded books to their places as Nithe reviewed the small stack to be certain of their selection. Her eyes roved over the shelves as she bade the books a silent, bitter-sweet farewell. When finished, Amirah turned back and watched with fascination as Nithe tucked the books they borrowed somewhere beneath his cloak. She ascertained magic was the way things disappeared beneath it, but it surprised her each time. Her surprise doubled when he produced a simple dark gray cloak and handed it to her.

When they returned downstairs to the main room of the observatory, Venincio awaited them by the front door. Nithe and Amirah cast one last look around the magnificent space before they met his weathered eyes. Venincio handed the letter for his son to Amirah. The crisply folded, cream-tinted paper had a blue wax seal. When Amirah accepted it, her eyes noted the wax appeared to have the impression of a thin crescent moon with three tiny stars sitting on its belly. She looked back up at the thin old man as she tucked it away on her person.

"Thank you for your hospitality and guidance." Amirah bowed her head toward Venincio to reflect her gratitude.

"And thank you again, Your Majesty. Know that once you accept certain things as easily as you have accepted this task, things will change." His wrinkled face pulled into a smile.

Amirah returned it. "Will it be alright if either of us were to visit in the future?"

"Of course, my dear! You must, and I am certain that you both will. Even if it is some years from now." Venincio's eyes twinkled. A subtle silver glow swirled in the depths of his eyes as if he were looking into the night sky. "When all is right, yet the world still quarrels, this old bag of bones will outlast many."

Amirah sensed a truth to his riddling words. She was certain that a message hid among what sounded like a puzzle. As if knowing this, Venincio chuckled and bid them a last farewell.

CHAPTER 17

Once more, they were on the road on foot. For a time, Nithe and Amirah walked in a comfortable silence, wrapped in their own trains of thought. The land changed as they drew farther away from the seaside cliffs of Isidris. Amirah took in her surroundings with a focused interest, pointing out plants, trees, and small creatures along the way. Brizia's lush, dark woodlands differed from Isidris. The roads snaked through the small hills of Isidris, flecked with patches of vibrantly colored forest and vegetation. Nithe smirked to himself at her wonderment and helped identify what he was familiar with as they went along.

They traveled until the sun disappeared below the horizon, leaving them with enough light to make camp away from the road. By the next afternoon, they would reach their destination. Nithe offered Amirah the rations and took a seat beside her on the fallen log outside of their tent. She took a handful of the dried fruits before returning it to him.

"You're not surveying the perimeter?" Amirah asked before she popped a piece of dried fruit into her mouth.

Nithe shook his head. "No, we're too close to the town and there are several farms in this area. A dragon flying around would draw more attention than it's worth."

"I couldn't imagine why," she snorted. She looked up at the star-dotted sky. "Do you think we'll be there before nightfall tomorrow?"

"We should be." Nithe took a strip of dried meat and returned the small bag to his pack by his feet. After a moment of eating in silence, he turned his attention to Amirah. "We'll need to be careful when we get to Ruya. I didn't get an opportunity to get more details from the Astronomer before you accepted the deal. There's a reason Venincio's communications were hindered. We're going into the situation blind."

Amirah winced. "I jumped at the opportunity to see more of the world, and I should've been more cautious, but I'm sure Venincio has good intentions."

"Your instincts about him are correct, but I don't think he is the one to be concerned about. Remember, not everyone is who you believe them to be. It's important, as a ruler, to know when to give trust, and when to withhold it. When you're making deals in the future, you want as much information as possible." He sighed and then smiled at her. "But all of that aside, you did get us into the library."

"I have a suspicion he would have let us in any way." Amirah nudged Nithe's shoulder with hers.

He shrugged. "Perhaps, given his powers."

"He referred to his type of magic as 'Cunning,'" she recalled Venincio's words.

Nithe nodded. "It's a general term for a complex set of magic that's related to foresight. It presents differently in each individual and often goes beyond the simple concepts of fortune-telling. Should you ever meet with him or Cicely again, they're great resources of knowledge about their own abilities and more."

"You don't have Cunning?" Amirah tilted her head sideways.

Nithe chuckled. "Of course not. Otherwise, I would have known better than to turn you into a swan."

They both laughed and continued the discussion for a few more minutes before Amirah yawned. She retired into the tent for the night while Nithe decided to keep watch of the surroundings. It didn't take Amirah long to fall asleep in the confines of the tent. Compelled to keep watch through the night, Nithe sat on the ground and rested his back against the log. After a few hours, he closed his eyes as he listened to the chirping of night-dwelling creatures and the steady whisper of Amirah's breath as she slept. More than once, he had sat cross-legged by the lakeside to meditate while fighting off the lure of sleep. He wondered if he would maintain the same focus when they were free of the curse. *What goal and purpose will I have then?*

In the early morning hours, Nithe woke Amirah. She groaned about the sun not being up yet but helped to pack up the tent and blankets. When he returned them beneath his cloak, he led her to the top of a taller hill nearby. At first, Amirah wondered why they hadn't returned to the road. Then, Nithe pointed to the skyline where the sun began rising. The light turned the sky into a vibrant shade of pink, warming the last of the blue night sky into a shade of lavender. Amirah gasped as the sun rose above the horizon, its rays casting a blinding light that split the cloudless sky and spilled over the hills and valleys below.

"Thank you," she said as they returned to the road. Nithe said nothing as they carried on in silence, a slight tilt of a smile on the corner of his lips.

RUYA WAS A SMALL BORDER town that sat at an intersection of three roads that crossed through three of the northern kingdoms. Along the way, several people on horseback paid them little interest as they passed. The road went up a steep hill, and when they reached its apex, a lower valley spilled into view. Nithe and Amirah were on the road that stretched to the capital of Isidris. The opposing two roads would intersect below the entrance of Ruya. Trees dotted the otherwise open fields outside of the small town that flourished with festival life below. Tents stood erected on the edge of the town's bordering wall and merchants lined the roadways, forming a bazaar that led up to the town's front gates.

Nithe cursed under his breath.

"That's a lot of people. How are we ever going to find Roman in all of," Amirah waved her arm in front of her at the massive gathering they faced, "*this?*"

"My thoughts exactly," Nithe grumbled, "but we better get started. The main road looks to be the most crowded right now, so we should probably avoid it."

Nithe and Amirah abandoned the road to go around the throngs of people. They wove through colorful structures and tents until they lost their sense of direction and emerged into an open field. Amirah spun in a circle, looking for any sign of where they had ended up.

"Let's cut straight through the field. We'll end up closer to the entrance. I can see the rooftops over there." Nithe pointed ahead to where the roofs of several buildings peaked above the tents and the wall that surrounded the town. She nodded in agreement.

They hurried to cross the perimeter of the expanse of the field, staying behind the odd stacks of scattered hay bales. Somewhere to the left, someone shouted in alarm. They ignored it and continued to move until Amirah's hand shot into the air. Nithe whipped around to find her frozen a few steps behind him with widened eyes and her fingers wrapped around an arrow. It had been inches from striking her. Their eyes went from the arrow to each other, then to the direction that the arrow had flown from.

A man with tousled, ash-brown hair jogged toward them from across the field. Amirah and Nithe noted the longbow strapped over his back. He sported a boyish smile that contrasted the scruff on his jawline. Amirah squinted, trying to place the familiarness of the stranger.

"Impressive catch! Did neither of you hear the shouting?" he asked.

"We didn't think it was meant for us." Nithe crossed his arms over his chest.

"The shouting was; the arrow, not so much. Sorry about that. Most people stay clear of the range during competitions. You must have some experience at archery."

"I'm good with a bow. Even better with blades. You might say I have some training and a good ear. Although, I prefer more advanced warning if I'm in a game of fire and catch. I assume this is yours?" Amirah handed the arrow back to him. Nithe arched an eyebrow at her with a look of curiosity.

"Ironically, it's another competitor's. Strayed a bit too far from their mark. You're too late to enter, but you're welcome to come to watch. We're near the end, so it won't take much longer. Although, that means the grouping is narrowed down to the best of the competitors. The most exciting portion to watch, if you ask me."

Amirah looked at Nithe, who shrugged.

"Why not?" She smiled at the man.

"Great! This way," he beamed at them.

"Do we have time for this?" she whispered to Nithe as they followed their new acquaintance to the opposite side of the field. "Shouldn't we be looking for Roman?"

"It's not the worst place to start a search. There are locals and outsiders here."

A short line of competitors with arrows stood facing them. Some looked onward in indifference, while others stared at them in annoyance. Amirah could pick out a few nobles based on their attire. No one seemed any wiser that she was foreign royalty, which made her grateful for the traveling clothes she wore. Their new acquaintance handed a competitor the arrow that had almost struck her. The man's face shaded like a beat and he turned away from them.

Amirah didn't have to look to know Nithe was staring holes into the man's back.

A short stack of hay bales separated the competitors from the small crowd that was gathered behind them. From this side, everyone faced the direction Amirah and Nithe had been walking moments earlier. The hay bale mounds in the field supported round wooden targets they'd been unable to see from behind. The man had been very off-target.

The competition resumed. Amirah and Nithe hung back to watch the event. Their new acquaintance assumed his position among the remaining competitors. The rounds were quick, with each person firing off their arrow, one after the other, down the line. They hit various locations on the targets. Some hit the center mark. After two more rounds of eliminations, three competitors remained—a woman, the man who had almost struck Amirah, and their new acquaintance.

A drum rumbled. The crowd held their breath in anticipation as each of the remaining contestants pulled back their bows and aimed at the same target. The drum stopped and their arrows flew across the field. It turned out that their new acquaintance was a near-perfect shot. His arrow struck, skewed a little to the right of the center, beside the woman's arrow. The other man's arrow was just below the two. The crowd erupted with delighted cheers. The gamekeeper examined the arrows on the other side of the field and proclaimed a tie.

"One more round! One more round!" The crowd chanted.

The gamekeeper signaled an additional round to break the tie, appeasing the crowd. This time, they took turns firing off their arrows. Each shot pierced the air, one after the other, aiming for that single target. Their new acquaintance went first and hit the target's center mark. Amirah admired the form of the woman who went next. The look in her eyes reminded her of Alonzo—calm and focused. He and Bradrick would have excelled at this event. The crowd erupted when the arrow struck the target, splitting the other down into the center. The final competitor took his shot, and his arrow landed on the side of the small center of the target, expelling him from the chance to win.

One final round remained to break the tie between the woman and their new acquaintance. The woman went first, this time hitting the center. Silence hung over the field as the crowd held their breaths in anticipation. Even the drum was silent as the bow creaked in protest of being drawn back. The arrow loosed, and a heartbeat later, it struck on the edge of the target. The crowd erupted into a roaring cheer. Prior competitors swarmed around the victorious opponents with congratulatory adulations.

A boyish grin plastered the face of their acquaintance as he departed the jubilant crowd, headed to Nithe and Amirah. She returned the smile with a soft clap for his performance. Nithe, who had watched the competition with veiled excitement, tilted his head in greeting.

"You did very well. We shall have a drink in your honor tonight," Amirah congratulated him.

"Thank you! Not first place, but I will take a well-deserved second. There will be another one tomorrow with crossbows. If either of you would like to attend—"

"We are just passing through," Nithe said. He exchanged a glance with Amirah.

"Right then. Well, if you haven't found your lodgings inside the wall by now, you may have to settle for the camp instead." He turned and pointed toward a bland mix of tents. "Non-merchant tents are stationed on this side of the fields."

"Thanks. Do you know how we could find someone who might be here?"

"Depends on how much time you need. I would start at the first tavern. Everyone at camp talks, so that's a strong second. You're welcome to join me for dinner around the fire if you've no luck. We get all sorts around camp. Bound to find someone with information." He gave Amirah a brilliant grin.

"The food from some tents smelled amazing. We'll try your suggestion first and perhaps see you at the fireside."

Later, after they had bid goodbye and parted ways, Amirah realized they hadn't exchanged names. Now, she and Nithe had gotten lost among a throng of people on the main road nearest to the gate. Jubilant faces bartered with tent merchants in every direction. Some tents had food, others featured artisan goods or hand-crafted items. While most stalls displayed items of the Northern Kingdoms, a few Southern Kingdom merchants offered a variety of their wares. Amirah looked over the items as they waded through the crowd. One of the merchant tents closer to the gates was a traveler with an eclectic selection that caught her eye. She paused for a moment in front of one of his cloth-draped tables.

Nithe noticed she was no longer beside him and stopped to look for her in the crowd. A few paces away, she stood in front of an orange and purple draped stall. He assumed a position beside her, looking over the display of curious goods. Her hand traced the daggers on a table, each sheathed in ornate scabbards.

A smile spread over her face when she looked up at Nithe. "Sorry. I got distracted. There is a lot more here than I thought when we first arrived."

He nodded in agreement. "Are you ready?"

Once again, her hands disappeared underneath her cloak and she nodded. The frown that flashed on Nithe's face when she looked back at the table was one Amirah missed. He withdrew a small velvet pouch from his cloak. Drawing her attention back to him, he tossed the pouch of coins to her. Curiosity furrowed her brows.

"There are a lot of food stalls here. We have yet to eat today. If you want something, there's enough coin in there for any of it."

"Oh," she said, blinking at him. "Thank you. Is there anything you want?"

"I'm not hungry yet." His gloved hand waved in the air, dismissing the idea.

Another smile crested her lips. On her tiptoes, she arched to look over the heads of the crowd. When she spotted a tent near the end of the festival bazaar, she bounced away. Nithe watched her go to get in line. Certain she had made it, he turned back to the traveler merchant's wares.

His eyes fell upon the selection of daggers she had admired. Each dagger was expertly crafted. Most were from the northern kingdoms with sharp-angled designs. One stood out to Nithe, neither the longest nor the shortest of the collection. The silver scabbard's lean, pointed shape featured twisting patterns that curled around tiny flowers. The patterns had ornate curves compared to those surrounding it. Black leather was wrapped around the hilt grip, and the silver pommel was encrusted with a magenta-colored gemstone.

The merchant approached him. "Anything I can help you with?"

Nithe picked up the dagger to better examine it. "This one seems well made. Where was it crafted?"

"The Southern Kingdom of Yaerel. Specifically, a family whose lineage was lost in the Khaos War. It's made from fine steel and silver. Not sure about the gemstone, to be honest. It's a deadly beauty, all the same."

Nithe pulled the blade from the scabbard and slid his fingers over the sharpened edges. Satisfied, he re-sheathed it. "Price?"

"Same as the others. Five gold coins." Nithe produced the payment. The merchant bit down on the coins before he stashed them into one of several bags that were slung across his body. "Pleasure doing business with you."

Nithe tucked the blade beneath his cloak. A few stalls down, Amirah finished making her purchase. Their eyes met as they found their way to the middle of the still-crowded road. The hint of a smile still pulled at the corners of her lips. She handed back the bag of coins while he motioned toward the gate. There wasn't a way they could talk over the noise of the crowded road. Amirah walked a step behind him, picking at a bowl of sweetened pieces of meat as the sun descended with leisure. It left them enough light to find lodgings for the night.

Inside the walls, Ruya was a small town with narrow cobblestone streets. Unlike the spired capital of Isidris, the only pointed roofs came from a small citadel that connect to the backside of the surrounding wall. The rest of the town paled in comparison with muted colors and simple rooftops. Most of the businesses seemed positioned on the road that led in from the gate.

They walked past an inn that posted a sign which warned travelers of no vacancies. As advised, they tried the taverns first. The first one had no rooms for rent, the next was full. A sign hung at the next weathered inn, symbolizing the same. Fortunately, at the third tavern, a spare room was available. The fact it had only one bed was the least of their problems at present. The place was in better shape than both of the inns. Nicks marred the worn wooden surfaces, and the floors creaked, but the paint was in better condition.

Satisfied enough, they took a seat at a table. The owners were an older couple that tended the bar with a daughter around the same age as Amirah, who brought their drinks over. The young woman's eyelashes fluttered as she directed her attention at Nithe. Amirah noticed how she dipped in a low curtsy to him that showed off her assets after she set the drinks on the table. It reminded her of some of the more annoying mannerisms of the women at court. Nithe gave no indication he noticed her flirtations. In fact, he didn't even look at her. When she asked if there would be anything else, her hand reached toward his shoulder. Amirah interrupted the movement when she spoke.

"That will be all. Thank you," she denied her with a pointed smile. Amirah may have been away from court for a while, but she could still command authority with little to no words. The young lady left them, her face falling as she turned away with embarrassment. Nithe stared at Amirah through narrowed lids.

She scoffed. "What?"

Nithe shook his head. "Nothing. We should start asking around for our contact. If he has been here for more than a few days, the locals should recognize him."

"That would be best if we want to get out of here soon. We should have asked at the archery competition." She frowned, wishing they had gotten the name of the competitor they'd made an acquaintance. "That guy seemed to be knowledgeable about this place. We should ask him."

Nithe thought for a moment before he nodded in agreement. "We should ask the barkeep first. If he isn't familiar with him, then we can go."

They both got up with their glasses to approach the end of the bar. The older man nodded in their direction, a sign he noticed them while he still tended to other clients. His daughter approached them, smiling at Nithe while she took his glass. The look dropped when her eyes landed on Amirah and she scurried away with both glasses. With a free moment, the barkeep came over to them. Nithe asked after a man named Roman, and the barkeep frowned apologetically. He wasn't familiar with the name, describing himself as good with faces, but terrible with names. The Astronomer hadn't given them anything other than the name for the sake of protection. Not only for himself, but also for them. They thanked him anyway.

When they turned to leave, the barkeep stopped them. "You should try the camp. If the bar and innkeepers around here don't recognize a name, but they have been here for any time, they are probably staying there. No sense to come inside the gate when everything they need is right there.

CHAPTER 18

A mong the sea of beige that made up the campground, boisterous gatherings formed around fresh fires. It was a stark contrast to the vibrant colors of the festival tents. The smell of earth mixed with the scents of hearty foods permeated the area. Amirah and Nithe stuck to the general direction that was indicated to them earlier in hopes of shortening their search. The last bit of sun had dipped below the horizon and stars began speckling the corners of the darkening sky, leaving less time to find Venincio's son. Most of those who stayed in the encampment appeared to be soldiers of Isidris. Amirah frowned at the failed attempts to find their contact.

Eventually, Amirah asked one of them where they could find the second-place competitor. They gave them a strange look until Nithe tossed a silver coin to them. In answer, they pointed toward a campfire across the way. Amirah had mixed feelings about how easily they had purchased the information. Like the other fires, several people gathered in a circle around the flickering blaze. Nithe pulled up his hood, covering his features as they surveyed the group. Several logs circled around the fireside for seating and most of the campers engaged in conversations amongst themselves. One was tuning a stringed instrument, checking the sound with gentle strums. Once perfected, he plucked a melody with graceful, knotted fingers. Another joined him, playing a rhythmic thump with a tan hide tambourine. Each time it was struck at the center, the sound of a small drum was accompanied by a jingle with each movement.

After searching each face, Amirah's excitement evaporated with no sign of the person they were searching for. Not the competitor, nor the Astronomer's son. Nithe clicked his tongue in frustrated distaste from losing both time and coin. Amirah shook her head. A tent flapped open no sooner than they had turned to leave. Just in time to spot their departure.

"Are you going to leave without a proper goodbye?" The new-yet-familiar voice called.

Their heads jerked toward the speaker in simultaneous surprise as they froze. Amirah ignored the deep huff Nithe made, which revealed his thoughts, and smiled brightly. In truth, her smile was more from relief that their coin had been well-spent. Nithe's greeting lacked the enthusiasm of Amirah's approach. She ignored his strange behavior toward their potential lead.

"I hope you will accept our humbled greetings instead. We were searching for you."

He looked between the two of them. "Glad you could find your way. Trouble finding a place for the night?"

"No," Nithe crossed his arms.

"We wanted," Amirah glanced at Nithe, "to thank you for earlier. This is our first time here and your directions were helpful."

"It was nothing. The people here are kinder than those in the capital. Anyone would have helped, but I know I'm not the only reason you're here. Come sit with us by the fire. There's stew if you're hungry."

His hand went to the small of Amirah's back and guided her to an empty spot on the log. Nithe's face darkened, and he took the seat beside her. Amirah thought she caught the slight flicker of the viridescent glow in his eyes. She saw his mood darken, something that happened whenever they were near their new acquaintance. The two men were night and day from each other. Not that either had done anything during their interactions to cause the tension that thickened with each exchange. Something more was behind Nithe's reaction, but now wasn't the time to question it. They were guests in a different kingdom, in a town they didn't know, and this was their only contact.

Their acquaintance passed a pair of steaming bowls to them. Despite the pleasant smell of the herb-infused meat concoction, Nithe still poked at it, his eyes hinting at his suspicion. He took an eventual bite and the look faded with each spoonful. She held back a chuckle at the sight and instead turned to their host. It was better to get to the heart of the matter if they had any chance of leaving the next day.

"Thank you, again. You're right, we have other business with you. We managed to find lodgings, but we haven't been able to locate the person we were hoping to meet."

"With the crowds from the festival, it's no wonder you've had trouble," he replied, taking a mouthful of stew.

"You seem familiar enough with Ruya, so you might be the best person right now to be asking," she admitted. "We already tried asking the tavern, and the barkeeper suggested the camps. Right now, you're our only contact here."

"I'm stationed here and have been for a short time. Enough to know the place as one would a new home," he nodded. "Who is it you're after?"

"I wouldn't say after," she peeked at Nithe. Despite his apparent concentration on his food, it was doubtful he wasn't listening to every word.

Amirah continued with a sigh. "We are looking for a man by the name of Roman."

Their host almost choked on his food. He stood, coughing, and pulled a flask from his belt. Several gulps later, he sucked in a breath of air. Amirah watched him with alarm, unsure of what to make of the incident. When he shook his head, he looked back up at her with a more guarded expression. Sensing the change, Nithe's gaze shifted to them.

"Why are you looking for him? Who sent you?"

"That's our concern," Nithe said with a flat tone.

The two glared at each other for a moment before Amirah cleared her throat. "I'm not sure we are at liberty to say. You must know him, though, judging by your reaction."

"Aye. I do," he looked back at her, "because I am him. My name is Roman."

Nithe straightened. His neutral expression gave nothing away, but Amirah heard the faint curse muttered under his breath. She couldn't contain the laughter that bubbled from her, interrupting the agitated silence. She clenched her sides to keep from toppling over. It earned a look of bewilderment from Roman and Nithe. Amirah wiped at the tears cresting the edge of her vision as she attempted to sober herself and pulled out Venincio's letter from her persons.

"All this time," she hummed in amusement and extended it toward Roman.

When he accepted it from her, a look of surprise crossed his face when he saw Venincio's seal on the other side. His fingers traced over the shape of the crescent moon embedded in the wax.

"Ah. That makes some sense." He looked back at them with an apologetic look. "Sorry about that. Given you've met my father, I hope you can understand my concern when a set of strangers comes looking for me."

Nithe agreed. However, Amirah crossed her arms in mock offense. "Strangers, are we now?"

"Newcomers," Roman corrected with a chuckle. "Although to be fair, I didn't catch your names either."

Amirah glanced at Nithe with uncertainty. She caught the mischievous glint in his gaze that he masked when turning to face Roman. "That is our mistake. We could have avoided this if we hadn't been rushing around. I'm Nithe, and this is Myrrh. We're travelers from the middle kingdoms."

"Nice to meet both of you. Nithe." The flask passed between the pair, then Roman looked to Amirah. "*Myrrh.*"

Her fake name was drawn out with a teasing tone that earned a scowl from Nithe. Amirah drank from the flask, letting the bittersweet liquid cover any hints of the thoughts that spun through her mind. As well as the guilt of the concocted name they had given him. They had been entrusted with his secret, yet they did not trust him with theirs. The way he drew out her name made her suspicious. *Could he know it was false?* Amirah wondered. This brought more questions about Roman himself.

There was something more to him than what met the eye. It wasn't the twinkling that matched his father's eyes, giving her the initial sense of familiarity. *No, something's off,* she realized. Nithe had sought to protect her identity. At least, that is what she suspected he was doing. It struck Amirah that, even with Nithe, it could be hard for her to interpret intentions. It was a weakness that could prove fatal in the Brizian courts. She passed the flask back to Roman, a flicker of uncertainty falling over her.

For the next hour, they conversed around the fire. People came and went from the surrounding circle. Each was eager for stew, drinks, and a sense of community that seemed abundant. Then, Nithe's quiet moodiness returned as Amirah engaged in pleasant conversations with Roman. Under the increasing starlight, he observed their exchanges in silence and frowned at their laughter. Most of which he masked with his watchful surveillance of their surroundings.

Eventually, the music players retired from their places beside the fire. Instead of silence, a boisterous group assumed the seats around another fire behind Amirah. Their laughter increased the volume of the area twice over. The sound acted as a cue for Roman to get more firewood. Nithe scanned over the neighboring occupants while he stoked the flames of the dimmed campfire in front of him. Someone bumped into Amirah's back in their rush to join the group. Before she could turn to confront the offender, Nithe's hand clamped around her wrist. He shook his head, glancing between her and the group. Her lips pursed, and she jerked her limb back.

Fine, she mouthed at him.

She wasn't sure she could tolerate much more of his mood. After pulling up the hood, she wrapped her dark gray cloak tightly around her body. The night air had chilled more than the fire could help, though it seemed she was the only one affected. Goosebumps rose on her skin as a shiver traveled down her spine. Nithe caught her eye and tapped beside his ear with a directed glance at the group. Their loud voices projected, making it impossible not to hear them. Still, she focused on the conversation that carried on behind her.

"All of that may be true, but what do you think of the Queen throwing a ball?" A gravelly voice asked between drinks.

"Queen Indra has never been a patient woman. I don't fault her for it this time. A ball might sound like fluff and excessive pageantry, but she uses them to her political advantage," said the one who had knocked into Amirah. Her eyes widened in recognition of the name. The sudden bombardment of news made her head spin.

"Of course, the Prurians will prioritize their political gain while leaving our kingdom to the wolves," a younger voice snapped.

"I wouldn't discount them yet. They're still allies to Brizia. Prince Bradrick may yet surprise us."

Amirah covered her mouth with her hand as she realized that the party behind her was from Brizia. She had seen soldiers earlier, but none donning the Brizian colors or emblem. She lowered her hand and looked at Nithe, who gave her a single slow nod, confirming her suspicion. His eyes trained on the group as they both continued to listen.

"Aye, but his mother won't make that easy. The whole point of the ball is to marry him off to the highest bidder now that our King is dead." The first speaker resumed the lead.

"Now, we have to clean up the aftermath alone. The members of court won't wait much longer before one of them beheads the other."

"They'll drag us all down with them in a bloodbath first. Family against family."

Amirah almost choked on her drink. Roman had finished putting logs on the fire and rushed to her for aid. He tucked a strand of ginger hair away from her face and plucked something away from her skin, causing Nithe to jerk in response. His hand smacked against his face as if a bug had bitten him. He rubbed the spot on his face with a contemptuous look shot in Roman and Amirah's direction. Roman chuckled while he observed the small in his hand object with intrigue. When he showed it to Amirah, she gasped. Nithe saw her eyes widen in alarm and moved to stand beside them. When Roman showed him the petite white feather, Nithe knew what it meant for Amirah.

"Intriguing." Nithe acknowledged the dainty thing without interest. "The pillows at the tavern must be made with feather down. That being said, we will need to get some rest before we set out tomorrow."

"You are welcome to stay longer if you are able," Roman invited.

"Thank you, but there are things back home that need our immediate attention." Amirah swallowed. It wasn't a lie. Not after what they just overheard. "Nithe is right. We should turn in for the night."

"Alright, then. It has been a pleasure making your acquaintance. I hope to see you again in the future when you have more time. Perhaps not while I am stationed here in Ruya."

Roman stood with her, offering a farewell embrace. Amirah welcomed the firm, warm arms that tightened around her. What she saw over his shoulder sent her heart racing. The group that sat at the nearby fire were indeed soldiers. Judging by their faded admiral blue surcoat uniforms, they appeared to be Brizian soldiers, which perplexed her. *Why are they so far north and dressed in old uniforms?* she wondered. Nithe cleared his throat drawing attention back to him. Roman released Amirah and turned to him with an extended hand. They shook and froze. A crooked grin pulled at the corner of Roman's lips as they stared each other dead in the eyes, hand in hand. Neither wavered their gazes that flickered with light, nor did they release each other. Amirah stepped between them and gave Nithe a nudge in the side.

"Thank you for your hospitality. I am sure we will meet again."

She smiled with an inclination of the head toward Roman. He mirrored her farewell and, with that, she tugged Nithe away from the campsite.

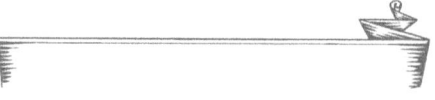

CHAPTER 19

Amirah tried to keep calm and walk at a steady pace to avoid drawing attention. Once they were far enough away from the camp, her steps quickened. When she stumbled, Nithe caught her before she reached the ground. More feathers cascaded away from her. All the distractions had caused the transformation to be forgotten. She normally would have been asleep at this hour. Reckless, she scolded herself.

Nithe looked her over for signs of injury. Finding none, he took her arm and pulled her along behind him through the gates. This time, Amirah's temper flared. She tried to jerk her hand away, but unlike earlier, he held an iron grip. When she tried again, he stopped to look at her.

"What?" he asked, bewildered.

His eyes bore into her. When she said nothing, he closed what little space was between them. Amirah caught his stare, her own mix of emotions causing her stomach to flip. A hand came up to dust a loose feather from her cheek and lingered a moment too long while Nithe searched her eyes. She resisted the instinct to lean into his touch. The moment passed when he gave a deep sigh.

"There's enough in the vial that you'll be able to change back if you want to stay here longer. We could always fly back after a couple of days." She didn't recognize the unfamiliar edge to his voice.

"Even if I wanted to—which I don't—it wouldn't be safe. Those were soldiers from Brizia. Their uniforms gave them away, but we weren't close enough for me to see if they had anything identifying which house they served. If the members of the court are ready to wage war with each other, it's strange that they are in a northern kingdom. Do you know why they would be here?"

"No idea, but what we need to worry about now is getting you inside before we run into anyone else."

She nodded in agreement. "Fine, but don't yank me along like I'm a child."

"Very well, Princess." He turned so she couldn't see the grin that played at the corners of his mouth when she growled. They stalked one after the other toward the tavern.

"Stop calling me Princess!" she snapped.

"Why shouldn't I?"

"As you once pointed out, I am your Sovereign. Everyone thinks the Princess of Brizia is dead, and she is indeed. So stop calling me by that title. I am the Queen."

Except for their footsteps on the ground, the world was silent. She didn't see his eyebrows arch upwards with her assertion. Of all the things he could have said, in that moment, they were better suited for another time.

"Good." He nodded as her words digested his mind, the word meant more for himself to hear than for her. "Good."

The barkeep greeted them with a wave when they returned to the busy tavern. Nithe gave him a nod of acknowledgement as they headed for the stairs tucked in a back corner of the tavern. It led to a hall with a handful of unmarked, aged wooden doors that matched the walls. If it weren't for the barkeep mentioning that theirs would be the first on the left, it would have been impossible to tell.

Inside, the small squared room was filled with simple furniture. A bed was tucked into a corner with a trunk at the end and an oval corded rug sat in front of a rickety-looking tub with a single window above it. To the left, a narrow table with a faded juniper high-back chair sat against the wall opposite the bed. Amirah's nose wrinkled at the faint musk of the room that was tinged with alcohol. Nithe cracked the window to allow the fresh night breeze to filter through the stale air.

"Take the bed," he directed.

Amirah scoffed. "You should stop bossing me around. I've never been known to be obedient. Where would you sleep?"

"Clearly, Pr..." he bit his lower lip and strained not to call her princess. The warning look she shot him as a reminder was venomous. "I can sleep anywhere; the chair or the floor. I plan to read the books from the library first."

"You have plenty of time to read. If we are leaving in the morn—"

"We do not have plenty of time." Nithe's tone darkened as he spoke.

His hands produced a book from beneath his cloak before he settled in the chair. Amirah's irritation over his ever-changing mood throughout the day superseded knowing he was right. Something was different about him today. Their situation brought them together, but it now served as an ever-present complication. Part of her pondered if it was the curse or if it might be something deeper. When she crossed her arms, feathers fell to the floor, ignored as they stared at each other. Both matched in stubbornness.

"I am aware we don't have the time. Not that it's my fault to begin with. More specifically, I don't have the time. The kingdom doesn't have the time," she spat.

Nithe stood up and took a few steps to cross the space between them. "Perhaps you would like to stay here with Roman and figure it out yourself? You're not a prisoner, so do as you please. Your soldiers were right there and you are more than welcome to go home with them."

"I have no reason to want to stay with Roman. I'm not sure what the connection is, or why you insist on me staying with him, but it needs to stop. He proved a reliable contact and could be a potential connection for Brizia in the future. Sabotaging that would be asinine. Right now, I need all the allies I can muster." She bristled, moving on without giving him the chance to interrupt. "As for the soldiers, they are not mine. We don't know who they have aligned themselves with in court. Turning myself in, here of all places, is a way to end up with my throat slit. An effective end to both of us and maybe the entire kingdom."

His jaw clenched as he stared down at her. If it weren't for her flaring anger, she might have felt nervous about their proximity. Refusing to cede a step, she stared up her nose at him.

"Then what do you want, Princess? Do you want me to share the bed with you?" he growled.

She blinked at his unexpected words. Nothing in his face or tone had changed. There was something unspoken, akin to a challenge, behind his relentless glare that she couldn't read. Her face heated with each word. Even the way he called her 'Princess' made the hairs on her arms stand on end. She crossed them, turning away from him, hoping to disguise the way her traitorous body reacted.

"I want you to get enough sleep for tomorrow's journey," she said. "Sleep where you want, and stop calling me Princess."

A moment of silence passed between them. She removed her cloak, placed it on top of the trunk, and climbed into the bed without looking at him. Nithe remained stationary. Although her eyes never went back to him, she could feel those dark green orbs following her. Once the blankets engulfed her in bed, she faced away from him, frowning at day's memories. It seemed as if one minute he kept her at length like a venomous snake and then the next he protected her as if she were some precious treasure. The undeniable pull between them was another thing to consider. Something her crown wouldn't give them time to explore.

A TINGE OF DISAPPOINTMENT nagged at Nithe. It joined the plethora of other things that devoured him from the inside out. Today would be added to the list of regrets that plagued him. The argument had been pointless. He knew she had been correct. Returning the book beneath his cloak, he fought the foreign emotions in silence, lending to his erratic behavior today. Either the curse or his probable madness caused the unfamiliar emotions within him to rise up. Regardless, no matter their origin, there was no reasonable explanation that came to mind. The dance he and Amirah were doing was a dangerous one.

Roman represented a multifaceted threat that he hadn't known existed to him. Neither party had been forthright. He could sense the magic that coursed through the new ally's veins. Unsurprising since he was Venincio's son. Magic was believed to have been wiped from the Continent, so the initial secrecy made sense while amid soldiers.

Once the connection had been made, it remained an unspoken matter. When they had shaken hands, a silent exchange of understanding passed between them. First, the recognition of the hidden powers that the other harbored. Second, an unspoken challenge where it concerned Amirah. Whatever magic he kept secret was not the same as the Astronomers. The ally Amirah hoped for was not the person Roman truly was. An alliance built on dishonesty would carry risk, especially when reclaiming a throne that was already in turmoil. *Thanks to me,* he shook his head at the thought. *A dangerous game we are playing, indeed.*

Amirah shifted under the blankets. The subtle rise and fall gave the rhythmic indication she was asleep and the winds of change would soon transform her peaceful form. The night drew closer to the early hours of the morning. Curiosity got the better of him and he folded the blankets away from her face. She remained, as suspected, unchanged for the moment. The cygnet feathers floated around her in a halo pattern and he plucked one of the downy feathers from her hair. It was like the one that Roman had pulled off her earlier. He resettled into the chair that angled toward the bed with the feather still cupped in his hand. It represented an unexpected sign of change. One they felt approaching. An unfamiliar feeling clenched his gut as he watched over her peaceful form like a sentinel until he was overtaken by sleep.

The next morning, Nithe was awoken by the loud flapping swan form Amirah had taken. It was easy to presume why she was in distress. If anyone nearby were to discover her, there would be many questions about where she was and where the great bird had come from. Though his tongue was like sharp silver, there was never a guarantee that strangers would accept any explanation he gave to them. The risk upon her was tripled with the number of skilled bowmen scattered around town. The sooner she returned to human form, the better for both of them.

The moon was fading with the dawn. The few eyes wandered into the streets in the early hours and dared to glance around in search of the commotion. Unable to soothe her distemper, he cursed under his breath. One hand flicked toward the window and a gust of wind produced itself from inside the room and slammed it shut. With a snap of his fingers, the coals sparked to life beneath the tub. The viridescent glint in his eyes flickered out quickly. The vial appeared in his hand moments later as the last drops of its contents dripped into the tub.

When he turned back to Amirah, she hissed at him. The first dive he made for her was a miss. So was the second. Yet, as she darted away, things knocked over in her wake and Nithe managed to wrap his arms around her, despite being battered by feathers. The water rose up and consumed her the instant her feathers made contact.

Nithe fell backward as the splash spread beyond the confines of the tub. The wave of droplets coated the floors, walls, and window. Another slosh followed as Amirah sprang up in human form with a yelp. The subsided water left her drenched in a half-full tub.

A persistent knock interrupted the glowering look she gave him. Nithe opened the door to find the old barkeep. His wrinkled face scrunched in alarm. Seeing Amirah, he stuttered an apology. Amirah splashed at both of them.

"Out," she demanded. "*Out!*"

The barkeep moved aside to make room as Nithe hastily exited into the hallway. The men audibly chuckled in the hallway after the door clicked shut. She climbed out and dressed, quietly muttering about Nithe risking the last of the vial. However, it worked. Despite her hair waving with saturation and the momentary embarrassment, they could go home. Soon after, they went down to check out of the tavern. Amirah, spotting the bar keeper's daughter, grinned from ear to ear.

CHAPTER 20

Not long after Amirah emerged, they left Ruya on foot for the remaining journey home. Amirah was content with their parting from Roman the prior night and had her mind set on the troubles of her kingdom. The unspoken weight of the crown called for her to return. Nithe seemed to have reverted to normal, though, the shadow of deep thought turned his brow down in silent concentration. Amirah was more than happy to let him keep whatever he bottled up to himself as they trudged along the road in silence. The few trees on the border of Isidris thinned until they crossed into Rapplend.

"Do you think we'll make it back in time?" she asked Nithe as they began up one of the rolling hills.

"In time for what?"

Amirah shrugged. "In time to prevent a war."

"Men will go to war, one way or another. It's only a matter of finding an excuse," Nithe said. "The absence of a monarch is avoidable only if you ascend to the throne, but it won't prevent fighting if they seek it."

They fell silent as a couple of horseback riders passed them with little more than a nod of acknowledgment. The people in this kingdom wrapped themselves in layered clothes of vivid pigments that flowed against the wind. While Amirah wished they had horses or could fly over the mountain, she couldn't help but enjoy the few encounters with those around them. Rapplend possessed a certain charm and its people that warmed her heart. By the end of the day, they found lodgings at a small farm that offered a room at the back of the horse stables.

The farmer and his young family were dressed in layers of clothes that protected their tanned skin like the riders. Greens and a deep purple seemed to be the popular colors proliferating the houses here. Three young children flitted around the skirts of their mother when the farmer called everyone for dinner. Their bright eyes glinted with youthful mischief as they circled her into the kitchen where a large table set with food waited. She clapped to grab their attention and motioned to the chairs. They ceased the bout of giggles and assumed their seats. When they focused on their plates, a smile crested her lips. Amirah consumed the food that smelled of warm herbs and delighted her tongue.

"Thank you for the meal," she said to the wife after finishing her plate. The woman grinned in response.

"You're welcome," her husband, the farmer, interjected, "and thank you for joining us. Elra is mute, but she will chastise you all the same. I would know."

He chuckled as the wife gave him a playful nudge in the side. When they had all finished, the children helped clear the table and went back to playing. The simple bliss of familial adoration warmed the place brighter than the hearth did. The beauty of the family enchanted Amirah, and she envied their reality. It was like looking through the window and being offered a sample of a life she could only ever look upon or imagine. A bitter-sweet peek into a world that promised delightful freedom and unhindered love. The thought of leaving it behind almost brought tears to her eyes.

In the morning as they turned to leave, the wife caught Amirah by the arm. She gifted her the vivid purple scarf she had worn. The kindred woman wrapped it around her shoulders and kissed each cheek farewell. Amirah returned her gesture with a hug. This time, tears escaped the corners of her eyes as she bade the family farewell.

Nithe observed her somber state but didn't bother her with an inquiry. He understood what she was feeling because he felt it himself. Despite keeping himself at a purposeful distance from others, especially happier families, he family had been as a window into what could have been, yet was not, and never would be. They moved along the road, each step closer to the mountains that separated Rapplend from the part of Brizia that hid the Duke's castle from the world. Its peak loomed over the land. It seemed as if they were chasing after a shadow—the closer they got, the farther it seemed to be. By nightfall, they would reach the base of the mountain and the shadow would elude them. The thought of home propelled them both for different reasons.

Without tree coverage, their plan was to camp somewhere away from the main road off the small trail they followed. The cool air glinted with sparkling stars as the night blanketed over the Continent. Both of them scanned their surroundings, cautious of the odd sensation of being watched from the hills at the base of the mountain. The path wound between them, dipping into tall blades of grass and boulder-esque rocks. Like Nithe, Amirah's kept a watchful eye, but couldn't find the source of their unease. She picked up her steps to keep closer to him. The silence that lingered around them was absent of any sign of life—no chirping insects, sleepless animals, or even the wind.

A resounding crack beneath their feet startled them to a stop. A brief screech escaped Amirah as they fell which came to an abrupt stop when the breath was knocked from her. Even Nithe grunted from his collision against the hard surface beneath where they had fallen. They were looking up from a small hole that was where they had stood moments before. Fragments of wood, dirt, and foliage littered around them and Amirah heard Nithe curse under his breath when he stood. He extended his hand and helped her stand up.

"What in the Twelve Kingdoms!?" Amirah scanned the hole a second time over. "Why would anyone put an animal trap all the way out here?"

"I'm not sure it's meant for animals," he said with a cautious gaze at the opening. "Hunters don't make a habit of putting traps directly on roadways. Not even small trails like that one. It's too small for me to transform or use magic without the risk of flattening you. We might have to climb out."

Amirah dusted off what dirt she could manage in frustration and when she looked up, an object glinted inches from her face. Her eyes darted up from the shining dagger Nithe held to his face. He nudged it toward her with a serious expression on his face. She raised an eyebrow at him and took it.

"What's this for?" she asked and examined the vaguely familiar pointed silver and the scabbard's twisting patterns.

"You need a way to defend yourself, even with me here. After learning you had some skill with weaponry, I bought it."

"Oh," Amirah blinked. "Thank you."

Nithe smirked as she fiddled with the gift. Her fingers danced over the designs and up the leathered hilt until they met with the pommel inlaid with magenta gemstone. A smile tugged the corners of her lips as she looked it over. The sparkle in her eyes hinted at the way the gift warmed her heart.

Twigs snapped above and stole her attention from the dagger. Nithe pushed her back against the wall, one hand resting firmly against her abdomen as he maneuvered his body to shield hers. Her breath hitched at the sudden contact but she remained silent as he held the index finger of his other hand to his lips.

He tilted his head down to whisper in her ear. "Be ready. We'll let them think they have us captured so we can get out of this hole. Then, we move. Don't hesitate."

Behind them, a rope ladder fell into the pit. A gruff voice called down, ordering them to climb up. Nithe's jaw clenched as he looked back at the rope. Amirah tucked the dagger in her clothes to make it well hidden, but still easy enough to access. Nithe ascended first. Amirah heard the shuffling footsteps and his grunt as she followed up the rope ladder. When she reached the edge of the hole, two pairs of rough hands latched onto her arms and dragged her the rest of the way out. Nithe was correct: it had been a trap.

An unkempt, mismatched group encircled the hole. They dressed differently from the rest of the civilians of Rapplend. Their outfits were a hodgepodge of garments, while some neglected to even put on a shirt. Nithe stared at the ground, his hands held behind his back by a guy with a brawny build. Amirah was handed off to a rounded fellow beside them with a patch over his eye. Boots crunched against the ground until they stopped in front of her. The man was older, just as dirt-encrusted as the others, but in a nicer coat. His thin hand clasped her chin, forcing her head from side to side. His dark eyes dilated and doubled in size with recognition. She jerked her head, attempting to escape the rough texture of his hands.

"What a prize we have caught today!" he crowed. She recognized his voice as the same one that demanded they ascend from the hole. The man's unfamiliar accent was not from Isidris, Rapplend, or Brizia. He released her face with a look of satisfaction. His body spun with his arms in the air to make a grand gesture to his underlings before he turned back to her. "The missing Princess of Brizia, Amirah Svana Landry. I must say your likeness really doesn't do you justice. A pleasure to make your acquaintance, Your Majesty."

Amirah sneered at the mocking bow.

"And whom are we now acquainted with?" Nithe muttered from beside her, his head hung low. Amirah noticed his eyes appeared to be shut, but she had the eerie feeling he still saw everything.

"I'll be the one asking questions if there are any to be asked. Who you might be? I know many faces, especially if there is money involved, but you are unfamiliar to me."

"He's a guide I hired," Amirah answered with authority laced in her voice. She stared the man down with the mask of indifference that had overtaken her face. Years at court and in training surfaced in an instant.

"You have been missing for some time, Your Majesty. I suspect there is more to your story than hiring a guide after that unfortunate accident. One that my curiosity begs to hear, but fate has decided otherwise."

"Fate or mortal commandment?" Nithe challenged in his unchanged posture.

The man, who seemed to be the leader of the surrounding crew, shot Nithe with a measured look. Around them, the group grumbled to each other, but nobody would have dared question him in such a manner. Unable to meet Nithe's eyes, he sauntered back toward the hole until his languid steps stopped and stared into the dark trap they had fallen in. When the group dissolved into silence, he answered, speaking to Amirah.

"Almost the entire Continent thinks you are dead. Yet, even as Brizia mourns, there are those who remain unconvinced until a body's recovered, like that of your father's. As it stands, there is a group of Brizian soldiers who would pay a large amount of coin for your head, dead or alive. Though, I hear the end will likely still be death, according to whom they're aligned."

"And who might that be?" She tried to mask the curiosity at the tip of her tongue.

He turned back toward her, purposefully retracing the steps he had taken away.

"Of that, I am uncertain. The soldiers mentioned their orders were coming from within the court. My interest is in nothing more than the bounty on your head. Nevertheless," his index finger tilted her chin upwards, "your ending will be kinder by our hands than those soldiers. We may be killers and thieves, but we still have more heart than those that pretend to be civilized."

"How considerate," she sneered.

The one who held Amirah released his grip on the demand of their leader but didn't step away. The whisper of a sword being unsheathed caught her attention, and one of the scruffiest of the crew handed a sword to the leader. It seemed they intended to kill her right here and now. Her heart beat faster as he approached her with the sword in hand. She wondered for a moment if they would let Nithe go after killing her, then laughed at the absurd thought. She knew the curse meant killing either her or Nithe would ultimately kill both of them. Fortunately, that wasn't something these brutes knew, but the thought was still amusing. As if Nithe would let the brutes have a chance. These were foxes in a wolf's den.

Amirah was forced to her knees. She stared in defiance at the leader while her hand felt for the hilt of the hidden dagger. Her fingers slid around the cool, leather-wrapped metallic hilt and waited. An apologetic smile crossed the leader's face as he poised to strike. A moment of confusion passed as she realized he didn't request any last words from her.

Nithe's head snapped up the moment the sword swung, and it was flung away by an unseen force. The leader faltered a step back from Amirah in surprise as his eyes followed the path from the sword on the ground, to the direction the force came from. The group's gaze followed along. Nithe stared back at them with venom. His dark gaze was lit with the bright viridescent color of his eyes. A hushed gasp, followed by the metallic sound of swords drawing, broke the silence. Amirah took the brief opening to move.

She yanked the dagger out and lunged at the leader. Her strike landed on his side—a quick blow—as the dagger sank in and out in a seamless motion. He cried out in pain and clasped at the wound that was blossoming red on his side. She moved for the sword, rolling away from the patch-eyed man who leapt after her. Her free hand grabbed the sword. Now upright, she found herself surrounded by at least three others. Her hand twirled the sword in a circular motion, testing the weight of it. This was a dance she had trained for.

Nithe fought off the ones who correctly assumed he was the biggest threat. He could tell, by the way they handled their weapons and their poor form, that they were less than trained. The unseen force of magic he emitted, knocked back the aggressors and his shifted hand tore apart those unfortunate enough to come within reach. Briefly, concern crossed over him when he saw Amirah surrounded. Her sword clashed with the first attacker as Nithe ripped his way through the group standing between them. Wielding a sword and dagger, she cut down her opponents.

As each fell, another replaced them. One moved to attack Amirah from behind and she spun, blocking their sword and striking at their open side with the dagger. They staggered back to look at the blood that now coated their fingers from the wound before they fell. A girl several years younger than Amirah, stepped up next to face her as the rest of them encircled her. The girl's dark hair was pulled back with braids which were interwoven with coin-like ornaments and the right side of her face donned a black eye. She crouched low as she and Amirah wove their feet in a circle around each other. In a flurry of combat, they landed minor blows on each other in quick succession. Amirah blocked the girl's advances and made intentional nonlethal attacks. She intended to only subdue the girl, if possible.

Nithe threw the remainder of Amirah's aggressors back, the last of the group turning their attention on him. One by one, he ripped out jugulers, eyes, and any manner of vital limbs, depleting them to nothing. When Nithe turned back, the leader now stood on the opposite side of the makeshift battle ring. Having somehow survived the lethal blow Amirah had landed earlier, he was pale from blood loss. One of his hands clasped over his side and the other bore a torch. He shouted senseless demands and threats at Amirah's opponent, urging her to fight as if he still had some hope for victory. Amirah pitied that this was the leadership the girl had endured for an unknown amount of time. The whirling of wind drew the leader's attention behind him.

The moment he spun around, his eyes met Nithe. Blood sputtered from his mouth in the place of words, and his eyes bulged as he watched as Nithe pulled a blood-soaked hand out of his chest. His collapse drew the girl's attention away from their fight. Amirah took the opportunity, swooping the legs out from under the girl, and pointing the sword within an inch of the girl's throat.

"Yield!" she demanded from the girl. Remembering the words from her training, she continued, "Cedere pugnae!"

The girl's lip trembled, and she shook her head in refusal. Amirah recognized the stubborn attitude. The soldiers who trained Amirah to fight had bested her countless times. Her refusal to forfeit when the loss was unrecoverable was a mark of her determinative nature. However, this wasn't training. She allowed the girl enough movement to sit upright.

"Yield!" she ordered again, this time with an outreached hand.

The girl rolled over to get up and Nithe saw the movements Amirah missed. As the girl moved, her hand reached for her sword. His eyes squinted in observation. Seconds of reality stole all the silent hopes that Amirah harbored and would go unfulfilled. The swing of the girl's sword ended quicker than it began.

Nithe knocked the girl over and snapped her neck in a swift movement. Her body slumped to the ground with the sword still in hand and Amirah screamed. Nithe stepped toward her, but she backed away, her face twisted in rage and sadness. She pointed to the dead girl's body with her sword. "She didn't have to die!"

"She was going to kill you."

"She was just a child! We can't kill everyone that opposes us, Nithe!"

Nithe held his blood-drenched hands up in silent surrender. Amirah's face crumpled as they faced each other, painted in the lives of the bodies that were scattered around them. She had proven herself as an effective fighter, but he wasn't sure if Amirah had ever seen bloodshed outside of when he had killed her father. Even with the risk of death, she found the innocence within someone who was attempting to end her life. He approached her like she was a scared, injured animal. In fact, the girl had gotten in a few blows. Nithe could now feel the secondhand wounds that replicated the ones on Amirah.

He wrapped his arms around her. Although she was furious, she didn't resist this time. Instead, she buried her face in his chest and sobbed. His warm scent that enveloped her, helped soothe the pain that linered in her chest. He rested his chin atop her hair for a moment before he spoke.

"My instinct was to protect you, nothing more and nothing less. I won't apologize for that. I can't promise to avoid it in the future, especially if someone is attempting to kill you, but I will try to exercise more... restraint."

The last word came out with a slow, hesitant drawl. She blinked, removing the tears that still clung to her damp lashes. Her face looked up from the dark safety of his body with a stern look.

"Promise." Her words were more a demand than a request as she stared at him.

"Promise," he relented after the silence became uncomfortable. "Now, let's dress your wounds before we get out of here."

Nithe's injuries were identical replicas of her own and he knew a few were deep. His own would heal before the end of the next day by the magic that coursed through his veins. While he could heal all the wounds on both of them, they needed to prevent infection—something his magic couldn't guarantee. He produced clean strips of cloth from beneath his cloak that they used to clean and bandage the most severe injuries. Then, Nithe used his powers to heal the smaller ones that scattered Amirah's body. She watched in a daze as his hands traveled over her limbs, leaving the familiar tingle of magic in their wake. His body healed its replicas as he worked over her.

After tending to each other's injuries, Nithe used his magic to cover the bodies with earth. It took minutes to carry the soil on the wind, unlike utilizing mundane methods. The task was more for Amirah's sake than for the dead. Turning them to ash would only draw attention they didn't need when Amirah was being hunted. Finding a place further away to camp, they settled into a restless sleep until the birds woke them in the morning.

The remainder of their journey home passed without further event, their path taking them through a pass that cut through mountains. Along the way, they gathered herbs for Nithe's collection from the green sides of the sloped pass. Many of them ended up stashed beneath in the mysterious shadows of his cloak. He made a few into salves and applied them to Amirah's wounds. A combination of the salve and touches of Nithe's magic hastened their healing. By the time they reached the welcomed walls of the Duke's Castle, only a thin pink scar remained on Amirah's upper leg.

CHAPTER 21

A messenger donning Brizian colors on his vestige rode through the gates of the Prurian palace. His horse came to a stop at the front steps, where he handed the reins to a groomsman as he dismounted. He patted the satchel that hung across his chest to ensure it was still closed as a castle steward in a blush and gold long coat greeted him.

"Good morning. I apologize, but Her Highness, Queen Indra, is not taking visitors today," the steward frowned.

The messenger bowed curtly. "My respect for the Queen. However, I am here to deliver an urgent summons to Lady Paget."

"I see." The steward looked around to be certain no one else was near enough to listen to the exchange. "Follow me. If anyone should ask, the Queen summoned you."

Once the messenger dipped his head to indicate his agreement, the steward led him inside the palace. All visitors usually met with the Queen in the throne or greeting room to pay their respects and disperse with any business. However, on some days, such as today, the Queen refused any visitors. The reason was apparent as the steward and messenger passed through the halls that bustled with life. They passed the cook, who lamented to his assistants about another menu with grandiose expectations. A man in a lace-trimmed velvet coat with a short black goatee and long bouncing curls that were tied back beneath a feather-adorned hat, leaned against a wall, tapping his foot. Two attendants stood beside him with a large trunk that sat between them. When the messenger and the steward passed the trio, the man called out and motioned for his attendants to follow with the trunk.

"Pardon me! Sir, sir!" He cried as the trio caught up.

The steward stopped at the base of the main stairway and looked patiently at the man. His eyebrows raised subtly with the expectation of hearing what the trio needed.

"Her Highness requested me to bring additional clothes for her to choose from for the final selection. Yesterday we met in the greeting room, but she is not there today."

"Ah yes, yes. Her Highness is not taking visitors, so all business will be conducted in her office. I shall take you up." The steward turned to the messenger with a curt bow of the head. "Please, excuse me. If you would please wait here for your appointment."

"Of course," the messenger returned the gesture.

After the steward, the dressmaker, and his attendants vanished from sight, the messenger busied himself looking around him. The palace was indeed busy. This allowed the time to pass quickly as he pretended to be interested in the ornate candelabras, rather than those who passed through the hall. He had almost forgotten his purpose until a sweet voice caused him to spin around.

"Excuse me. I understand you have a summons for me." Gabrielle Paget flew down the stairs as quickly as her slippered feet would allow.

"Yes, my lady, from your father." The messenger bowed quickly at the waist in greeting. From his satchel, he produced a parchment letter sealed with wax.

Gabbie accepted the letter and broke the seal. Her eyes scanned over her father's writing while two conversing voices reached her down the main stairs as their owners approached. The messenger bowed at the waist when Prince Bradrick and Lord Macanay came into view. Bradrick stopped when he realized Gabbie was standing at the foot of the stairway.

"Is it bad news?" Alonzo inquired of the messenger as he and Bradrick came to stand beside them.

The messenger straightened as he answered. "Lord Paget has sent a summons for Lady Paget to return to court with haste."

"And a letter," Gabbie sighed as she finished reading, "without any good news. The mourning period for the King is coming to a close in Brizia. Some lords have become quite vocal about their ambitions and..."

Bradrick shook his head in disbelief as his brows turned down. "What about the searches?"

Gabbie frowned. "There was a vote, Bradrick. The lords have discontinued all searches for Amirah. I should have returned to Brizia with the rest of the nobles. At least I would have been more useful there."

Bradrick swore under his breath and disgust laced his voice. "How could they do this? They don't even know what happened to her! There was barely any discord when there should have been an outrage that their King died in such a manner on Prurian soil. Instead, they're vying for power for a throne that is not theirs to take!"

"It's not your fault, Gabbie," Alonzo offered in reassurance, though the brightness in his tone was gone. "Thirst for power fuels the hearts of men who have little other passions. Their decision was made long before a vote was cast. I understand Lord Paget's concern for you and the kingdom. However, with the kingdom headed for upheaval, wouldn't it be safer for you to stay here?"

"Perhaps, but even so, I will return. My father needs my help at court and will feel more at peace if I am near. There are ways I can still aid him with the nobles. The influence I have garnered among the court member's wives and daughters has proven helpful on a number of occasions. It might buy us more time."

Alonzo rubbed his chin in thought as he tossed a suspicious glance at the messenger. Upon seeing this, the messenger shifted on his feet nervously. When he offered his opinion, there was a subtle quiver to his voice. "Not that my opinion as a lower noble matters, Lady Paget, but I believe that you have the right idea. It is rather difficult to accomplish anything when the ladies of the house are unhappy. One would imagine that usurping a throne when your house is not in order, would be a nary impossible feat. More so, when your allies have similar plights to contend with."

"Thank you. My house comes from lower nobility, so I care as much for your opinion as I do your loyal service." Gabbie gave the messenger a kind smile before she turned her attention back to a brooding Bradrick and Alonzo. "I should change and prepare for the journey back. Father will be less nervous when he knows I'm safe. I'll ask Kamille to send my trunks back to Brizia. If we leave on horseback, it will be a faster journey."

Bradrick crossed his arms. "We were planning to depart with the hunting party at noon and will stay at a border village. Gabbie, you and—"

"—Sir Tristan, Your Highness" the messenger answered at Bradrick's pointed look.

"Right, then. You and Tristan meet us at the gates with the rest of the hunting party and we can escort you. It's one of the few ways I've been able to leave the palace without my mother fussing. I will have Kamille write to you to keep you abreast of my search for Amirah. Please keep me updated on the situation in Brizia."

"Alright. I'll see all of you soon. Tristan, will you please do me the kindness of having a horse prepared for me?"

"Of course, my lady." Tristan bowed and excused himself. At the same time, Gabbie headed for the guest halls, leaving Bradrick and Alonzo to continue their own preparations.

With the approaching ball, more hunting parties were being sent out than normal. This had been Bradrick's cover to look for Amirah ever since his mother ordered him to stop. He was the last of the dwindled number of those who believed she was still alive somewhere. Now, it seemed Brizia had given up all hope and concern for her. Disgusted by this, Bradrick resolved to take up the mantle of continuing the search for her on his own for the sake of both kingdoms. There was a limited time left to find his missing fiancé, a fact that hung over him like a dark cloud.

Alonzo noticed Bradrick's mood as they rode out into the crisp autumn air that stole the color from the tree leaves across the Continent. He looked around to ensure no one appeared to be within listening range. Most of the hunting party observed the surrounding natural world or immersed themselves in conversations. Gabbie and Tristan followed behind on horseback, carrying on a hushed discussion. Certain that he was safe to speak, Alonzo steered his horse closer to Bradrick.

"We're staying at the tavern tonight, your favorite getaway, and we left the place without incident. Usually, this would be a cause to celebrate with a tankard of ale. I assume there are a number of things weighing on you."

"You assume correct," Bradrick admitted.

"Word of the ball has reached beyond the Continent. I'm sure you've heard since that is almost all your mother talks about. Given your mother's precedent for any manner of party throwing, it's expected to be grand. It's keeping her busy enough for now. So, what's the next phase of the plan?" Alonzo glanced sideways at Bradrick, who shrugged.

"Keep searching until we are out of time. Same as before."

"What happens when time runs out?" Alonzo pressed.

"If," Bradrick corrected. "If time runs out. Then we have no choice but to move forward to the next part of the plan. I haven't committed to it yet, but essentially, that would be to remove my mother from power, whether I am married or not. I am hoping it doesn't come to that." He sighed. "Even if the crown is rightfully mine."

Amirah awoke to the fresh sunlight casting through the window in her swan form. Her eyes blinked against the fog of sleep as she looked around the study. She and Nithe had fallen asleep reading over the books they brought back from Isidris. In truth, Amirah had skimmed more than she had actually read through. Most of the books were written in an unfamiliar language and contained more depth of magic than she was familiar with. The looming need for her to stake her rightful claim to the Brizian throne left her anxious. She spent as much time beside Nithe as possible, knowing it would soon draw to a close.

The seasons had changed, bringing patches of warm-colored leaves to some of the trees nestled among the evergreens. After their return, Amirah spent time with him lounging in the courtyard. When they were in the study, she peppered Nithe with questions about his childhood and the places he had traveled. Part of her wanted to know everything about him. Curse or not, she accepted these moments would engrave themselves upon her memory. Nithe warmly recounted what he remembered of his father and the time spent in his mother's homelands—one of the island nations beyond the Continent. She was captivated by his vivid description of the island, a place she could only dream of one day seeing herself.

"They sound delightful." Amirah smiled at Nithe after he had described growing up with a cousin in the home of his aunt.

"Most of them are or were, yes." Nithe stared at the star-painted ceiling above the lounge chair he was draped lazily over that was situated in front of the dragon-shaped fireplace.

Amirah sat in the opposite chair, eating one of the small twisted pastries he had made for them. When Nithe picked one up off a plate on the small table between them and bit into it, she found herself staring at his lips. She turned away, mentally chastising herself for the ridiculous thoughts that had no business traversing into such obscurities.

Oblivious to the pink suddenly coloring her face, he recollected a time the sweets reminded him of. "After my aunt had taught my cousin and I how to make these, we thought we'd surprise her with them. So, when the entire clan gathered one night for dinner, we served them dessert. The thing was, my aunt never labeled her spices. So I added what I thought was cinnamon, but turned out to be cumin. Everyone took a large first bite, and it quickly became a memory I may never outlive."

Amirah made a face at what she could only imagine the pastries would have tasted like. The look earned another chuckle from Nithe. He continued to explain the punishment he had earned, which equated to some task that usually had another tale to go with it. Once, she asked if he missed them, and learned that only his cousins and one uncle remained with the living—of which he had no particular attachment to.

It occurred to her that, during their journey, she had found a sense of forgiveness toward Nithe for her father's death. Although, she couldn't pinpoint the exact point in time. It was strange, yet she understood his motivations. The past affected them both in unexpected ways. Yet, despite the problems between their parents, Nithe still sought to protect her. If it hadn't been for the curse and her recurring transformations, she might never have learned about her father's terrible past. All things considered, she would still have been married off. If whoever was plotting her demise didn't succeed at ending her life, then her mother-in-law-to-be would have called the shots. Her heart ached for Bradrick, knowing that his mother still intended to use him as a pawn in her own political games.

How will I explain it to Bradrick or anyone? Even if I can explain it, will everyone I've known hate me for staying away and breaking the contract between our two kingdoms? Her pessimistic thoughts carried on with worry. She hoped her disappearance had not made an enemy of Bradrick. Though their courtship had only begotten a strong friendship, she had abandoned it, along with everything else in her quest to stop being a swan.

Now, once again, Amirah sat with Nithe in his study in her pristine avian glory. Lost in quiet reminiscence, she considered his sleeping form for a moment. His head rested half on an open book, the other half on the arm tucked beneath him, the edge of Amirah's purple scarf from Rapplend intertwined with his fingers. If she were in her human form, she would have reached to brush the pieces of long strands of black hair that draped over his face. She studied his peaceful countenance and its stark contrast to his formidable waking form. If a swan could smile, she would have.

After committing this image of him to memory, she hopped down from her chair. It was still early, but she wanted to stretch her wings in the courtyard. Flying felt like freedom and was the most favorable part of being a swan. However, she would prefer to remain a human, even at the cost of never flying again. Cicely had given a riddle to her that she gave much thought about, trying to solve whenever she took to the skies.

Outside, the sunlight warmed the surface of the lake. With the water still too cold for her liking, she rose into the air, eager to stretch her feathered appendages. Nithe had relaxed considerably since their initial agreement, giving her enough space for herself. It felt as if he had given her the freedom she had never been allowed, and would likely never possess again after she returned. She vowed to herself that she would find some way to show her thanks for the precious gift.

Her wings glided her in aimless circles above the surrounding forest. During these flights, she explored the land below. After the numerous leisure flights she had taken since their agreement, she had almost memorized the land surrounding the Duke's castle. There were hidden paths that wound through the forest, each one overgrown and reclaimed by nature in the efforts to erase all traces of the Duke and the lack of travel in the near two decades. The main one led from the gate of the castle's wall to the main road that stretched between Brizia into Pruria. Nature had kept it a secret by covering it from view.

Amirah suspected that, somehow, the forest had worked alongside the magic concealing the Duke's castle from the world. Nithe had never elaborated on the specifics of the enchantment on the lake or the magic that kept it a secret. Nor had she ever considered asking about it. It was strange to think of how many years she had passed the road without knowing it existed. If it was not for Nithe, the place would have been forgotten forever. Amirah wondered if she could see the castle once she returned to the throne.

Lost in thought, she glided down to a small pond hidden away by brush from the intersecting roads. The water was still cool, but warmer than the lake had been. She dipped her head into the water, bathing by instinct. As she preened the feathers between her resting wings, the snapping sound of a twig interrupted her, and her head popped up in alarm. At the edge of the pond stood a familiar face, staring at her with wide, turquoise eyes.

"Well, aren't you a beauty," he whispered.

Alonzo was a welcomed sight. She glided through the water toward him, hoping he might recognize her somehow. After all, she was still herself. When he stepped back toward his horse with a cautious look on his face, she paused.

"Perhaps we won't return without fresh game from this hunt," he said as one hand carefully reached toward the horse, while the other took the bow from his back.

Amirah flapped her wings, busking at the perceived threat. His movements faltered as she rushed toward him. The surprise gave her enough time to take flight before he could string an arrow.

As she flew, an arrow whisked past her a moment later. She heard him curse below as she increased her speed. *Bradrick has always been the better shot. Thankfully,* she thought. The frantic rhythm of her heart and the pumping of her expansive wings propelled her away from him. She didn't have time to admire his ability to track from the ground as he followed behind her. He didn't seem to notice that his horse galloped on the hidden road. She needed to escape Alonzo without leading him all the way back to the castle.

Two more narrowly missed arrows passed her. She veered toward a thicker growth of forest in hopes he would follow away from the road. With a dive, she disappeared from his line of sight into the thick of trees. The closer she drew to the walls, the thicker the forest grew. Fortunately, she had practiced gliding in between the trees. Her body moved through pockets of sunbeams that were scattered between their dark canopies like a well-rehearsed dance. When she could see the walls, it seemed as if she had lost him.

Good. Perhaps he will find something else to hunt, she thought as her white body rose above the treeline at the edge of the wall that surrounded the Duke's castle. Below, the lake came into view just beyond its border. The pristine surface mirrored the sky, dotted with a few small puffy clouds. Its waters called out to her like a welcoming song. Amirah heard the almost silent creak from not far below and she moved to turn toward the hiss that sliced the air a moment too late. When the arrow struck, time seemed to freeze for a moment before the wind began rushing around her. She hadn't lost Alonzo in the woods after all. Her vision tunneled too quickly to feel the glitter of pride for his ever-impressive hunting skills. The world faded to black before her body could register the approaching impact of it hitting the forest floor.

NITHE FLIPPED THROUGH the tattered pages of a Mage's Almanac that he had pulled from the Astronomer's library. If any written text were to give them an answer, it would be in books such as these—knowledge that was almost forgotten to the entire Continent's history. He had poured through them, looking for any morsel of information that might help rid them of the curse. So far, the text was giving him nothing more than lessons in magic. While he held adept knowledge, there was plenty more to learn. Some of the text seemed to slink around certain subjects; death, love, and hate—though these could be construed as the same thing—repeated the most often. Words danced around the pages in vagueness and riddles. Some caught enough of his attention that he thought it better to revisit them. He used the corner of Amirah's scarf as a bookmark on a page he wanted to return to later.

The object reminded him of her and the trip to Isidris. He could tell it already smelled of her without lifting it to his nose. The corners of his mouth quivered upward as he rubbed the smooth cloth between his fingers. It was a slight comfort while she was gone—a fact he'd struggled to adjust to, though he would never outwardly admit to it. He didn't want her to feel bothered by his constant presence or like a prisoner. Which, as he promised before, she was not.

He found himself restless, despite the considerable amount that their trust had grown. Amirah was an undeniable distraction. Even when she wasn't here, his focus was unstable. He felt the sand of time pushing them to opposing ends. He knew, soon, the glass would shatter, and they would be carried away from each other. He frowned at the thought. *For the love of the Continent, I must be a fool.*

There was a tug inside him. It pulled at his mind and body like an unseen line. Somehow, in the silence of the study, something felt off. It was easy to explain away his wandering thoughts about Amirah and their wretched curse. Although he had tried to keep a distance, their relationship had still grown closer than should have been possible. When he held her in his arms following the attack in Rapplend, there was no more denial left in him. He could blame the curse for many things, but it was not what drove him to rip out the heart of the man who dared to threaten her life. It didn't make him kill any of their assailants. While he made a promise to her, he also promised himself that he would protect her. Even if he had to destroy anyone who would harm her. The truth of it all could be the beginning or end of them.

The lonesome silence of the room daunted him like an unwanted reminder. With a sigh, he turned back to the tomes. Within moments, his eyes glazed over the lines of text he meant to study. They focused and unfocused until the window pulled the attention away. The familiar tugging sensation still pulled at the back of his mind, constantly drawing him toward her. It had grown stronger since they first met. He resolved to ignore it, to give her the space she needed, and wondered if he had been inside too long. *Tug.* The courtyard had a lure of its own, with the way evening rays of the sun danced on the lake surface in a dazzling display. He considered taking one of the books down to read and resting on the steps that disappeared into the lake.

Tug, tug, tug.

Nithe moved to stand up. When he rose to his feet, a jolt of pain struck him. He bent over, clutching at his side with a hiss at the pain. It seared through him from his arm into his rib. The smell of copper tainted his air as he forced his eyes to remain open. He held his fingers up before his eyes, noting the fresh crimson that stained the book's pages, his clothes, and Amirah's scarf. Alarm bells sounded in his head. He didn't need a mirror to know his eyes had come to life with the magic that allowed him to move with the speed of a tempest.

Nithe moved with the wind churning around him and grabbed bandages on the way to the courtyard. Seconds later, he was there. He scanned the surroundings, searching the lake, the trees, and the sky until, finally, movement snagged his attention. Dropping the bandages, his vision tunneled in on a blur of white in free fall from the sky. Realization dawned on him, along with dark dread and fury. A beastly roar ripped from his throat as his magic whipped the wind around him like a savage storm. It propelled him through the sky, partially transformed—not a complete human, not a complete dragon, but a creature born of fury. The magic was fueled by his rage as he realized that an arrow protruded from the swan. She had almost made it to the wall. Almost. When she was seconds from the ground, Nithe reached her. His arms ensnared her body like a safety net and sent feathers scattering. For a moment, he hovered there, looking over her limp body. Emotions washed over him like the rapid waves in a storm as it built to a peak—worry, rage, guilt. With no immediate view of her attacker, he raced back toward the castle. There would be time to hunt the perpetrator down. First, they needed to survive.

CHAPTER 22

Two loud knocks, a slap, and two softer knocks sounded against the wooden door of the room at the tavern Bradrick kept rented. It was the coded knock he and Alonzo had used whenever they were staying away from the castle. Bradrick rose from his lounging spot on the bed to let his friend in. Before he could, Alonzo burst into the small room where two thin beds tucked against each wall and a map that covered the table near the window. Sweat beaded Alonzo's dark brows, dripping down his face with each heaving breath. Bradrick looked him over with a touch of bewilderment before his friend waved him away.

"What in the Twelve Kingdoms have you been doing?" Bradrick asked.

"You wouldn't," Alonzo panted between words, "believe me."

Alonzo braced his hands against his knees to steady himself. Bradrick took the moment to check the hallways for tavern patrons. It was empty except for the merry sound that carried through the building. He shut and bolted the door, then reeled back toward his friend, who seemed to have steadied himself against the wall, staring wide-eyed at the ceiling. Bradrick cleared his throat to draw Alonzo's attention back to reality.

"Try me," he encouraged, while taking a seat beside the map-drawn table.

Instead of responding, Alonzo shook his head. He removed the satchel and maroon leather jacket from his body, tossing them at the foot of his bed. The bed gave a quiet groan when he sat down. For a moment, he stared at his hands in contemplation. Then, he began to recount his morning hunting trip that was anything but productive. The beginning sounded ordinary until he stumbled upon a hidden pond near the road. Bradrick noted his change in tone. There was an edge to it as he went on.

"Gabbie and Tristan continued on to Brizia earlier today when the hunting party began tracking their marks. By the afternoon, most of our party had returned to their lodgings. I continued to hunt while there was still daylight and fewer people. As I was watering the horse, the strangest thing happened. This gorgeous bird glided down and landed in the middle of the pond like it didn't even see me! It had the longest neck I have ever seen on a bird, and these large, pristine, white feathered wings. It goes on, minding its own business, until I take a step. Next thing I know, it turns in my direction. I thought this would be the perfect shot, but I swear it knew what I was doing before I even touched my bow. It came at me before I could get an arrow laced and then took off into the sky. Of course, I missed the first shot, but I followed on my horse," Alonzo continued.

He recounted his chase from the forest floor and the additional missed shots until he was forced to climb down when it veered off into thicker trees. He recalled how the area of the forest he traversed was covered in unnatural darkness as he had continued tracking the bird. Near ready to give up, he had found a tree to climb up for a better vantage point. Bradrick hung onto his every word.

"I thought that I had lost the creature when, suddenly, there it was, above the trees. The way it hovered in the air, floatingthere, staring off into the distance, seemed strange. I had one clear and final shot to make. I let the arrow loose while holding my breath. It hit its mark! So, I climbed down the tree to collect my bounty. The spot the creature had landed was peculiar. I could hear water, but there was none to be found. I was certain the spot was correct when I found traces of blood and feathers, but no bird. Nothing."

Bradrick nodded. "You're sure it didn't get back up?"

Alonzo blinked at him. His hands reached for the satchel on the bed. From it, he pulled out a long white feather. Bradrick froze. His eyes widened with realization. He tentatively took it from Alonzo. It didn't take much examination for the familiar shape to send his mind in a frenzied attempt to connect the dots. He ignored the concerned look that washed Alonzo's face, knowing where his thoughts had ventured. His own eyebrows furrowed together as Alonzo answered his question.

"Besides a few drops of blood, this was all I found. I saw it go limp and fall from the air. Then there was some kind of roaring screech that carried over the trees. But I found almost nothing. It was like it never even hit the ground. Whatever was in those woods spooked the horse. She was eager to get out of there and almost ran off without me."

"Do you think you could pick the location out on the map?"

"The pond, yes. Where I found the feather... would be more of a rough estimate. It wouldn't be difficult to retrace my path in person." He hesitated, giving Bradrick a knowing look. "What's going on in that head of yours?"

"I found feathers identical to this, near where Landry was killed. Remember? This might be the same beast that attacked them." Bradrick stood to look over the map. He used the feather to point from the town and looked at the range around where Alonzo would have traveled. He drew an invisible circle around the area between the mountains and the road that went through the kingdoms. "This forest here. This land has been a neutral territory in Brizia since the death of the Duke. You recall the stories?"

"The Dark Duke?" Alonzo's words came in a whisper, but Bradrick could see the wheels turning in his head. Alonzo traced the path he had taken, part of the way on the road, then cutting over the Brizian border. His finger was outside the edge of the invisible outline drawn by the feather. He drew a breath inward in thought before he nodded. "The pond was about there. Even on the map, there is nothing but trees here. Where is the water? The pond isn't even marked. What does this have to do with the King's daughter?"

"Most of the stories all say Duke Sorgin was secretly a sorcerer. What if sorcery wasn't the only thing he was hiding?" He looked up at Alonzo, whose raised eyebrows puckered with a surprised realization that the question had probable merit. "I am saying, we have some exploring to do with this last lead. Let's plan it out and leave before the first light. We don't want to go unprepared."

They discussed what they were going to do into the deep hours of the night. Once a plan was formulated, they gathered provisions and ensured the horses would be ready for the early ride out. The options in the small town were limited, but they managed to get enough supplies for a couple of days. They agreed that they should exclude the other members of the hunting party. On more than one occasion, Bradrick and Alonzo dared to slip away from guards and other soldiers who were unfortunate enough to be assigned to watch over the pair. This was no different. Bradrick mused over the memories as he sharpened his sword before climbing into bed for a few listless hours of sleep. Those fragments of the past reminded him of a time when they learned that if they left before daylight, Queen Indra would be none the wiser to her son's schemes.

Exiting the small town on horseback, they made quick travel on the main road. The thickening trees were the only obvious sign they crossed into Brizia. Overgrown grass and wild shrubs filled the pockets that were without trees. Alonzo steered his horse away from the road where one particular spot was more like a clearing that dipped into the woods with some shrubs off to the side, than an actual road. They slid down from their horses to examine their surroundings. The pond, where Alonzo first saw the bird, was hidden behind wild shrubs and bushes. Now, there was no obvious sign that it had been there. Tracking the trail of hoof prints leading to the edge of the woods was a simple task.

However, they paused and crouched down at the prints as they disappeared ahead. Bradrick stood slowly, tilting his head from side to side. He pulled Alonzo up beside him, pointing into the wood. They tilted their heads from left to right in unison. There before them appeared to be an overgrown road that stretched into the woods. Nature had reclaimed the floor as her own, tree roots disrupting the surface. The trail was difficult to differentiate between what was forest and what might have once been a road. It was swallowed up by the forest in the distance. Bradrick made a point to update the map before they remounted the horses. The forest loomed over them, the dense canopy of branches casting shadows as they followed the near-invisible road. Both remained quiet while they scanned their surroundings with caution. The farther they went, the gloomier the forest seemed. They paused on occasion to check the trail when the road seemed to curve away, or there was too much growth to be certain they were still on it. Broken branches, stomped-down grass, and hoof prints steered them forward.

Despite spending nearly the entire afternoon on this trek through the forest, their nerves still hung on the edge. Bradrick studied the map he had updated with every pause they took. He slid down from the horse with his eyes scanning the canopy that would soon blend with the night sky. Alonzo moved to follow, his eyes darting from Bradrick to their surroundings. Bradrick raised a finger to his lips before cupping his fingers behind his ear. Alonzo noticed it then—the silence. The horses shuffled and snorted against the eerie quiet. Bradrick noticed their agitation increase without provocation. The trail of hoof prints and a footprint that matched Alonzo's, retreated from the road, disappearing into the thickening trees. He nodded to Bradrick, confirming this was the spot. Here, the bird had tried to throw him off its trail by cutting into the trees.

"I am going ahead. Your tracks disappear into the trees here, and the horses won't be able to follow much farther in. Lead them as far as you can, then follow behind me once they are secured," Bradrick directed his companion. He ducked beneath a branch before Alonzo could offer an argument against him going forward alone. Alonzo gritted out a curse as he gathered both reins to follow where Bradrick had already disappeared. Both men were confident he would catch up.

The blazing sun left a final stream of embers to trickle through the darkening forest. Patches of ember light trickled down, offering little reprieve. The air here felt different. Bradrick moved through thick trees and bushes, even as the forest was cast in shadow. First, he found the barren tree Alonzo had climbed the prior afternoon. Still, he pushed forward until it was too dark to see properly. It was then that the sound of water drew his attention. Using his ears as a guide, he emerged to a small clearing. Yet, there was no water here, despite the dew-laden scent that carried on the air.

The early twinkles of stars winked down through the pockets of open holes in the canopy. He noticed a few branches were broken, some scattered around. Dried blood still speckled the ground where it was apparent that something had happened here. The trail wound back on itself from here; the tracks disappearing the way he had come. Soon, Alonzo would arrive in the clearing. He surveyed the surrounding area to look for the water while he waited, but the darkness inhibited his range of sight. He found nothing but an evasive dry maze of forest as he returned to the clearing. A heavy feeling filled the area and caused the hair on his arms to stand on end. Birds startled from their nearby hiding place in the trees and several trees worth of them went squawking into the early evening sky.

THE DUKE'S CURSE

Bradrick scanned the branches and sky above him with slow, steady steps as he moved away from the epicenter of the clearing. The sound of large wings cut through the air, circling somewhere unseen above, and was joined by a nearby screech. His hand held tight to the golden-plated hilt of his sword as he waited for the right moment to unsheathe it. A snap behind him pulled his attention sharply to the left. His hand followed his body, and with it, the sword that glinted in the darkness. Something heavy swooped down from the darkness of the canopy. He managed to roll away from the great beast's attempt to tackle him. As he returned to his feet, his eyes widened at the sight of the creature. Before him towered a tree-high dragon, black as night, with viridescent lit eyes that were currently narrowed on him. The magnificent being was a stark contrast to the bird that Alonzo had described. His mind plucked at the possible connections.

However, the dragon gave him little time to think as it made a swipe at his torso that knocked him over again. Back on his feet, he dodged another swipe that narrowly missed his chest. He took the opportunity to make his first attack against the creature. The sword arced downward at the dragon's center, blocked at the last moment by a clawed digit. The dragon unleashed a ferocious roar that sent a gust of wind into a torrent around him. Bradrick's arms flailed in an attempt to maintain a semblance of balance. When the winds subsided, he wrapped both hands around his sword and resumed an offensive position. The dragon narrowed its unnaturally bright eyes on him as if he were prey. When it moved to tower over him, a low, predatory growl emanated from its throat. Ever defiant, Bradrick glowered back at his impending death dealer.

Inches from Bradrick's face, the dragon began to morph at a furious speed. The black scales smoothed back into the shrinking form, becoming human skin. A familiar face, lit by the same menacing, forest-green eyes, glared back at him. The shock on

Bradrick's face was replaced with outward rage at the tall, dark-haired intruder from the ball. Even though it seeped into the more distant past, that time haunted him like an unending nightmare. His presence made more sense than anything else Bradrick could have imagined. Venom laced his tongue and he couldn't help but spit at the ground when he spoke.

"You!" His voice came out with a growl. "Where is she?"

Bradrick was yanked to his feet by the collars of his shirt and jacket at a speed that seemed unnatural for a human. A single hand gripped the fabric so tight that it left little room to breathe. Bradrick's hands fumbled for control, but the sword clamored to the ground. Their noses could almost touch as the man snarled at him. "You come uninvited and hunt without permission in my forest, and have the audacity to ask me questions? You draw blood within my land and dare to question me?!"

Bradrick blinked at his words as confusion marred his speech. "The bird?"

The man released his physical hold, dropping him. He stared at Bradrick through thinned eyes. "Yes, the swan. Or any creature on my lands, but especially the swan."

Bradrick knew better than to ask much more of the imposing figure that stood before him. The aftermath of what was left in his wake in the past was evidence enough for caution, but what he said struck Bradrick as strange. For all he knew, this was neutral territory in Brizia. He scanned over the dark cloaked figure, noticing the combination of fresh and dried blood that riddled the man's side, arm, and hands. Most of it had been concealed by the black cloak, but the moonlight revealed enough. His gaze didn't go unnoticed, judging by the darkened glower over the already ominous look on the man's face. His boot lashed out at Bradrick's sword, kicking it away with more force than necessary.

"Well, that doesn't make for a fair fight, does it?" Bradrick asked incredulously.

"As if she was given a fair fight," the man snapped. "No. Despite how much I would enjoy ripping your head off your royal shoulders right now, I have a promise to keep as long as she still breathes."

A fist met the side of Bradrick's head. The force of the hit sent him flying sideways, where he collided on the ground. While his vision was dazed, he felt the tug and tight binding of rope around his wrists. He considered fighting back, but something told him this might be the fastest way to discover where Amirah had been hidden. His captor seemed to think he was the one who shot the swan from the sky. Hidden away in the darkness of the night-shrouded forest, Alonzo remained unnoticed at the edge of the clearing. That gave them the edge they needed.

Bradrick was pulled back onto his feet by the collar of his shirt while his vision still wavered. Even when he was steadied, the world seemed to move. There was a notable change to their surroundings. Sound returned to the world as the veil fell. Where dense trees previously stood, a stone wall encased in sprawling vines, crumbling to the ruins of time appeared. Bradrick gaped in wonder. He knew it was implausible that both he and Alonzo had missed this. The rope irritated his wrist as he was tugged forward through a narrow opening. It was more surprising that his captor let him pass through the walls while conscious. *Not a good sign,* he thought. Through the wall, his grim thoughts gave way to the sight of a lake glistening with starlight and the reflection of the imposing castle beside it.

CHAPTER 23

Darkness seemed to stretch on for eternity. It was a warm, welcomed embrace of nonexistence. When Amirah finally awoke, she was in an unfamiliar room surrounded by a familiar smell of spice and ginseng. The bed was massive enough for a dragon to sleep on, soft layers of deep burgundy and black swallowing her. One look around made it obvious who the room belonged to, but she was uncertain why she was there.

A stone fireplace, the fire cold hours ago, claimed the wall opposite of the bed. In front of it sat two dark wood, ornate sitting chairs, one with a pile of folded clothes on the seat, and a small table. Thick drapes encased the windows, one drawn back to allow light in, the other, blocking it completely. The walls were empty of any pictures, barren of decoration. Sitting angled into the corner of the room was a writing desk with a small duo of painted portraits in golden frames. From where she laid, it was difficult to make out the faces or identify specific details.

She pushed the crust of morning away from her eyes and sat up. She clasped at her side with a grunt at the sudden throb in her side; the pain calling forth her last memories. The hazy visions of the forest, her race toward the castle, and the sudden pain of an arrow striking her down before darkness became all she knew. Her hands went beneath the thick, black silk robe that was too big to be meant for her. The tips of her fingers prodded at where the arrow should have been, but where the area was tender, she felt bandages wrapped around her bare torso. Their texture was rough, more so by the dried blotches of blood soaked through them than the cloths themselves. She could feel the wrappings around her arm without seeing them.

A headache followed the memories of Alonzo; his arrows flying from his bow as he chased after her. It was a wonder that the fall didn't completely break her. Given the care her wounds received, it was apparent Nithe had come to her aid. The curse would have alerted him. *Any harm that comes to you, comes to me.* His past words echoed like a whispered taunt. Concern twisted her gut at the thought of him being injured and bleeding because of her.

Her vision focused enough for her to slide out of the enormous bed. The movement irritated a dull ache in her limbs as her feet padded over the ornate rug. She stopped at the chair with the folded pile of clothes that turned out to be a dress left for her. It was a black velvet dress with long fitted sleeves marked at the shoulder with golden trim which matched the ribbon that laced the square-necked bodice. When the robe slipped from her body, she looked at the dried blood on the bandages with a wince. The room was chilled and made her quick to re-clothe herself. It was a relief that the dress fit to her body without squeezing. It wasn't one from the collection her mother had left behind, and she made a mental note to ask Nithe about it when she found him.

Leaving the room behind, she first checked the door that led into the study. Finding it empty, she turned to the second door that led into the hallway. The castle was quiet, no more than usual, but it felt eerie, almost lifeless, lit only by the light that shone through the windows. She had become familiar with the castle enough to move through it, even in darkness. Her feet carried her through the corridor to the stairs, where she descended to the entrance room and into the hall that led to the kitchen. Even if Nithe wasn't there, she could use the dried herbs to brew a tea that would help ward off her headache before she continued her search. A clatter sounded which stilled her feet on the steps. Then, a heavier silence followed the noise.

Amirah ducked into the shadows outside the kitchen doorway. Keeping her back pressed to the wall, she craned her neck to peek around the corner. The kitchen looked empty and undisturbed. Certain that she had heard something, she scanned the hall from one end to the next. But, as before, no other sounds or signs of life in the castle. Eventually, she dismissed the pestering nerves that made her arm hair stand on end.

The tea didn't take as long once she lit the room with a small fire. When it was ready, she filled a cup and put the remainder in a pitcher for later. While cleaning up, a shadow flickered past the doorway in her peripheral vision and her head jerked up, only to find an empty doorway.

A feeling of unease knotted her stomach as she inched toward the silent hall. Once more, her head dipped into the hallway with caution, only to find it empty. The warning signals in her mind cautioned against her leaving the light of the kitchen as she ducked into the shadows of the corridor. Silent step by silent step, she retraced her path to the stairs and around to the base. She scanned the area, finding no one. With a deep sigh, she hugged her aching sides, ready to return to her tea.

When she turned, arms enveloped her from behind. The startled scream that escaped her lips was muffled by the hand that clamped over her mouth as a male voice hushed her. Her response was violent. She bit into the hand and thrust an elbow into the stomach of the would-be assailant. With a grunt of pain, the attacker released her. Prepared to strike again, she turned but faltered. A familiar face crumpled in surprised pain, stared at her in shock. He extended one arm up, signing his surrender.

"Alonzo!?" she gasped.

"Yeah. That would be me," he wheezed. His eyes appraised her when he straightened. "You are a sight for sore eyes, Amirah. I apologize for scaring you, a debt you repaid well."

They smirked at each other. The nature of his appearance made it apparent that he was not invited to the castle. She felt a pain of guilt that he might have discovered the castle by following her. She felt the guilt even more so, knowing he was endangered by entering uninvited. Amirah hugged him before tugging him back to the kitchen. Alonzo's turquoise eyes scanned the room, which was now more lit than any other part of the castle. Curiosity sparked behind his eyes as he scanned the details of the space, then looked upon Amirah herself.

"Why are you here?" he asked. The perplexed sound in his voice was genuine.

Amirah felt as if the bandages hidden beneath her dress showed. If he had followed her, then the question wouldn't need to be asked. "It is a long story, one we don't have enough time for. I should be asking you the same thing. We need to get you out of here quickly."

"I can't do that." He shook his head. The look of curiosity was displaced by one of grim determination. "Bradrick and I have been looking for you. There was this bird—"

"I know." She said, looking away.

Alonzo paused. "How?"

"You wouldn't have found this place if I hadn't been such a fool."

She subconsciously rubbed at her aching side. Alonzo noticed. When his mind snapped the pieces of the puzzle together, he grimaced. "You were the bird."

"The swan, yes. I did say it is a long story."

"I returned with Bradrick. We followed the trail to where the bird—you—disappeared. He was captured. Then, it seemed like a veil of magic was lifted, and I followed them here," Alonzo shook his head. "I'm sorry, I had no idea it was you. This mess is my fault."

"No," Amirah patted his arm in reassurance, though a tinge of panic pricked at her. There was only one person who could have captured Bradrick and had control over the magic the Duke used to conceal the castle. The situation was more precarious than she first thought. "You had no way to know it was me, and my wounds have been tended. It's not me that we need to be worried about. I have an idea where we could find Bradrick. If I can help you get to him, both of you need to leave."

Alonzo wanted to argue, as he knew Bradrick would when they reached him. He thought better of it as he heard the urgency in her voice.

He nodded. "Lead the way."

Guessing where Bradrick was being kept was a simple task. Amirah had explored almost every inch of the castle and knew exactly where Nithe would have imprisoned the Prince. She guided Alonzo through the corridors and rooms with expertise, careful to stick to the shadows. Uncertain of where Nithe was, she didn't want to risk running into him yet. Their agreement didn't include prisoners, especially ones that she knew.

Alonzo explained in a near whisper more details about Bradrick's capture. Amirah listened to the summation with her heart hinged on the hope that Nithe had kept the promise he made her in Rapplend.

The risk of being caught depended on luck alone as they descended into the dungeon, filled with tension. It was below ground at the bottom of the keep, and only accessible by a dark, narrow, spiral staircase that ended in a tight squared room. Amirah was relieved to find the space empty. On each of the three walls was a door with a small, iron-barred window. Beneath a torch, held by an iron sconce, was a ring of similar-looking keys as lackluster as the doors they fit.

The sound of clanking chains came from behind the door opposite the stairway as Amirah snatched the key ring from their place. She tried the first, then fumbled with the second until the lock clinked and released. Amirah flung the door open and Alonzo followed her into the cramped cell. It was a cold, damp space with a single iron-barred, drain-sized window near the ceiling that served as the sole light source. There was no warmth to be found or any comfort items. They could barely make out the sullen figure slumped against the shadows of the wall.

Bradrick's golden hair framed his grim face but his soft brown eyes sparked to life at the sight of them. Disbelief and concern twisted his features. His arms stretched achingly high above him by the shackled chains, allowing very little movement. Amirah sighed at the rush of relief at finding him alive. As she worked a smaller key into the shackles, Alonzo helped the Prince off the floor. They embraced each other when Bradrick stood free from his chains. Rubbing his wrists, his eyes darted between his friends.

"How in the Twelve Kingdoms did you find me?" A victorious grin flitted toward Alonzo, who acknowledged it with a chagrined nod before Bradrick turned to Amirah. "Do you know how long we have been looking for you? Were you here this whole time?"

Amirah dodged his questions. "Not enough time to get into everything. We need to get you two out. Now."

They raced against time now. At some point, Nithe would return. The fact she hadn't found him earlier when she ventured into the kitchen, meant he was apt to return soon. She jumped when Bradrick's arms ensnared her in an embrace.

"I knew you would be here. Everyone else doubted you were still alive, but I knew. We should leave—"

"I can't go with you." A pang of guilt sprang up as she pushed away from him.

"My lady," Alonzo stepped forward, "your kingdom needs the rightful heir to return to the throne. The mourning period for the King has passed, leaving the kingdom vulnerable without a ruler in place. War is brewing between the members of your court and the people of Brizia will suffer for it. They need you."

"I know," she stated as she stepped further back. "I intend to return and take my place as the rightful Queen soon."

They looked surprised. Bradrick tried to step toward her, but Amirah continued to back away. A frown tugged the corners of his lips. "We can keep you safe and our kingdoms strong if we—"

"I don't need to be kept safe," she snapped with more venom than she'd meant.

Bradrick looked as if she had slapped him. Amirah had never yelled at him. Despite all the time they had spent in courtship, there remained sides of her that he'd never seen. She felt a pang of regret, softening her tone it to ease his hurt.

"I meant that I am safe. I will be, even when I return, which will be soon, but not today."

"Your people need you now," Bradrick repeated Alonzo's words. "You can't stay here with him. He killed your father, Amirah."

"It's more complicated than that. I'm sorry, but I can't go back yet."

The door behind her creaked farther open. Startled, Amirah spun around and Alonzo moved in front of Bradrick with a dagger in hand. Nithe emerged from the shadows with an unreadable expression, his boots the only sound against the stone floor. Amirah stepped toward him and searched his eyes as they flicked from the others to her. He stood like a picturesque statue, clad in regal black, as he stared down at her.

"You can," he said finally, "and you should."

Amirah gaped at him in disbelief. His words felt more like someone had thrown cold water onto her. She had expected anything other than his dismissal. When he moved closer to her, Alonzo pushed himself between the two of them with his dagger pointed expertly at Nithe. Nithe's eyes narrowed at the weapon, then landed on Alonzo.

"Let them both go," Alonzo said with his chin tilted up. "Your quarrel is with me. It was my arrow—my mistake alone. I led Bradrick here, not knowing what we would find. There is no reason to keep them prisoner for my error."

Amirah scoffed behind him. Bradrick tried to grab for her arm, but she shrugged him off. She pushed between the two, her back to Nithe as she poked a finger at Alonzo's chest.

"I am not a prisoner! Put that away. Now."

All three men looked at her with surprise. Alonzo, who was also unfamiliar with this side of Amirah, looked to Bradrick for direction. Unable to make heads or tails of the situation, Bradrick shrugged. Amirah wasn't discovered chained to a wall like Bradrick, and she certainly didn't behave like a prisoner. He observed her with his captor with growing discomfort. Something between the pair that bothered Bradrick, although he couldn't pinpoint what.

Nithe resumed his indifferent countenance. "You can put away your weapon. I have no intention of keeping any of you here. I grant you safe passage to leave."

"What?" all three voices gasped.

Amirah turned to frown up at him. Stepping between him and Alonzo had put them inches apart. Though his face didn't reflect it, his eyes looked upon her with an unspoken ache. Her dark doe eyes stared at him from beneath the fine furrowed brows that matched her hair.

"What do you mean by 'any of you,' Nithe?" Her voice was almost a whisper.

"I mean for you to leave as well," he said. Although he spoke gently, she still flinched, as if someone had struck her.

"What if I don't want to?" She prodded, as her hands reached for him and came to rest against his chest.

Nithe brushed a lock of ginger hair from her face. His thumb rubbed the side of her face with gentle strokes. "Your friends are right; the people of your kingdom need you. The sands of time have run out."

Amirah opened her mouth to argue. Before a breath of argument escaped, Nithe leaned down and brushed her lips with his own. He lingered a moment, as if they remained in their own frozen bubble created by the whisper of a kiss. When he pulled away, she stared at him with confusion. Her heart raced, but it felt as though a cruel trick was being played as she searched his eyes. His face drew tightly downwards, almost scowling as if angry. His arms slipped away from her, then paused for the briefest moment. His fingertips lingered with hers for a fraction of a second until he stepped completely away and looked at each of them directly.

"Leave. *Now,*" he growled, his voice as cold as the expression on his face. Amirah flinched again at the bite of the words. "I order all of you to leave my lands. Immediately."

Nithe stepped back from the door to allow their departure and refused to meet Amirah's eyes. She felt frozen, as if suspended above a floor of glass that had shattered beneath her. Bradrick grabbed her arm and tugged her toward the door. Her feet dragged as she considered fighting them. Nithe's sudden refusal churned her mind into a dazed confusion as she was led away. Nithe released a burdened sigh when their footsteps scuffed over the steps as they ascended the dungeon.

The facade fell. Alonzo cleared his throat, pretending not to notice as he moved for the door. Nithe caught him by the shoulder. Alonzo looked at him with surprise, not at the move, but at the gentleness of the touch. His eyebrow arched upward toward him questioningly.

"I want to commend you for the loyalty you displayed for your Prince."

"It was my mistake," Alonzo admitted. "I didn't realize it was her."

"Forgiveness isn't always in my nature, but I admire that you owned up to it. The Prince is lucky to have you. The brand of loyalty you have is a rare gift. One that she will need. I have a request, and I think you might be the only one I can trust."

Alonzo observed him. "Thank you, I think. What is it that someone of your power would need from me?"

"It isn't for me, it's for her. Amirah and I are bound by a curse, courtesy of our father's errors. It has intertwined our fates so that our survival depends upon the other. If either of us is injured, so is the other. I would prefer this secret remain between us three and the dead. You were right about the disturbance among the noble court members of Brizia, but I cannot return with her. Amirah's life will be at a greater risk upon her return. I ask that you help keep her safe during her ascension to the throne. The union of the two kingdoms should be enough to solidify a finite peace. Can you stay by her side until that time comes to pass?"

"I think I can agree to that." Alonzo offered his hand. Nithe accepted it with a sullen smirk and an understanding passed between them.

If Nithe couldn't break the curse, he could at least ensure her safety. It was an unlikely alliance, but both were decent judges of character. Amirah hadn't seemed to notice her decrease in transformations. They'd become more farther apart, meaning she had almost freed herself—something he had overheard Cicely say to Amirah before. Nithe didn't relay this to Alonzo, knowing that, if the need arose, Amirah would only need the lake. When Alonzo left, Nithe didn't follow. Instead, he stood for a time in the dungeon as a pit formed in his stomach. If it weren't for the curse, he wasn't sure his heart wouldn't feel as sorely wounded as it did as the impenetrable distance between them grew.

CHAPTER 24

A lonzo caught up to Bradrick and Amirah as they went back to the horses without alluding to the pact he had made with Nithe. Neither of his companions appeared to suspect anything else had occurred during their exit.

Bradrick offered his hand to Amirah after she fastened one of their spare cloaks around her shoulders. She hesitated and looked back toward the castle. A tugged at her insides that beckoned her to turn back, but it needed to be ignored if she was going to step off the precipice to return home. Bradrick, unaware of her internal conflict, extended his hand further until she took it, pulling her onto his horse.

They mounted the horses and raced back through the woods. There was an urgency to return that propelled them forward. Alonzo was the one who pulled his horse to a slow canter near the edge of the woods. His mind had been racing along with the speed of the horses. Bradrick slowed his horse to a stop until they trotted side by side.

"What is it?" he asked.

"I think we are hurrying back into the unknown without much of a plan."

Bradrick nodded in agreement. They hadn't planned any further than finding Amirah. Now, they coasted forward blind. Though they knew some of the various obstacles in their path, that didn't account for what they didn't know.

Behind him, Amirah scoffed. "Don't forget to include me. My father may have had the ultimate say in my life while he was living, but now that he isn't, I can make decisions for myself. I know the ball is almost here, but I need to address the issues within my own kingdom first."

They pulled the horses to a stop. At first, surprise crossed Bradrick's face. Then, it was replaced with a contemplative look. She was shocked when both men gave indicative nods of agreement and took the opportunity to slide down from the horse. The edge of the woods was feet away, the only offering of concealment from the main road ahead. She looked to the sky with a heavy sigh from the way her heart ached.

"Why didn't you return?" Bradrick prodded.

Alonzo shook his head and turned his horse away to give them a semblance of privacy, although he still listened.

"It's complicated. There are deep-rooted secrets almost no one alive in the kingdom is aware of. Few within the whole Continent. On top of that, I heard of the plots among the members of my court and discovered there's been a bounty placed on my head by one of the lords," she explained, ignoring the shocked expression on Bradrick's face at the new information. "I knew and I had planned on returning soon, bringing Nithe back to court with me. Now, plans seem to have changed."

Alonzo dared a glance back at them as the Prince scoffed in disbelief. "Bring the sorcerer? That's absurd. What has happened to you?"

"Everything and nothing has happened. Not everything is what it seems. Don't be so quick to judge the actions of someone you don't know," Amirah asserted with a warning tone to her voice. Her fingers curled into fists until her nails bit into her flesh.

"He killed your father! That tells me enough. I saw the aftermath with my own eyes!"

"After my father threatened to kill me!" Angry tears crested the corners of her eyes. Even Alonzo turned to look at her. The silence stretched as her words settled over them.

Bradrick's face fell as he whispered the only question that could form through his shock. "What?"

"That night, after my father finished off our Captain, he turned his blade on me." She lifted her chin to show the faintest silver scar. Her hand grazed over it as she felt the phantom of cold metal against her flesh and the resulting sting until Nithe's hands had healed it. "He held a sword against my neck until I bled, threatening my life quite vocally. There are many terrible things my father has done that deserved death, and even that may have been too kind."

Bradrick battled internally with himself. He had wanted her to stay after the disaster at the banquet. He had wanted to follow after them when they fled. So many times that their parents had used them as political pawns to ascertain power, but King Landry threatening to kill his own daughter was a kick in the stomach.

"Fine," he relented through gritted teeth. Amirah may have forgiven the sorcerer, but he refused to relent. "No matter the reason, he committed regicide on Prurian soil, and for it, he's condemned. If he steps into Pruria again, he will be arrested. I have to get back before my mother suspects I have snuck off again. I'll return with the hunting party, and Alonzo will go with you to offer Pruria's support of your ascension. If we can keep things quiet until your coronation, preferably until the ball, then that keeps my mother off the playing field in Brizian politics for the time being."

"A quiet return might be the best option," Amirah agreed, as a few early droplets of rain fell from the sky. "It will make any opposition to my crown easier to deal with. Can Kamille be sent with Gabbie?"

"Gabbie has already returned, as well as the rest of the Brizian court. However, she returned only after her father sent a summons.

Kamille is under the employment of my mother. I would send her anyway, but her absence would be noticed."

Alonzo remained silent as the two royals continued their next phase of plans and offered a nod of agreement when needed. Bradrick's instructions for him to leave with Amirah made keeping his compact with Nithe easy to do. The two royals needed support in their quest to obtain the crown of two different kingdoms. They were no longer the same children, scheming against an arranged marriage.

Amirah schooled her face when the ball was discussed and, when they parted ways, she couldn't help but glance behind her. Alonzo caught her look as he led their horse by the reins toward the Brizian capital. He suspected that the Duke's castle wouldn't remain a shadow of her past. Later, when they mounted upon the horse, he felt her head each time she turned to look back. Everything she searched for had been swallowed by the magic within the sparse forest until even the mountain peak was a speck in the distance that could be mistaken for a large, pointed tree.

When they were closer, Amirah pulled up the hood of her cloak and ensured her hair was secured beneath it. No one stopped them when they rode through the city toward the familiar castle. The rain had kept the streets clear of prying eyes. With no one on the throne to protect, even the guards left with their families until duty called them again. Alonzo rode through the courtyard gate and steered them toward the stables on the side. To their fortune, a young stable boy greeted them. Alonzo jotted down a note on a piece of paper and asked if he could deliver it. The stable boy raced off with a youthful smile on his face and a gold coin in his pocket. Alonzo secured his horse in an empty stall at the back before they set off for the castle.

Unlike the palace in Pruria, the Brizian castle was older, built mostly of stone with few entrances. The one they headed for was tucked away on the side, close to the stables. Often, it was used by soldiers or servants, and the kitchens had a separate door not far from it. When she was young, Amirah used the heavy traffic from both of them as a distraction to slip away from her guards. She knew every way in and out. Even the secret interior room had an escape tunnel that led deep into the woods. Now, Amirah pulled the hood lower on her face with the same hope of getting through unnoticed as Alonzo took the lead. He recalled the layout from memory from the times Bradrick and Amirah's courtship was spent here.

Inside, it was unusually quiet. The castle wasn't abuzz with life as her memory recalled. They passed by rooms and went through corridors without seeing more than two servants the entire time. Neither servant lifted their head from their tasks. Alonzo and Amirah reached the base of the stairs that lead to the next two upper levels. Frustrated by the emptiness, Amirah threw off her hood when they rounded into an empty corridor with an evergreen rug that stretched the length of the hall. There, they froze at the sound of a familiar voice that prattled on incoherently somewhere. Alonzo smiled at Amirah and bowed at the waist with his hands extended in the direction of the voice. She took the invitation to assume the lead with a straightened back. Although her black dress was worn from traveling, she wanted to enter with the presence worthy of the throne she was about to claim.

When she rounded into the open door of the room where the voice emanated from, she almost stumbled into the person. They stood with their back to the door but turned around with a start, the shock immediately replaced by a huge grin. Gabbie always seemed to glow when she smiled, but after being apart for so long, Amirah felt blinded. They threw their arms around each other in an embrace and delighted cries. Beside them, Alonzo tossed the stable boy another coin before he scampered away.

"Look at you! Aren't you a sight to behold?" Gabbie gushed as she pulled away to examine Amirah from top to bottom. She was quick to resume her proper court mannerism and offered a low bow to Amirah.

"None of that," Amirah waved off the propriety. "I haven't even announced my arrival. I know that the soldiers are, for the most part, on leave until they are recalled to duty, but the castle seems...dead. Where is everyone else?"

Gabbie looked wary. "After the King's funeral, some members of the court became unsettled. To minimize disputes, several went to their homes and will only come to court for urgent matters. Fortunately, there hasn't been much in the last month. With them gone, there is less to do for the remaining castle staff. There are fewer of them now, and the royal coiffures are closed until someone takes up the crown."

"The nobles have not been quiet about their political aspirations. Even the farthest reaches of the Continent are aware of their maneuvers," Alonzo added.

"Too bad for them that I made it back alive," Amirah said with a knowing smile. There wasn't enough time to explain how she was already aware of the power plays for her crown. Not when she was here to claim it. "If we are to succeed, we need to move quickly and quietly as we gather allies to my bloodline and to me. Gabbie, I know we can count on your house, so inform your father first. I would like to have a meeting before the night is over with whoever can be here. We don't want to draw too much attention, but we need a few more members of staff, including no less than two private guards. Were any of my trunks sent back from Pruria?"

The shake of Gabbie's head told her enough. Amirah looked down at her black dress with tight lips. There was a part of her that was reluctant to take it off to primp, but court politics were half impressions. Gabbie offered to lend her a gown, but she declined with another solution in mind. With any luck, one of the remaining servants would be skilled with a needle.

Gabbie set off to her tasks. Alonzo stuck with Amirah, who was following nothing more than the shadows of her memory through forgotten corridors. Somewhere in the castle was a room stuffed full of various items her father wished to forget, and she aimed to find it. Finally, they happened upon a wooden door at the end of a solemn-looking stone hall. To her dismay, it was locked, as she remembered it. Alonzo bent down to examine the door's lock and pulled a thin iron filament from his pocket. He fiddled with it for only a moment until the handle turned and swung open.

Amirah stared at him with a gaping jaw. "Can you do that with every lock?"

He shrugged as a mischievous smile spread over his face. "Almost. Although, I haven't failed to open any yet."

They chuckled until they entered the room, where the dust shifted into plumes that made them cough. It was crammed with various items: paintings covered with gauze cloth that stacked against the back wall, furniture in every direction, crates, trunks, and decorative items, all forgotten over time. Amirah uncovered one of the paintings to find a likeness of her dark-haired mother dressed in a regal gown with fitted layers of gold and red. Hope sparked in her chest as her eyes flitted to a series of trunks pushed against the wall beside the paintings. Unlike the door, they were unlocked.

With Alonzo's help, lid after lid was lifted to reveal her mother's wardrobe in pristine condition. Amirah examined them closely and became certain they would fit the same way the ones at the Duke's Castle had fit her.

Amirah had the trunks brought up to her room. When she changed and the bandages removed, she was glad to see the wound had healed completely, thanks to Nithe. Now, a different ache tormented her body as she parted with the black velvet dress. One of the servants helped make minor adjustments to a shimmering gray dress that hugged her shoulders with belled sleeves that left her arms bare. There was enough happening around her to be a distraction and, by the evening, the beginnings of their efforts became realized.

Gabbie and her father, Lord Paget, had gathered more supporters within the court than Amirah had expected. However, she was surprised at the amount of approval her return had garnered. All the years she had disobeyed her father and mingled with others around the castle now proved advantageous in garnering allies. It was favorable to have fewer opposed parties, but just as dangerous. Messages were quietly suspended from leaving the capital until after the coronation. This kept Pruria and the rest of the Brizian court blind to her movements. With Alonzo's advice, a private guard was hand selected. The Captain she chose happened to be one of the soldiers she had taken lessons from and sparred with, despite her father's misgivings. He was about a decade older than her and his family began to serve under the crown when her mother was alive.

After several days of meetings and preparations, the Brizian castle began to buzz with life again. It was time to call the remaining nobles back to court. Upon their arrival, they were shocked to find her standing in front of the grand silver throne, centered on the elevated dais. There was a simple grandeur in the squared room, which was made of time-tested stone. For all of her royal blood, it felt like being on a performer's stage as she looked out at the gathered nobility. Other than the throne, she had the room decorated with deep shades of green found in the forgotten storage room for the spectacle. Even the floor-length gown she donned was such a dark shade of green it was almost black, standing out against the pale stone of the room. The item that demanded the most attention was the emerald-encrusted, silver crown that adorned her head, as it had her mother before her, in a display of power.

She announced her claim on that dais, then paused to allow the members of the court to voice objections or challenge her if they chose. Some spoke out with grumbling complaints about her disappearance and delayed return. There was little demand for details, as most had seen the state of the late King's body when it was returned to the capital for his funeral rights. It was known that she had returned with healed injuries, so no one felt the need to pry, though some expressed concerns over the collapsed arrangement with Pruria. Alonzo's presence squelched by his presence as a supportive emissary of Pruria.

One lord proved more stubborn than the others. Lord Theorin wore the usual scowl on his middle-aged face, and all but called her a liar. As he entered into a long-winded rant, she began to suspect he might have been the one to put a bounty on her head. Alonzo stepped forward to intervene, but stopped when Amirah raised her hand. Lord Theorin continued with a reddened face while a few of the nobles nodded in agreement at his every statement.

"A woman on the throne?! The day that happens will be the day this court turns on itself. Mark my words, we'll be fighting each other from within. My blade and the blades that serve me are for the throne alone, not for some female. This is why our King tried to arrange a marriage. So we would have a proper King to follow in his stead. We will not be called to heel by a woman! It's blasphemy!" He huffed and crossed his arms. The display was reminiscent of a child having a tantrum.

With a steady stride, Amirah descended the steps of the dais until she stood inches from him, her nose nearly touching his. Her guards pulled their swords, ready to address any physical threat to her life. When she spoke, her voice was low and filled with bridled anger, but clear enough that anyone in the room could hear every word.

"I formed political allies before I could walk. I grew up among our soldiers, learning to wield a sword alongside them. I am my father's daughter, but also my mother's. Which is fortunate for you and the soldiers who have been following your orders. If the vote today is in my favor, then I am your Sovereign Queen. So, if you want to challenge me, do it now. However, if you want to make threats of treason, I can act more like my father."

"And what, girl? Have your guards slaughter me on the spot?" He turned his head and spat onto the stone floor beside them, narrowly missing the hem of her dress. The remainder of whose blood coursed through her veins seemed to sober him, despite his obstinance.

"No," she said and turned back toward her guards. She took a sword from the hands of one and tossed it at the feet of Lord Theorin. Everyone in the room looked from her, to the weapon, and back again. "You threaten my life, I defend it. You threaten my crown, I defend it. You threaten my kingdom, I defend it. Whether you want to challenge me or overthrow me, then it will be me that you contend with. That goes for anyone here."

Theorin looked at the sword, and the muscle in his jaw flexed as he contemplated whether or not to pick it up. His arms unfolded from his side. Alonzo offered her his sword with a bow, more to hide the smirk on his face than to show reverence. Nevertheless, she took the weapon from him. Her next words addressed everyone before her.

"This court was meant to function as a unit to represent our people. If we go to war amongst each other, the divide will spread through the kingdom and take them with it. My gender has nothing to do with your loyalty to this kingdom. It takes an effort from all of us within the royal court to protect the people. They are worth more than anyone sitting on the throne. If you won't be loyal to me, at least be loyal to them."

Silence hung in the air following her last words. It was Lord Theorin who nodded first and took a knee to bow before her. The rest of the court members followed suit. When the final vote was taken, it was unanimous. Amirah allowed herself a wry smile of victory, though this was a mere battle in a longer war. Their next meeting—the coronation—determined the next phase. Even when the crown rested on her head, there would still be obstacles and threats. Especially while her reign was in its infancy.

After the room cleared, Amirah breathed a sigh of relief and slumped onto the throne. Alonzo clapped for her as he came up beside her. The smirk he tried to hide during the whole scene burst into a full smile of pride. Calling the court was the pageantry of politics required by old traditions, but her words were honest. Amirah returned a weak smile, her mind already having ventured onto the next task and the hollow space that tugged in her chest. Despite her fight to suppress it, he noticed her mask fall away, though he didn't pry.

"Well done," Alonzo commended.

"Thanks. Do you think it will be enough?"

"I think it will carry you through the coronation. What you did here today showed them you are worthy of that throne. I would be surprised if whatever bounty on your head isn't canceled immediately. The army will need to be brought to heel, so choosing your generals should be high on the list."

She looked back at her guard. The silent message passed between them and the Captain dipped his head in agreement. "I am sure we will find suitable candidates before the coronation. A formal announcement will be put out throughout the kingdom of all the changes the people should be aware of."

"Bradrick would be proud," Alonzo said. Amirah grimaced at his statement as she straightened in her seat. "Is something wrong?"

A somber, distant look clouded her eyes for a moment. She sighed and looked up at her friend. "Many things are wrong, but that comes with the job. Have we heard from Bradrick?"

"I expect a message from him will arrive when your trunks do. An invitation to the ball should be with it. Those things are our golden ticket to get you back into the palace unnoticed until it is time. Everything has otherwise been locked down and, other than myself, there won't be any visitors in or out. All messages are being screened at the borders by the soldiers you sent to secure them. Any other kingdom will assume this is the result of internal discord. I will have to leave for Pruria before you, but I'll wait until after the coronation."

"Thank you, Alonzo. Time is slipping away before I can grasp it. There is something I need to do before the coronation. With everything going on, I don't want to weaken my position by showing my hand, and I'll need your help. Most of the records are kept here at the castle, but I've checked all the obvious places without any luck. What I am looking for was too important to destroy. My father would have hidden them somewhere, but I can't fathom where."

Alonzo rubbed his chin in thought for a moment. "It might be that they aren't hidden in the castle. It isn't uncommon to have additional records kept somewhere else. Pruria has an entire catacomb full of records instead of within the palace, though your architecture here is different. Have you checked the royal treasury?"

"Royal coiffures are closed until someone takes the throne. Going there would attract attention. Although, it would make sense..." Her eyes grew wide with realization. "Land records hold value, so many of them are kept there."

She continued to elaborate to Alonzo the specifics of what she was looking for and he volunteered to go search the records on her behalf. He set out on this task the next day as she continued with meetings.

As predicted, there was no further resistance from the members of the court. Lord Theorin appeared in better temperament and was almost tolerable. The meetings took up the latter half of the day until it was beyond time for a meal. With her stomach knotted in concern, she paced the floor of the private office adjoined to the sitting room, like the bedroom and washroom, unable to eat. It was adjoined, like the bedroom and washroom, to the sitting room. All of the Queen's rooms were larger than the ones she had been in while growing up, but equally dreary—something she would inevitably take the time to fix. She recalled the warmth of the Duke's castle and found she missed the fireside in the study. The hollowness in her chest eased at the memory. It was at that moment that she realized she hadn't transformed into a swan since she left the Duke's castle. With this epiphany came a wave of relief and simultaneous sadness.

Cicely's words echoed in her memory, "*...You're stuck, so the magic is stuck. You have to choose to release what binds you.*" Amirah thought back to the last few times she had transformed at the Duke's castle. So much had changed since the first time she had shifted. She better understood the past, found forgiveness for Nithe, and sought to remedy the wrongdoings against his father. Since she was forced to leave his side, she had resolved to become a queen worthy of her throne. No longer was she a young lady kept like a caged bird or forced to bend to the will of another. She was free in a way only she could accomplish. Cicely had said it was an answer only she could find, and indeed, Amirah had found it.

As she stared out of the window in her private office, she was filled with a sense of accomplishment. She would miss being able to fly and preen by the lake. Now that she would no longer become a swan, she had no excuse to visit the Duke's Castle without an invitation. Alonzo returned to find her staring, transfixed on the distance beyond the window. She remained that way until he set the full satchel down. Eyeing the bulk of the papers, she knew that she would end up spending days and nights pouring over the documents she had requested.

"All of this?" Amirah asked in disbelief. She looked from the stack to Alonzo.

Alonzo nodded. "Everything, or at least everything that still exists."

"I can't thank you enough, Alonzo." She smiled at him, at a loss for better words. These would give her both the information she needed and allow a welcomed distraction from the silent grief that ate away at her.

A servant knocked on the door and announced that her trunks had arrived from Brizia. As predicted, with the delivery came the invitation to the ball. The invitation to the ball was on gold spun paper, and Amirah couldn't help but cringe at the sight of it. A small number of invitations for her coronation had gone out to the intended parties and nowhere near as exorbitant and gaudy as the thing in her hands. Alonzo also shared the letter Bradrick had written to him.

His absence from Pruria was noticed by Consort Foley, although Bradrick was doing his best to provide cover for him. Alonzo reluctantly agreed to return to the Prince's side. Not because of either royals orders, but his promise to Nithe. He hesitantly agreed to return only after her generals were selected. With the knowledge he did everything possible to ensure her safety in Brizia, Alonzo departed for Pruria. He and Bradrick needed to ensure their efforts in Brizia carried over into Pruria.

Amirah had asked Alonzo to deliver an invitation to her coronation to the Duke's castle on his way back. It was a small deviation on his return home, and wouldn't cause much delay. However, when he arrived, no one appeared to occupy what seemed to be a forgotten place. He pushed the invitation beneath the large front door and left, wondering if Nithe would ever see it. Alonzo knew that, if the man never saw it or gave it any credence, it wouldn't impact the coronation. He was confident that, when Amirah's coronation came around, she had everything she needed to execute a plan of her own, without any of them.

CHAPTER 25

To Queen Indra's pleasure, Bradrick returned with the hunting party. She cooed at his greeting and agreeable mannerisms when he walked into the throne room to give her a proper welcome. Any other time, she would have needed to send someone to fetch him once she learned he had made it back.

"I have to say, Bradrick, this is a welcomed change in you," Indra praised him.

"Much change has been needed," Bradrick agreed, though his words had a doubled meaning.

Since finding Amirah, he felt different—a sense of newfound hope which renewed his resolve to obtain his crown. Her reluctance to leave the castle behind and return had been alarming. Although, after everything was explained, she astounded him. He had spent the ride back in deep thought about everything Amirah had said and their renewed strategies. Bradrick made a point to stay in his mother's good graces and acquiesce to her requests until he could execute his part of the plan. That included avoiding bickering by ensuring he followed the expected protocol. Queen Indra took his behavior as a sign that her son had finally relented in his frivolous search for the missing Princess. Appeased, she dismissed him, almost nonchalantly, from what might have been the most peaceful exchange they'd had since he was a child.

While the Brizian nobility had returned to their kingdom, Amirah's belongings were still in her room. Bradrick needed her trunks to be sent back with an invitation to the ball. On the way to his chambers, he requested a servant to retrieve a blank invitation to the ball, then summon Kamille. By now, everyone in the castle had heard of the Prince's return, so moving around unnoticed would have been a futile endeavor. Later, a knock came at the door and the servant delivered both the invitation and Kamille. When the servant left, Bradrick looked down each side of the hall. Seeing it was clear, he tugged her through the chamber doors and shut them.

"What is it?" Kamille asked as she watched him stalk over to a desk in the corner of the room.

Bradrick shuffled through a pile of things until he found a quill pen. As he began scrawling on the invitation, the words rushed out of him. "We found her."

"You don't mean..." Kamille's hands cupped over her mouth as her eyes widened in realization.

Bradrick turned to her with a wide grin and nodded as he approached with the invitation in hand. "Yes! It's Amirah. We found her, Kamille."

"Is she alright? Where in the twelve kingdoms has she been?" Kamille's voice cracked, overwhelmed with relief.

"Closer than we ever thought possible, though it's not my story to tell. She is safe and whole, but it is important we keep it that way. No one else in the kingdom is to know. That's imperative for her continued safety. Her coronation will happen in Brizia first, then at the ball, her return will be announced to the whole Continent. I need you to pack any belongings she has left in her room here and have them sent back to Brizia, quietly. Send this invitation with it. If anyone, or rather, if my mother finds out, then everything will be ruined."

Kamille nodded, understanding the order. She took the invitation from Bradrick with one hand and wiped the corner of her eyes with the other. "Her trunks are already packed. It may take a few days to avoid notice, but I'll have them sent back as soon as possible. Thank you, Bradrick."

When she left, Bradrick prepared himself for the next phase of the plan. The first few nights at dinner, Alonzo's absence from his side went unnoticed. Instead, arriving guests for the ball filled his seat. Everyone's attention fixated on Consort Foley, whose stories served as an unwitting distraction. Being the socialite that he was, Foley was the only one that took notice of Alonzo's absence.

"Where is Lord Macanay? I miss his witty humor," Foley asked one night, looking around the table.

"Alonzo has been tending to forgotten business and catching up on training. I hear there will be some amusing stories when he rejoins us." Bradrick excused his right hand's absence with a simple, yet vague, explanation. Bradrick had expected it wouldn't have gone unnoticed the entire time.

Despite the Consort's return to his fellow socialites, Bradrick suspected he noticed Alonzo's absence every dinner afterward. He addressed these concerns in a letter he drew up for Alonzo. He was grateful to have gotten it to Kamille in time to send it out with the trunks. By now, Brizia would be under a lockdown, and fewer things would get through. Queen Indra herself was too busy with trivial details for the ball, or reveling in the attention of the new guests to notice anything else. This offered Bradrick some relief. However, the approach of the ball still put a sour taste in his mouth.

Once again, Queen Indra had outdone herself. As the days dwindled, it became more apparent that, while the ball was purportedly meant to find Bradrick a suitable wife, every detail was to Indra's preferred style. The halls now dripped with gaudy gold decorations that overflowed into every room the guest's eyes landed. Even the kitchen was outfitted for the occasion. Coordinated gold uniforms were issued to the entire palace staff, while dressmakers and cobblers frequented the palace to outfit the court nobility. Indra and

Foley had extravagant matching outfits of layered gold and white fabrics.

Whenever possible, Bradrick stayed out of sight to avoid all chances of running into his mother unless he was summoned or his presence was required for regular court activities. Most meetings remained boring, except for one note regarding Brizia's closed borders. One lord brought the issue up in the throne room.

"Your Highnesses, should we be concerned with the growing tensions in Brizia?" The noble, in a pastel, lilac-colored coat and periwig, asked. Bradrick recognized Foley's sharp attention drawn to the man and realized this was one of the Consort's friends.

"What do you mean?" Queen Indra asked passively. Her face was blank, and she appeared to be preoccupied with a selection of hand fans being presented to her on a tray that was held by one of the staff.

"Well, we have heard very little from the court there. They refused my messages at the border, which it appears they have locked down."

"Is that all, then?" Indra sounded bored, but her eyes lit up as she selected one of the hand fans and opened it. When the noble said it was, she turned her eyes on him. "Unless they present a threat to us, there is little else we can do. They have not called on us as allies. As such, we must be careful when we choose to interject into another kingdom's affairs. Otherwise, we may unintentionally start another Khaos War. If Brizia begins posing a danger to us or the other kingdoms, that is a better time to interject. However, if they have simply secured their borders during the internal upheaval, that is of little concern to us. Better they keep it from spilling over into other kingdoms of the Continent."

To Bradrick's relief, no other complaint on the matter was presented at court, so he turned his focus to preparations for the ball. The castle filled with guests, who had poured in from every corner of the Continent and beyond, with each passing day. Alonzo arrived amidst the final influx of visitors, which allowed him to maneuver his way to Bradrick without notice. He explained the opposition Amirah faced. Bradrick's muscles tensed until he heard the tale of her confronting Lord Theorin. The coronation was happening as they spoke, and he felt relieved knowing that all they needed to do now was wait for her arrival.

"Do you think there will be any trouble while she is on her own?" Bradrick pressed. "She had mentioned there was a bounty on her head."

"She has created a personal guard, and they are loyal beyond question. They are always near, working in shifts, so I do not fear for her safety," Alonzo reassured Bradrick. "Kamille has already prepared a room for her. I'll meet with her when she arrives, and when everything is ready, we'll make our move."

AMIRAH'S CORONATION was not the extravagant event most royals had. She'd never dreamt one for herself, unattached to Bradrick, or without Indra's full authority over every detail. Nothing could match the opulence of the events that happened in their neighboring kingdom. When the ceremony began, most of Brizia still slept. Amirah took her oaths as Sovereign, on her knees in front of the throne and the court she would serve. The early rays of sunlight streamed through the throne room, casting a gentle glow over her fair features, loose ginger hair, and burgundy ceremonial robes. Without the grandiose fanfare preferred by Queen Indra, the ceremony only took a couple of hours.

Perfectly timed, the morning bell began to ring out the moment the crown was placed upon her head. The images engraved on the relic had faded into the tarnished silver that served as a base for the empty golden cage that arched upward and curved into a point. The heavy weight of it distracted her from the whirlwind of emotions she kept behind a blank expression. Deep chimes from the outer wall's tower bells echoed over the capital as she walked to the throne. The last ring fell quiet when she turned to sit upon it as the new Sovereign of Brizia. The timing of the bells, which roused anyone within range of the capital, was perfect; ringing in both the rise of the sun and the dawn of a new ruler.

The citizens of the Brizian capital had been the first to learn of Amirah's return and coronation. Despite the short time frame of the notice, the people wasted no moment organizing celebrations across the kingdom. Before the court members could partake in these festivities, formalities needed to be completed. First, the doors to the palace opened to allow all nobility to come before the throne and welcome their new Queen. Some faces she had known as a child, but there was one particular face missing that pained her treacherous heart. She powered through the day with a smile pasted on her face, despite the way her stomach felt plagued.

The announcement of newly appointed titles of nobility came with other necessities that took up most of the time. Amirah's coronation rights came to the last portion, where she announced her first acts as Queen. First, she ordered that the entire kingdom's food stores be inventoried, no less than quarterly. The information she had gleaned from the records Alonzo retrieved had allowed her to outline a suitable plan to present to the noble houses in advance. With this order, she followed it with a promise of transparency to reconcile past mistakes under her father's rule. As a show of faith, she sent heralds and dispatchers throughout the kingdom to hang copies of her plan and announce the new appointments throughout Brizia. Her final act was a further testament to the promise. Stillness overcame the room as she rose to speak.

"Due to misunderstandings during the Khaos War, Duke Sorgin Vivek passed without being given a fair trial. Therefore, I decree, as Queen Amirah Svana Landry, that the crown hereby grants absolute pardon to the late Duke and all of his house." She motioned to Gabbie, who passed out stacks of parchment paper. "These are copies of the official report on the evidence found from a private inquiry that further supports this act. I have made it available as a public record in the royal archives, should anyone wish to read it."

Everyone read over the report with interest. A few nobles dared to attempt to read over the court members' shoulders with wide-eyed curiosity. With Alonzo's help, she uncovered the records proving her father had placed the Duke's lands in a private trust. The same happened with all manner of his private property, and her father never reassigned the territory. No official decree existed that turned the area into neutral territory. The accounts of the forced removal of the small towns drew frowns from readers. The old maps reflected the towns that once stood where Amirah had witnessed ruins and marked the castle. Any newer maps included none of these details, as if King Landry had tried to erase them.

The report concluded that her mother, Queen Rana, had died from poisoning, as supported by the notes from medical staff. Near the conclusion, the report cited the King's handwritten accounts. Most of what the selection told of was the Brizian royal's souring friendship with the Duke that devolved during the war. It wasn't the whole truth, but it was enough. Most of the court was already aware of some of her father's dark history and didn't need every detail. As the sound of pages turning filled the room, a low thrum of voices began as the court muttered amongst one another. The sound grew until Lord Theorin stepped to the front of the room. She wasn't sure what to make of the twinkle in his eye as he stood on the first step.

"I move to vote in support of the Queen's acts," he announced.

There was a gasp throughout the room, and Amirah couldn't keep the look of surprise off her face. Her eyebrows rose further when a second, third, and more votes cried out in succession. The room erupted in applause, and their warmth bit against the cold harboring inside of her. This time the smile that turned the corners of her lips was real.

After her crowning ceremony reached its conclusion, anyone who wasn't a court member dispersed. Most of which left the castle and joined the crowded streets already ripe with celebration. By the afternoon, bonfires were lit as the nobles departed individually after swearing fealty to her as their new Queen. Throughout the capital, anyone present recounted the events from the throne room. Amirah's first acts as Queen began spreading throughout the kingdom.

It surprised the remaining court members to learn Amirah had received an invitation to the Prurian ball. Lord Theorin, who was among them, was the most elated. He was the leading voice in the group that outburst their cheers of full support of a continued courtship. They would take almost anything to secure a continued alliance with the neighboring kingdom, and nothing cemented that more than marriage. To Amirah, the arrangement's support felt like a blow to the gut, but she owed it to Bradrick to help him secure his crown.

CHAPTER 26

B radrick studied his mother's sour face. Everything within sight dripped with gold except for his black, formal attire that was stitched with ornate gold details on the lapel of his dress coat. Queen Indra was covered with more gold than anyone or anything else in the ballroom. If he hadn't showed up in a room that was filled with people, she would have ordered him to change into something more suited to her chosen color palette. Instead, she could only scowl at him from behind a golden mask. Every guest wore a mask of the same color, some provided at the door. Bradrick selected one that was nowhere near as flamboyant as the mask Foley wore—a golden ribboned mask with pearl drops around the eyeholes. Without the luxury of time, his mother forced a foreign smile onto her face.

Arm-in-arm with Consort Foley, she traversed the dense crowd until she reached a long table draped in white and gold silk clothes. The other tables that sat around the edges of the room had gold-spun tablecloths with gaudy centerpieces and mounds of food. This ballroom was the largest of the three in the palace. Yet, it still seemed too small for the number of guests present. Somewhere in the room, the Master of Ceremonies announced the dinner portion of the night. The nobility at the royal table waited for Queen Indra to sit before taking their seats. All except for Foley, who tucked the Queen into her chair before assuming his seat beside her. Bradrick sat on the opposite side of Foley to avoid eye contact with her.

Servants circled the tables with golden trays filled with the same golden-colored appetizers. Bradrick politely declined the food, already having an untouched plateful, and pretended to focus on his drink. In truth, his eyes searched every table for the duo he needed here the most. They would arrive at any moment, but the anxiety of waiting soured his stomach. When the main course came out, the chattering lowered to a hum and combined with the metal clank against plates. He could feel the hungry eyes of each woman in the room bore into him from every corner of the room. It did nothing to help his appetite as he picked at his plate, which was one of the few reprieves from the ongoing stares.

When Queen Indra finished eating, everyone else was required to do the same. The crowd rose as she and Foley made their way toward the seating area for the royals. Everyone followed as they stood in front of their throne chairs that sat upon a low dais in the center of a pair of staircases. The steps curved up in a wide arc and ended at another set of doors above them. The Prince followed studiously behind his mother until they assumed their positions before the thrones. Above them, the Master of Ceremonies stood at his station beside the doors. He overlooked a list as the crowd separated into onlookers and those to be presented to the Prurian royals.

Consort Foley waved at the musicians stationed in a corner of the room. At his signal, gentle string music engulfed the hum of chatter. With the room in order, the Master of Ceremonies announced each suitress with her accompanying parent or guardian to Queen Indra and Prince Bradrick. The ladies and their escorts looked at him like ravenous wolves with fresh meat being dangled before them. More than once, he resisted the urge to roll his eyes at the bland conversation and over zealous compliments.

Introductions continued as Bradrick stood beside his mother and discreetly searched the throng of bodies for any sign of his two comrades. He was so engrossed in looking for them that he failed to notice the approach of a petite young woman in a pink chiffon dress with curl-piled hair, and her father. Her attempt at playful banter fell upon deaf ears while their parents engaged in delighted conversation. Queen Indra caught onto his lack of attention and gave him a gentle nudge in the side. He shot his mother a disgruntled glance at her prodding as his senses snapped back to the woman in front of him. She was an elegant little creature, one that his mother had probably assessed as easily malleable under her control. There was a subtle spark to her gray eyes when he absentmindedly nodded to whatever question she had asked.

He realized his mistake too late when she grabbed his arm and led him away with a squeal of gratitude. Fortunately, she seemed oblivious to the terrified widening of his eyes or the way his mouth fell open as she carted him to the center of the ballroom. Bradrick did his best to recover and mask the shock from his face when the woman waved back at her father as the surrounding crowd made room for them. A four-four beat with a sweeping melody enchanted the room as all eyes turned upon them. Bradrick resumed his composure and his hand slid to the small of his new dance partner's back as he took the lead. Whenever their eye contact broke, he scanned the faces around the room.

"I apologize for being forward, but you hadn't asked any other ladies to dance yet, so I thought you might be shy. Thank you again." Her voice was a whisper, different from the playful pitch she had around their parents as other dancers joined them on the floor. Onlookers watched with keen interest, including their parents.

"You're welcome," he murmured. When he glanced at her gray eyes that searched around them, he knew that she was putting on a show as much as he was. "May I ask who you are looking for?"

"I am so sorry. I was... I didn't intend..." She flushed with embarrassment. He chuckled softly, causing her face to redden further still.

"It's alright," Bradrick said with a reassuring smile. "I was looking for someone too."

"Is that why you haven't asked anyone to dance yet?" She pried with a coy smile.

"Yes. Although, my mother might have my head if I were to say so within her earshot." They laughed. There was a charming ring in her laughter that reminded Bradrick of Amirah years ago. "What about you? Why haven't you danced with anyone?"

"Me? My father insisted I dance with you and no one else. He's been trying to find me a good match for a while. I was exchanging letters for several moons with a Prurian suitor he'd chosen until we received the invitation for the ball. Of course, for him, marriage is all business."

"A likewise story for me. We can only hope to be better parents than our own in the future, Lady..." He gave her a curious arch of his brow.

"Mallory Devon," she mimicked his expression. "From the Kingdom of Allerie, the Queen's southern houses."

"Lady Mallory Devon," he repeated as the music crescendoed and started to draw to a close. He spun her away from him, then back in close enough to whisper in her ear. "Let us vow to be better parents in the future. Should you find your suitor in the crowd this night, bring him to me, and, if you wish, I will give the Prurian crown's blessing."

Lady Devon swallowed down her surprise. She gave a small nod of agreement and dipped into a low curtsy on the last note of the song. When she arose from her position, her face beamed brighter than the largest star in the evening sky that night. He helped her stand steady as they faced the crowd. Countless eyes stared back at them with a mix of admiration and jealousy, none-the-wiser to their agreement.

"I will do my best," she said in a low voice so none of the onlookers would hear. "What will you do, Prince Bradrick? Doesn't your mother intend to announce a new fiancé for you by the end of tonight?"

"That won't be a problem," he started as he flashed her a bright-toothed grin worthy of his title, "when the lady makes her appearance."

The crowd clapped for them and he could see his mother's eye as they twinkled with approval. Sir Devon stood beside her and Consort Foley with a prideful grin. Someone in the crowd called for another dance between them and it spurred another round of applause. Queen Indra dipped her chin as an indication for him to submit to the request. Bradrick cursed under his breath through the gritted teeth of his unwavering smile.

The sound of the doors opening at the top of the staircase saved them from the crowd's demand. Silence fell over the ballroom as curious eyes drifted up to the balcony and the source of the disruption. The Master of Ceremonies looked over a golden invitation from a man's leather dress gloved hand. He did a double take at invitation and then paled as he looked up at the enigmatic couple that had interrupted with their late arrival. Bradrick couldn't help the triumph that infiltrated his face. With a smug grin, he strolled to the base of the stairs as the couple descended.

"Now presenting, Lord Alonzo Macanay of Pruria accompanying her Royal Highness...," the Master of Ceremonies inhaled and looked again at the woman, "Queen Amirah Svana Landry of Brizia."

Audible gasps rippled through the room. Every eye zeroed in on Amirah as she descended on Alonzo's arm in a flowing gown of black and a delicate golden lace mask. A cloak of black feathers trailed behind her as they descended the stairs. Most notable, especially to Queen Indra, was the pointed silver crown that was perched atop Amirah's coiffed hair. Alonzo's outfit, devoid of any gold except for the simple mask, completed the matching trio. The mouths of Prurian nobility gaped at the sight of her as if a phantom haunted them. Those who weren't from the Continent watched with interest, despite the lack of context for the reactions at the pair's arrival. Many faces turned to Queen Indra, who tugged at Foley's sleeve with a paralyzed expression.

Alonzo bowed his head to Prince Bradrick when they met at the bottom of the stairs. Now that Amirah carried a higher title than him, it was no longer appropriate for her to lower herself. She stood straight with her elbow-length black, silk gloved hand offered to him. He took it, bowed at the waist, and placed a gentle kiss upon her knuckles. Together, the trio turned toward Indra with the straightest faces they could muster.

Indra's face changed from the palest white, to red, to an impossibly vivid pink in rapid succession when they stood before her. Even Foley looked Amirah up and down as if she were a ghost, or wore the same outfit better than himself. Both equally horrifying to him. Indra whispered frantically into his ear and tossed a seething glance of a mother's rage at her son. The trio waited patiently for her acknowledgment.

Bradrick whispered from the corner of his mouth to Alonzo. "I was concerned something had happened."

"Timing is everything. No one here can say they didn't see her tonight," Alonzo whispered back. A crooked grin flashed over his face and stayed there. Bradrick arched an eyebrow at him, impressed with the strategic forethought.

"Well," Indra snapped, as if she had been waiting for them to speak. Her eyes latched onto each of their faces, pausing a moment longer on Amirah. "Will someone explain what is going on?"

It was Amirah who stepped forward. Her voice sounded stronger than any of them had ever heard it, unwavering before Queen Indra. "An invitation arrived for me after my return to Brizia. Please excuse my delayed response, as there were urgent matters needing to be settled within my court. Since my father is no longer with us, Lord Macanay was kind enough to be my escort in his stead. I have come to honor the arrangement between our kingdoms. That is, if it still stands."

Queen Indra gave her an appraising look. This was not the Amirah she was accustomed to knowing. The person before her now was as much a stranger as any of the guests in the ballroom. Her eyes turned to Bradrick with a grin that looked pleasant to anyone but their own children. Even if she wasn't sure how, Indra knew that somehow, they had duped her through some scheme. With a full ballroom, she had to reign in the maelstrom temper that surfaced whenever she felt crossed in order to save face. A wrong step could give an unfavorable impression, costing Pruria allies. If any of the guests felt that the ball had been pointless showmanship, there would be unfortunate consequences. While everyone was surprised and brimmed with curiosity, she was the sole person who suspected foul play. Bradrick knew all of this as he waited with a calm countenance.

"And you, Bradrick?"

"Details aside, Mother, it appears I was right about her being alive," he responded with a curt smile.

"So it does," she relented with pursed lips. Foley leaned down to whisper into her ear. With a deep exhale, her eyes fluttered with exhausted nerves. "We will discuss this later. For now, our guests should be allowed to enjoy the remainder of the night as intended. My announcement regarding your engagement is postponed until tomorrow. Amirah, you are welcome to stay, of course. Will you excuse my delayed answer until the morning?"

"That will be satisfactory," she replied. "I will inform my guards."

Indra nodded at Amirah's acceptance and hooked her arm into Foley's. She waved at the Master of Ceremonies, who announced their departure as they disappeared from the room without a word to anyone else. Amirah took a seat with Alonzo at an empty table nearest to the stairs and observed the ballroom as Bradrick continued meeting with guests. Some were curious, while others seemed dismayed at what Amirah's appearance tonight meant for themselves. One lady approached Bradrick with a gentleman in tow. Both appeared to be near Bradrick's age, the man about the same height, but with short brown hair. Amirah recognized the lady's pink dress and watched with interest.

"This is the man?" Bradrick asked her.

The couple both blushed at his attention. The girl nodded in response.

Bradrick continued a hushed conversation with them—too low for Amirah or any of the other guests to hear—before he raised his hand in the air to gather the room's attention. The few eyes that weren't already upon him, turned with everyone else as he spoke. "My mother has retired for the night, leaving me in her stead. Let it be known that the Prurian crown grants its permission to marry between this couple. May their union be blessed and strengthen the ties between our noble kingdoms!"

It was not the engagement announcement the crowd expected. Still, they clapped in response to the Prince's announcement. Lord Devon seemed confused as he looked between Prince Bradrick and his daughter's fiancé. Both of whom smiled at him in return. Bradrick offered Lord Devon his hand with a firm pat on the shoulder. At first, he seemed as if he might protest, but then he turned to his daughter, Mallory, and it melted away. She radiated a joy that spread to her father when she enveloped him in a hug before she returned to her fiancé's side. Bradrick glanced at where Amirah and Alonzo sat together nearby.

Amirah's eyes glazed over with a faraway look as she watched the small family. Bradrick recalled what she had revealed in the woods as they left the Duke's castle behind them. For the first time, he wondered as he scanned over the woman in black, if he still knew Amirah, or if he ever truly had to begin with. Another courtesan group approached to meet him, distracting him for a moment. When he finally got a chance to look back, Alonzo was engrossed in a conversation with a couple at the table, and Amirah was nowhere to be found. Bradrick followed the gazes in the crowd to her back as she disappeared through the ballroom doors.

CHAPTER 27

In the hours following Amirah's shocking appearance at the Prurian ball, word of her return and ascension to the throne of Brizia began to circulate. It spread from the palace and throughout the Continent with rampant fervor. The next day, everyone from the ball awaited Queen Indra's decision while Amirah stayed in her room. Her guards denied anyone's requests for an audience with stone faces of indifference. That included Bradrick and Alonzo, who were even more bewildered when Kamille was also turned away. If it weren't for their presence outside of the door, Bradrick wouldn't believe she was in there. She had kept a quiet distance from everyone since her sudden departure from the ball.

Queen Indra had her own surprises in store. The trio had fully expected her to dispense with business as usual in the throne room. Bradrick and Alonzo waited at the front of the gathered crowd. Queen Indra carried herself toward the throne with a reverent poise, despite the disgruntled faces of some guests. When she sat, she smoothed the ruffled fabric of the ivory and gold laced gown in no particular hurry. Bradrick braced himself for a public scolding that he would usually receive whenever he outmaneuvered his mother. She looked at him with a sly grin before speaking.

"First, I must thank our esteemed guests, who have traveled from far and wide to be here. Your presence is a joyful highlight to our kingdom after we endured such an unfortunate period of loss. Through tragedy, we have been given a most welcomed gift. As it is known, Brizia's former King fell before the contract that would have secured our alliance was fulfilled. In the wake of his death, we all presumed that his only heir, Bradrick's betrothed, was lost in the tragic accident as well. As everyone witnessed last night, she has returned, reclaimed her throne, and offered to honor the contract. I have given much thought to these circumstances and to you, my honored guest. As the Queen of Pruria, I must also honor the contract as it stands, lest all of our prior contracts, and my word as Queen, no longer hold value. My son, Prince Bradrick, will be crowned as our new King of Pruria following his marriage to Queen Amirah."

Bradrick and Alonzo both looked at each other in wide-eyed shock, their surprise reflected through the crowd's audible gasp. Some of those gathered began shouting their protest while the rest engaged in the growing hum of gossip that followed in the wake of her announcement. The engagement's reinstatement was expected, but Queen Indra's announcement of Bradrick's ascension astonished everyone. The crowd quieted as Indra rose again to depart from the room, pausing in front of a stunned Bradrick, who could do nothing else but bow to his mother. After which, she left the room with a victorious smirk painted upon her face.

Bradrick and Alonzo rushed down the halls of the palace, eager to be away from the crowds and prying ears that would surely report back to his mother.

"How? Why?" Alonzo wondered out loud.

"If any of us knew that, it wouldn't be such a good plan. She's up to something," Bradrick grumbled in response.

"I don't disagree, but it is so...strange. Your mother giving up power seems like a poor strategy," Alonzo said with a huff. "It truly baffles me."

"That is just it. It's a strategy, which means she still holds power in the situation somehow," Bradrick pointed out as they made their way from the palace toward the stables. "I know my mother. She is self-serving first and foremost, Alonzo, so we know that there is no possible way she would cede power without a fight."

He dismissed the stable hands and groomsmen as he began pacing the length that ran between the stalls. Alonzo proposed a few theories, to which Bradrick added. They debated the motivations behind his coronation being moved forward, which was the most flabbergasting part. Not only was Indra turning power to her son—to whom, at all times, she preferred control over—but she was doing it quickly. It confounded every theory they could come up with to make sense of her actions.

"The Prince dismissed everyone; you may go," Alonzo directed the groomsman who had re-entered the stable a few hours later.

"Beg pardon, sire, but Queen Amirah ordered her carriage ready for departure," the groomsmen explained as he bowed to Bradrick. "Shall I wait longer?"

Bradrick frowned. "No, no. If the Queen wishes to leave, we mustn't keep her. However, take your time and prepare another set of horses. Alonzo, I want you and Kamille to accompany her to Brizia and stay until she returns."

"That won't be until spring," Alonzo reminded him. "The snow is ready to fall. We won't return for a full season if we go with her."

"I know, but the way things are developing here, we can't be certain of anything. If she is leaving without notice, then she doesn't mean to see me beforehand. She will need familiar faces around her to keep her company while Mother keeps me busy with wedding and coordination preparations. Offer her support in my stead."

Without further protest, Alonzo complied with his friend and Prince's order. By the time Amirah's carriage departed, he and Kamille rode beside the carriage into Brizia. As predicted, the snow began falling the day they arrived in the capital. The northern kingdoms were known for their chilled climates and harsh winters and the one that blanketed the center of the Continent in gusts of the soft white powder was more bitter than usual. The road between Brizia and Pruria became impassable for four moons. During this time, Amirah's first act as Queen proved to be beneficial for Brizia. Before the first snowfall, the kingdom's food stores were counted and reported upon her arrival. There was no surplus this winter, but proper rationing ensured no citizens starved.

Alonzo stuck by her side at Bradrick's request. The Prince had wanted him to be there as protection, but she had already proved capable of handling herself, in addition to her private guards who took their duties to heart. Instead, Alonzo remained as a temporary emissary for Pruria and a friend of the Brizian Queen.

He observed the mask fall away whenever others weren't around. At times when he caught her staring out the window with a book sitting open and unread in her lap. Her vacant expression would shift when he announced himself, but he had already seen the cracks in her facade, which deepened his concern for her. When Kamille and Gabbie were present, the smile she kept plastered onto her face would falter when they weren't looking. Alonzo didn't dare to point it out, but he instead, stood as a silent sentinel, always present if she needed him. Sometimes, the best friends stood in silent support of the ones who needed the company more than any advice. Gone was the vibrant Princess. In her place was a forlorn Queen.

The ground thawed and birds began serenading the mornings as the roads opened between the two kingdoms. With spring's arrival, Alonzo was summoned back to Pruria, where Bradrick awaited him at the stables with a look of nervous impatience. Their brief embrace gave way to the barrage of questions that occupied Bradrick's mind the whole winter. His nerves were rattled by the lack of communication, increased by the hovering of his mother. As usual, Queen Indra had dictated every detail of planning the coronation and the wedding. He spared Alonzo most of the boring details of the cold months he spent dwelling on the matter. In turn, Alonzo answered his questions to help settle the Prince's worrisome disposition and made a point of mentioning that Amirah had ascended to the throne with unparalleled expertise.

They strolled through the frosted courtyard toward the palace as the conversation carried on. "I am glad to hear Brizia has welcomed her transition to the throne. It's good she's adjusted to her role as Queen seamlessly, but how does she fare?"

Alonzo's footsteps stopped and he looked at Bradrick with contemplative hesitance. He didn't want to divulge in excess, but Bradrick needed to know that something was amiss with her. He decided the best option was to ease into the topic.

"Amirah appears to be in better health than when her father was on the throne. Her people adore her, the Brizian court is in order, as far as one can tell, and the winter passed without issue. However, we both know that every royal in existence has at least two sides to themselves, and—well, perhaps I shouldn't read into things."

Bradrick felt the creeping of nerves once again. "Read into what things?"

"Did you notice how much she has changed while she was gone?" Alonzo asked suggestively. When Bradrick looked at him with confusion he continued, "Even in the small amount of time you have seen her since she left those woods, it is undeniable. She blossomed and has made a worthy Queen, but I feel that her spirit has dimmed since we brought her back. She presents herself to the world, family, and friends with a fortress around her. Wearing a mask in public is necessary for anyone in the royal courts, but the cracks that reveal the truth when that mask slips, speak more than words. I-I find myself worried for both of you as this wedding draws nearer."

Bradrick nodded and looked to the sky as if the answer to their predicament was hiding behind the gray clouds. The mere glimpses he saw of Amirah radiated with the stranger she had become. First in the woods. Then again, for the briefest time, in Pruria. She had kept herself at a distance, preventing Bradrick from the chance to discuss their options, as he had intended. Everyone had barreled ahead with plans without consideration of her desires the entire time he had known her. She had offered to honor the arrangement if it stood, but never said if that was what she had wanted. Concern plucked at him until it left him with a pit of irritation.

A sigh of exasperation escaped him. "Do you think I should call off the wedding?"

Alonzo shrugged. "I might not be someone prone to singular, rigid relationships or love, but I know a broken heart when I see it. Birds with clipped wings don't need a cage to ensure they won't fly away."

Alonzo's words hit Bradrick's heart like an arrow of clarity. Spring was finally arriving and soon, Amirah would be here. He resolved to amend the situation by giving Amirah the one thing no one else had given her yet.

AMIRAH ARRIVED THE week of Bradrick's coronation and found Queen Indra in the depths of handling the final details of the events to come. A small supply of invitations was provided to Amirah in case any important guests had not been included. Queen Indra's normal fanfare would be on full display during the coronation, and, unlike the first attempted wedding celebrations, this second one would be an uncharacteristically smaller event.

Kamille and Gabbie, along with Amirah's private guard, remained at her side from the time they arrived in Pruria. The pair only left to work on tasks or to sleep. However, the guards slept in turns and refused any visitors at night. Bradrick was kept away for longer than the sun was up by his mother's increased demands and the continued arrival of guests. He suspected Queen Indra's antics were intentional, but held his tongue with limited patience. Alonzo, knowing Bradrick's concern, which mirrored his own, took the opportunity to visit Amirah. He noted that she was much the same as she had been when he left her side in Brizia. While it still concerned him, there was nothing that could be done at the moment, and there was no immediate remedy in sight. After his visit, he headed off to deliver invitations to the Brizian court, at her request. A task that needed to be done quietly before either of the Prurian royals could question it.

Amirah's mood was darkened further by boredom. Few tasks to keep her occupied from the wretched thoughts that plagued her mind. Sleep eluded her, leaving her perpetually exhausted. The few hours she did manage to rest were restless. She knew the cause: a combination of the impending events and the unexplainable pit in her stomach whenever she thought of Nithe. The unanswered messenger hawk she sent to inform him of the pardon and transfer of the trust that held his father's properties did not surprise her. After all, he was notably absent from her coronation. Even so, the silence stung.

She wondered if, somehow, Nithe knew that she had stopped transforming into a swan and he had no further reason to be in contact with her. Their connection through the curse came with so many surprises that she never considered how her transformations might affect it or not. It had taken a few moons for her to realize that the transformations had stopped. If he somehow sensed it, then he had little other reason to be concerned until they had a solution to the curse. Now, she wondered about the state of the curse that bound their fates long before they had met. She recalled the feel of his lips against hers for the first and last time as some cruel twist of fate.

A knock on the door interrupted the intrusive thoughts. She had dismissed her guards in the late hours of the night so they could all rest. They had hesitated a moment, but they were as obedient as they were loyal. Since the threats appeared to have either subsided or at least grown quiet, she kept the guards more for the comfort of having another breathing human being around. With a groan, she crawled from the bed to answer the errant knocker. She jerked the door open with unintended force and, to her surprise, found the culprit to be Bradrick, who stood with a charming grin.

"Did the door offend you?" He asked, chuckling when she rolled her eyes at him.

"Only when someone is knocking on it," she huffed halfheartedly.

She sidestepped and motioned for him to enter the room. While it was smaller than her usual room in Pruria, she liked the snug simplicity of the space. Bradrick seated himself on one of the blushed sofas that sat facing each other at the end of the bed, and Amirah positioned herself on the opposite one. He noticed the sleepless shadows under her eyes in the candlelight, something he was familiar with.

"Sorry for intruding on your sleeping hours. Things have been busy, and I needed to steal a moment to speak with you. All the same, I'm sorry for my lack of attentiveness."

A nervous smile played at the corner of her lips. "It may be the most boring time I've had since being crowned, but that is quite alright. Fortunately for you, I wasn't sleeping."

"That makes two of us. I haven't slept well in weeks. Mother and Foley circle everyone in the castle like ravenous hawks. No bites yet," Bradrick joked.

Amirah laughed, a sliver of her old self shining through as it rang through the room. "What will she do with herself after your coronation?"

"Hopefully, host fewer parties. Although, I am sure she will find some way to remain involved in court. She may eventually marry Foley," he paused at that and the smile faded from his face. Amirah straightened at his change in demeanor. Her skin prickled at the serious tone that cultivated his voice when he began talking.

"Speaking of marriages," Bradrick said with a pause. Summoning his courage, he took a deep breath and continued. "I meant to discuss our engagement prior to the announcement, but there wasn't time before you left. Everyone is pleased with your ascension, including myself. While we may not be a lover's match, I still care for you a great deal. The day you went missing, I regretted how we had fought against this arrangement. I thought that, if I had complied with the arrangement, if I had fought harder for you to stay, then perhaps everything would have been different. When it seemed we had lost you to the world, I refused to believe it. I've failed in so many ways as a friend, an ally, a protector, and a royal. Finding you was the only chance I had to remedy each and every way I let you and our kingdoms down.

"Since your return, you have focused so much on your duties that I feel you are forgetting about yourself. I want whatever will make you happy, Amirah. I want you to have a choice in what happens in your life. No one should ever dictate what happens in your life or treat you as nothing more than an ignorant pawn again. You are, and deserve, so much more than that. If at any point, you wish to stop the wedding—"

Amirah stood abruptly and strolled to the window before he could finish. Bradrick waited patiently for her to speak, knowing she needed time to process. He was certain in what he had said, so he would not rush her. But when she continued to stare out at the night sky, he went to her side with concern. Moonlight made her skin glow like an ethereal goddess and her eyes had a faraway look. The gentle touch of his hand gave her a start. She frowned further at the empathetic look that he cast over her. She patted his hand that rested on her shoulder.

"I apologize if I offended you." He spoke to her with the gentleness of someone who approached a timid animal that might frighten away.

Despite his efforts, her heart weighed like an anchored ship that fought against the waves of an ocean. Somehow, his voice reminded her of Nithe, though they sounded nothing alike. Reminders of him now felt like she was consistently being stung by a swarm of angry hornets. She gave Bradrick a wry smile as steel wrapped around the blistering wounds of her spurned heart.

"It's not you who offends me. I appreciate your efforts and that you care for me. You are right. We may not be a love match, but we are a good match. Above all, I owe a duty to my people. If anything happens to me, I must ensure the kingdom is in capable hands. A marriage between us secures that. I have already had an attempt on my life, and who knows when another might happen."

"What?" The question came as more of a gasp from Bradrick's lips. "Who? When?"

"While I was gone, Nithe and I encountered a group who caught wind of a bounty placed on my head. I have suspicions about who placed the bounty, but I haven't been able to confirm it. I survived, and now the issue seems to have resolved itself."

"Survived a group? Where are they?"

Amirah's voice was devoid of emotion as she began explaining. "They're dead. They captured us and explained that they intended to kill us. When they attacked, we fought back. We're the only ones who walked away that night. I have blood on my hands, the same as Nithe. Bearing royal blood within the Continent carries risks, and I embraced the weight of my crown's responsibilities when I took the throne. I accepted the duty to the people of my kingdom when I fought to survive so that I could return to them."

Bradrick listened with rapt interest. He was in the dark about everything that happened to her while she was missing. Now, there stood an invisible wall between them, and it left him curious with a pinch of sadness at the increasing distance between them. It was as if she had opened a window so that he could glimpse at that part of her past—a past he couldn't fathom for her. She had surely been through an unknown amount of ordeals, and despite everything, her growth into the Queen that stood before him was a marvel to behold. Of all the emotions swirling within Bradrick, he felt pride for her the most. His eyebrows raised higher than Amirah had ever seen them as he settled his conflicted feelings for her.

She gave him a hard look and added, "If I wanted to rescind the engagement, I would have done it at the ball."

"Very well," Bradrick said gently as he stepped back. Despite the matter being resolved, he still felt unsettled by her acceptance. While their romantic feelings for one another remained unchanged, Amirah's decision to abandon hope in favor of duty was unsettling. "If you change your mind in the future, or wish to be unburdened by marriage, you only need to ask and it will be done. As we agreed in our previous schemes, we can peacefully divorce."

"The same goes for you. Although, the faithful members of our courts might take issue if we do something like that."

"Perhaps," Bradrick shrugged. "You are elegant, whether you are a swan or a woman, and well-liked without a husband at your side. You don't need magic to hold your power. You are an enigma, even without a crown upon your head. They would be utter fools to oppose you."

A smile blossomed over her face, the first genuine one she had given in a while, although she felt a dizzying mix of emotions. Nithe occupied her mind, but Bradrick offered her comfort. Bradrick saw the light of life seemingly seep back into her. Even if it was temporary, he reveled in the sense of peace that now the air between them seemed to be cleared. Amirah accepted the embrace he offered her at that moment. Her mind couldn't help but compare the feel of

Bradrick's gentle encompassment to Nithe's arms wrapping around her body. When they parted, she was grateful for the natural concealment the darkness offered as she wrestled with the thought.

When Bradrick left the room, she crawled back into bed. Sleep embraced her with dreams that re-lived moments with Nithe. She found herself faced with him in a dark, blank room made of a sea of stars. When his arms wrapped around her, she felt small, safe, and at peace. His voice whispered in her ear like a ghost in the wind, "*Your blood is bound to mine. Forever.*"

CHAPTER 28

B radrick's coronation was full of splendor. His mother treated it as yet another one of her parties; a last hurrah of her own taste. Indra's attention to detail had been as impeccable as ever. The ending result was an elegant affair that showed her power while celebrating her son's ascending to the throne. She spared no expense to ensure decorations hung through every street in the capital. Her own gown was at its usual level of excess. The white and gold details complimented her son's attire beneath the oversized regal ceremonial cape.

All eyes in the throne room watched as Bradrick entered at the start of his crowning ceremony. It was the longest process of the entire coronation that started with a ritual that was unique to Pruria. First, he washed his hands in an ancient basin that sat carved atop a waist-high pillar of stone. After which, a Pruria citizen—an individual chosen ahead of the coronation by the priest—poured a few drops of gold-tinted oil to anoint Bradrick's hands. Properly anointed, Bradrick proceeded up the dais. His mother followed from the front of the seated crowd until she stood behind him. He stopped before the priest, who awaited him before the single golden throne.

Amirah remained focused through the droning recitations. She wore a gentle smile on her face that was partially genuine. *It feels as if this destined day were no more than a dream*, she thought as she watched the priest place the crown upon Bradrick's head. As if to confirm her thought, Indra turned. Her piercing stare drifted from Bradrick to the front row, where Amirah sat behind them. When Amirah noticed, they smiled at one another and turned their attention back to Bradrick. As he stood to face the crowded room, a brief tune of trumpets erupted, followed by a unified chorus of proclamations.

"Long live the King!" Amirah joined the chanting of the crowd.

After the lavish ceremony, Amirah joined Bradrick in a white and gold carriage, both eager to escape the excess attention and relieved to be done with it. Alonzo bade them goodbye before closing the carriage door. Once they passed the palace gates, the carriage rolled through crowds that had gathered along the main road. Like Brizia, this was the heart of the civilian celebrations. Pruria was familiar to Amirah, but it had always differed from her own home. Still, the welcoming waves of the warmhearted city brought their own warmth. Despite having known Bradrick his whole life, each citizen was eager to catch a glance at their new King. As the beginnings of the tour continued, Amirah reflected on how much Pruria had grown to love Bradrick as their Prince, and how much they would love him as their King.

The tour through the kingdom served a dual purpose. First, for Bradrick to meet his people as their new King, something that was both a custom and a necessity. Second, Bradrick and Amirah are to be presented to Pruria as a couple ahead of their upcoming nuptials. Bradrick had monitored Amirah for any sign of wavering in her decision, but had found none. In fact, in the quaint coastal town that sat on the coast, she almost seemed happy. They were the picturesque royal couple their parents had trained them to be. Exhausted after wrapping up their last stop, they climbed back into the carriage and collapsed onto the long cushioned seat.

"Perhaps we should do this again after the wedding," she proposed sarcastically.

Bradrick groaned in response.

In truth, tours had become achingly repetitive for Amirah. Her face ached from constantly smiling and her body was sore from long carriage rides–though she thought the impression she had made was good. Her lap was filled with bouquets and gifts from Prurian citizens who had welcomed her with the same warmth they had for Bradrick.

Lassitude became Amirah's taxing nemesis. By the time they returned, less than a week remained before the wedding. She sought sleep whenever some last-minute task didn't need attention. The few guests she had invited began trickling in, all demanding attention from her until the eve of the wedding. She began feeling less present and more like she simply floated through the motions. The wedding feast, which went without incident, was the worst. Thankfully, it required minimal mental presence of mind, and she needed to only smile or clap. Bradrick was otherwise occupied with his own nobles who vied for his kingly attention. The politics gave Amirah a reprieve from the dancing expected of them at the previous wedding-eve banquet. When it was late enough, Amirah excused herself for beauty rest and retired to her room.

Gabbie followed behind her, once again, the dutiful lady-in-waiting. Kamille joined them in her room and helped to strip away the ruby, multi-layered gown Amirah had worn. Kamille spirited it away to be cleaned while Gabbie worked with diligent hands to prepare the bed. Amirah slipped into a simple white chemise nightgown, aching to dive beneath the covers. Kamille returned to help ensure everything was prepared for the morning when a knock sounded at the door. Gabbie gave her a long white silk robe to pull on while Kamille answered the door.

Indra barged into the room without introduction from Amirah's private guard. A look was shared between Amirah and the maidens in the room. Her soon-to-be mother-in-law wore the same shimmering, periwinkle gown from dinner, which must have finally come to a close if she was here. They dipped their heads to each other in a show of mutual respect, then Amirah made a wide sweep of her arm toward the sofas. She followed behind Indra and assumed the sofa opposite her while the two maidens busied themselves.

"I came for a brief visit. With a busy day coming, I brought some tea for the night. A small gift for my daughter-in-law. Though you have always been like a daughter to me, tomorrow we will become an official family. Your father would have been proud of your decision to honor the arrangement."

Her words made Amirah shift in her seat. She disguised the discomforted movement by reaching to accept the offered small box of tea leaves. "Thank you. It has been a busy week. Your gift is very considerate and should help me achieve some much needed rest."

Indra instructed Kamille to bring some hot water to steep the leaves. Amirah opened the lid of the box to inhale the bittersweet herbal aroma, different from the floral blend of tea leaves Nithe would make for them during late nights in the study, as Indra chatted. Her unexpected visit tonight was reminiscent of their first meeting. Many years of their lives overlapped until they were irrevocably intertwined. This side of the woman was so seldom seen that Amirah had almost forgotten it existed. The casual conversation with Indra came to a natural end by the time Kamille returned with the prepared tea. She urged Amirah to drink a full cup for the best sleep, then took her leave.

Amirah drank through two cups of the rich-flavored drink. The taste of it matched the aroma and the bitterness clinging to her tongue. It was far too late to request honey from the kitchen, so Kamille set the remaining brew and box on the small table in the corner. Amirah slipped beneath the covers and bid her friends goodnight as they moved to depart for their own rooms. Sleep consumed her before the door clicked shut behind the two women.

As Amirah slept, she dreamt of being an elegant white swan that was lost amid the night, a familiar voice calling to her as she circled a pool of moonlight. Its mass shrank and shrank as she drew closer until her body landed on the black waters that burst into all-consuming flames around her—an inescapable death.

Violent shaking woke Amirah from the haunted dream. When her eyes jerked open, she saw Kamille's contorted face of concern. The dark-haired beauty stood at the bedside with her hands on her hips. She sighed, the sound both frustrated and relieved. Amirah pushed away the wavelets of ginger hair pasted to her sweat-drenched forehead. Her body felt as if it burned from the inside out, much like the dream. The light that poured through the windows hurt her eyes and every inch of her wanted to curl away into a dark cocoon.

"I could hardly wake you! We are behind schedule, and if we don't hurry, you will be late. I'll prepare the bath for you, soggy thing." She clicked her tongue. Amirah's stomach flipped, an onset of nausea that made her lurch upright with a hand cupped over her mouth. Kamille gave her a wary look. "Perhaps a bucket first?"

Amirah nodded in silent agreement.

The nausea gave way to cold chills and her teeth chattered while she drove through the aching movements to climb out of bed. The misfortune of illness striking when this day was finally coming to pass was a grim omen. She refused to allow it to cause a delay. Her resolve to see this through to the end, whatever the end might bring, had become ironclad. Kamille helped her keep steady until she reached the private wash chamber. Centered in the tight room was a round tub filled with floral bath water.

There was an inkling of déjà vu as Kamille tended to her mess of hair, but Amirah found it difficult to focus on memories through the churning in her stomach. They worked in brisk tandem to finish the task. Her hands quivered as she climbed out. She felt chilled from the water, despite its warmth, but her insides felt like an inferno.

Gabbie stood waiting with her dress when they returned to the bedroom. Both maidens helped Amirah slip into it without upsetting her coiffed hair. Their assistance allowed her the grace to breathe through her unrelenting nausea. The almost sheer sleeves of the gown billowed out, hanging from her shoulders. They contrasted the smooth fitted bodice, which led to the flowing fabric that moved around her hips and legs like water. Her skirts dusted the floor, keeping the short-heeled boots hidden. A delicate cape draped over her shoulders with a jeweled chained clip over her chest to keep it in place. Gabbie stepped back, examining her as Kamille pinned pearl drops into Amirah's loose hanging waves before adding a small silver crown that glistened with gemstones as the final touch. Finished, Gabbie gave Amirah an approving nod.

Amirah was grateful there was no time to eat before being ushered from the room as her stomach began to churn anew. She sent her guards ahead to the throne room with Gabbie, leaving Kamille to accompany Amirah through the halls. Every corridor was barren except for a few floral arrangements that remained from Bradrick's coronation. This was the least amount of decorations Amirah had seen for any event in Pruria. The contrast was a minimal distraction from the heat that prickled the back of her neck. It might have upset someone else, but Amirah preferred the lesser exuberance. Her bones ached in protest with each step, and she stumbled over her own feet as her vision blurred from a dizzy spell. Kamille offered her arm for support and when Amirah accepted the help, they continued. When they stopped before the throne room door, Kamille stepped back for a final examination.

"Will you be alright, Your Highness?" The maiden dabbed sweat from Amirah's forehead with knitted brows.

All she could offer in response was a thin smile. Kamille's brows furrowed and unfurrowed until she relented with a subtle nod. Another smile fluttered on Amirah's face in thanks and Kamille left to inform the Master of Ceremonies of their arrival. His voice bellowed from within before the doors swung open. Gabbie emerged and took up the back length of Amirah's bridal cape and followed behind her with it in hand.

The interior was as barren of decorations as the hallway. The few floral arrangements that remained washed the space with their gentle scent and melodious music wove throughout the familiar pillar-lined room. Sunlight and candles offered gentle lighting that streamed down on the few faces that stood between the pillars. Each person turned, one by one, as she passed with careful steps upon the pale runner that stretched down the center aisle, all the way to the dais at the opposite end. Crested banners for each kingdom hung from the ceiling on each side and if she had felt better, she might have smirked at the irony that a dragon was featured on the center of the Brizian colors.

Instead, she focused to keep her steps in time with the sweet song selected for this procession and moved toward the blurred faces that stood at the dais. She fixated upon them to avoid any suspicion that something was amiss under the watchful eyes around her. Even without precise details, she could tell Alonzo stood on the floor below the dais, which hosted the throne that was hidden somewhere behind Bradrick. Both men were oblivious that anything was amiss as she approached.

Like everyone present, they dressed in pristine finery for the occasion. Alonzo's juniper green velveteen jacket sporting a white flower was the lightest jacket he had ever worn. Meanwhile, Bradrick wore a clad white ensemble, except for the gold threaded pattern—a detail that was likely selected long before his coronation by his mother. Now that Amirah was closer, she could make out some of the finer vine-like stitching on Bradrick's clothes and the edge of a slight smile that played on the corners of his lips. She tried to smile back, but her sense of balance betrayed her careful maneuvers and her facade fell as her footsteps stumbled. Indra, who stood in her spot of honor with Foley at the front edge of the crowd, lanced an arm out in support.

She whispered so no one else could hear. "Are you alright? You look deathly pale."

"Just a misstep," Amirah tried to reassure her. "Nerves, I think. Thank you."

She lied in hopes not to cause alarm, although concern and worry already painted the few faces that she could make out. Her back straightened as moved on alone, determined to ward off any further suspicion. The taste of bile in the back of Amirah's throat rose as she continued, despite the wavering floor, until she found herself beside Bradrick. Behind her, Gabbie mirrored Alonzo's position. The duo shared a concerned look with Bradrick as he turned with Amirah to face the bishop, who stood a step above them on the dais.

The bishop appeared dressed in a simple robe of white, gold, and black. His aged voice cracked as he opened the ceremony with a blessing as Bradrick and Amirah knelt upon instruction. Pain emanated from her bones and she clenched Bradrick's hand harder than she intended. She tried to ignore the sensation of his eyes boring into her as their heads dipped down before the bishop. Sweat beaded her brow as the ceremony continued. She hoped Bradrick wouldn't notice her distress, but when they turned to face each other, he mouthed a silent 'what's wrong' at her. She gave a weak smile in response, not knowing what ailed her beyond the relentless toll it was taking on her body.

She heard only muddled words from the Bishop when Bradrick grasped her hands in his, each movement based on memory. When they stood, the Bishop guided Bradrick through his half of the nuptials. She didn't notice the Bishop speak to her until Bradrick tugged lightly on her hand. Once again, from memory, she repeated the vows. Each word that passed her lips was clear, though her vision faded in and out of focus. Her words faltered on the last line and silence followed the incompleteness. Her hand slipped from Bradrick as the room appeared to spin in multiple directions and she wavered with an involuntary step backwards.

The doors to the throne room burst open, light spilling in and startling the crowd. Each person turned toward the interruption and their eyes landed upon a dark figure that staggered forward. His black, leather-gloved hand stretched out before him as if to reach for Amirah. Darkness threatened the edge of her vision as her eyes landed on the familiar face that was contorted in agony with each wavering step forward. She could hear the trembling in her voice as the blackness consumed the last of her vision.

"Nithe?"

CHAPTER 29

B radrick, distracted by the intruder, reacted a moment too late. The audible thud of Amirah's body colliding with the floor divided the room's attention. Luckily, her arm had cushioned her head from a bloodied end. Bradrick rushed forward and knelt beside her, taking in the deteriorated state of the woman's shallow breathing. Several people swarmed around Amirah's collapsed body with concern. Bradrick directed Alonzo to help their new guest, who appeared in the same shape Amirah was moments before the collapse. Gabbie fell to her knees beside her Queen and began crying as she aided Bradrick's continued attempts to rouse her.

Amirah had called out to the man as she collapsed—Nithe. Bradrick realized only he and Alonzo recognized the name. This version of Nithe appeared different from the man who had imprisoned him in the Duke's Castle. Perhaps it was the state of his body, haggard from unknown pain, or the wild look on his face as he slowly approached. Bradrick made no move to stop his advance, which appeared strenuous as he struggled forward. He stumbled, much as Amirah had done moments before. A few of the guests squinted at the vaguely familiar face, unable to place it, as whispers began spreading among their concerned faces. Half of the room hadn't been present when Nithe had made himself known the night Amirah had disappeared from Pruria. Bradrick's mother, however, tilted her chin back with indignation as Alonzo met Nithe in the middle of the room.

Bradrick couldn't hear the words passing between them, but he felt relieved when Nithe allowed Alonzo to wrap his arms beneath the man for support. His mother gave an audible huff before her hushed murmurs to Foley continued. As Alonzo passed with Nithe, his eyes darted toward Indra and Foley, who remained whispering to each other in their original positions. He continued to the dais, despite his deep down-turned brow that matched his frown at whatever he heard from them. The small crowd that gathered around Amirah gave him and Nithe birth to approach until Nithe was able to kneel beside her.

"Why is no one stopping him? Guards, arrest this intruder!" Indra shouted.

Bradrick stood abruptly and signaled the guards, who had drawn swords, to stand down before he shot an angered warning look at his mother. While Bradrick had once told Amirah that Nithe would be arrested if he stepped onto Prurian soil, he wasn't prepared to do it under the current conditions. Additionally, he wasn't about to allow his mother to continue her reign of control and power now that he was King. Indra looked at him with squinted eyes as if she were about to reprimand him, which Bradrick dared her to as he stared back.

"Why is he still here, Bradrick? This man wasn't on the guest list and should be removed," Indra challenged with balled fists.

Nithe pulled an invitation from beneath his black cloak and waved in front of him. His darkened eyes shot toward Indra as a cold declaration left his lips. "I oppose the marriage."

Every eye in the room darted between the royals and Nithe. Many studied the man with leveled concern, while others now looked upon him with intrigue as Alonzo took the invitation. He stepped forward with it held into the air for the entire room to see, before passing it to the Master of Ceremonies. The stout man scanned it twice before he looked at Nithe and then Alonzo, who wore a smug grin directed at Indra. The Master of Ceremonies cleared his throat and made his announcement.

"Please allow me to introduce the Duke of Brizia, Lord Nithe Vivek."

The words ricocheted off the throne room walls, followed by an audible gasp from the surrounding audience. Indra's face twisted in malicious indignation, and Foley quirked an eyebrow at the unexpected surprise. Bradrick felt a small twinge of satisfaction watching them. *Well played, Amirah,* he thought. Her first acts as Queen had outwitted a number of people, including his mother. Bradrick wondered, with increased interest, if his own threats to arrest the man were moot due Amirah's pardon. He and Alonzo shared a crooked grin.

"The Duke is a welcomed guest here," Bradrick announced to the room. He turned to his guards with a direct command, "No one else is to come in or out of this room until I command otherwise. Send someone to fetch the royal physician. I want him here immediately."

Five of the guards left the room while the rest stayed to lock down the room and guard their King.

"How do we know he isn't the cause of all this?" Indra's accusation was vague, but it was there, and it gave away more than she intended. At least, it was to Bradrick, who knew his mother well. Several gazes fell upon her with reproach.

"The cause of what, exactly, mother?" Bradrick deadpanned with an irritated frown, irked by the suspicion that she held some hidden knowledge of the situation.

The old royal physician shuffled in before she answered, approaching with haste. His beady eyes glued on Amirah well before he reached the dais. The slight hunch in his back arched further when he stooped to examine her without instruction. Gabbie moved back to allow him space to work, unlike Nithe, who stayed steadfast at his Queen's side. He watched the Physician with intense observation, without care toward the crowd that studied every movement in the room. The Physician lifted Amirah's eyelid, checked her pulse, observed her hands with a squeeze to each fingernail, and peered into her mouth with a peculiar sniff of his sharp nose. A thin line of blood pooled at the corner of Amirah's mouth and when he opened it, the first drop trickled in a long crimson trail down her jaw. The Physician's face paled in alarm.

"What is it?" Bradrick prodded.

The Physician gave a grim frown. "Poison."

Time stood still in the Prurian throne room. Bradrick broke it with a curse under his breath. Nithe's face was unreadable, half of it masked by the long black hair that cascaded down from him and over Amirah like a protective curtain. Bradrick could tell from the rasping, rattling sound of the breath he drew that the man was in dire shape. Those around them wore forlorn faces and Gabrielle sobbed into her father's chest, who frowned down at Bradrick.

"How could she have been poisoned!?" It was more a demand from Lord Paget than a question.

A number of the Brizian court members were present, each of whose faces reflected a question similar to Paget's. This was especially true for the attending members of the Brizian court. The threat of hostility was a palpable taste, one Bradrick was not looking forward to entertaining as the same question tumbled around his own head. He rubbed his chin as he puzzled over the information available to him. His eyes fell upon Alonzo, who stared at Indra and Foley. His mother flashed a twisted grin at Consort Foley, unaware her son had seen. However, it was the Physician who would provide the first clues.

"What do we know?" Bradrick asked him.

"It would've had to have been within the last twelve hours, given her condition. There are no signs of puncture and no residue. I would look into who had contact with her majesty within that time."

Bradrick looked at Gabbie, who attempted to wipe away the tears that still streamed down her cheeks. "She brought her private guards. Gabbie, you and Kamille saw her the most yesterday. What can you tell us?"

Gabbie gulped in the air as she recalled her memories of the prior afternoon. "She was tired after the wedding-eve feast and didn't eat much, but she hasn't been hungry as of late. Kamille and I attended her until our dismissal from her room when she went to bed. The guards remained at their post until their dismissal this morning. Lady Indra was her only visitor last night, and she left before we did."

Bradrick nodded while a growing suspicion nagged his brain. Nithe seemed to have become more alert to his surroundings as the exchange continued.

"When was she last served anything to eat or drink?"

"Before she turned in for sleep," Gabbie said, as a horrified look overcame her face.

"Who served her?" Bradrick felt a swell of foreboding even as he asked it.

"Kamille," she looked at Indra. "But it was nothing more than a fresh tea that was brewed right there in her own room. Lady Indra brought a box of loose blended tea as a gift. I watched it brewed and poured. Kamille would never harm her."

Nithe's eyes went wide. He stood up amidst a coughing fit where blood began dripping from his own lips. Alonzo and Bradrick looked at him with concern. Alonzo moved to help him, but was pushed away. Nithe's eyes met with Bradrick's.

"Get her to a bed," he instructed no one in particular and turned away.

"Where are you going?" Bradrick asked.

"To get a remedy," Nithe called back over his shoulder without pause.

Bradrick signaled the guards to move and let him pass. He then spun toward Amirah's guards, who were nearest to them. A moment before he spoke, a deep and terrible shriek pierced the air outside of the castle. Everyone around them ducked their head and searched the air above them in alarm as if they would be able to see the creature there. It was a familiar sound to Bradrick and Alonzo, who appeared unaffected after having encountered Nithe's irritated dragon form before. There wasn't time for the questions that lurked behind the numerous eyes that turned back upon them.

Bradrick fixed Amirah's guards and his soldiers with a stern look. "Amirah's rooms are to be searched for anything that could have been drunk, used to drink from, and for any parcels of tea. My mother and Lord Foley Osman are to be confined to their rooms until further notice. No further orders are to be taken from either of them for any reason. Send in a gurney so we can transport Queen Amirah to the Queen's chambers on the second floor. Inform her guards so they can be there when we arrive."

"Wait! Bradrick, I admit, I did bring her a gift." His mother protested and chuckled with a dismissive wave of her hand. "It was a simple tea blend, nothing more than a gesture of goodwill from me as her mother-in-law. How could you suspect me of poisoning her? There is no way I could have also poisoned the Duke. You saw the state of him—identical to the poor girl's condition. How could I ever have managed to poison both of them?"

Alonzo let out a deep sigh that sharply drew everyone's attention in his direction.

"We can thank the blood curse for that." Bradrick threw a puzzled look at Alonzo, who scrubbed the back of his neck. A battle with his conscience relented when his eyes met with Bradrick and he lamented with another sigh. "There was a curse laid upon King Landry by the prior Duke of Brizia. There isn't much known about it, but this curse has affected their children. The Queen and the present Duke's fates are bound together by this curse. Which means, if Amirah is dying, so is he."

The smile fell from Indra's face as though someone had slapped her. Bradrick signaled the guards to escort his mother and Foley to their rooms. He glared at his mother, a silent challenge that dared her to further defy his orders. His heart ached at the bewildering betrayal that came from his own flesh and blood. Alonzo clapped his shoulder, a silent apologetic comfort, as they watched his mother being taken away. Nothing could make him question Alonzo's allegiance to him, but what surprised him was that this was the first time he was hearing the information. He considered Amirah could have sworn him to secrecy, and if Alonzo was nothing else, he was loyal. The curse puzzled him. Endangering one life through the other was never something Bradrick had considered fathomable before.

Gentle hands helped place Amirah on the gurney that carried her away to the private bed chambers that had been prepared for after the wedding, which was adjoined to Bradrick's chambers. The members of the Brizian court were malcontent with the information available. They left grumbling louder than the rest of the guests after Amirah was carried from the throne room. All except for Gabrielle, whose father hesitated to let her out of his sight. The deadly assault upon their Queen had everyone on edge more than the day Amirah had gone missing. After the throne room had cleared, Bradrick and Alonzo went to the Queen's chambers. Bradrick's staff transferred Amirah's limp body from the gurney to the plush comforts of a luxurious bed, and Gabbie joined the maids in their efforts to fuss over her.

Behind them, the royal physician arrived with a guard and Kamille in tow. The Physician set to work checking Amirah over once more. Her skin had an unnatural pale sheen to it. He rotated her onto her side at the end of the examination to prevent her from choking on the blood that continued to trickle from her mouth.

Kamille cast forlorn eyes down upon a tray she carried. It held a pitcher of unfinished tea, a single cup, and a wooden box with an engraved floral pattern. Bradrick picked up the familiar box, trying to recall where he had seen it before. Inside it was the bitter-sweet scented tea leaves Gabrielle had described.

When he asked Kamille to recall the night before, she confirmed Gabbie's version in her own words. The young woman had been under the employment of his mother for years and had volunteered to take the position as Amirah's maid early in her employment. Bradrick could tell by the look on her face that she felt burdened with guilt. Guilt that was not meant for her, judging by the information he had gathered. What was more, the Physician himself pulled Bradrick aside to confirm his suspicions. Alonzo followed him like a shadow and they listened intently to the beady-eyed old man.

"My King, the prognosis is grim. I know what this tea is and I must confess my own guilt in the matter." His aged voice sounded hoarse and his beady eyes became glossier as he continued. "Queen Indra often asked me to bring various things back for her from the markets of the other cities, where I traveled to fill the royal apothecary. She had a particular fascination with a rare tea blend that was near impossible to find. It's made from a single plant, a rare herb, known for its malicious effects upon the body. It carries no benefits and its sole use is poisoning. It took years to find it for her. This very blend came from a merchant in Brizia. I never questioned why Her Highness wanted it, and for that, I have to blame for the death of the Brizian Queen. I will accept any punishment you deem fit, my King."

The old man shook as he knelt to bow at Bradrick's feet. Bradrick ran a hand through his messed blonde hair before he pulled the Physician to his feet. He remembered the moment his mother had received this box from the Physician. That was before they had found Amirah and before anyone knew she was alive.

"I cannot, in good faith, punish you for following my mother's orders while she was upon the throne. There is some fresh paper on that desk over there. I would like you to provide written testimony under the witness of this guard." Bradrick pointed to the one closest to them and then asked, "If there's a remedy for this, how long will it take?"

The Physician's frown sagged further. "The herbs that are needed to make a remedy do not exist within our apothecary or within the borders of our kingdom, your Highness. They would need to be foraged from the mountainsides in Brizia and most likely are not available at the capital markets. We do not have the luxury of time."

"How much time do we have?" Alonzo asked.

"She has a few hours, at best."

Bradrick cursed loudly and everyone nearby jumped at his outburst. He was familiar with defeat, but none such as this. All they could do now was sit and anxiously wait with the hope that Nithe would return within time. Or at all, given the state he'd been in. The Physician gave instructions on how to keep her last mortal hours comfortable. Bradrick issued an immediate order that the apothecary was to be updated to include remedies for all poisons known to the continent. It would be a long and daunting task, even with assistants, but the grievous-voiced Physician agreed with his King. The evidence and testimony met with Bradrick's own memories, painted a vivid picture of a long-planned betrayal—an issue that would need to be dealt with in the coming days to prevent war between Pruria and Brizia. Though, there was no certainty that it would be possible when Amirah passed.

Kamille, Gabbie, and the maids took a break from Amirah's side when they had nothing left to do. All anyone could do was watch Amirah's still body tapered out and wait until her last mortal breath slid past her lips. Something none of them were prepared to do. Gabbie and Kamille held each other up as they departed from the room in tears, glancing at Bradrick as he paced the halls. He did not look like himself with the way his blonde hair hung in disheveled loose waves against his rugged face. His eyes were wide and held the glint of a man on the brink of a crazed outburst.

Bradrick offered Amirah's private guards a break from their sentinel post at the doorway, but they refused, a mix of rage and the grief of loss tainting their faces. The mood had spread throughout the castle, darkening the halls in spite of the streams of sunlight that fought the sullen shadows through the windows. Alonzo left and returned to Bradrick's side with a full bottle of spirits. When Bradrick finally took a seat beside him, Alonzo pushed it into his hands. Alonzo pulled a metal flask from beneath his coat, and together they sat in a miserable silence on the hallway floor. Besides defeat, Bradrick recognized another feeling that reveled in haunting him. Guilt was his own personal plague that, once again, ate him from the inside out. This time, he was sure it was here to stay.

Distant screams broke him from his spiraling thoughts as screams carried to him from the crowded Prurian streets, as if the war had already broken out.

A shadow flickered through the rays of afternoon sunlight and something large impacted the palace, which caused a rumble of aftershock to vibrate the walls and floor. The sound of a crash echoed through the halls, followed by screams of panic, and Alonzo and Bradrick jumped to their feet with a start. The sharp sound of metal came from Amirah's alert sentinel guards, who withdrew their dual swords from their backs. They each tossed one over to Bradrick and Alonzo, then assumed defensive stances in front of Amirah's door. Bradrick mouthed a silent thanks to them and received a grunt of acknowledgment. Then, with a glance at Alonzo, he led the way toward the main stairwell that led to the lower floors.

The duo approached with their swords poised to strike, apprehension beading their brows at the sound of trudging of heavy footsteps. As the sound neared, their adrenaline soared until they jumped into view of the stairs. When their eyes fell over the steps, Alonzo cried out as he moved to strike, but was blocked by Bradrick's sword. Their metal clashed, and Alonzo was pushed back so that his blade didn't hit its mark. Both of them dropped their swords in recognition of the sagging black form, whose steps faltered. Nithe struggled to drag himself up the steps, his bedraggled long black hair sodden with sweat as blood streaked down his lips, painting his chin crimson. Bruises and scratches from unknown tribulations riddled his body and clothes.

They rushed down the steps and each took one of Nithe's arms over their shoulder and carried him to the Queen's chambers. He collapsed into a chair that sat at the bedside where Amirah lay. His eyes snapped to her, a spark of life lingering in their green depths that flickered with viridescent light, there one moment and gone the next, as his power wavered. The hands of time ticked closer to the cusp of running out for the both of them. Amirah had the pallor of a corpse and Nithe appeared as a walking one. A cough full of blood interrupted Nithe's ragged breathing and Bradrick passed him a cloth from the pile the maids left on the bedside table.

"Did you find what you were looking for? Do you have the remedy?" he asked. Nithe gave a single nod of his weakened head in response. "The poison was a tea that was made from some herb only found in the Brizian mountains. Are you sure this will be the cure?"

Nithe nodded again as his eyes fluttered until they shut. Bradrick cursed and moved to check if he still breathed.

Alonzo patted Bradrick's shoulder. "We should go find the Physician. There isn't much time, but we'll need his help with both of them. We need to be sure this is the right remedy. If it isn't, it could kill them."

"They're already dying," Bradrick hissed with frustration.

"All the more reason to be safe and not speed it along."

"Fine." Bradrick shook Nithe's shoulders. His eyes opened in a half-lidded gaze to Bradrick. "We are going to get the royal physician. I suggest staying put for now so you can reserve any remaining energy."

Nithe gave him a slow blink. Bradrick assumed he either agreed with the plan or was too far through death's doorway to comprehend. With no other options, Bradrick begrudgingly signaled for Alonzo to follow him out the door with a slight jerk of his head. Alonzo registered the message and moved for the door. Then, he paused, casting a look backward at Nithe and Amirah before following after his King.

CHAPTER 30

Nithe groaned as the sound of chamber doors shutting roused him back to a wavering consciousness. Amirah lay before him on a bed, fresh blood trickling out of the side of her mouth. It took an agonizing effort to shift his body away from the chair to sit on the bed beside her. She didn't stir at his presence and Nithe frowned. If she were in her natural state, she would have squirmed at their proximity. The connection between them had always set her on the edge. It was an instinct, the same as his, to inevitably fall for or fly away from the other. He pulled the sullied gloves from his hands, letting them fall to the floor. One hand grazed over the ginger hair that fell around her. The vibrancy of it made her an ethereal vestige of the moment that bridged life and death. Nithe pushed back the threads of her hair, exposing her ear, and he bent closer so she might hear his strained voice.

"I am sorry," he rasped. "Sorry that I wasn't there, and that I let you down. I am sorry for the fool I have been. By sending you away and by keeping a distance between us, I thought I could protect you. I am sorry for the selfish bastard that I am in asking you to fight to survive this, Amirah. I need you to be okay because I still have a promise to keep, and because I love you."

There was no response, no stir of movement to his hushed confession. It was doubtful she heard him while passing through death's door. His hand reached beneath his tattered black cloak that clung to his battered shoulders and a small violet-hued glass vial emerged in the palm of his hand. A twine cord with a small label attached at the neck of the vial bearing his father's handwriting, sealed shut with wax.

The Prurian King had told him enough to confirm his suspicions about the poison, and Nithe didn't have enough time left to wait on Bradrick's return with the royal physician. The wax was brittle from age, making it easy to break. He put the bottle to Amirah's lips and the small amount of liquid that went past her then dripped back out the other side. He frowned, wiping the droplets away from her jawline. The motion caused the wet and dry blood trickling from her mouth to smear.

He didn't have the energy to swear. The magic that coursed through his veins had barely kept him alive. He felt the power draining away, along with his life force, as it fought against the relentless effects of the poison and the dark pull of the ache within his heart as he looked upon her near-lifeless body. Her breaths were so shallow they weren't even visible. Nithe wondered if he had it in him to curse the whole Continent before the last breath left his lungs as his father had done to King Landry. If it wasn't for the curse, he might have more power to save Amirah.

His eyes snapped to the vial clenched in his hand. The train of dark thoughts led him to an idea. There was enough in the vial for a single antidote. Enough to save one person. He poured the contents into his mouth and held it there while casting the vial aside. It rolled onto the floor with a clatter. Gently he maneuvered Amirah's head, his palm cradling the back of her head. The thumb of his other hand pulled against her chin so that her lips parted. The unnaturally sweet scent that accompanied the poison's effects, mixed with the pungent smell of copper that drifted toward him with her feather-light breath. He sealed his lips to her and used his tongue to siphon the antidote to the back of her mouth. The liquid left in a slow stream until there was none left. Then, he withdrew and observed her through blurred vision. When Amirah didn't show any signs of distress from the exchange, he placed her head back in its original position. Darkness encroached on his sight. Nearby, the door clicked open as his hands slid away from her fragile form and he was swallowed by the black shadows as he collapsed beside her.

A TEAM OF PEOPLE ENTERED the Queen's bedroom behind Bradrick. They froze at the sight of Nithe collapsing beside Amirah. Bradrick and Alonzo bolted forward as his limp body crashed into the floor and Alonzo began checking his vitals. Bradrick bent to pick up a shining object from the floor, his fingers tracing the empty violet vial with a small label attached. He cursed, unable to read the hand-scrawled words. He didn't need to read it to know that Nithe had already administered it. When the royal Physician approached with an outstretched hand, Bradrick gave him the vial. The old man put it under his sharp nose, which scrunched as he sniffed it. With a finger, he rubbed the opening, then brought it to the tip of his tongue. His lips smacked as he squinted at the small attached label. A smile spread across his face that reached all the way to his widened, beady eyes.

"Your Majesty, it's the antidote. A rare enough find." He handed the vial back to Bradrick as the smile sobered from his face. "I hope that it was administered soon enough to be effective against the poison. There is little more that can be done. We must wait a while longer."

A flicker of hope breathed relief into Bradrick as the Physician departed and he turned to the servants in the room. "Prepare the adjacent chamber rooms for our guests here. The Duke of Brizia will stay until he has recovered."

"You sound hopeful," Alonzo muttered, who still knelt beside Nithe.

"Indeed. I'm afraid it's the last left within me," Bradrick said, glancing at his friend. "Issue an order for the arrest of Lady Indra Balthasar and Lord Foley Osman. They will face a tribunal for their crimes."

"You wish for Foley to be prosecuted as well?"

"As my mother's Consort, he has been her confident in all things. He was at her side the day she received the tea. At minimum, he is an accessory to her crimes. There may be more we don't know. The tribunal will determine if he played a larger role in this conspiracy."

The servants returned with the gurney to transport Nithe's unconscious body to the adjacent chambers where he would have his own bed. He was heavier to lift than Amirah, so Alonzo helped them move his body. Bradrick stared at the empty space on the floor where Nithe's body had once lain, lost in thought. The movement of Alonzo at Amirah's bedside drew his attention back to reality. Nimble fingers tucked the sheet around her form as one of the servants cleaned the blood from her chin. Sweat glistened her brow, but her breathing had strengthened. Exhaustion began to pull at Bradrick. One look at the window told him it was the middle of the night.

"Go get some rest," Alonzo said, turning to him. "I will stay here and watch over her. Let the guards take a break for a shift. We can send some of our own men to stand at the door if it appeases them."

Bradrick hesitated for a moment. He didn't want to give up hope for the fear that troubled him—the what if's that plagued him at every turn. If it were anyone else, he would have refused. Trust within his own home had been cut thin by the day's events. For the time being, he would give no faith to anyone outside of his own inner circle.

"Alright," he relented. "Report to me in the morning. Send for me immediately if anything changes."

With that, Bradrick left for his own chambers at the end of the hall. The air felt thick and unbearable, so he stripped until only a pair of loose black trousers remained on him. Even then, sleep continued to evade him. He left, strolling past the guards to wander the dark halls in a thin open robe that flowed away from his bare chest and skirted behind his feet. As King, no one questioned his movements through the deep hours of the night. Eventually, he found himself wandering down an obscure stairwell hidden in a seldom-traveled back hall on the main floor and into the deepest part of the palace.

Sunlight never touched these damp stone tunnels with iron doors evenly spaced down each side. Torchlight was the only source of light. The holding cells of the palace dungeons were always empty under his mother's rule. If some unfortunate soul earned a place here, they were never here very long once guilt was determined, sometimes at the detriment of limb or life. Bradrick stopped in front of a cell that held a single person in the quiet lonely halls. Foley looked up from his sitting position on the dirt and straw-covered floor with a defeated expression. The Consort was a shadow of his earlier self—the bright, flamboyant colors of his outfit faded by dirt, smeared makeup, and disarrayed hair. Bradrick ordered the guard that stood by the door to bring him to the interrogation chamber down the next hall.

Bradrick intended to spend the coming days doing unspeakable things to glean every piece of information from Foley Osman. It was something he detested doing and avoided at all costs, but for this situation, he made an exception. He couldn't be weak so early on in his reign, nor could he tolerate threats that came from within his own house.

When Bradrick reached the interrogation chamber, the guard had already begun to strap Foley down onto a table that sat at the center of the room. The leather straps had held an uncertain number of people down under his mother's command—not that they ever lasted long enough to tell about it. It was a simple enough room meant for unpleasant things. It smelled as damp and musty as it looked, but it wasn't the worst of the options. As Bradrick walked around the perimeter of the room, he noticed that the room itself seemed quieter than the others. In the hall, he hadn't heard Foley's protests, which were somewhat muffled within the room as the guard finished strapping him down.

"You know your mother only acts in the best interest of the kingdom, my dear boy," Foley groaned as Bradrick dismissed the guard to stand at the door.

Bradrick ran his hand along the wall of tools before he tucked two behind his back and walked over to the disarrayed Consort. He lowered himself within an inch of the man's face. "For a long time, I think you have mistaken our relationship. Just because you took a place in my mother's bed doesn't mean you took my father's place or possessed an ounce of power. Let me be clear: I'm not your *dear boy*, I am your King."

With that, he began the agonizing process of extracting every detail possible from the man. By the end, Bradrick had a foul taste in his mouth. He might not have been a fan of torture, but he had a knack for it. Fortunately, Foley was quick to fold. When he was finally ready to crack, Bradrick summoned a scribe to the room. He hardly noticed the scribe's unflinching attention, likely a result of working under his mother. Within a matter of hours, which seemed like days, Foley dispelled the whole truth.

As he did, Bradrick wondered what few redeemable qualities a selfish man like Foley Osman possessed. His rise in status at court was a mystery to everyone, as much as his ability to garner Queen Indra's affections, one that would remain a puzzle not meant to be solved. Yet, before Foley spilled the details of a long-planned conspiracy, he struck a deal with Bradrick. He asked, not for his own life, but for Indra's to be spared; a flicker of nobility from a man who reportedly schemed his way to the top. The scribe took down each detail, which Bradrick ordered Foley to sign in blood. With everything finished, Bradrick felt as though he had satiated a strange hunger. His mind, though haunted by thoughts, finally gave way to sleep.

CHAPTER 31

Familiar voices echoed through the darkness with soft murmurs. The sense of existence faded in and out into the dark void of nothingness that was wrapped around Amirah. She could still feel the terrible burning in her body that consumed her in the pockets of silence. At some point, a familiar voice whispered close to her in the darkness. The words brought with it a warm caress and familiar scents—woods, fresh flowers, spices, and ginseng—words she could hear, but blended together in the void of endless black space. Overwhelming peace followed in the wake of their absence.

An unknown space of time later, the fresh scent of a garden breeze followed the sound of cloth moving as it danced in the wind. The warmth from unseen sunlight trickled through the layers of the open glass doors and sheer curtains that stirred her sense of existence. Her eyes took in the red backs of her eyelids and then the canopy above a bed as she opened them. Her skin prickled to life with the feel of the cool whisper of a mid-spring breeze. The croak of a groan that fell from her lips warned her of a long, unabated thirst. She became more aware of the luxurious surroundings that sheltered her in an otherwise lifeless room. A cry sounded from the other end of the room when she pushed away the plush comforter and sheet.

A maid rushed to her bedside, pulling the blankets back up. Amirah fixed her with a look, but the lady chided her with a tsk-ing sound. "Don't get up yet, Highness. The King has commanded I summon the Physician to examine you once you awoke."

"I need a drink," Amirah's voice cracked. She needed to whisper to keep from straining. "Please."

"Of course, my lady. I will tell the kitchen to send up food and drink."

Amirah relented at this and laid back. The room wavered and her stomach harbored a subtle ache, whether from hunger or residual illness, she couldn't tell. The maid rushed from the room and, not long afterward, the Physician hobbled in wearing his usual white habit. Years of knowledge etched his face, but there was life behind the beady eyes that looked at her with relief. A wide grin spread over his face.

"It will please King Bradrick that you are awake. Lord Alonzo is on the way to alert him as we speak. If I may, I'd like to examine you before he arrives." He gestured toward her arm. When she gave him her wrist, the examination began. He checked her pulse, her breathing, and prodded at her stomach and ribs. Then he observed all aspects of her head, including her mouth. The only points of interest seemed to be the lingering tenderness in her joints. "Do you know who you are?"

She chuckled at the peculiar question. "I am Queen Amirah Svana Landry of Brizia. What in the Twelve Kingdoms happened?"

"I think it might be best that I answer that question."

Bradrick stood in the doorway with his arms crossed, a smile spread across his face. Despite the upgrade in the title, he continued to dress like his old self; leather and clean, loose tunics cut from the finest woven fabrics. The only sign of his title was the golden ring on his finger and the crown that circled his head. The Physician cleared the room, noting as he left that, although Amirah seemed recovered, she should take it easy for a few days. Bradrick sat at her bedside and she tried to sit up, her stiff joints aching in protest.

"You should stay put for the time being." Bradrick frowned, an unfamiliar look of concern on his face.

She laid back into the pillows layered beneath her head. The small amount of energy she had gathered seeped out of her, along with any will to fight.

"What happened?" she asked him. The weak edge in her voice was unfamiliar to her.

"In short?" He paused at the rhetorical question before his eyebrows furrowed downward as he stared at her. "You were poisoned."

"Oh." Amirah gaped at him. It was difficult to find an appropriate response.

Bradrick chuckled at her passive acceptance. "That's enough for you, is it?"

"No," she admitted, "but it makes sense. My memory is fuzzy. I don't know how I got here."

"You were carried here from the throne room after your collapse. Our royal physician identified the cause of your sudden illness. We were without an available cure; helpless as you deteriorated. Ultimately, it was your Duke who saved you."

Amirah bolted upright, ignoring the pain that shot through her body. Her last fuzzy memory was of him in the throne room doorway before she could remember nothing else. She searched Bradrick's face with a questioning look as he nodded his head.

"You should tell Nithe he needs to work on his timing. I can't imagine the Brizian court members are going to be thrilled with frequent tardiness." A mischievous grin lit his face before he shifted to a more sobered expression. "There is a lot that you have missed. Once the tea my mother gave you was confirmed to be poison, the rest of the investigation was quick. She and Foley faced tribunal last night."

Amirah sucked in her breath with a grimace. Then she gave Bradrick an empathetic look of sorrow. "Bradrick, I'm sorry I—"

Bradrick held up his hand. "No, please don't apologize. This plot was a long time in the making. If it weren't for a deal Foley struck with me, the tribunal would have sentenced them to the sword. Instead, they will be exiled to an isolated island off our coast. Both have been stripped of titles and any remaining power. They will live out their life in hermitage. It's not death, but I hope the consequence will be sufficient for you."

Amirah thought of her father's demise. "As someone with both parents dead, especially one deserving of the fate they met, I could never fault you for saving your mother. It's hard to believe she would do something like this after years of pushing for our marriage. Bizarre, even."

"Power taints the mind. My mother planned to take out anyone she couldn't control. One day, that might have included me. When you went missing, their plan was to continue control over the crown through me and whoever I married. Part of the reason Foley never got further than being her Consort was because of my mother's love for power. After the inquisition into the poisoning, there was enough to convict them. However, Foley gave up his silence in exchange for their lives." Bradrick sighed, but a gentle smile turned his lips when he took her hand in his. "Now that this has passed, we have the freedom to make an honest decision."

Amirah's eyes widened. "We were both at the wedding, we both said the—"

"You never completed your vows." He squeezed her hand with a widening smile. "It means the ceremony is incomplete. I know that you are putting duty before your own well-being. My admiration of you has grown tremendously, and I love you the same way I did before your father died. Yet, my own feelings about marriage are unchanged. Therefore, I release you, Amirah. I release you from the contract of betrothal."

"What? Why? You know as well as I do what our kingdoms stand to gain if we marry." She shook her head in confusion.

"As King and Queen, we can guarantee our kingdoms remain allies. As King, I swear that Pruria will always be an ally to Brizia while the crown rests upon my head. We have the same gains through a written contract now that we both sit on the throne. What's more important is that you will always have a friend at your border. Two, counting Alonzo," he laughed. The sound rang through the room like a deep bell. There was an unmistakable glint in his eye as his laughter quieted. "We have the freedom we have longed for."

Amirah stared at the canopy of the bed she rested upon, as if she could find the answers to the world's problems somewhere above her. This would have a rippling effect on both kingdoms. She was the first Queen to inherit a throne by blood and not through a husband—the first to rule without marriage. Now, the long promise of one would be dashed away before her people's eyes. It came with the inherent risk of retaliation against her. One she would face head-on with a sword. She regarded how Bradrick carried the weight of his kingdom with confident grace and realized that the two of them had changed.

"Thank you," she whispered. She got up then, not considering the thin night dress someone had changed her into, and hugged him. Bradrick stiffened at the initial contract and faltered back a step as she wrapped her arms around him. "Thank you for everything, Bradrick."

"You're welcome." He hugged her back. Relief washed over him at the acceptance. Clearing his throat, he stepped back from the embrace. "Speaking of thanks, I should reward your Duke somehow. I already granted a pardon to mirror your own. It should prevent any potential distress about your father's death on Prurian soil if anyone makes the connection. Still, I feel it's not enough."

"He has very particular taste," she mused.

"Clearly," Bradrick gave her a pointed look.

She blushed but pretended not to catch the meaning as her mind recalled how he appeared before she collapsed. Even from a distance, the curse held power over his life. She grimaced at the thought. "Where is he?"

CHAPTER 32

Orange afternoon sunlight spilled into a simple, elegant bedroom that was bathed in cream paint and gold trim details. Amirah scanned every detail of the chambers adjacent to hers. The rooms appeared coordinated in the same fashion, including the furniture and linens, with some subtle exceptions. By now, she had each detail memorized.

Nithe rested beneath clean blankets on a canopy bed almost as large as the excessively plush one she had awakened in. The servants charged with his care had stripped and cleaned his olive-tanned skin as well as his clothes, leaving them mended on the bedside table. With them sat a Prurian bottle of spirits, left behind by Alonzo during a prior visit.

Amirah approached the bedside, as if drawn to it under a spell, and looked over his peaceful, chiseled face. The rhythmic rise and fall of his chest beneath the blankets comforted her against the guilt of causing him to be in this bedridden state. Unlike her room, no chairs sat beside his bed. If she attempted to drag one over, it might startle him awake. Despite having woken up days ago, the physician insisted on giving her restrictions and would frown upon her attempting to do such a thing. Still, she hoped every day to discover him conscious. Her delicate brows knitted as she wrestled with the feelings that churned in her stomach. None of which matched the other as they spun through her head in a relentless conflict.

Smoothing the emerald dress over her knees, she sat carefully on the edge of the bed. Nithe's black hair scattered about the pillow in a fan of long tendrils that normally hung below his shoulders. She brushed a stray lock of hair away from his forehead and tucked it behind his ear. The touch didn't disturb his sleep, and she wondered why he remained unconscious. Bradrick said he had given her the antidote but hadn't taken any himself. He healed faster than her the last time they were injured. *Why now does it seem he's suffered more than I did? Shouldn't we both have been cured?* she wondered.

Curse or not, she couldn't deny that the void haunting her chest for months now disappeared at the sight of him. Although her feelings might not be reciprocated, she was content with knowing he would respond if she were in danger—a small token of peace or, at least, a semblance of it.

Amirah stayed beside him for a time, though Bradrick had told her of a small banquet he was hosting tonight that would begin soon. Kamille had already helped her dress in the emerald-colored corset she now wore and had tied her hair halfway back with a matching silk ribbon. With Kamille's help, Gabbie made the simple style work with the silver crown. Prepared, she had nothing left to do but summon the will to leave Nithe's bedside. There would be a newfound tension from her court members tonight and being late would not help her impression upon anyone. The risk of furthering potential dissent motivated him to leave the peace of his chambers.

The banquet hall was full of smiling faces, some familiar and some not. A mass of nobility had gathered, most of whom wore deep-colored dinner attire, and took this banquet as a jovial celebration of Amirah's return to health. Each face beamed at her, their greetings filled with wishes for her good health. Food piled at the center of the tables in combinations of sweetmeats and savory sides. At the King's table, Bradrick stood enduring similar conversations with a wide-toothed grin.

His long ornate robe of bitter orange and gold offered the appeal of formal wear that was typical of his title, while also hiding his usual tunic and breeches. Amirah had finally reached his table after wading through the gathered crowd that was eager to speak with her and assumed the empty seat to Bradrick's left. Alonzo passed her a full goblet from the opposite side of Bradrick. She accepted it and took a deep drink. It satiated the constant thirst that followed her since she had returned to the waking world. Bradrick finished a conversation with one of his court members with a polite dismissal. When he rose to his feet, silence came over the room without the need to clank a glass or pound the table to call attention to him. All eyes turned to the table with keen interest.

Bradrick thanked everyone for attending the banquet, then raised his glass and waited for everyone to follow suit before he announced his toast. When a hush fell over the crowd of guests, he began.

"I want to thank everyone for their patience. These have been times of great sadness and confusion, but out of it, we have found ourselves resilient. We have found joy within the fog of despair and are better for it as we emerge into a new age. Tonight, raise your glasses, not in honor of me, but in honor of our kingdoms and the good health of our friends and allies."

After everyone drank, a murmur of conversation followed. When Bradrick did not return to his seat, the sound died out as looks of confusion passed around the tables. A lone cough from farther down the King's table drew a few gazes as Alonzo produced a scroll of papers from beside him. Following a drink, Bradrick took them in hand and looked at the crowd.

"The pages of this scroll are the contract for marriage between the Kingdom of Pruria and Brizia, signed by the former royals. Given the attempts on Amirah's life by one signee, these contracts are no longer valid. Furthermore, I hereby rescind the agreements and the

Prurian Crown's intent, releasing Queen Amirah from the contract. There will be no further attempts to achieve such a union between our houses."

The words fell over a hushed room as speechless faces looked upon them with a shock that shifted into varied other emotions. A unified gasp carried over the quiet as Bradrick dipped the scrolls into a candle flame and set it into a metal bowl. The onlookers stared as the fine roll of papers turned to ash before the entire room. Even Amirah's mouth gaped at the display. Bradrick looked around the room with an expression of indifference. A murmur passed between clusters of people at the tables, each arguing over details they saw outside of the act of marriage.

"What about the alliance between our kingdoms?" one Brizian noble asked.

"As King and Queen of our two perspective kingdoms," Bradrick started as he held out a hand to Amirah, who stood and sent a smile out toward every table, "we are committed to this long-held alliance. Instead of marriage, we will forge a contract as allies to cement a bond between our kingdoms that is greater than that offered by the previous arrangement. Both parties will maintain their benefits and our neighboring friendship will become stronger than it has been in generations."

Those present turned back to their discussions, their tone different from before. It sounded lighter than Amirah expected, and the nodding of several heads allowed her and Bradrick to resume their seats in confidence. Alonzo and Bradrick shared a smirk of victory as everyone began moving about the room, taking new audiences at neighboring tables.

Alonzo moved to the empty seat beside Amirah when Bradrick's attention became preoccupied with another Prurian noble. He passed her one of the warm dinner rolls before he continued to load his plate. Amirah smiled as she watched him set the full plate on the table.

"Do you think there is enough for seconds?" she asked.

He shrugged. "Not sure about this batch. However, there is plenty left in the kitchen. You do know you can ask the servants to take him a tray up, right?"

Red colored Amirah's cheeks. "I thought I would take something small in case he wakes up. Although, I was more thirsty than anything when I came back to reality."

"Never underestimate a man's stomach." He tore off a chunk of bread and followed it with a deep drink from his goblet. Then, a second later, he leaned in closer and whispered, "I have a confession to make."

"Oh?" An amused smile twisted Amirah's lips.

"I think the two of you are blind. You and Nithe see each other without seeing each other. Now that you are free to open your eyes, you should do so."

She let out a nervous chuckle. "I'm not exactly sure what you are suggesting, Alonzo."

"Look at me, Amirah." He gave her a sobering stare. "You're a dutiful Queen. You put your people first and betray your own heart. Yes, Bradrick asked me to escort you to and from Brizia, but it was Nithe who asked me first. Before we left that castle, he entrusted me with your shared secret and asked me to protect you. Which, I might add, I was a miserable failure at doing. We all were. I hope both of you will forgive me for it."

"There is nothing to forgive," she said as she patted his arm. "But if you feel in need of my forgiveness, you have it. I do not need constant protectors. I may have been a naïve Princess in the beginning, but now I am a Queen. It is my burden to be perceptive and guard myself, which I can do on my own."

"Everyone needs someone to watch their backs. He isn't a bad choice."

There was a heaviness to her sigh; a brief lapse in her mask where the troubled depths of her heart's mind were visible as her head tilted upward to search the ceiling. "That might be true. I can't ask him to do what he has already done for me for the better part of a year. I know I was a complication in his plans—a liability. When we couldn't find a way to break the curse, I no longer interested him. His recent arrival was because of the ties of the curse. I was almost the death of us both, and I won't ask more of him because of it."

"Doubtful! All of it. Both of you have built walls around yourselves for your own reasons. No man is dense enough to ask for protection for someone they don't hold a flame for. Not the way he did. They especially wouldn't oppose their marriage to a King."

Amirah's mouth gaped in surprise, and her eyes became saucers of shocked disbelief. "He didn't!"

"Oh, but he did." The bright smile on Alonzo's face widened with the increased burning in her cheeks. "He did indeed."

The words registered with a deep ring of truth that sent her heart fluttering. Her eyes darted around the room as if to search for something or someone, but no one seemed to notice the onset of wild panic that stole her mind. When she turned back to glean more details, Alonzo had already left her alone at the table.

She was in no state or mood to deal with the onslaught of inebriated questions from either court's nobility. Gabbie and Kamille had both disappeared into the night, Bradrick was smiling through the conversation he carried with the crowd that gathered around him, and her best option was to retire for the night. Not wanting to disturb anyone, she rose quietly from her seat and left without drawing attention to herself.

She had noticed that her personal guards had rotated out with some of the Prurian guards. The constant presence of well-meaning soldiers outside her door made her feel like she was under lock and key but her closed chambers brought a sense of peace that outweighed the discomfort of constant vigilance. Soon, the promised contract would be signed before the end of her trip, signifying an end to her time here, and she would return with her court to Brizia.

The unrestricted safety of the bedroom offered solace to sort, through her thoughts as she prepared for bed, and her lungs breathed in relief when the corset gown fell away. The replacement was a soft black nightgown of almost sheer fabric that flowed away from the snug, fitted strip of fabric around her chest. The design was more revealing than she was used to wearing, but she relished the comfort of it. Her long ginger hair fell past her shoulders when released the loose waves from the ribbon and when she finally laid down, they spread around her like a wild halo. Yet, the moment her head touched the pillow, her thoughts became louder.

She tossed and turned into the night while Alonzo's revelations tunneled into her heart and made a home there. The idea of sleep taunted her from the twinkling starlight outside her windows. When she burrowed beneath the blankets, she thought of the warmth of darkness that enveloped her whenever Nithe had embraced her. A pang of guilt nagged her for not checking on him before going to bed. She hadn't asked the kitchen to send him a tray and wondered if they would have done it without her instruction. Unable to take much more of the incessant worry, she threw off the covers and slipped a matching silk robe over her nightgown.

When her head poked out of her chambers, she saw the length of the hall disappeared into the darkness except for a few candlelit sconces on each end. She could see the back of a guard as he marched on patrol down the corridor. She shut the door with the handle remaining turned to prevent it from giving away her movements. A neighboring Queen was no exception to life at court. Each step toward the adjacent door was a threat to the current state of peace she felt since discretion in private movements kept rumors from the political floor. With the marriage contract dissolved, interest in what she did unsupervised would increase. She considered it might be better if she weren't fighting rumors off before she returned home with the news.

When the door to Nithe's chambers clicked shut, she breathed a sigh of relief. Except for a single candle on the sitting room table, the room was dark. A tray of food from the banquet sat beside the candle, waiting to be consumed. Someone had added extra bread rolls to the pile. She took the tray and candle into the bedroom where Nithe rested beneath the blankets. Candlelight illuminated the room with a soft, orange-tinted glow as she set the tray on top of the dresser. One servant had rotated him onto his side so that he faced the window so that Amirah sat on the now vacant side of the bed. The space between them was more than there had been in the tents during the voyage to Isidris. She studied the steady rise and fall of his breath, unsure of why or how long she lingered on the edge of the bed. One moment turned into another and, before she had the chance to realize it, the lure of exhaustion consumed her.

CHAPTER 33

A soft growl that purred in Amirah's ear interrupted the fabric of her dreams and emanated from the darkness where a warmth snaked around her torso like a blanket. She felt an urge to bolt upright at the warm, prickling sensation that tickled the back of her neck and she struggled to roll away from it in her sleep. The arm helped her roll over as her eyes opened and her breath hitched when her fingers felt a wall of flesh beneath them. She gasped at the sight of heavy-lidded green eyes that bore into her.

Delight and relief washed over Amirah as her face brightened at the sight of Nithe awake. If his arms hadn't weighed her down, she would have tackled him with a hug. She moved her hand away from his bare chest, curling it into her own. Her face reddened, realizing all that stood between them was the sheet and her satin robe-covered night clothes. The expression on her face changed from joy to mortification, causing a light chuckle rolled from Nithe's throat as she gaped for words.

"I-I'm sorry. I didn't mean to fall asleep here," she stammered.

"You mean you were watching over me?" His eyes twinkled down at her when he spoke. The slight tilt of his head when he quirked an eyebrow made her stomach flip.

Her mouth opened, ready to argue, but she paused, realizing he was correct. The crooked smirk on his face widened when she nodded. What she didn't realize was that he had been awake for a while watching over her. The color of death that had washed over them was now replaced with the burning shades of life. That brush of mortality drew them nearer in this moment as they reveled in the sight of each other. The flame in Amirah's core flickered to life, alert to their proximity and ready to spread if fanned. Her face attempted to summon the facade of regal propriety as if she weren't lying in the naked man's bed.

"It was the least I could do as your Queen to return the favor of saving our lives." Amirah shrugged against him.

Her mask slipped when his arm tightened around her. His embrace was firm but gentle; safe but dangerous as it kindled something within her. She bit her lip as his face drew so close that their noses nearly touched. His eyes narrowed in on the movement, a low hum emanating from him.

"That's the least you could do?" Amusement lit the morning rasp in his voice, sending a shiver down Amirah's spine. Although the question was rhetorical, Nithe lifted his eyebrows expectantly. Her head bobbed, but he could see through her lie and a serious tone replaced the playful note in his voice. "Understand there is no equivalent exchange between us. No such thing could exist, and not because of the curse. I placed too much blame on that to avoid the truth of what was happening. I fought every instinct to follow you. I forced a distance that should have erased every feeling I thought the curse had fabricated. Still, the pull to you managed to reach me."

"If that were true, why didn't you reply?"

Amirah's words trembled, and disbelief creased between her brows. The tiered wall of protection that fought to keep the stronghold around her heart shuttered at the hint of truth. Her words belayed the many things her wretched mind whispered to explain the pain of his absence. She didn't push him away, and yet, his head reared back as if she had slapped him. Several unreadable emotions flicked over his face until he settled on her with fixed attention.

"There isn't an excuse or valid reason. I was a fool for fighting the urge to come to your side and keep you for myself." The growl in his voice hinted at anger that wasn't toward her. "I won't ask your forgiveness. My actions put you in danger. I see that now. Even if it was the curse, or even if you didn't want my affection, I should have been at your side when you returned. I should have been here."

"Affection?" Her attention caught on the word.

A wicked grin spread across his face at the question. Every hair stood on end when he brought his lips next to her ear. His breath tingled against her skin, igniting her senses like the kindling of a flame. "Yes. Of all the times I have touched you, held you, and even when I kissed you, it was a taste of the longing for you that pulled at my soul. I would give every bit of the essence of my wretched existence to you if you asked it of me. "

She couldn't repress the sound of the gasp that escaped her lips before he pulled back. The candlelight had flickered out and left them in the gray-blue light in the early hours before dawn, but even in the dim light, she couldn't hide the glassy sheen in her eyes. Every fear she had was rebuked with the raw words that pummeled at the gate around her heart as it fought to keep the walls from crumbling—a last stand as Amirah and Nithe balanced on a precipice at the moment. She shifted and glanced over that edge with a guarded heart that feared where they would land.

"When you didn't respond, I thought your feelings weren't the same as my own," she confessed, the vulnerable words bringing her near to tears. "When you returned because I almost got us killed, I thought of how much of a burden and liability I'd become for you."

"See how foolish I have been?" Nithe shook his head. His eyes never left her as he propped his head up on his free arm so that his face was now above hers. Threads of his black hair cascaded down like a curtain to mingle with her own. "For all the fight and distance in the world, there is no life without you, Amirah. Not because of the curse, but because my world is empty without you. I was doomed even before I knew who you were the moment our eyes met. Curse or not, I need you. All of you. Everything and nothing. If you ask me for it, I will give it. I will take every burden you have to give me if it means I can stay by your side. All or nothing."

Amirah's breath hitched at his words as a whirlwind of emotions slammed into her. She saw the searing honesty behind his eyes and the walls inside her crumbled away, and though her eyes watered, no tears followed. His words stoked the starved flame like oxygen within her. She could feel them about to tip over that edge. Once they fell, she knew they could never go back.

One of her hands slid over the muscles of his bare chest when his face dipped toward hers. There was a darkness that flickered in the depths of his green eyes, a primal glint that studied her.

"What will it be?" he whispered.

A question. A challenge. A promise.

No matter the answer, they were about to fall.

"All of me," she answered. "If that includes all of you."

He smiled. "It does."

CHAPTER 34

Nithe tore them from the edge they had been teetering on, sending them in a free fall as his lips met hers. They crashed together like a rolling wave, each caress leaving a prickling trail of excitement on Amirah's skin. Nithe's hand slid from his head to cup her jaw as he devoured her. His tongue grazed her upper lip, earning a soft moan from her. The kiss deepened by the insurgence of his tongue, coaxing hers to dance with him. She reveled in the taste of him as he washed over her and her hand slid from his chest around his neck as the burning fire spread heat through her body, relentless and full of need. When he pulled away, she couldn't help the whimper of disappointment.

He grinned, a mischievous hunger in the look. Using the arm encircling her waist, he shifted their bodies so that one of his legs was pinned between her thighs and his hips pressed against hers. They were close enough that she could feel the hardness of him as it lengthened beneath the blanket. He pushed his hair back as his face angled toward her again and she shuddered when his mouth met the sensitive skin of her neck. A fresh wave of sweet torment came with each caress of his tongue and nibble of flesh.

An unhindered moan purred from her throat as his hand pushed away the robe from her shoulder and he began working his mouth down from neck to collarbone. She arched into his touch as his lips moved over the thin cloth of the nightgown that hugged her breast. A hungered groan came from his throat as one hand molded over her other breast while his mouth found the peak of her nipple beneath the black cloth with a teasing exploration of his lips. Her hips moved, rolling with the sensations that trickled from his every caress. A grunt of pleasure escaped him as her hips pressed against him like a wanton nymph and his lips traveled back up in a trail of sensual kisses. Her skin was on fire, lit by the graze of his hand as it moved away from her breast in a path down to her navel. A shiver ran up her spine as his fingertips brushed the flimsy cloth that tangled around her legs. He pulled his head back, face alight with deviant need.

"I never told you how ravishing you look in black."

A blush tinted her face beneath a wild smile. She propped herself up on one elbow and traced a single finger from his chest to his now-exposed navel, and he hissed at the touch.

"Ravishing, am I?" she asked.

"Completely," he purred. "May I?"

She nodded and the warmth of his fingers slipped beneath the tangled hem of her nightgown. Slow burning trails followed the wake of his long fingers, firm and direct in their hunt to find the center of her heat. A curse slipped through her lips at his touch, her head falling back onto the bed. His fingers encircled her mound and moved with expertise as he hummed in approval at the way she responded when he stroked her clit with a rhythmic glide of his fingers. A mewl came from her as he rubbed her clit until her heat pooled into his hand.

"Perfection," he growled before his lips crashed into hers once again.

The fingers that were soaked in her wetness came up to brush her mouth. She took his index finger into her mouth, tasting her slickness intermingled with his flesh. A sound emanated from him, a mix between a groan and growl as he dipped a second finger in, eyes fixated upon her. Something within her felt feral with need, and, as if he could read her thoughts from his half-straddle position over her, he leaned close to her face.

"Tell me what you want, Amirah," he demanded as he pushed himself back. The blanket fell away from him, and she let her eyes wander over his exquisite form. She paused on his full erection, her eyes widening with the desire to touch and taste. When her hands reached for him, he pinned them on either side of her head. She gave him a look of bereft confusion, but the raise of his eyebrows prompted her to answer.

"You," she panted. "I want you."

"We already established that. I mean, tell me what you want *now*, Princess."

"Queen," she corrected with a brief flicker of annoyance.

"Queens make demands and give orders. Right now, you're not doing that. You need to be specific about what you want. Remember, I said: ask me for it." The mischievous glint in his eye danced with amusement.

"No, no, no. That's not what you meant when you said it." She flushed.

"I meant every possible interpretation, including that. But if that's not what you want, then I can continue where I left off."

Another wicked grin flashed over his face and he moved her wrists above her head, his long fingers of one hand pinning them to the bed. Her mouth dropped open as she watched the flex of his muscles as he trailed his free hand down her body. He untied the robe that had already half abandoned her body and even with the thin clothes of her nightgown; she felt exposed. The gown remained pushed up from his previous explorations, exposing the bare skin of her thighs. He released her wrist and repositioned himself at her feet. This time, there was no exploring as he leaned over, exposed her mound, and devoured her with fervor. His lips came down on her with that same ferocity and his fingers pressed into the sensitive folds of her heat. The firm pressure of his thumb as it circled her clit sent her over the edge and she cried out in ecstasy, reaching the peak of pleasure before crashing down. It didn't diminish the second wave that coiled in her core when he continued. Each stroke against her heat was a faster demand for more until her hips began rocking. She bucked against him, searching for the right friction.

"Please," she moaned out.

"Please, what?" It wasn't a question, but a demand.

Waves of desire coursed through her as Nithe dragged her near the edge once more, but refused to let her fall. Each time, she writhed beneath his hand, building closer to that peak, only to be shoved back. One of her hands slid down between them, wrapping around his length, and he stiffened, surprise and pleasure twisting his face. He faltered and released a low growl that felt like velvet against the skin. She pumped his length, which made him buck against her hand in erotic pleasure. He released her sweet core and pulled her hand away.

"Not yet, Princess," he chided in a husky voice.

"I need you, Nithe. Please," she whimpered in a desperate plea for release.

"How do you need me? Where?"

Her mound throbbed—an ache not yet quenched that demanded relief. Amirah huffed, but there was no edge to it. Nithe let the errant wrist go and watched the subtle tremble of excitement in her body that followed in the wake of his hand as it slid over her curves. He kneaded her breast as his mouth ducked to consume hers again. She drank in the taste of him as he devoured her, and when he tugged at her hips possessively, she gasped against his lips. He pinned her bucking hips with one hand, and with the other, left a trail of sparks as it ventured back to her sensitive folds. Her breath stilted in ecstasy when he found her clit and toyed with it. She tried to repress the moan that escaped her throat.

"I want to feel you," she panted. A furious blush colored her face as she explained, "Inside me."

"There it is," he hissed. His teasing fingers moved away to rub a piece of her gown between his index and forefinger. "But first, I want this off."

She couldn't help the surprised expression on her face. With a lick of her lips, she gave a slow nod of submission. He released her and sat back with an arm draped over his knee. He looked like an ethereal being that should have been carved from polished stonework, poised like the statues in the courtyard of the Duke's Castle—dark, masculine, and every alluring inch of him displayed with easy confidence. Sitting upon her knees, she drank in the sight of him.

There was a brief glint of viridescent light in his eyes when he flicked his wrist and caused a slight breeze to tug at the dangling ties to her robe. It slipped from her arms as she shifted and tugged with slow, deliberate precision at the fabric around her arms. She smirked, her own dark desire dancing as she watched the hunger darken his green eyes when they followed the movement. The strip of black around her chest fell away to hang on her hips, and with a push from her hands on each side, she pulled it to her knees. She turned to swing her legs over the side of the bed and held the fabric in place as she stood on the floor. Then, she bent to drag the bunched fabric of the gown down to her ankles. An excited chill ran down her spine when he groaned at the sight of her on full display.

Piles of fabric now at her feet, she turned and crawled her way back over the bed. She watched his intentionally slow approach. His eyes danced with deviant thoughts, matching his fully displayed approval. A finger slipped under her chin and she followed the gentle guide up to him. He bent his towering form to meet her and their lips coalesced into a roaring wave of heat that added fuel to the fire.

A slow burn turned into a fevered dance that spoke of longing that was filled with endearment.

"I love you," she whispered against his lips when the kiss slowed to a cinder.

The feather-ight words offered affirmation, fueling the intensity between them like fresh kindling to a fire. Nithe kissed her again, the touch of their lips speaking more than simple words. Unabated, raw emotion trickled between the collisions. He pulled her closer with the hands that caressed her body in a concerto of heated desire. One of his hands grasped her hips, the other encircled her torso, his fingers pressing firm into her skin as he guided their descent toward the mattress in fluid movements. She couldn't help it when she grabbed his shoulders, stomach churning with butterflies as he tugged her with him. Yet, his hands guided them down until she straddled on top of him and his body formed a shield beneath her.

Her bottom lip caught between his teeth, a gentle nibble that pulled a soft moan from her throat. She needed more, and he gave it willingly—more sucking, more biting, as if Nithe wanted to devour her. Her hips sought friction against her sensitive apex as his erection teased just below her slick entrance. The sensation of it as it grazed her flesh tightened the coil and sent moisture pooling between her thighs. His fingers traced up the curve of her neck and bunched the hair at her nape. She froze at the sudden broken contact of his lips from her own. The flick of his tongue against the sweet spot behind her ear made her whimper. She could feel the feral smile on his face as he teased the spot.

"Take what you want, Princess." The husky rasp of his voice against her ear made the coil with her tighten further. "Take it."

With the command, his hips tipped upward, the tip of his erection nudging against her opening. He tilted her head back toward him until their noses and foreheads touched as Amirah lifted her body to angle over him. They stared into each other's eyes as she sank down until he was buried to the hilt. A shiver of pleasure rolled down her spine as she adjusted to the fullness of him and Nithe hissed through his teeth. They sat there, staring into one another for a moment before his entangled fingers released her to stroke her face.

His hips bucked, encouraging her to move against him. She responded with slow, steady rolls as his deliberate languid thrusts drove rivulets of ecstasy through her—a dance in perfect tandem that sped up with frequency. He groaned at her delicious responses and the pinch of her nails as they dug into his back. She drove down onto him while his hands clamped onto her hips, giving and taking everything they could with each tandem thrust in synchronized balance. She leaned into him against a wave of pleasure as it rippled through her while his mouth sought hers like a ravenous beast. A flurry of uninhibited moans tore from her throat as their movements became fevered. His moan against her lips drove her to oblivion, and she cried out. The feel of him swelling inside of her until her walls clamped around him drove them closer to the edge. Even as she neared the apex, his hands slammed her hips against him to push him deeper, harder, and faster, again and again, until she writhed against him. The final thrusts threw them from the edge in a blissful free fall of exploding stars as he pulsed within her.

His breath shook as he kissed her forehead. They lay there, intertwined together for what seemed to be an eternity—a bubble of frozen time sheltered from the world. Amirah's head rested on his chest, her hands toying with a stand of his long black hair. The hollow space in her heart filled with truth, his confession, and left her marveling at the road that led them up to this point until her eyes shut. There was more to discuss, more to explore, but for now, they resigned themselves to the peace of the moment. Their minds burned it to memory until they drifted to sleep.

It wasn't until late morning that they returned to consciousness. Amirah and Nithe jerked awake at the sound of the door clicking open, followed by a trio of chattering maids stepping into the room. A shriek from one pulled the other's eyes forward and their footsteps froze when they saw the bare forms of Amirah and Nithe enthralled in each other's limbs without a scrap of cloth to cover them. Amirah and Nithe glanced from maids to each other. Then, without a word, the women retreated from the chambers. Amirah threw an arm over her eyes.

"So much for preventing rumors at court," she mused.

Nithe chuckled. He pecked her lips, her cheek, and trailed a line of kisses to her delicate collar cone. "They'll have plenty to talk about while I'm around."

Her eyes brows ticked up at his tease and the realization that something else hid beneath his words. Her hand toyed with his hair and a gentle tug drew his attention. He came back to her, recognizing the vulnerability in her gaze.

"Are you coming back to the capital with me?"

"Yes," he answered without a pause or waver. The word struck like a bell tolling as his eyes bore into hers without blinking. "We can go after I deal with our attempted murderer."

She shook her head at him. "It's already been dealt with."

"The King's mother? Dealt with?" Nithe scoffed in disbelief and shook his head.

"It was. Bradrick ordered for her and her companion to be arrested the same day. A tribunal happened while we were both incapacitated."

He looked surprised at the news. "I didn't think he was capable of killing, let alone his own mother."

"He didn't." She caught the dark irritation shift over him. "Her companion betrayed them to save her life, and they struck a deal. I'm not sure if Bradrick realizes it yet, but she might have received a fate worse than death."

"They are a threat to you as long as they are alive," he argued.

"When someone who had the world eating from the palm of her hand loses everything and has to live with the consequences of their actions, it is more difficult than the ease of death. While it might seem insignificant for her punishment to be living out the remainder of her life in a hermitage on a tiny forsaken isle, she lost so much more. Not only did she lose all of her power and influence that stretched beyond the Continent, but she also lost her son. Her *son*, Nithe. Somewhere behind all the scheming and manipulation, there was a mother who once loved her son. I don't know how long it will be before she reflects upon that, but it won't be any different when that day finally comes. When it does, the regret will eat at her lonely heart in that isolation."

Nithe considered this for a moment before he sighed, the darkness in his mind relenting. "Alright, I can see a point. I'll let the Prurians deal with their own for now, but only because you ask it of me. I made a promise, so this is an act of good faith. However, if they ever step off that isle, I will kill them myself."

Amirah smiled at him. "And I will help you do it."

CHAPTER 35

Amirah and Nithe remained in Pruria a full day after the completion of the contract for alliance to join the celebrations. News poured out from Pruria into the Continent. Bradrick's announcement and variations of the story that surrounded Indra's involvement in Amirah's brush with death held lasting interest throughout the Continent. It was no surprise that the Brizian nobility who had come for the wedding sent word back to those who remained in the capital. What surprised Amirah was the welcoming crowds that gathered to rejoice in her return to health and the kingdom, making her return far from a quiet affair. This was something she had never seen under her father's rule. The warmth that spread through her heart made her hope the people's endearment would stay the length of her tenure. She promised herself to do everything she could to achieve that.

Nithe held true and stayed by her side, much to the chagrin of the court members. His presence alone caused a stir before he even stepped foot into the carriage home. The title, pardon, and slowly improving relationship with King Bradrick bought a berth of silence from her people until they reached the Capital.

In Brizia, news of a new Duke accompanying the Queen spread, along with everything that transpired at the Prurian palace. People looked upon Nithe with curiosity more than anything else as they passed through the welcoming masses. Few remembered Nithe's father or made any connection between them.

It was the court members who displayed any mix of displeasure. Most of which came from the fact that their young Queen had played them with enough finesse to secure his position—even if it was rightful. Even if the maids in Pruria said nothing of what they saw that morning. However, Brizians began to whisper about his close companionship when Amirah was out of earshot. Even Gabbie wondered about the constant presence of the enigmatic man beside her Queen. She watched Nithe and Amirah with piqued interest but avoided prying and silenced anyone getting too carried away with gossip.

Nithe concealed his magic around everyone except Amirah, but there was still the occasional breeze that would erupt indoors or in the gardens that playfully tugged at her in public. After which, Amirah would chuckle to herself as everyone would look around the room in bewilderment. She enjoyed their private moments of reprieve and stolen kisses as usual activities resumed following their arrival.

The first Meeting of Nobility brought stacks of papers for Amirah to shift through; a task that consumed the better part of the day. While the nobles took their leave for a mid-day meal, she stayed behind to finish the review. The food stores had promising signs of growth; she had worked with one lord to expand the plan to include storage for droughts and shortages. The parchment in her hand included a civilian stabilization project that required her authorization. She finished attaching her name to the last paper when everyone reconvened. As everyone took their seats, she handed the project proposal and plans off to a youthful lord that sat to the left of her. Nithe joined them and took his seat to her right.

Amirah glanced at him as he contemplated a particular passage of the document in front of him. His transition into the role his title demanded quelled conflicts, and his impassive nature left the members exasperated. Amirah and Nithe had been careful not to unintentionally disclose their private affairs. However, rumors had begun to circulate the castle. She knew the issue would need to be dealt with before it grew out of control and turned into a scandal.

As she smoothed a wrinkle that had formed on her red skirts, the lord with a youthful face brought forward another small stack of papers. He nervously shifted on his feet as she took it from him. She raised an eyebrow at the awkward exchange as he scurried back to his seat between his two elder noblemen. One laughed haughtily, clapping him on the back, and suspicion prickled down Amirah's spine as she looked at the papers he had given her.

The first two pages looked to be a list of names, specifically of men from noble houses, some of which she recognized. Beside each name was a brief subtext profiling the individual. The third page was a proposal outline signed by less than a third of the court. She reread the document to be assured she hadn't misunderstood, but the purpose was perfectly clear. Her eyebrows scrunched together as she stood and drew everyone's attention.

"What is this?" Her voice quivered as she shook the papers. The subtle hint of suppressed rage drew Nithe's attention. When no one answered, Amirah rolled the papers into a singular scroll and pointed it at the nobleman who had brought it to her. Speaking to him through gritted teeth, she demanded, "Explain."

He flinched and shifted under the full scrutiny of the room. "Apologies, Your Majesty. My understanding is that it's a collective list of bachelors in suitable stations that was put together by the Lords for—"

"Me, perchance?" She arched her eyebrows and pursed her lips, silencing the rhetorical question. Her attention turned back to the court and a few of the Lords looked away in guilt. "Do I look like a prize to you? To any of you? Is that how you see your Queen, a royal-blooded woman, or any woman at all?"

Nithe stiffened in his seat beside her but said nothing as he cast a dark glare around the room. Amirah continued, uncertain of how he might react. If they made a mistake, they could unintentionally reveal their private relations before either of them was ready to deal with the fallout. Court politics held power over her life more than it ever had before, and she needed to end that. She thought there would be more time, but time was a fickle thing. Lord Theorin stood up opposite her. *Of course*, she thought.

"Majesty, we meant no offense and did not intend to upset you." Lord Theorin began with a calm air of authority he had not possessed when she had returned to claim the throne. The false smile on his face irked her. "This proposal is about the security of the kingdom, not about you personally. As the last of your bloodline, it's imperative to produce an heir to keep the throne secure, thereby keeping our kingdom secure. Please consider the candidates the Lords have proposed at your leisure. There is no rush. "

Amirah shook her head with a sarcastic smile. "Indeed, there is no rush. Tell me, Theorin, has everyone in this room been privy to this petition disguised as a proposal, or just the men who think it's within their authority to advise me?"

A crack appeared in the old man's facade as he failed to continue with his forced smile. "No, not everyone, Majesty. We gathered enough support for it to be presented to you."

Amirah passed the papers over to Nithe. His face remained blank, but she caught the subtle tick in his jaw as he reached the third page. Their eyes met for a moment before she continued. "If a petition or proposal of any other sort were to come before my desk, the whole of the Brizian court would be included. We should, therefore, include everyone else present in this one. While this little conspiratorial attempt is passed around, let it be known that I decline the proposal. My answer is final, and that answer is no."

The elderly Lord beside the young nobleman rose to his feet. He stood less than half a foot taller than her in his age and barely tipped his head in a quick bow to her. It was more an act of formality than respect for Amirah, and they both knew it.

"Your Majesty, it doesn't matter if the entire room is aware. You are being asked to ensure the security of our kingdom by the body of this court. Brizia would benefit from the reinvigoration of your bloodline. A male heir—"

"Enough," Nithe cut in, his voice laced with venom. All eyes turned upon him as his chair scraped the floor. He rolled the papers up and passed them back to Amirah, who watched him with intrigue. "It's a wonder that anything gets done with this court. Schemes and plots are simply well-intentioned roads for selfish benefit. The prior King excelled at that and it appears those of you who happen to still live are not. If you weren't such cowards, you would have proposed this openly, to begin with. Since you presented this matter to the Queen without proper entry before the court, then it is for her alone to decide if it's accepted."

Lord Paget, who sat absorbing the information spilling before him, joined with Nithe. "That's correct. Procedurally, if a petitioning party submits a proposal or petition to the crown without involving the court in whole, no member of the court shall have the right to voice the matter, and the final ruling is left to the crown."

Nithe sported a wicked grin. "Well, then you have your answer, gentlemen."

Nithe resumed his seat with a dark look of satisfaction as the elder nobleman stuttered, but didn't dare argue with him. It was Lord Theorin who had a false sense of security when he dared move to speak again, but Amirah had enough of his antics. While she didn't have a sword in hand like the last time he had challenged her, she was no less able to cut him down. Transparently several of her court members thought it wise to become snakes. They slithered outside of the walls of her home, plotting to enforce their will upon her. What they forgot was that she was there to rule, not to *be* ruled. Least of all by the men who thought of her more as a broodmare than their Sovereign Queen. Amirah spoke before the lord could utter a word.

"Lord Theorin, this is the second time you have made an issue of my marital status. Since your initial objection to my claim to the throne, I have ruled without a husband, proving I am more than capable of doing so. I made it clear what would happen should you challenge my rule again, and for some reason, you have chosen to do just that. Each signature on this proposal is from those who think it is appropriate to advise me on the Kingdom's security, when this court barely held itself together, let alone all of Brizia, before I returned. You bring a petition against me without the consideration that a marriage could undo all the progress we have made since I assumed the throne. There is no proposal that could be made where my answer will be anything different. If I want a husband, then I will take one. If I want a child, then I will have one. If I want to sleep with half of the Continent to achieve that or for the sake of my own desires, then I will do so." A noise between a grunt and a cough came from Amirah's right. She could feel Nithe's gaze as he stared at her, but she didn't dare turn to meet it at that moment. "This court will have no input into the affairs of my bedroom *or* my marital status, nor will I allow it to be weaponized against my position."

"This isn't about your rule, your personal affairs, or your gender. There is no directive on who rules in your stead, and you have no advisors to offer your guidance, so we tenured court members must make up for that flaw. We don't have to crown whoever you wed as King. So long as an heir is produced, the throne remains secured by—"

"Your Queen has already given her answer!" Nithe's voice boomed with an ominous undertone. It carried a darkness that matched his face and Lord Theorin's mouth snapped shut.

"So having no advisor is the reason you keep spearheading these attempts to usurp my crown? It appears we need to make some adjustments to address these matters. First, I appoint Lord Nithe Sorgin as my advisor, and Lord Paget as my second counsel. Do both of you accept?" Amirah looked at each of them, who nodded in agreement. "Secondly, there is no diversity in the age or gender of this court. If the court has no equality, then it cannot justly represent its own people. I will resolve this by appointing new heads to the vacant seats belonging to the three new territories in the western part of our kingdom. There will be no less than two women appointed."

She picked up the roll of papers and tapped her desk with it.

"I have been upon the throne not yet a full year, and some of you continue to work against my interest. A viper is loyal to no one but himself. I am inclined to remind you why that is a mistake, but my words tend to fall upon deaf ears. If you want to ensure the kingdom's security, then make certain even the neediest of children within your territories are cared for. I'm not a broodmare to be given as a prize. I am your Queen. If you want security, start with loyalty."

No one dared breathe a word as she dipped the roll of papers into the edge of the dancing candle flame. Nithe passed her a metal bowl, and she set it at the center of her desk so everyone could watch as it burned into a pile of ash. Lord Theorin resumed his seat with a deep-set frown of defeat and once the roll of papers burned away, Amirah dismissed the nobles. No one objected as they scurried from the room like nervous rats. *That's exactly what they are, the whole lot of them,* Amirah thought.

Nithe, who lingered behind with her, showed nothing short of pride when she looked up at him. He was the one person who might ever hold any power over her. *Power indeed,* she thought when a playful smirk twisted his lips. He bent down with a dangerous glint and whispered teasingly in her ear, "Sleep with half of the court, eh?"

CHAPTER 36

The end of summer brought much-needed changes to the Brizian court. Amirah had hand selected the new members of the court and with it, power shifted in her favor. Although there remained some tension and unease with her father's remaining members, Nithe's presence quelled their vocalized attempts to control her. He commanded respect in a way that gave her a fever pitch and the result caused her to flourish behind closed doors. His position came with the authority over the court that didn't need a crown. Instead, he acted as an impenetrable wall that surrounded her from opposition.

With his promoted title, he brought life back into his lands; a project which required him to depart from the capital. He was less than pleased that Amirah had stayed behind. It wasn't their first disagreement about her safety since he had joined her at the capital. The fact that it remained unclear which of the court members placed the bounty on her head before she ascended remained a hovering issue. She knew Nithe despised leaving her in a castle full of conspirators. The work required of them superseded the risk, so she agreed to keep the dagger he had gifted her strapped to her at all times. In the Duke's territory, the wood-dwelling villages needed direction to be rebuilt, and the castle needed attention. This required Nithe to remove the glamoured barrier surrounding the Duke's Castle and lake. Despite the abundance of the area, food stores need to be built for his territory as well. Each task was a long endeavor alone.

Gabbie began attending the Meetings of Nobility as Lady Paget. Her father was preparing her to take his seat as his successor, but he would continue to act as the Queen's second advisor. Amirah was glad to have another friend at court. After the last meeting, Kamille stepped in time beside them when they entered the hall. The trio had been inseparable since her arrival. Amirah spent an increased amount of time with them to distract herself from Nithe's absence, and the last hours of daylight were no different. They dressed up in form-hugging gowns before dinner for the simple fun of it. Amirah took to wearing dresses that flowed and were slit to the hips. It gave her better access to the dagger if she needed it and complimented her figure. Tonight she wore a glittering gown that flowed around her from the hips down like the wisp of angered storm clouds.

Together, the three of them ate a full meal in one of the smaller dining rooms. At some point, the newest members of the court joined their little group for an evening of entertainment. Before they knew it, several nobles filled the room, and it turned into a small party. Amirah allowed herself a lighthearted night of drinks, cards, charades, and music. It had been so long since she had let go. By the time they finished, the sky was pitch black as the trio left the room in fits of giggles. Kamille hiccuped on the way to their chambers and, with it, they collapsed into piles of laughter on the stairs.

"Aren't you glad I finally persuaded you to redecorate these horrid walls?" Gabbie slurred between breaths.

"They were dreadful, weren't they?" Amirah mused as she looked at the subtle elegance of the new decor—some well-placed paintings, silk tapestries, fresh rugs, and banners with ribbons. They all marveled for a moment before Kamille stood up, clasped Amirah's arm, and pulled her to her feet.

"Up, up, up ladies." Her words encouraged them in a sing-song voice.

They continued their march toward the promise of a comfortable bed, but reaching the top took longer than normal. Gabrielle looked weighted, tired from the party and drinks as she leaned against a wall with her eyes closed. Gabbie's room was down the hall, but from the look of her, she wouldn't make it there alone.

"She might need an escort," Amirah observed.

"No," Gabbie cooed as she tossed an arm over Kamille and sagged against her with a smile. "Kamille, you'll go with me, won't you? Both of you can spend the night in my chambers. I don't need an escort."

Kamille cast a reassuring look at Amirah. "You go on. I'll stay with her."

"Okay," Gabbie agreed on her behalf.

They laughed and split ways. When the ladies moved out of sight, Amirah changed direction. She needed the fresh air of the garden more than the lonely silence of her chambers. They had restored the small square stretch of green following the winter. It was encased in high walls with a tree at each corner and covered in sprawling vibrant greens and perennial blossoms. She sat upon the stone bench in the centered wood, surrounded by wild-grown plants. It had become her favorite place—a small sanctuary with a view of the star-studded sky. It wasn't near the size of the one at the Duke's Castle, but the small pond at the center reminded her of the lake. This was especially true at night when the world was quiet and the only sounds in the little biome of creatures living there and the ripples of the water.

She laid back, staring up at the world that shimmered—the universe's perfect blend of light and dark in a never-ending dance. She lay there for ages, admiring the show, unaware of how much time passed. When she finally sat up, she could feel the daze from the night's festivities. The end of her nose was numb with warmth and her vision swam. One more drink and she would have been in the same state as Gabbie. She made a mental note to be more responsible next time. Then inhaling the cool night air, she savored the tranquility before she decided it was time to return to her own room.

Somewhere in the garden, a twig snapped and stole her sense of comfort. She went rigid as her eyes scanned the area, but she saw nothing out of place. Every sound in the garden seemed to cease. The only thing she could hear was her breath and the elevated heartbeat in her ears. Her heart raced, sensing something was wrong. It knew she wasn't alone. Something or someone was there in the garden. Amirah sighed as if she was dismissing the noise, attempting to fake the relaxed posture she previously had. She needed to buy herself enough time to reach any of the guards. At night, there would be fewer of them. Especially near this area. Another reason she liked the garden was the privacy. Not that it did her any favors now.

Her hands smoothed the skirt of the gown, feeling for the dagger hidden there. With slow steps, she exited the garden the same way she entered. Apprehension swelled her body as she paced down the hall, each step evenly paced and quick. Her path would split in two directions at the end, giving her a chance to glance behind her without being noticed. The urge to look back tugged at her gut, but she knew better than to give in. Predators chased down prey that recognized they were being stalked.

Rounding the corner to the right into a shorter hall, she glanced, not more than a flash, but only enough to see what she needed before she slipped out of sight. A pit formed in her stomach after she saw the massive, black-cloaked form that inched after her. Whoever it was moved without hiding at the center of the hall. Out of sight, she burst into a run. It was a risk, sure, but that might be the single opportunity to create some distance between them. It was a risk she had to take. If they caught up, she would have to fight. Given the size of them, she wasn't sure if she would win, but she would at least get in a few critical strikes.

Amirah heard voices around the corner ahead. Her feet pounded against the stone floor as she pushed forward, unable to predict the distance. In truth, the drinks earlier did nothing to help, but she knew her assailant would round the corner at any moment. Reaching the corner, her body slammed into a wall and she tumbled to the ground. At least, that is what it felt like. The voices stopped in unison and she looked up to see the wall was actually a group of soldiers. They looked down upon her sprawled figure on the floor with surprise. Something about them seemed familiar to Amirah, but she couldn't connect them with any specific memory through her blurred vision.

"Well, would you look at our fortune," a gravelly voice cooed as he came to stand in front of her. She could see the crow's feet beside his cold, hazel eyes, sun-weathered skin, and the shadow along the jaw that needed a morning shave. Amirah blanched, realizing what made these soldiers familiar. "Get her up."

They wore faded admiral blue Brizian surcoats, with more leather than metal armoring. She noted too many vulnerable points and that one soldier wore the emblem of one of the noble houses around a leather cord. Her vision failed to sober enough to comprehend the distorted-looking animal wrapped around a twisted branch. Instinct fought against training when hands dragged her back to her feet. The men all chuckled as the largest one encapsulated her in his brawny arms. She grunted in discomfort as his leather bracers dug into her flesh and she felt for the cool touch of metal strapped beneath her skirt. With it in her grasp, she needed to wait for an opening. She counted her odds against the number of attackers. There were at least five.

Six.

The black-cloaked pursuer rounded the corner, freezing dead-center of the corridor. The soldiers didn't notice the shadow of death at their backs while they circled her like a predator with their next meal. Much to Amirah's annoyance, the exception was their terrible formation and stances. She couldn't keep away the sneer that crept over her as one soldier snapped his fingers in front of her face.

"There you are. Aye, it's her all right gents. Pity for us to meet like this. What's that look for? Who do you think you are to look down your nose at us?"

"Queen," she snapped. "Which you would know if whatever house you served ensured their soldiers kept up with the basics of their profession rather than hunkering around like civilian drunkards."

The smell of alcohol lingered around them, hitting Amirah wave after wave. The breath of their leader clouded the air around her whenever he spoke.

"You're not everyone's Queen," he sneered. "Least of all to us or the lord we serve. Part of the reason we're here, isn't it gents? Would be easier for you to play nice."

The others nudged one another and laughed. The big one that held her squeezed tighter as a sinister chuckle rolled through him. The hall wavered behind their ringleader, the mass of black moving with it. She cursed herself for overindulging earlier as the sound of metal drew her attention back to the current problem. Her vision narrowed as the leader passed a short sword to the man to her right.

"What are you doing?"

"Unfortunately," he sighed, feigning empathy, "we've been ordered to kill you. It'll be easier if you don't fight."

She spat at him. His two-step retreat gave her brief satisfaction until he came back. The impact of his hand on her face blacked the edges of her vision. Staring at the floor, a bubble of laughter coiled within her. She choked, trying to keep it down until she looked up.

Then she really did choke.

His hand clasped around her throat and cut off the sound, along with her air. In the silence, her choking was replaced by a deep, animalistic growl that emanated from behind the old soldier. Her attention sharpened on the black-cloaked figure as air refilled her lungs; a reprieve when the hand fell from her throat. Amirah tilted her head for a better view and her breath faltered. Viridescent light glared out from the darkness of the hooded figure, licking with power, and a primal chill swept down her spine. Her numbed senses prickled to attention when the hood was pushed back. The men surrounding her exchanged confused glances.

"Five against one is hardly a fair fight." Nithe's chilled glare fixated upon them.

"I don't see why that's any business of yours," scoffed the leader.

Amirah suppressed a dark chuckle. She rolled her head to the side to see around the old soldier and Nithe's vision narrowed on her. She caught the flash of a crooked grin that faded before the group returned their gaze to him. She beamed despite the angered faces around her, even Nithe, who she had thought a moment ago was the visage of death's wraith. Perhaps he was, because death was waiting impatiently behind his glare.

A glint of metal caught her attention in her peripheral sight, and the boulder of a man behind her used one of his hands to force her face skyward. There wasn't enough time to wait for the icy touch of metal to her throat that she knew was coming next as she plunged the dagger in her hand into the brute holding her. His grip faltered, and she freed herself from him, pulling the dagger with her. His howling scream was the trigger, one she silenced when she slid her blade across the side of his exposed neck. The room erupted into chaos.

The leader swore, knowing someone would have heard the scream of his fallen comrade. With a drawn sword, he dove toward

Amirah, forgetting Nithe at his back. A mistake he realized too late. An unseen force that moved with the flick of Nithe's fingers tossed him back and the impact against the wall knocked him unconscious. Nithe shifted his hand into a claw and turned toward the others as Amirah jumped back from a series of swings.

Metal sliced the air and she ducked the wide swing of the short sword. Her mind picked apart the problems with the form and speed born from experience as she backed toward the wall. It reminded her of training. The trio of remaining soldiers surrounded her, attempting to coral her into a corner. Each of them had a weapon, but the one with the ax to her left attempted to grab her first. She used her free hand to strike at his unguarded face and the hit landed with an audible crack from the impact to the cartilage and bone. Her hand that wielded the dagger found the tender, weak points; like a fang that sank into flesh. Two quick bites brought him to his knees.

A ragged cry burst from the one who had been swinging the sword at her. It missed by an inch when Nithe jerked him back and his claws plunged into the man's back. The last soldier reacted to the piercing scream with a raised sword. Amirah took the opening to wrap around his body and slide her dagger over his throat. The screaming stopped with the gut-curdling sound of bone snapping before both soldiers' bodies fell to the floor in bloody heaps.

CHAPTER 37

Nithe transformed the claw back into a hand that was now saturated with blood. When their eyes met, they encased each other in an embrace that said more than words could. Her arms circled his neck as he pulled her tight against him. They stilled, relieved at that moment. When Nithe pulled away, he tilted her face up. His eyes searched hers as a mix of emotion marred the pinch between his brows.

"You didn't recognize me?" The hint of concern tinged the question.

"No." Amirah felt heat rise to her face with the admission. "My vision hasn't been clear since I left the party. I wasn't sure who was following me. I just... fled."

"Party?" A frown and grin interchanged his face a few times. At last, a chuckle curled from his throat. "You've been drinking and could still draw blood from the attackers. Beautiful."

Warmth fluttered in her stomach at the praise. "Would have missed the chance if you hadn't shown up. Their poor training was helpful. We should have saved one for questioning."

Nithe nodded his head to the slumped form against the wall. "He's not quite dead."

"Yet," Amirah added.

She removed herself from Nithe and headed for the fallen group leader. A swift kick to his side was enough to rouse him as a painful cough pushed his awareness forward. Amirah knelt beside him with her dagger pressed against the side of his neck as Nithe stood behind her with malignant interest. The man's eyes widened as he realized his predicament.

"I know who you are," he rasped at Nithe with weakened venom.

"Could have fooled me," Nithe mused.

"You're the Dark Duke's son," he hissed. "Just as evil as your father."

"No," he stated coldly with a wicked smile. "I'm far worse."

The responding scoff earned a coughing fit from the would-be assassin leader. Amirah noticed a corded string that stuck out from his collar, and she used her free hand to yank it off. The man glowered at her but said nothing in protest. A painted crest danced in the dim torchlight of the hall. Closer to her face, she could recognize the emblem she had seen on one of the other soldiers earlier—a gold-eyed wild dog that twisted around a scrawny branch of yew. She passed it to Nithe, who tucked it beneath his cloak after studying it.

"Are there more of you?" She pushed the dagger into his skin enough to pierce the surface layers.

"Just kill me," he spat and shook his head. "You'll get no information from me, false Queen."

There wasn't enough time to react. The man latched onto her wrist and forced the blade to slide deep against his neck. Amirah jerked back from the blood that spurt forth, the hot copper-scented liquid splattering the side of her face. Nithe ripped her away before more damage could be done but it was too late. He cradled her head to his chest as the traitor bled out. Amirah had no tears or signs of remorse. However, the words 'false Queen' shocked her mind and lingered there. A group of running soldiers peeled to a stop. Their eyes darted around the scene, one of her personal guards among them. When he bowed, the rest followed suit.

"Captain," she acknowledged him.

"Your Majesty." His eyes scanned her blood-covered body. "Are you injured? What happened?"

She shook her head, not mentioning the scratch. "The work of treason from within the royal court. Have this cleaned up. Not a word of this is to leave these halls. Whoever does will go straight to the dungeon on charges of sedition. At sunrise, summon every court member to the throne room. Post extra guards at the door and perimeter of the room. I will retire to my chambers until then."

"Shall I accompany you, my Queen?"

She gave the Captain a faint smile. "Thank you. With traitors within our walls, I need you to see to this. Nithe will escort me."

He bowed to her and the rest of the soldiers followed suit, then set to clearing the bodies from the hall. Nithe steered her away from the crimson-drenched stones and toward her chambers. Although the house emblem confirmed her suspicions, who she trusted was further limited. She knew that, before sunset tomorrow, more blood would spill in the name of her crown. The thought both empowered and petrified her as they drew closer to her room.

Locked within the privacy of her chambers, Nithe helped her strip off the ruined gown. The stains had soaked through the layers into her chemise. She slipped it from her body, letting the cool night air chill her skin. Nithe left to find a bowl to fill with warmed water; leaving her to the silence of her mind. Several hours before the sun would open its warm face to the soil of Brizia. If the sands of time had a sound, it would have been the steady beat that drummed against her ear.

When Nithe returned, he led her to a chair to sit. Her skin pebbled against his touch, and she was vaguely aware of his eyes apprising the state of her fight-disheveled body. With tender diligence, Nithe worked a soaped cloth over her flesh. He started with the near-dry splashes of crimson that painted her face and worked his way down. Amirah looked at the red stain, the clothes, then the streaming water as it rinsed away the blood that wasn't hers. He repeated the actions to wash, rinse, and regathered the cloth, working his way down to the tips of her toes. When he reached the cut that she had called a scratch, he avoided running the cloth over it. Instead, his hand gently touched around it, allowing the wound to heal itself faster with the subtle assistance of his magic. A frown flickered on his face and left when he kissed the cleaned skin near it. When all traces of red were gone from her skin, his fingers worked to unpin her frazzled hair. Crown set aside, his fingers combed through the ginger tendrils until they smoothed under his touch.

Finished, he wrapped a blanket around her shoulders and placed a kiss on her bare shoulder. It simultaneously burned and melted into her, a familiar flame to sear away hidden wounds. She hummed at the sensation as he came around to stand face-to-face with her. His presence replaced the darkness from the halls; a gentler side to the dragon of a man that was reserved for her alone. One she came to know while at the Duke's Castle. With it came the intensity of a blazing star.

"Have you sobered yet?" he asked.

"Suitably enough," she sighed. The tingle at the tip of her nose was gone, lost in the unpleasant events of the night. The back of his fingers grazed down the side of her face and stopped to hold her chin between his index and thumb. She savored these moments of delicate peace beside him. "I have missed you. I thought spending more time with Gabbie and Kamille would distract me from that."

He picked up the unspoken words like she was a book to read. "Don't blame yourself for tonight. You did what needed to be done. I hated leaving. If I had returned later, who knows what the treasonous leeches might have done. They're lucky it was you who ended most of them."

"Your timing was perfect. My inebriation and carelessness led me straight into their hands. Even without the legacy of my father, there's already been so much bloodshed."

Nithe lowered his hand as he gave her a serious look. "You can't tolerate treason, Amirah. If that means more blood spills, then so be it."

Amirah shook her head. "I know I can't, but I don't want to become like him. Threats to my life come with the weight of my crown, but how much blood is a throne worth?"

"You won't become like him. If you are worried about bloodshed by your hand, do what you must, but know I will take up that mantle. I would decimate the Continent if it meant your peace and safety. Threats come with the throne, but so do you. And where you go, I will follow. Set the precedent now on how you will deal with traitors who are closest to you."

"That's too many people. This lord has a following and influence. Mass executions will lead to dissent from all corners of Brizia."

Nithe considered her. "You don't have to kill everyone, just enough. There are punishments that can be equal to death. Consider what King Bradrick did to his mother. Being on the throne comes with moments where you will have to bend your personal morality in favor of sustaining the Kingdom. To quote a philosopher named Vendrigoth, 'Execute the head, exile the body.' There are options within your grasp. All you have to do is command it."

She sighed and lowered her head for a moment, knowing he was right. When she raised it, there was a look of steeled resolve in her eyes as her heart finally hardened itself against those who had wronged her.

"So I shall. Call my General here immediately. We have work to do if we want everyone here by first light. If I'm to set an example, every noble house under my rule will bear witness to it."

Nithe bowed to her at the waist with a wicked grin. "As you wish it, my Queen."

CHAPTER 38

At the first light of dawn, Capital soldiers knocked on the door of every Brizian court member. Even the farthest-reaching head of the noble houses was available thanks to the Meeting of Nobility yesterday. They filed into the throne room with weary, bewildered faces. Soldiers lined the halls and those on the interior perimeter of the throne room dressed in full armor. The court nobles noted the increased presence as quiet murmurs of concern shifted between neighbors. Several questioned Gabrielle and her father, who were equally perplexed as their peers. The throne dais was devoid of anything save the empty silver throne. Not one person seemed to be aware of why they had been called and several grumbled in malcontent for being roused.

The heavy thud as the throne room doors shut quieted the room and everyone turned to see who had entered. A few muttered when the guards closed the doors and stood stationed in front of them. What drew everyone's attention was their Queen, who parted the crowd with a sword strapped to her side over a black gown embroidered with creeping ivy. A stiff metallic crown with dangerously pointed spikes jutted toward the sky from the tightly bound nest of her ginger hair. Behind her followed Nithe and an entourage of her personal guards. The hard, unreadable expression on her face made some of the nobles shift uncomfortably. They stared in silence as her guards took formation around the dais with their unsheathed swords pointing to the floor. Nithe stood off to the side below the dais; a strategic position that allowed him to both listen as a fellow noble and become an equally threatening buffer of the personal guard.

A disgruntled voice called out from the crowd. "What is the meaning of this? Why have we been summoned here so unreasonably early?"

Angered chirps of agreement echoed his sentiments and a sinister smile pulled at Amirah's lips. She handed a long rectangular box to her Captain. He took it to the Brizian General, who stood opposite of Nithe in fully decorated armor, and stopped in front of him. The cacophony of grumbles died down to murmurs of curiosity. When the Captain opened the box, the General retrieved a large scroll. He scanned the length of the document with no more reaction than a curt bow to the Queen. Unknown to the nobles, it was a document he had helped create. As he left the throne room, attention turned back to Amirah.

"Unreasonable is a word," she started as she addressed the crowd. The smile had fallen from her face, replaced by a coolness that matched her weighted tone. "A word used to describe women that cannot be controlled by the will of others. One that is being used to call to question my summons, my power, and my rule. A challenge to my position that has manifested in those who seek to usurp the throne from within this court."

Amirah paused, allowing the message to settle. Several gasps and exchanged glances with their peers, yet no one denied it. Most refused to let their mask falter, knowing when a political game was afoot, while some had long been players on the unmarked board. None dared speak or question her until more was revealed. Amirah paced the dais with intentionally slow steps, her hands clasped behind her back. She waited patiently until the opening and closing of the throne room doors interrupted the silence. The steady thrum of soldiers' boots as they marched over stone floors around the perimeter of the crowd silenced their whispers. Amirah exchanged a glance with Nithe before centering the dais again.

"My mother once sat on this throne in the stead of my father during the Khaos War. Some of you may remember that time, some of you may be too young, and some of you have chosen to forget. No one objected to that based on the simple fact she was married, but her word was as good as that of my father's. When I claimed my place as the rightful heir to the throne as the flesh and blood of both bodies, I was not afforded the same courtesy. Instead, I now face an accumulation of challenges and the workings of treason from my own court."

Lord Theorin scoffed from the front of the crowd. "What evidence is there of this? Every ruler that has and ever will exist, face challenges to their rulings. That is the function of the courts."

Amirah gave him a pointed look. "Lord Theorin, fascinating for you to ask. First, let it be said that the function of this court is to represent the interest of the people, not to seek control where it does not have the authority to do so. The evidence you ask for works against your favor and of several others aligned with you."

"Absurd! If such evidence existed, we would already have been in chains."

Amirah's eyebrows raised in an expression of indignation that was mixed with mock surprise. Nithe came up to the dais without the need to be summoned and Amirah held her hand out to him, although her eyes never left Lord Theorin. Nithe's fingers lingered for the briefest moment on her as he slipped the item she needed to her. It was Lord Theorin who let his mask slip as he watched her present the evidence to the court. She saw it, the seething hatred for her that was masked seconds later by indifference. She raised the amulet that bore the crest of a noble house high so that all eyes in the room could look upon it. Only then did her attention revert to the entire throne room.

"Last night, there was a deliberate attempt upon my life within the halls of this castle," she started, addressing the entire room. "A group of mercenary soldiers who sought to carry out an act of treason. Around the neck of one was an emblem belonging to house Theorin."

Shocked gasps, whispers, and glances passed through the gathered nobles. Amirah allowed them a moment to digest this revelation, and Lord Theorin released a boisterous laugh, drawing everyone's attention. Its condescending undertone rang throughout the throne room. Amirah noted the few who joined him while their eyes shifted around them. *Perhaps nerves, perhaps not.*

"You mean to tell this court that you escaped a group of soldiers unscathed?" Theorin chuckled again and turned to the room with a question meant to mock her assertion. "Where are these soldiers then? Hmm? If this attack were real, then the capital would have been flooded with armored search parties. We would lock the noble families safely behind their own doors, not parade them into the throne room. Yet, we're called here from the comfort of our beds to witness empty accusations. This is a false pretense of power from someone who grapples to maintain absolute control of every one of us."

"It might disappoint you, Lord Theorin," Nithe's contemptuous voice interrupted, silencing the traitorous laughter around the room. "But they are dead. There are those who can attest to the skill our Queen possesses with a blade. Several guards witnessed the devastation of their bodies, and I witnessed the attack. I admit, I had the pleasure of taking out one myself. They're buried in the prisoners' graveyard, where all traitors rest."

The smile fell from Theorin's face and Amirah kept her inscrutable countenance as she addressed the room once more.

"It seems to have been forgotten that I grew up training among our soldiers, much to my father's dismay. Like many of you, I suspect he is rolling in his grave that I wear the crown and rule from the throne alone. These mercenary soldiers were seen as far north as the Continent of Isidris. They hunted and spread the word of the bounty placed on my head from someone within this very court before you all voted in favor of my rule. Their apparent lack of training was a poor representation of Brizia, which is treasonous enough without an attack. The whisperings between your house and allies that have called me a false Queen have challenged my right to rule after ascension has been consecrated by the people through the very body of this court.

"Your allies scheme alongside you in political attempts to usurp or control this throne. This could have gone on ignored like the complaints of spoiled children, but then, last night, it was pushed too far by the tip of a hired blade. Now, I have to choose how much blood will stain my throne as we witness what happens to traitors under my rule. *This* is the reason I've called all of you here. General, if you would please."

The General bowed to Amirah then marched up to a step below her on the dais and unrolled the scroll that was passed to him earlier. As he did so, the soldiers he brought back with him into the throne room spread throughout the crowd. Several protests and cries of anger rang out as they began to make arrests. A few nobles ran for the throne room doors and windows, but the stationed guards blocked them. Each person struggled against their arrest, but the soldiers quelled them into agitated compliance with ease.

"By order of her Majesty, Queen Amirah Svana Landry, an arrest warrant has been issued for Lord Theorin..." The General continued to bellow out a list of names and charges, some of who had previously aligned themselves in the attempt to force her into marriage. The guards placed a third of the room into chained cuffs before the General had finished. The soldiers brought every court member who aligned with Lord Theorin before Amirah, and forced them to kneel before below the dais.

With arrests completed, the General addressed the room again. "The aforementioned nobles will be subject to an expedited hearing on their charges following the presentation to the Queen."

Amirah looked out at the remaining members of her court as the General finished. "Due to the nature of the offenses, we are holding a trial hearing immediately. I have already presented evidence and witnesses regarding the attempt upon my life and Lord Theorin's involvement as the leader. If there is more evidence during this trial, we will hear it. As for the rest of the accused, we will question them and hear from witnesses. In the end, the remaining nobles present will decide the matter of guilt or innocence."

Amirah turned and finally took her seat on the silver throne. Nithe came to stand beside it, his eyes swirling with the glint of viridescent light that was only noticeable up close. His presence reassured her as the trial carried on through the morning and staff members, guards, and nobility were presented as witnesses. The offenders had been reckless in who they held private conversations with, which, left unchecked, could have led to a risk in the kingdom's security. The room held a mix of emotions that spread across the faces of everyone in attendance.

The process was the same for each one that was brought to kneel before the dais, with some witnesses turning against one another. Almost all of them confirmed the accusations about Lord Theorin's plots to claim the throne for his own, even after Amirah had returned. They confessed their own involvement with remorse in the hopes to be spared. *How fast they have turned on each other,* Amirah thought behind her stonewalled expression.

At the end of it all, the remaining court members were called upon to vote for each charge. It was the sheer number of confirmed allegiances with Lord Theorin that surprised Amirah the most. She expected that some of those arrested would be freed since their confessions served as enough recompense through their own evidentiary involvement with Lord Theorin. She had known loyalty and witnessed it but their willingness to turn upon him and each other was far from loyalty. Lord Theorin's face was twisted in disgust, his ruddy nose shoved into the air with unrelenting arrogance, and each noble's admission was more convincing than the evidence. Papers trails could be forged and false evidence could be planted, but combined with the word of these men, everything was solidified for the peers who stood in judgment.

One last person came before the General and cast their vote. Amirah's breath caught, knowing that it could be one vote that tipped the scales of justice. Nithe's hand squeezed her shoulder, his firm grip offering silent support that was intermingled with the desire to tear Lord Theorin to pieces. They both knew it was Nithe's allegiance to her alone and the promise he made to her on that bloodied path in Rapplend that kept him at bay. A thin line he would easily cross if not for the fact she was about to cross it herself. The wait for the verdict spanned the length of a noon bell toll, as if time ticked down to a certain doom. The question was, for who? When the answer came, it was but a fragment of time that was not longer than it took to bat an eyelash.

Lord Paget let the word fall from his lips like a weighted anchor. "Guilty."

Horrified rage twisted onto Theorin's face as he fought against his cuffs, cursing everyone around him. Amirah dipped her head back and watched the man unravel. Beside her, Nithe openly grinned at her victory. Then, Theorin spat at her in his rancor. The wet glob fell inches from the hem of her dress, and she sneered at the offensive mass. When his shouting continued, Amirah began to feel the weight of dread. The court and nobles had rendered judgment, but she alone would deliver fate. For it, she would be judged by the masses.

Standing, she looked at each of the faces that knelt below the dais. Some hung their heads in shame, others looked upon her with silent pleas for mercy. All except Lord Theorin. His hate boiled behind a glare that could melt her silver throne, if spared the chance. His family, no doubt, would harbor the same resentment toward her after this day. She used that molten heat to steal her nerves as she withdrew the sword from her side. Its meaning was symbolic as she pointed the sharp tip at them, one by one. Each flinched as she guided it in their direction save for Lord Theorin, who stared at her with contempt from his centered position.

"Those present have rendered judgment upon those of you who remain on your knees before justice. At this moment, that is the duty of this crown. Many recall what type of finite justice stained my father's crown. Now, it will stain mine. Lord Theorin will face the sword. His execution will be delivered at sunset. As the fallen head of his house and having ruled by treason, so will the punishment extend down upon its entirety."

Theorin cursed her and strained against the confinement of his shackles.

"I do not recognize the rulings of a false Queen!" Amirah flinched at his venomous words and looked to her personal guard. Nithe moved forward but stopped short as he watched the scene unfold as Theorin's ravings continued. "How can you accept orders from her slithering tongue? How do you think she escaped the same fate as the King? She's no innocent maiden—"

Whack.

The Captain's booted foot struck the side of Theorin's face and he fell with a quieted thud. Curled up into a ball, he coughed painfully until he was tugged upright again. He spit out the pool of blood that formed in his mouth and with it flew three haggard teeth.

He ogled them, along with the bright red drool that ran from his lips. The Captain said nothing but pulled a cloth and began gagging the man. When finished, he turned to Amirah, bowed, and returned to his post. No one uttered a word. Amirah looked at Nithe with shock and she caught the light of amusement in the tilt of his green eyes. She cleared her throat, ready to be finished with the wretched business.

"The house of Theorin will be demoted and their purse is forfeit to the treasury. Then, they are to be exiled from the kingdom. The remaining of those accused will witness the execution before being exiled into individual servitude with no more than the position's pay. Your families may remain if they choose, but your houses are, henceforth, demoted. For three full generations, none will receive an appointment of land or position at court through blood or marriage. Anyone that is exiled attempting to return will be put to the sword without trial. So has judgment declared, so is justice done."

"So is justice done," those standing repeated in unison.

The soldiers that stood behind the prisoners hoisted them to their feet. Most looked relieved not to share the same fate as Theorin, though disappointment still haunted their brows. Theorin's head sagged from defeat and the assured headache that the Captain's heavy boot had delivered.

Inspired by Nithe's words last night, Amirah had decided to spare as many lives as possible. Leniency did not mean freedom from punishment. The remaining nobles had watched in judgment of the prisoners and their Queen, and their verdict aligned with the charges. Time would reveal how those outside of these faces would interpret her rendition of the verdict. New houses would take the place of fallen ones and the people would learn of the transgressions and form their own opinions. When you cut off the head of a snake, it died. If you cut the head off a hydra, three more grew in its place. Sparing lives could solidify the foundation of her rule, as much as it could shatter it to ruins, but it was a risk Amirah was willing to take to prevent further bloodshed.

No one stayed to converse after the offenders were carted away and Amirah would hear no audience in the throne room this day. Instead, the executions would take place; an example and a message solidified. The veil of death would hang over the Capital until it shuddered with the last breath of light.

CHAPTER 39

Nithe steered Amirah away from the emptied hall and her personal guard followed behind them. All that remained were the cold stone walls and the soldiers that lined them. When they reached her chambers, some guards remained posted at the door, while the others took their turn to rest. The Captain left them before she could to express her thanks for his assistance at the trial. Amirah allowed Nithe to pull her into the inner rooms of her chambers as exhaustion weighed her limbs.

"I need sleep," she sighed, falling into a heap on a chair.

"That you do," Nithe agreed, leaning against a wall. A knock sounded at the door and Nithe answered it, reservations about their relationship being suspected, and forgotten. He returned with a letter in hand and passed it to her. "For you."

Amirah groaned as she sat up to read it. The golden seal revealed it came from Pruria, and piqued her own curiosity. Bradrick had sent a letter earlier than planned. Worry creased her brow as she broke the seal. Her eyes flicked over Bradrick's handwriting as she took it to her desk. To her relief, it didn't contain ill-begotten news.

"A welcomed surprise on such a bleak day. Bradrick says that he and Alonzo will pass through in a month's time. They're headed to the southern kingdoms of the Continent. If memory serves me, some of Alonzo's family is from there."

From Amirah's recollection, Alonzo had not seen his family since he was a young child. She wondered what the reason might be for going to them now, but was certain they would fill her in on the details when they arrived. She glanced up at Nithe, who had plopped himself onto an overstuffed couch.

He tilted his head as he spoke. "I wonder how long they intend to stay. The weather there is balmy during our winter months, which makes for an appealing place to rest. Will their borders be secure while they're gone?"

"All of Pruria falls at Bradrick's feet, as you've seen. If there are any concerns from outside or within Pruria, our alliance would act as a buffer. All the more reason to fill the gaps in my court with haste."

Nithe sat up and followed her as she exited the bedroom. A distant look haunted her eyes and her hands twisted nervously in front of her. Behind her, Nithe wrapped his arms around her middle and hugged her against him. Without his cloak, he had nothing dark to wrap her in besides himself. Hugging her tighter, he rested his chin on her shoulder, a strand of his black hair falling over it. Still lost in thought, she twisted the inky end between her fingertips.

"Something troubles you." It was a statement, not a question—an acknowledgment whispered into her ear.

"I just sent a man I've known my whole life to his death," she said matter-of-factly.

"Ah, yes. That is true, but there is something else," Nithe hummed.

"Many things trouble me. Sometimes, I suspect it will be that way my entire life," she lamented with a sigh.

"Did they not teach the Princess to share?"

She spun around to face him with a warning look. "No, I can't say that they did."

A chuckle sounded from his throat. "We share a curse. Why not more? I am your royal advisor, after all."

He pulled her with him toward the bed until they both fell. Amirah tumbled down beside him with laughter and their bodies arranged until they were fitted to one another. Pressed together, Amirah rested a bent leg over his. His arm snaked around her from shoulder to hip where his hand rested, while the other tucked beneath his ebony hair. Her head leaned into the alcove between his chest and shoulder, where it fit perfectly. Her hand glided over the fine fabric of his shirt, feeling the familiar muscles beneath. She wanted nothing more than to curl into the warmth of his firm chest and rest. She craved nothing more than to sleep beside him, but her chaotic mind would not cease its tumultuous voice until they had further discussions. She was certain of her decisions, but the softer side of her heart harbored guilt.

"We both know that you are more than that. Something that will need to be made public by us, rather than someone else," she attempted to change the subject.

"Oh? I had the mind to rip out the wiggling tongues of snakes. Did you have something else in mind?"

He grinned down at her gawking expression, his teeth gleaming like the hungry predator he was. There was no telling if there was a hint of truth to his words, or if it was a complete jest so she poked at his rib with her index finger. He grunted, and a frown replaced the smile.

"I need you to be serious about this, Nithe, if you aren't already. No cutting out tongues over gossip. It wouldn't be fair since they would have some merit. I was serious when I said that I am certain my father is rolling over in his grave that I sit unmarried on his throne. I can imagine his corpse bursting into the throne room one day to throttle me for my brazen volley upon the remnants of the court."

A shudder ran through her at the imagined scene.

"He would have to have a heart to care," Nithe said with intended irony. He stared upwards, searching the world above for a muse. "I have seen that organ, and there was not an ounce of love for anyone or anything outside of his own gluttonous power. It would save your conscience to think less about how he ruled and more about how you want to rule. The past cannot be changed, and you do not want it to influence the future more than it has. Balanced is the crown where justice has a conscience. This is your time to make changes for the betterment of your people, as much as for yourself. The key is where you place the weight upon the scales."

"Spoken like a true advisor."

Nithe shrugged. "Because it is true. You have mentioned the weight of the crown. If it is heavy, you might as well make it comfortable."

"What if it is too heavy for me to bear alone?"

Nithe looked down at her, but she didn't meet his eyes. "Alone? Even as I am beside you?"

"And in my bed," she reminded him with a brief smirk. It flitted away with the tide of serious, forbidding emotions. "Eventually, people will talk. They did when we first arrived together, but it faded. I am surprised gossip hasn't followed us from Pruria. Testing time has never worked in my favor and I don't want us ruined by the inner workings of life at court. I could announce a courtship between us. It would keep the peace for a while, but it would come with watchful eyes that have nothing better to do but wait with impatience for gossip."

"We could escape to my castle. It's not a home without you anymore," he admitted.

"Or we could get married."

The words slipped from her mouth before she could stop them, and Nithe bolted upright. She flinched at the loss of heat around her as he looked down at her with a guarded face. Already, she could feel the sting of rejection as panic rose in her chest, even as he bent over her. His dark hair cascaded around them like a curtain of night and confusion marred her face. He stroked down her jawline, attempting to ease the pain.

"No. I'll not steal what you craved before my blood called to yours. Not your freedom or crown. Neither will be shadowed by me. Instead, I will protect these things without you having to barter them away."

"Y-you're worried about my freedom?"

The slow bob of his head confirmed her suspicion.

"I only know freedom because of you, Nithe. The request to marry and bear children will come again and again. We could rid the world of every domineering old man that is concerned with a woman's place, and more will replace them. The crown has expectations of me. I wanted freedom, yes, but I wanted the freedom to choose my fate. I could marry anyone else, and I would not know the same freedom I have with you. Being at court threatens the peace we have found. If we begot a child, it would be all the worse for them."

A unique expression spurred his face. "Are you with child?"

"For the love of the Continent, no. We've been fortunate, but I don't know that luck will hold for long." Her hands cupped his face. "I am not asking this out of duty. I am asking you because I want all of you. If that means I must forfeit the crown for us, I will."

"That would still equate to me having stolen it from you," he groaned. "I don't want your crown."

"Then don't take it. It's mine to give and take as I see fit. The receiver is to accept or decline. Your titles outrank almost everyone at court, which already positions your claim to the throne if anything should ever befall me—assuming you survived, that is. Curse or no curse, duty or not, I want you."

His resolve was chipped away by her reasoning and the revelation of her desire. He hovered closer and embers like the breath of a dragon licked at her core.

"A year," he conceded. Her heart fluttered as his breath tickled her lips and he laid out his terms. "A year of courtship to keep the peace at court. A year away together for harmony, and every third year after. Whether we retreat to the walls of my castle or travel, I do not care so long as we have a semblance of peace away from the public eye. The majority of court affairs can be dealt with through documents and messenger, or so I learned under my father's tenure. That is one year for each promise I've made on this path we have walked together. If our blood is bound by a curse, then so shall our flesh be bound by love. I'll not take the mantle of the King, for it is not what I desire. I have enough power to bend the will of Kings without the need of a crown. To mitigate risk, the laws will need to change to allow magic back into Brizia. While I do not fear the might of men, there are others to consider, including yourself. If we ever have a child, they could have powers of their own. I know we want a better future than what we've inherited. Will this satisfy you?"

"Yes," she breathed, "that will do perfectly."

His lips crashed down on hers and the warm, inviting fire consumed them in a white, scolding flame. They danced there until their bodies disintegrated from their present troubles. Afterward, sleep chased Amirah with its welcomed blanket and she curled into Nithe's side, content, despite the chaos they had endured. There they slept in their own amorous cocoon. In her sleep, she dreamed of the world she would build with him at her side. Her kingdom would flourish like her love for him had, small hands would clasp around her fingers, and the dance of a viridescent flame would nourish the surrounding land. She was already bound to him. Not by the Duke's curse or any external force, but by her own heart. Sometimes the villain and the curse are the salvation. Sometimes they aren't a villain or a curse at all.

LOLA KNOES

The End

Acknowledgements

This book would not have come into existence nor this dream into fruition if not for the support of family, friends, and the indie author community. My mother and husband encouraged me to write again and their continual support helped me get the words on paper. For that I am thankful. A special thanks goes out to my beta and alpha reader groups for their helpful insight, diligence, and wonderful encouragement. You all helped make this book so much more than it initially was. To my ARC team for giving my book a chance and taking the time to review it. Special thanks to Tasha, Amy, Rebecca, Tess, Ari, and many others who helped out with this book at various points in the process. I'm so glad to have met you all. Your support, guidance, and friendship kept me going. To Art Lynx Covers for designing my amazing cover. To RS Fantasy Maps for bringing the map of this world to life. Thank you to my developmental editor Ashton Taylor for everything you have done with this book. Special thanks to my editorial team for helping improve all versions of this book. Finally, thank you to each reader who gave my book a chance. I couldn't do it without all of you! So if you enjoyed reading this please consider leaving a review. Welcome to the Darkened Kingdoms Collection, I hope you're ready for more adventures in the twelve kingdoms! For updates please follow my socials, join my ko-fi, or subscribe to my linktree: linktr.ee/ LolaKnoes

Don't miss out!

Visit the website below and you can sign up to receive emails whenever Lola Knoes publishes a new book. There's no charge and no obligation.

https://books2read.com/r/B-A-QNFZ-UFBLC

BOOKS 2 READ

Connecting independent readers to independent writers.

About the Author

Lola Knoes is the author and creator of the Darkened Kingdoms Collection. She writes dark fantasy, romance, and snack-sized poetry. Although she always adored reading books, Lola's storytelling journey began with a second grade class assignment: a self published book. She would later go on to take creative writing classes, participate in poetry competitions, write short stories, and content for businesses. When not writing Lola can be found creating art, listening to music, reading, creating chaos, and spending time with loved ones.

Read more at https://www.lolaknoes.com.

www.ingramcontent.com/pod-product-compliance
Lightning Source LLC
Chambersburg PA
CBHW070841260626
47170CB00007B/2459